THE AUTOPSY

I clamped back the skin flaps while Tonetka prepared the rib-extension unit. I cut through the tough, inner-abdomen cavity lining. Fluid shimmered beneath the laser in a black pool. That was odd. Jorenian blood didn't turn black, even when it coagulated.

"Internal viscera and skeleton are obscured by what appears to be a necrotic fluid." I took a sample. "Suction, please." Tonetka applied the extractor's tip and evacuated the fluid for what seemed like an hour.

The internal organs didn't appear. Neither did the bones. She was only emptying the abdominal cavity. We exchanged a look, and she shut down the extractor's pump.

The Senior Healer averted her gaze as I put my gloved hand into the body and searched with my own fingers. The black fluid felt thick and cold.

"Tonetka." She didn't want to hear this, but we had to include it in the data record. "His internal organs are missing. His ribs. Everything. They're gone. . . ."

StarDoc II:
Beyond Varallan

A NOVEL BY
S. L. Viehl

A ROC BOOK

ROC
Published by New American Library, a division of
Penguin Group (USA) Inc., 375 Hudson Street,
New York, New York 10014, USA
Penguin Group (Canada), 90 Eglinton Avenue East, Suite 700, Toronto,
Ontario M4P 2Y3, Canada (a division of Pearson Penguin Canada Inc.)
Penguin Books Ltd., 80 Strand, London WC2R 0RL, England
Penguin Ireland, 25 St. Stephen's Green, Dublin 2,
Ireland (a division of Penguin Books Ltd.)
Penguin Group (Australia), 250 Camberwell Road, Camberwell, Victoria 3124,
Australia (a division of Pearson Australia Group Pty. Ltd.)
Penguin Books India Pvt. Ltd., 11 Community Centre, Panchsheel Park,
New Delhi - 110 017, India
Penguin Group (NZ), cnr Airborne and Rosedale Roads, Albany,
Auckland 1310, New Zealand (a division of Pearson New Zealand Ltd.)
Penguin Books (South Africa) (Pty.) Ltd., 24 Sturdee Avenue,
Rosebank, Johannesburg 2196, South Africa

Penguin Books Ltd., Registered Offices:
80 Strand, London WC2R 0RL, England

First published by Roc, an imprint of New American Library,
a division of Penguin Group (USA) Inc.

First Printing, July 2000
20 19 18 17 16 15 14 13 12 11 10 9

ROC REGISTERED TRADEMARK—MARCA REGISTRADA

Printed in the United States of America

PUBLISHER'S NOTE
This is a work of fiction. Names, characters, places, and incidents either are the
product of the author's imagination or are used fictitiously, and any resemblance
to actual persons, living or dead, business establishments, events, or locales is
entirely coincidental.
   The publisher does not have any control over and does not assume any responsibility for author or third-party Web sites or their content.

For my son, Michael Edward Viehl.
May you alway choose the path
less traveled.

ACKNOWLEDGMENTS

Many thanks to my terrific editor, Laura Anne Gilman, and my friend Holly Lisle, for all your wisdom, guidance, and most of all—patience!

I'd also like to thank Chris Ryan for his invaluable insight and advice on fighting techniques and the honest realities of hand-to-hand combat.

PART ONE:

Departure

CHAPTER ONE

The Sunlace

I will give no deadly medicine to anyone if asked,
nor suggest any such counsel.

Hippocrates (460?–377? B.C.)

Hippocrates never got smacked in the head by a patient, I
thought as I ducked to avoid a wildly swinging counter-
weight. That, or he'd kept them all in restraints.

My first patient, Engineer Roelm Torin, had been admitted to the ship's inpatient ward late yesterday. He wasn't
happy about it, either. According to the nurses, he had
already destroyed an infuser array, knocked his berth monitor over twice, and kept all the other patients awake half
the night with his grumbling.

I grabbed his traction rig before the blue-skinned patient
kicked it off the berth mounting. "Good morning, Roelm."
I performed a visual examination and adjusted the rig's
clamp. His left leg, while plainly mobile, was badly swollen.
"Feeling a little restless?"

"Your pardon, Healer." Roelm made a swift, apologetic
motion with one six-fingered hand, then turned to address
the Omorr making a chart notation. "Release me."

I looked over at the ship's senior surgical resident, too.
Squilyp had gone and started rounds without me. Again.

The Omorr never glanced up from his data entry. "That
is not possible, Engineer Torin."

"We'll see," I said, purposely contradicting him.

That got my rival's attention, and Squilyp's round, dark
eyes glared at me. I was a few minutes late for my shift.
My braid, still damp from my shower, hung over one shoulder. He'd probably make note of both crimes.

In contrast, Mr. Punctuality appeared immaculate and

authoritative as ever. Despite his pinkish derma, Squilyp's green resident tunic actually looked good on his tall, lanky frame. Not that I planned to tell him that. I didn't like the pompous little ass. Since I was in line to be Senior Healer—the job he wanted—Squilyp didn't like me.

That had been the status quo for nearly two months now, since I'd joined the crew of the Jorenian star vessel *Sunlace*. I'd agreed to replace the retiring Senior Healer, Tonetka Torin, but there were problems. I was Terran, not Jorenian, and had only a year's experience treating nonhumans. I was also a fugitive with a bounty on my head.

Hardly a sterling resumé.

I held out my hand. "Chart, please." The Omorr shoved it at me. "Thanks, Squilyp." I gave him a broad, friendly smile. He hated that even more than my untidy hair.

"Dr. Grey Veil." Squilyp didn't call me Healer. I'm sure he called me plenty of names, but not Healer. "My latest scans are annotated."

They'd be perfect, too. Squilyp ranked first among the *Sunlace*'s five surgical residents, for good reason. I'd never seen him make a single error on the job. The Omorr's knowledge of procedure rivaled that of the diagnostic array.

The known universe would collapse before this guy ever screwed up.

"Did you run a hematology series?"

"Of course." The hundreds of gildrells that covered the Omorr's oral membrane muffled his offended tone. The white, prehensile filaments measured half a meter long, and tapered from a thick base to slender, fingerlike ends. I'd never seen Squilyp eating or drinking. That wasn't a big priority for me.

"Good." I reviewed the rest of his notations. "Nice work."

His gildrells stiffened as though I'd yanked on them. "Excuse me."

The Omorr stalked off. He had four limbs, but used three like arms, leaving the fourth to stand on and hop around with. It should have looked silly, but Squilyp moved with what I could only call a *stately* bounce.

Like me, the Omorr was something of an oddity. On his homeworld, touch healing and ceremonial prayer were the preferred methods of medical treatment. Yet he never attempted to use his spade-shaped appendage ends (no fingers, just incredibly dexterous membranes) to touch-treat a patient. Squilyp also had a bit of an obsession with cleanliness. Mere dust motes seemed to aggravate him. Almost as much as I did.

Oh, well, I thought. Can't expect *everyone* to adore me.

"Healer Cherijo!"

I turned to my patient. Roelm pushed himself up, too quickly, and impatiently jerked his leg. Before I could grab it, the traction rig crashed onto the deck.

Roelm's white eyes—Jorenians had no detectable pupils or irises—widened as he looked from the ruined equipment to the sight of the Senior Healer stalking toward his berth. "Healer, aid me to convince Tonetka this was none of my doing."

I got the usual crick in my neck as I greeted the Senior Healer. I'd become resigned to feeling like a dwarf ever since I'd boarded the ship. Nearly everyone, including my boss, was at least a foot taller than me.

"One more mishap, and I vowed to put you in restraints," Tonetka said, and gave the rig an ominous look. "I shudder to think Pnor trusts *you* to keep the stardrive operational."

Roelm's chin jutted. "Which I cannot do, unless you release me!"

The Senior Healer muttered something rude. The patient growled something back at her. I had no idea what they said. The flat, square-linked vocollar I wore around my neck wouldn't translate Jorenian profanity. I'd been told it had little equivalent in any language.

"Why don't I take a look at the leg?" When Roelm made an impatient sound, I patted his shoulder. "Let me do a proper evaluation, Roelm. The boss will fire me if I don't." I picked up a scanner. "Relax."

Tonetka kicked the rig out of her way. "You may wish to sedate him first."

One side of my mouth curled. "I don't think that will be necessary."

She moved beside me to observe. "More scans?"

I nodded across the ward toward the Omorr. "Just in case Mr. Wonderful missed something." I performed three passes over the leg, then studied the readings.

Roelm tried to get a look at my scanner display. "Well?"

"Well, if you were on my homeworld, I might think this was a form of filariasis," I said. "The readings are consistent."

The big man frowned. "What is that?"

"Swelling caused by parasitic worms that block the lymphatic vessels. Very nasty," I said, deadpan. Roelm's skin rapidly acquired a greenish cast. I took pity on him. "Luckily, it isn't that."

"Thank the Mother." Roelm closed his eyes and exhaled dramatically. One of his big, work-roughened hands pressed over the twelve-valve heart in his chest.

I said aside to Tonetka, "Surgical history?" She shook her head. "Okay." I put his chart down. "Tell me what you've been doing over the last few days, Roelm."

He looked indignant and virtuous. "I have been inspecting the port thrusters, every shift."

Yeah, right. Jorenians worked hard, and played harder. Then there was all that warrior-training stuff they did in between. He'd either injured himself on the job, gotten clobbered during combat training, or done something even stupider off duty in the dimensional simulators. I picked probable idiocy number three.

"Try out any new programs during your recreational interval?" I asked. "Wrestling some swarm-snakes, maybe? Rappel down any Andorii cliff-plateaus?"

"I made two visits to the environome, both for—" He paused. "Nothing physically strenuous."

"Come on, Roelm," I said, prompting him with a roll of my hand. "Details, give me details."

"I merely sought to increase my manual dexterity. The program employed fine manipulative skills. My work demands that I keep my fingers . . . flexible."

I considered this. "Flexible like . . . grav-rowing down the white-water rapids on Radonis?"

"No." He hunched down. If his shoulders got much higher, they'd be covering his ears.

"You did not think to attempt blade dancing?" Tonetka asked, horrified.

Our patient simply shook his head again and looked more miserable than ever.

I sighed. "Roelm, don't *make* me walk all the way over to that environome and access your program."

"You will laugh at me."

My boss and I exchanged a glance.

"We won't," I said. "Physicians' oath. Right, Senior Healer?"

Tonetka nodded vigorously.

"Very well." Roelm looked around and lowered his voice to a whisper. "I have been learning how to weave."

"Weave where?" My boss moved closer, ready to throttle him if necessary. "Between blade dancers?"

I could barely hear him now. "I have been weaving baskets."

"What? You mean—" I bit my lip. "Oh. Right. *Baskets.*"

Here we'd been thinking Roelm had tried to half-kill himself in some intense physical challenge. In reality, he had been teaching himself the gentlest—and definitely the most *feminine*—of Jorenian art forms.

"Yes," he said. *"Baskets!"*

Tonetka whirled away just as I caught the expression on her face. I stepped between her and Roelm, so he wouldn't see her shoulders shaking, and cleared my throat.

"Well, that sounds nice, Roelm." If this got out, he'd never live it down. "Um, very interesting."

"It is not amusing," he said. "A male can learn such skills as easily as a female."

A cough that didn't do much to cover a laugh burst from the Senior Healer. I jabbed her in the back with my elbow. My calm, understanding expression never wavered.

"Of course they can," I said. Tonetka snorted and I elbowed her again. "What else have you been doing?"

"No more than is usual. Eating. Sleeping. Working."

That reminded me of what he'd said before. "Describe how you inspect a thruster."

He elaborated. The *Sunlace*'s colossal engines required careful maintenance and regular inspections. As a supervisor, Roelm directed most of the stardrive operations, and routinely inspected the work performed by his subordinates. Not surprising. He'd been one of the ship's primary designers.

From what he told me, a new design concept required him to perform several comparison tests on the thrusters. I recalled what I knew of the equipment from the lengthy tour I'd been given during my first week.

"Roelm, when you were running these tests, did you have to balance yourself against the edge of the access panel?" He nodded. "On one leg, maybe?" Another nod. I lightly patted his swollen limb. "This leg?"

"Yes, but—" He stopped and looked sheepish. "I did spend an extended interval in such a position, recalibrating the directional relays and checking circuit tolerances."

Tonetka had gotten over the giggles. Now she glowered over my shoulder. "*How* extended?"

Roelm made a weak gesture. "A double shift."

My boss tossed Roelm's chart up in the air and stalked off. I caught it neatly when it came down, then made the appropriate notation.

"Well, that explains where the edema came from. We'll keep your leg elevated for now. The diuretics will reduce the swelling." I tried to look stern. "No more twisting yourself into a pretzel for a whole day, Roelm."

"What is a pretzel?"

I laughed.

Tonetka didn't appear at all amused when I entered her office. She shoved aside a touchpad onto which she had been pounding data. White eyes glared in the direction of the Engineer's berth. Then she exploded.

"That stubborn *t'lerue*!"

I closed the door panel, sat down, and calmly completed my chart entry while she vented.

"Males will be males," I said when she started to run out of bad words I couldn't understand. "It's the reason the female of most species invariably lives longer."

"Hmph. I should like to divert his path."

That constituted a declaration of ClanKill, or—in Jorenian idiomatic terms—a death threat. I knew she wasn't serious. Tonetka often blustered to vent her frequent frustrations.

"Give him a day or two on a restricted diet," I said. "That should teach him a lesson."

"He's fortunate we don't perform amputations in this age." Tonetka rubbed her fingers against her brow. A reluctant chuckle escaped her. "Weaving. Mother of All Houses."

"Think of it as great blackmail material," I said. "He could be your devoted slave from now on."

"At the very least. Ah, well. Here are the current cases." She indicated a short stack of charts. "Roelm constitutes the only new admission. We should prepare for transition in a few hours. I want to put Hado back in sleep suspension."

Tonetka and I had performed open-heart surgery on Navigator Hado Torin a few weeks before. Despite his steady recovery, his condition remained guarded. The extra precaution of putting him in a sleep suspension field before the *Sunlace* dropped out of dimensional flightshielding would protect his still-healing cardiac organ.

"Are we getting near that planet Captain Pnor told me about?" I asked. "Ness-something?"

"NessNevat. You haven't been accessing your relays again."

"I keep forgetting." No, I didn't.

"Program an alarm," my boss said. "As Senior Healer, you will be required to review intership communications daily. Even," she said when I tried to interrupt, "the ones to which you do *not* desire to respond."

I rolled my eyes. "If you only knew how many times I get invited to someone's quarters for a meal interval. . . ."

"You are a popular member of our HouseClan." Tonetka had no sympathy for me. "As Terrans say, get used to it."

That was the whole problem. My life had never been this complicated before. On my homeworld, for example, I worked, ate, and slept. After I'd left Terra and transferred to Kevarzangia Two a year ago, I made a few friends I never had time for. Worked. Ate. Slept.

However, here on the *Sunlace,* I found myself up to my eyebrows in nice, sociable Jorenians who had absolutely no intention of leaving me alone. Ever since I'd been formally adopted by HouseClan Torin, I'd been under siege.

They signaled me constantly. Invited me to eat, talk, or spend recreation time with them. Stopped by my quarters to chat. Would have stayed and sung me to sleep if I'd asked.

My biggest problem? *Guilt.* I suspected all the attention I was getting sprang from sympathy over the death of my

Jorenian lover. I was considered a widow in the crew's eyes. Yet Kao's death had been *my* fault.

Then there was the Allied League of Worlds' failure to recognize me as a sentient being over the matter of my being a genetic construct—a clone. That ruling had ultimately prompted Joren to rescue me from K-2, adopt me, then break off all relations with the League. Added to that was the bounty the League had put on my head, which constituted more credits than a raider could make in ten lifetimes. Half the mercenaries in the galaxy were probably out hunting for the *Sunlace* by now.

In light of all that, *I* felt the HouseClan should resent me. *They* thought I should just ignore the whole distasteful business, and stop by for a meal when I was free.

Eventually (I hoped) I'd get used to it. The *Sunlace* was currently en route to Joren, HouseClan Torin's homeworld, in the Varallan Quadrant. Since the journey would take a revolution, equal to a standard Terran year, I had ample time to adjust to my new family. Or to get off the ship.

"Caution." Tonetka's vidisplay sounded an alert. "Multiple incoming emergencies."

The Senior Healer and I dropped what we were doing and hurried out into the bay. Squilyp intersected our path. A pair of female educators limped in, carrying an unconscious child between them.

They were a mess. Shredded garments. White eyes wide with shock. Serious lacerations all over them. A spattered track of greenish blood on the deck trailed behind them back to the gyrlift panel.

"Here." Tonetka helped them place the limp little girl on an open exam pad. Her experienced eye evaluated case priority in a blink. "Cherijo, the child. Squilyp, with me."

I performed a visual first. She had a minor head wound, dozens of shallow contusions, and a few deep ones, all on the front surfaces of her body. Her powder-blue skin felt cool and clammy; her respiration sounded jerky and labored. A quick pass of my scanner revealed the rapid drop in her blood pressure.

"I need hands over here!" I yelled as I put aside the scanner, then yanked a thermal cover over the child. One of the junior residents joined me at the exam pad, and monitored while I quickly sterilized, masked, and gloved.

I checked the child's airways, and found them mercifully clear. "She's in shock. Oxygen, stat." The resident took care of that while I attached a fluidic infuser to the small arm.

"Uhhh . . ."

"Easy, sweetheart," I said as her eyelids fluttered. "You're going to be fine." My gaze shifted to the resident, who adjusted the monitor's sensors from adult to juvenile levels. "What's her name?"

"This is Fasala Torin."

"Fasala." My hand lightly stroked her brow. "Honey, can you hear me?"

"Yes . . ." Dull with pain, the child's eyes opened.

Her gaze made a tight knot form in my chest. Had mercenaries attacked the ship again, without an alarm sounding? What else could have done this? Fasala couldn't be more than five years old. Just a kid. Bleeding because of me?

"Heal . . . er . . . hurts . . ."

I could agonize over the possibilities later. She needed me now. "It's okay, honey. We're going to take care of that." To the resident, I said, "Twenty-five cc's of pentazaocine."

After administering the painkiller, I watched the monitors. The vise on my lungs eased as her levels began to stabilize. Although Fasala slipped back into unconsciousness, the immediate danger of traumatic shock was over.

She wouldn't die. I wouldn't let her.

The resident rapidly prepared an instrument tray while I ran a second scan series. By then the shallow head wound had stopped bleeding. That was odd; the shallow ones usually gushed like fountains. I frowned when I saw none of the other open gashes were bleeding, either. Jorenians had wonderful physiologies, but their blood didn't coagulate *this* fast. Especially not with multiple breaches of the subdermal cartilage layer.

"Tonetka?" I called out. "She's stopped bleeding. For no apparent reason."

"This one as well," Squilyp said.

"Scan the lacerations for foreign material," Tonetka said. I glanced back and saw her bent over one of the educators with a magniviewer. "Do either of you see anything?"

Squilyp's gildrells flared with agitation as he scanned the

other female. "I cannot find visible debris here," he said, and glared down at the moaning patient. He probably thought she was hiding it from him.

Tonetka addressed the educator she was treating. "Tell me, ClanCousin, what caused these injuries?"

"I do not know, Senior Healer." Pain made the patient's voice sound reedy. "Fasala did not return from our group environome activity. We found her an hour ago, on the fourteenth level. The interior buffer . . ." Her eyes closed briefly. "It shattered."

I knew vaguely what an interior buffer was—some sort of security barrier inside the hull that prevented accidental decompression. Too bad I couldn't apply some of that to the Omorr's mouth.

"That's impossible!" I heard Roelm Torin yell from his berth across the ward. "No buffer could—"

At the same time, the Omorr said, "Interior buffers are indestructible. No—"

"Quiet!" Tonetka cut both men off, then asked the educator, "How many others were injured?"

"Only the three of us."

"You are certain it was the buffer?"

"I felt it implode back on us." The educator shuddered. "As if we had been slashed by a thousand unseen knives."

Squilyp stopped probing his patient and stared at the educator in horror.

Roelm gasped. "Mother of All Houses."

I guessed that meant these buffer things *did* shatter. The constriction in my chest started to loosen. Maybe it hadn't been from an attack on the ship. Plus Squilyp was actually *wrong* about something. The known universe was going to collapse. Right there in front of my eyes.

"Cherijo, Squilyp, set your scans for adaptable sonic alloy debris in the wounds," the Senior Healer said.

"What, exactly, is 'adaptable sonic alloy debris'?" I asked.

"It's what they make buffers out of," Squilyp said, overjoyed that he knew something I didn't. "Sonic-based matter. It will not be visible to your eye, nor can you feel it. Use the most sensitive setting."

Invisible, untouchable debris. Lovely. Could this possibly get any worse? "When we're done here, I hope someone will explain this stuff to me," I said as I recalibrated my scanner's range.

Sure enough, when I made another pass the display revealed innumerable tiny shards lodged in each laceration. Tightly meshed together, which explained the coagulant effect—the ghost-debris had sealed off the wounds. When I applied my probe tip, the debris immediately surrounded it. Like sticking a finger in water.

"Any suggestions on how to remove something I can't feel?" I asked. "Or grab?"

"Roelm?" Tonetka raised her head to consult him. "What is used to fit the alloy during construction?"

"Resonant harmonicutters," the engine designer said.

My ears perked up at that. "Resonant?" I glanced over the edge of my mask at the engineer. "You mean you cut these buffers with sound?"

My terminology made Roelm look pained. "They are sonically fitted to each vessel."

Same difference, I thought, then addressed my boss. "Tonetka, remember when I told you about the ultrasound diagnostic imaging once used on my homeworld? We can adapt something like that to remove these shards."

"Ultrasound?" Squilyp sneered at the archaic word. "Why don't you simply hack them out with amalgam blades?"

I ignored him. It was easy, I'd had lots of practice. "We can modify our scanners to emit a low-spectrum sonic field."

Tonetka saw where I was going. "The buffer alloy will vibrate, but how will we extract the shards?"

"Connect your dermal probes to the scanners," Roelm called out. "Calibrate them to match the alloy's frequency."

The Omorr resident nodded his approval to Roelm. "Buffer alloys are self-restorative. The nature of the matter is to be attracted to itself." He then gave *me* a surly look.

Yeah, I thought, the dumb unqualified Terran does it again. Doesn't it just make you want to scream?

The resident assisting with Fasala urged me in a low voice to make haste.

Once I'd modified my scanner, I connected a dermal probe to it and started on one of the larger wounds. A low

sound like tinkling glass hummed as I probed the gash.
Gently I tugged, and felt something slide from Fasala's
flesh.

Green blood flowed at once. *Got it.* A pass with an alternate scanner revealed no more shards in the site. I held up
my gloved fist. Saw nothing on the surface of the probe.

"Uh, Roelm?" I raised my head and held up the instrument. "How do we dispose of stuff we still can't see or
touch?"

"Seal the probe in a vacuum."

It took fourteen more probes before the child's wounds
were completely shard free. Sealed vacuum containers littered the deck. As we worked, a nurse summoned a team
from Environment Operations to remove the dangerous
shrapnel.

I finished first, so the unhappy task of signaling Fasala's
ClanParents fell on my shoulders. I broke the news to
Darea and Salo as gently as I could. Both were on their
way to Medical as soon as my signal terminated.

Once I was assured the Senior Healer didn't need help
with the educator (Squilyp would have slit his membrane
junctures before asking for my assistance), I went to talk
to Roelm. He was staring at Fasala, whose critical-care
berth was only a meter away from his.

We both got to watch Darea and Salo rush in and hurry
to their child's side. Salo turned pale the moment he saw
her. Darea pressed her fist tightly against her mouth.

"Roelm." I sat down and patted his good leg to get his
attention. The accident might not have been due to my
presence on the ship, but I wanted some more details. "Tell
me about these buffers."

Glad for the distraction, Roelm explained the theory behind Jorenian ship construction. How the long, uninter-
rupted spiral design was so great for interdimensional
jaunting. He used terms like "subatomic constants," and
"spontaneous symmetry."

Quantum mechanical construction, I discovered, was
about as riveting as a hematological abstract.

At last the engineer got to the important part. Evidently
the exterior hull, while incredibly resilient, could still be
breached by extreme forces, such as multiple displacer
blasts. When that happened, the ship's interior adaptable

sonic alloy mantle, commonly referred to as "the buffer," immediately sealed itself over the rupture. No matter how big it was.

"Not today," I said.

"Buffers cannot be shattered." Roelm was insistent. "It would require the complete destruction of the ship."

"This one did. You saw those wounds."

He muttered and pressed a huge hand over his eyes. Engineers didn't like it when you messed with the universal principles of matter and interaction.

"Cherijo." Tonetka gestured wearily for me as she transferred the last educator to a berth.

I left Roelm and joined her. "How are we doing?"

"The women will recover. Fasala?"

"She's stable," I said, glancing over. Salo was kneeling beside his ClanDaughter and holding her small hand. His other arm was around Darea, whose face was pressed into his tunic. "We'll have to watch her, though."

"Keep her on close monitor. I must report to Command Level. Captain Pnor requires my presence."

Squilyp hopped over to join us. He was only nice to one person in the Medical Bay, for obvious reasons. "Senior Healer, you need to rest."

I resisted the urge to make a kissing noise. Barely.

"After I make my report to Pnor." She was curt; Tonetka disliked being treated like a doddering old woman. Too bad Squilyp hadn't noticed *that*. "Have the accident site on level fourteen secured immediately," she said to me. "Tell Ndo I demand a full investigation be conducted at once."

The Omorr cleared his throat. Or had a moment of flatulence. It was a tough call. "Senior Healer, surely you don't believe—"

"It matters not what I believe!" she shouted at him. "No more of our ClanChildren will be carried in here bleeding!"

"Of course." Nervous, gildrells twitching, the surgical resident hopped away.

Probably off to sterilize some already clean part of the facility. I wondered if the Omorr had a term in their native language for "obsessive-compulsive disorder." Or "insensitive jerk."

"Cherijo!"

"Sorry." I shook my head. I'd been so busy glaring at Squilyp I never saw the data pad Tonetka was holding out to me.

"The statement from the educator." She thrust the data in my hands. "In the future, attend to *me*, not the surgical resident, when I am speaking to you!"

Tonetka was right. We couldn't fool around with this situation, not with all the curious kids on board. I needed to focus on that. Not the insensitive jerk.

"Sorry," I said. "I'll see to it right away."

As I rose, she put a hand on my arm.

"Your pardon, Cherijo." She lifted her fingers to push them through her disordered hair. The purple streaks of age seemed more pronounced. "You would think after all these revolutions, I would learn to distance myself from a pediatric case."

I gently put my hand on her shoulder and squeezed. "I hope you never do, boss."

I signaled the Ship's Operational Officer, Ndo Torin, and relayed Tonetka's orders. I quoted her using the same tone and expression she'd used to singe my eyebrows off. It was the simplest way to let the S.O. know *The Senior Healer Was Not Happy*.

Ndo, who was second in command on the *Sunlace*, vowed to conduct the investigation personally. I didn't blame him. Tonetka in a rage was awe inspiring.

"How is Fasala?" he asked. Like all Jorenians, he was very protective of the kids, and appalled to learn of what had happened to her.

"Serious, but stable. Salo and Darea are with her. We'll take good care of her, Ndo," I said. "Let me know if you need any further data from Medical."

"I would also like to interview the two educators after we inspect the damaged cargo section. Thank you, Healer."

I made rounds and kept a close watch on Fasala's vitals. Poor kid. Her small, motionless body huddled in the center of the berth. Her ClanParents said little, and didn't move an inch away from her side.

I kept thinking about how I'd feel, if she was my child. Kao and I might have had a little girl like that. If I hadn't killed him, trying to save his life.

After discovering I was the result of a highly illegal genetic experiment, I fled Terra for the multispecies colony on Kevarzangia Two. There I had worked as a FreeClinic Trauma physician, and fallen in love with a Jorenian pilot named Kao Torin.

A mysterious epidemic decimated the colony. I didn't become infected, but thousands did, including Kao. Quadrant cruisers arrived to enforce planetary quarantine. The colony erupted into hysteria, then violent anarchy. Thousands died. Plans were made to sterilize the planet.

During the worst of the chaos, Kao stopped breathing.

In desperation I injected my lover with my own blood, which revived him and destroyed the contagion. However, my genetically enhanced plasma went on to attack Kao's own cells, and eventually killed him.

I'd live with that forever.

The Jorenians didn't blame me for what I'd done. Instead, they seemed to want to help me get over it—even Xonea Torin, Kao's ClanBrother. Xonea and my Oenrallian friend, Dhreen, spent plenty of off-duty hours with me, the two pilots making it their mission to keep me busy. Xonea tried so hard to be the brother I'd never had.

Speak of the Jorenian. Xonea appeared at my side, his large frame tense as he spotted the unconscious child and her distressed ClanParents.

His gaze went to Fasala's head wound. "She will live?"

I nodded, lifted a finger to my lips, and led him off to Tonetka's office, where we could talk in private. Xonea immediately eliminated at least half the available space. Maybe because his shoulders were as wide and solid as a deck support strut. Or the two and a half feet he had on me.

Kao had been almost as tall, I thought, then thrust the image away.

My ClanBrother was still wearing his uniform, which meant he had come here directly off shift. The silver tunic complemented his dark azure skin. A warrior's knot secured the long, straight black hair at the back of his neck. Like all the Jorenian males, he didn't wear any ornaments. They didn't have to.

Compared to him, I resembled a scrawny child. Like the Jorenians, I had black hair, but mine possessed a silvery sheen theirs didn't, the same "grey veil" passed down from a distant Native American ancestor. My pale Terran flesh made me appear ghostly beside my sapphire-skinned Clan-Brother. We looked a lot like disproportionate, negative photoscans of each other.

I gave him an abbreviated report on the child's condition.

"She is so young," he said, then gave me a thoughtful look. "You are blaming yourself for this."

Another annoying thing about Jorenians. They were incredibly perceptive. "Not really," I lied.

He didn't buy that. "The ship was not under fire when this happened, Cherijo. There have been no League vessels within a light-year of our position since our last transition."

"A mercenary vessel—"

"Would still show up on our perimeter scanners," he said.

"All right." I scowled at him. "It wasn't my fault." I didn't say *this time*, but Xonea picked up on that as well.

"Cherijo. You must release Kao to his journey."

Easier said. "We did that, Xonea. Remember? I gave part of the eulogy." I had nearly cracked into a heap of small pieces doing it, too.

One big hand settled on my shoulder. "We sent his body to the embrace of the stars. Yet his memory remains with you."

"I'll never forget him." What was wrong with his memory? It was all I had left. The stars weren't getting it.

"No." Xonea's hand tightened, then drew away. "I do not believe you will." He made a graceful gesture that was the Jorenian equivalent to shaking his finger in my face. "Only know, Healer, you cannot walk two paths."

Jorenian journey philosophy was full of little gems like that. "You cannot walk two paths" *(make up your mind)*; "select the journey to complement your destination" *(make up your mind and decide where you want to go)*; and the ever-popular "a wise traveler knows his direction" *(do you even know where you're going, stupid?)*.

What else could be expected from a species whose idea of a good time was to travel a thousand light-years? For no particular reason, either. The mood hit them and *wham!*, they were firing up a stardrive.

"Don't worry. I'll stick to one path, Xonea."

"You *are* my worry." Xonea gave me a chiding look. "I remain your ClanBrother, Cherijo."

In the usual Jorenian roundabout way, he was saying I didn't have to be so touchy, and I wasn't alone. "Thanks."

He glanced back through the viewer at Fasala. "What made those wounds on her?"

"One of the educators claimed a buffer shattered on level fourteen. I know, I know." I stopped him with my hand before I got another lecture on astroengineering. "The adaptable sonic alloy can't be breached or smashed." I thrummed my fingers on the surface of the desk. "Xonea, we spent a good hour picking pieces of this indestructible buffer out of those three patients. What is going on?"

Xonea regarded me steadily. "A buffer does not simply collapse. It *never* shatters."

Even the laws of science bent, on occasion. "If the hull panel *was* breached, why didn't the buffer explode outward, into space?" I asked.

"The buffer would contract and reform. Any weakness would be immediately arrested by the self-restorative nature of the alloy. Here, I will show you."

Xonea used Tonetka's display to key up a component schematic on the alloy, then programmed it to display the buffer under breach conditions. The simulation resembled something trying to make a hole in a thin sheet of water.

One long blue finger pointed to the screen. "See how the weak point is drawn inward at once? The expanse closes in upon itself. No alloy material is separated or lost. Nothing may penetrate the buffer thus." He advanced the simulation, and showed me how the buffer instantaneously reformed over whatever had tried to make a hole in it.

"Wouldn't a breach cause at least some of the alloy to detach?"

"No. Sonic-based alloy bonds at the subatomic level. Nothing can separate it except—"

I remembered the term Roelm had used. "A harmonicutter?"

"Yes."

My fears about the mercenaries resurfaced at once. "What about a sonic-based weapon?"

"There are none in existence, to my knowledge." Xonea collected weapons, so he'd know that. "Harmonicutters require tremendous power to operate, more than any star vessel could generate alone. It would require planetary resources. The buffer did not shatter."

We weren't anywhere near a planet. So it hadn't been a League attack. "I personally removed fourteen containers of that stuff from Fasala's wounds. Believe me, Xonea, you lost a good-sized chunk of your impervious alloy today." He straightened and made a gesture of frustration. "Yeah, I know exactly how you feel."

I studied my friend's face. At that moment, his resemblance to the man I'd loved had never been more acute. Soften the chin, add a few laugh lines, and he could have been Kao's twin. If only . . . no, I wouldn't do this. Kao was dead.

"Caution," Ndo's voice said from the console panel. "Transition in fifteen minutes."

"I have to see to the patients." I rose to my feet, and his hand reached out to catch mine.

"Cherijo, I would speak to you further." His fingers skimmed up my arm, briefly touched my cheek. An affectionate gesture between Jorenian siblings, one he made often. "What say you meet me at my quarters later?"

His quarters? With the way I felt right now, thinking about Kao, missing Kao, wishing Xonea was Kao? "Maybe." Over my dead body.

"I will see you then."

I hurried past him. *Later* was a flexible word. It could mean hours. Or days. Or months.

When Captain Pnor relocated the ship from one spacial dimension to another, the transitional effect created stress. Stress some of our patients, like Fasala and Hado, didn't need. I joined the residents and nursing staff as we raced to prepare our more fragile cases. Once that was done, I strapped myself in next to Fasala's berth as an extra precaution.

I never liked transition. The first time I'd gone through it, a League ship had disrupted the flightshield. The *Sunlace*'s altered molecular structure had allowed them to momentarily focus a containment beam around me. They'd tried to pull me out as the ship transitioned. Luckily, the attempt had failed.

Unfortunately the resulting strain had caused me to suffer a cerebral seizure and two consecutive myocardial infarctions. Not an experience I cared to repeat. I closed my eyes as the colors and shapes around me began to run together.

A moment later, we were clear. I went first to Fasala, who emerged from sleep suspension with no ill effects. My hands stopped shaking almost at once. Neither Darea or Salo commented on the fact I had bitten my lower lip hard enough to make it bleed.

"Doctor," Squilyp called from Roelm Torin's berth. The big Jorenian thrashed wildly under the Omorr's restraining grip. "He was trying to release the support braces harness again," the surgical resident said when I got there.

I grabbed one big arm and hung on. "Did you ask him what's wrong?" He gave me the usual haughty glare. "Oh, for crying out loud, Squilyp. You have to *talk* to them sometimes! Roelm?" When I could get it close enough, I ran my scanner over him. "What is it? Are you in pain?"

"The stardrive!" Roelm's eyes bulged as he grabbed at my sleeve and came close to breaking my arm. "There is something wrong with the transductors! I could hear it as we transitioned!"

CHAPTER TWO

Two Sides of Wanting

Squilyp hopped off in disgust while I took care of our frantic mechanic. Intimidation and a mild tranquilizer worked just fine. Still, I'd never seen anyone work up to a near-seizure over something that was—what? An engine rattle?

The drug calmed Roelm. So did my threats to put him into sleep suspension. He agreed to my suggestion and let me relay a message for him to the S.O.

From Ndo's reaction when he got my signal, I gathered the way the stardrive rattled was fairly important.

Ndo dispatched an entire engineering crew to check out Roelm's claim, then had me set up a terminal by the Engineer's berth. Relays flew fast and furious between Medical and Operational. Only the threat of plasteel restraints kept Roelm from tearing off his suspension harness and going down to inspect the engines personally.

The remainder of my shift was filled with the usual duties. I supervised the residents. Ignored the Omorr's irritating sneers and patent condescension. Gave orders to the nurses as they made the daily evaluations. Thought up unique excuses, should Xonea press the "stop by my place" issue. Performed afternoon rounds.

As she was improving, I updated Fasala's condition from critical to serious. She woke up once, and I removed the dermal regenerators for a few minutes so her ClanParents could each give her a careful embrace.

"She is always so impatient to explore," Darea said to

me as her hand smoothed Fasala's tangled black hair back from her small brow.

"Ring . . ." Fasala, who had fallen back asleep, muttered under her breath. "Ring . . . light . . ."

"What is this ring and light?" Salo asked.

"Probably nothing." I scanned the child and made a chart notation. "She's talking in her sleep."

"Fasala has an abundant imagination," Darea said, and straightened the pillow beneath the small head. "Her enthusiasm to explore springs from that, I fear."

"She needs to temper such enthusiasm," her ClanFather said. Salo Torin worked on the Command level as the Senior Communications Officer. Like Xonea, he also wore the warrior's knot that symbolized combat experience. Both men, according to Tonetka, had served together during several Varallan conflicts. Despite the tough appearance, I suspected this quiet man was as shaken up over Fasala's injuries as Darea.

Squilyp bounced by the berth and stopped when he saw me working on Fasala's chart. He got there in time to hear the last part of our conversation.

"An extended interval of discipline will do much to curb her inappropriate behavior," the Omorr said. "Punishment often discourages children from repeating thoughtless acts."

I saw the identical reactions of Fasala's ClanParents as they swung around, and shook my head sadly.

Squilyp, Squilyp. This was not going to be pretty.

"You speak of *punishment*? With my ClanDaughter here as she is?" Darea rose, every muscle on her substantial frame tensed. An assistant in the subexecutive level, she hardly resembled an administrator now. If there had been a pointy object within her reach, Squilyp would have had it sticking out of some part of his body.

"Omorr." Salo took a step toward the resident. His six-fingered hands knotted into very large, resident-flattening fists. My vocollar didn't translate the rest of what he said, much to my secret disappointment. Squilyp's gildrells twitched and he backed off a good meter. Fasala's Clan-Father smiled.

I was enjoying this a little too much, I thought. Time to break it up before we finished with Omorr smeared all over the decking.

"Okay, Mom, Dad." I stepped between them and the intended victim. Jorenians were wonderfully nonviolent beings, except when someone threatened their kin. Then they made the Hsktskt look like League Armistice Envoys. "Calm down." I looked over at Squilyp. His derma was turning as white as his gildrells. "Resident, go check on those patients at the far end of the ward."

"I just examined those patients."

This was the thanks I got for saving his miserable hide?

"Do it now, Squilyp, or you'll end up in surgery as a patient." I even gave him a push with one hand to start him hopping.

"Squilyp needs a refresher course on Jorenian HouseClan protocol," I said to Salo and Darea. "I'll schedule him for one as soon he untangles his foot from his gildrells."

My little joke didn't make a dent in the thick aura of anger emanating from Fasala's ClanParents. They eyed each other, with that silent form of communication Jorenian bondmates lovingly shared. Only now it seemed much more ominous.

"Darea, Salo," I said, and my sharp tone got their attention. "He's insensitive and ignorant, but he's not a threat to Fasala. *Stop it.*"

All those bunched blue muscles relaxed a degree. Darea glanced at her ClanDaughter. That gave me an idea.

"Concentrate on your child. She needs to be lo—" I hastily recalled there was no such word as *love* in their language. "She needs both of you."

I took a cautious step, placed my hand on Fasala's brow, hoping to draw their attention away from the Omorr.

"Salo, would you lift her for me?" I asked. "I want to change her bedding. Good. When we've done that, Darea can help me put the dermal regenerators back on line."

The nurses and I kept the couple busy for the next half hour, while their tempers cooled down. Their stares at Squilyp, however, remained lethal.

Tonetka came into Medical to relieve me. I could have kissed her. Between Roelm's ceaseless agitation over the engines and Fasala's parents being prepared to jump Squilyp at any moment, my nerves were frayed. I updated her on each case, and we examined the child together. She ordered the Omorr go off duty a half-shift early and compose a formal apology to Darea and Salo, then asked me to join her in her office.

"I spoke to Pnor about the buffer. He agreed with Roelm that it could not be breached so," the Senior Healer said as she sat down at her desk. "You can imagine his surprise when the Environment Operations Station reported extracting over a kilo of buffer alloy from our containers."

"So the educators *were* right." Xonea wasn't going to be happy to hear that.

"The site has been closely inspected. There was no hull breach or plate damage. The buffer is intact. It is as if it never happened."

I described Roelm's wild reaction after transition, and she decided to have the Captain interview the engine designer personally.

"I have little knowledge of engine design or tolerance. Pnor will sort this out." Tonetka completed her notes. "Now, regarding your upcoming sojourn." She handed me a data pad. "Here is a list of your assigned objectives."

My first diplomatic mission. Lovely. "Couldn't you send Squilyp to Ness-whatever instead of me?"

"NessNevat." She made an impatient gesture. "Squilyp has created enough difficulties at present. He stays here."

"Okay." I watched her smother a yawn. "Want me to stick around for a while?"

"No, I am well," Tonetka said, then sighed. "I look forward to returning to Joren. I can think of nothing better than basking in the radiance of our sun, and compelling my mate to cook for me."

"Sounds great," I said. "Maybe I'll join you."

The Senior Healer snorted. "I do not care for the warmth of mercenary pulse fire."

The careless remark stung, but I only sighed. If I wasn't the most wanted being in the galaxy, I certainly took second place. "Good choice."

"Forgive me." Tonetka made an embarrassed gesture. "I did not think before I spoke, Cherijo."

"It's okay. Besides, even if I left the ship with you, I'd have to eventually find another job."

A nurse signaled from the ward and indicated that Roelm wished to speak with Tonetka.

"Now that gives me an idea," I said, and grinned.

"Maybe I'll find a new vocation. Something like . . . basket weaving."

"I would not consult Roelm Torin about your proposal," Tonetka said. "His pressures would remain permanently in the red range."

Jenner woke me early the next morning, the usual way. Fifteen pounds of Terran Tibetan temple cat landed on my chest. I opened my eyes and got the Imperial Glare.

"Hungry, Your Majesty?"

Jenner's silver fur rippled as he drew himself up and thumped his haunches down on my rib cage. I could almost hear his disgusted thoughts. *After nine years of training you, you still have to ask?*

"All right, all right." I made him his breakfast and a server of tea for me. Once he'd wolfed down his portion, my pet padded off to find a comfortable perch. "Hey, don't wreck my favorite chair."

Jenner ignored me and jumped up on it. *Was your favorite chair. It's mine now.* He began kneading the cushion with his paws, preparing for the first of his hundred or so daily naps.

"Don't push your luck, pal," I said. "I'll make you take a feline exercise program. You're getting fat, you know."

His large blue eyes became indignant slits. *It's not fat, it's muscle.*

"I see you . . . running laps around a track." I grinned. "Being chased by Terran hounds."

I got my chair back.

After a light meal, I dressed and I headed out for the launch bay. I still got lost in the spiraling turns of the vessel's expansive twenty-eight levels. Some crew member always found me and sent me in the right direction. They treated me the same way they would a little kid. It was understandable. I was roughly the same size as Fasala Torin.

Fasala. She had come close to being cut to pieces. What had happened to make that buffer explode?

I kept mulling over the possibilities throughout my shift that day. Still lost in thought as I came off duty, I turned to enter the gyrlift, and walked into the only other Terran on board the *Sunlace*. Startled, I backed into a corridor panel and bumped my head.

"Reever!" Automatically I rubbed the sore spot on my skull. "That's it. I'm going to strap a proximity alert beacon on you."

"Perhaps *you* should wear the device." His voice sounded as bland as his expression. "*Your* lack of attention invariably causes such incidents."

Tall, fair-haired Duncan Reever was a handsome specimen of Terran male, if you skipped the unemotional face and cold eyes. As usual, he was wearing uninspiring black garments. In one hand he carried the portable database unit he was upgrading to allow our vocollars to continue to function away from the *Sunlace*.

Reever, who had been K-2's Chief Linguist, had come on board the *Sunlace* after my rescue. He'd offered his services to Captain Pnor in exchange for transport to the Varallan Quadrant. Since he was a telepathic linguist, and knew or could learn every language of every species the *Sunlace* might encounter, Pnor had welcomed him with open arms.

I, on the other hand, wasn't so crazy about the idea. Reever's main motive for joining the crew, I suspected, had nothing to do with getting a free ride, and a lot to do with me.

"Are you trying to be funny?" I asked.

Reever simply gestured for me to proceed him into the gyrlift. He was always so calm, so controlled. I could smack him just for that.

The gyrlifts whirled around the outer hull spirals, transporting crew members from one end of the ship to the other. The concept that you *could* walk one corridor and tour the entire ship from top to bottom always confused me. Apparently Jorenian engineers had planned vessel construction very cannily. How the tech involved worked was far beyond the limits of my attention span.

It worked, that was the important thing.

The *Sunlace* resembled an elongated Terran nautilus sea shell in design. The hull was one big, revolving corkscrew, while the vessel's stardrive had the capability of boring through dimensional barriers. That enabled the Captain to whisk the *Sunlace* away from any threat in a hurry.

A shame I couldn't do the same thing whenever Reever showed up.

I shouldn't have felt that way about another human being, but Reever wasn't exactly an ordinary Terran. He'd been born and raised in space, and had traveled extensively around the galaxy with his parents. During his childhood, something had happened that prevented him from displaying normal human emotion. Or maybe he never learned how. Reever didn't exactly gush at length about himself.

He turned to me. "You are scheduled for the sojourn to NessNevat."

"Yeah, I am. Have you ever been on this planet before?" I hated to make small talk. I was lousy at it.

"You haven't been accessing your relays again." At my blank look, he frowned. "I sent you a concise briefing on the planet's native inhabitants."

"I'm so sorry." A lie. "I've been busy." The truth. "Why don't you give me the short version?" Wishful thinking.

"According to available commerce reports, the Ness-Nevat are humanoid, warm-blooded, five sensory, verbal, highly intelligent life-forms."

"Why are we relying on traders for data?"

"They have had the only contact with this species. The information appears to reflect relatively accurate accounts."

I didn't question his opinion. Duncan Reever's parents were the first intergalactic anthropologists to leave Terra. He knew more about alien species than anyone on the ship. I'd never even met a nonhuman until I'd left Terra.

He continued briefing me. Knowing him, I'd eventually hear the entire textdata on the NessNevat, down to how many crops they planted per season, or whatever. I held up one hand when he took a breath. "Never mind. Why are we stopping here?"

"The NessNevat species are not on the Jorenian database. The Captain considered our close proximity to be an excellent opportunity to make initial contact. The planet is one of the few in the region with compatible fuel sources, as well."

"Sounds great." I stopped the gyrlift at level ten. "Excuse me, I'm going to get something to eat."

Reever followed me out. "I'll join you."

Lucky me.

Located three levels below the Medical Bay, the Galley was a popular gathering spot for communal meals and conversation. Although a portion of the crew (like me) usually dined in their quarters with their families (unlike me), others preferred a more sociable atmosphere. Part of the level was sectioned off and used as a recreation area. I spent considerable time there losing my credits to Dhreen and Xonea at the whump-tables.

Reever and I went to the prep units, and selected our meals. The usual post-shift tension, combined with worrying over Fasala, had ruined my appetite, so I chose something light.

"Healer Cherijo."

I glanced over my shoulder to see a tall, stunning Jorenian woman walking toward me. I didn't know her name, but judging by the color of her tunic, she was one of the teachers. Since I couldn't make a clean getaway, I set down my tray and waited.

A Terran gazelle bounding across the Serengeti would have looked knock-kneed compared to this goddess. My envy of the natural, graceful beauty of the female Torins was a familiar pang now. They were both ethereal and earthy. Long-limbed. Generously curved.

Oh, to be honest, they were *all* goddesses.

This one possessed exquisite features: feathery black brows, slanted white-within-white eyes, lush lashes, an aristocratic nose, and sculpted lips. Emerald gem clips studded her thick crown of intricately coiled raven tresses. Her embroidered aquamarine tunic was immaculate. More green gems winked at her ears, wrists, and fingers.

I could hate her without much effort, I decided. "Hello."

I got the usual supple gesture of salutation in return. I couldn't do that, either. Not without extensive remedial training.

"Ktarka Torin," she said, introducing herself. "Educator, Talot Province."

The Jorenians liked to give me name, occupation or rank, and birthplace when we chatted for the first time. I had no idea why. "What can I do for you, Educator Torin?"

Ktarka smiled at Reever, who stood waiting next to me. "I desire but a moment of your time, ClanCousin. The educator staff would very much like to give you this." She thrust a small folded package into my hand. "A token of our appreciation."

I unwrapped it. Inside was a pendant, the kind Jorenian females sometimes wore attached to their vocollars. The dark, polished stone felt cool against my fingers as I touched it. I knew better than to refuse. Jorenians were very sensitive about things like personal gifts. "This is gorgeous, Educator. Thank you." And why was I getting it?

She took it and attached it to my vocollar. "You devote much time to the children, Healer. The teaching staff has been negligent in expressing our gratitude."

All I'd done was play some games with them and put together a sandbox for the littlest ones. "You really didn't have to do this. I think I have more fun than the kids do."

She adjusted my vocollar, then smiled. "You are as generous as you are wise." With another fluidic gesture, she returned to her table, where four more educators sat beaming at me.

"The crew has grown extremely fond of you," Reever said as he dialed up a strange-looking concoction of vegetables and protein for himself.

"No kidding." I gave the educators a little wave.

We sat down and I eyed his meal. Whatever he had programmed resembled organic refuse. It smelled worse. It couldn't be a Jorenian dish. Their noses weren't as sensitive as mine, but they still *functioned*.

"What's that?" I asked.

"Serada baked with shredded nyilophstian root. A favorite of mine from childhood."

"Your childhood where?" I leaned over and sniffed. Yep. I'd smelled nicer backed-up disposal units. "A waste-recycling facility?"

"No." He didn't elaborate. Reever was an expert at that.

"I need to program a meal for you sometime, Reever. Remind me."

My own selection smelled great, but was too hot to eat immediately. While it cooled, I sipped my herbal tea and nibbled on a synwheat cracker. The silence went from there to noticeable.

I tried again. "So, what's the problem?"

"There is no problem I am aware of," he said, giving me another of those enigmatic looks.

"You just *felt* like having a meal with me?"

"I desired your companionship."

"Uh-huh." I tasted my dish once more. The prep unit had successfully incorporated my recipe program. It was delicious. He still wasn't talking. "Well, here I am."

"Yes."

This was going to be as challenging as performing open cranial surgery while wearing a blindfold. "Did you have a particular topic you wanted to talk about?"

"Yes."

Make that a blindfold and one hand tied behind my back. "What is it?"

"I would like to know your impressions of the Jorenians."

That was innocuous enough. "They're an interesting people. Great to work with. Extremely friendly. Why?"

Reever lifted his server of tea and gazed over the rim at me. His eyes were nearly as dark as mine today. I didn't look into them for very long. A soul could get lost in there.

"Would you prefer less attention from the crew?"

I shrugged.

Reever swallowed. Replaced the server. Took a bite of his baked garbage. He chewed it and swallowed again. A faint line appeared between his light brows. "This is not as I recall. My data must be in error."

"At least. Here, try mine." I held out my spoon.

He looked like a man being asked to sip hydrochloric acid.

"Liquified synprotein, reconstituted vegetables, and carbohydrates. A dash of sodium chloride. Go on, Reever. Try it. It has to be better than that stuff."

Cautiously he tasted it, and his eyes widened.

"Good?"

"What do you call that?"

"Chicken noodle soup." I gestured toward the prep console. "Go dial some up for yourself. I left the program on the main menu."

He left and returned a moment later with his own bowl. The serada was summarily disposed of. I was glad I didn't have to smell it anymore.

My turn to initiate polite conversation. I noticed his skin

tone was paler than it had been on K-2. No botanical gardens for Reever to dig in on a ship. At last! A neutral topic. "What have you been doing these past weeks, Reever?"

"Extending the linguistic database. Exploring the ship. Interacting with the crew." He finished his soup in record time. I was impressed. Not one slurp. "And you, Cherijo?"

"The same, work, finding my way around, making friends. Though I keep getting lost and everyone wants to be my friend." The intense way he watched me made me self-conscious. I lifted a hand to smooth my hair, then dropped it. "Stop doing that."

"Stop doing what?"

"Staring at me."

"I've missed you, Joey."

The words hung between us. His fair head inclined as one of the crew greeted us in passing. I tried to think of a witty reply. Encountered a blank wall.

"Reever, I—" I downed the rest of my tea in one gulp. "You always do this to me."

"What do you mean?"

My lips thinned. "We get to a certain point in the conversation, then you get enigmatic and call me Joey." And here I'd put all that effort into making polite small talk, too.

"I have no demands. Only a request."

Oh, *this* I wanted to hear. "What?"

"Will you spend some off-duty time with me?"

Now I was getting suspicious. I knew what part of me Reever was really interested in. The convoluted grey stuff between my ears.

From the first moment we'd met on K-2, Reever had repeatedly established a connection between our minds. Through that telepathic link, he could completely paralyze my body, and access my long-term memories. That was how he'd discovered I was a genetically engineered clone.

This ability of his didn't thrill me. In fact, after the first time he'd done it, I'd punched him out.

Reever claimed he'd never achieved that type of link with another human being before. He could even do it without touching me. Another first. The unique connection we shared was, beyond a doubt, the only attraction I held for him.

Or was it? Suddenly I felt rather warm.

He repeated the question. "Will you spend some time with me?"

"Doing what?"

"Cherijo." One badly scarred hand crossed the small gap on the table and took my wrist. I pulled back automatically, but he held on. "No. I won't force you to link with me."

"Good idea. You wouldn't look good with lukewarm chicken noodle soup all over your face." I let my hand stay where it was, for the moment. Why was it so damn stuffy in here? "Just what do you want, Reever?"

"I *am* human," he said, while his thumb moved back and forth over my knuckles.

The small, intimate gesture had the most embarrassing effect on me. I could literally feel the color creeping up my damp neck. "Uh-huh. And?"

He threaded his long fingers through mine. "We share more than you will admit, Cherijo."

Okay, I knew what he meant. Although I'd been created in an embryonic chamber, I had the same natural, healthy urges of any human female. Reever knew that from personal experience.

I felt a trickle of sweat inch down my cheek. "I take it you want more than just the pleasure of holding my hand."

"Yes."

He'd had more than that already. Reever, manipulated by the Core life form, had attacked me in an isolation chamber back on K-2. Assault quickly turned into a weird kind of seduction. I *didn't* cherish the memory of what Reever and I had done on top of that exam pad. That didn't mean I'd forgotten what it had felt like. In fact, parts of my body were reacting in much the same way right now.

I cleared my throat. "You're interested in the more . . . biological stuff." What was wrong with me? I was acting like a overly hormonal adolescent.

"Yes," he said again.

You're not a virgin, I reminded myself, so quit acting like one. Kao and I had spent one glorious night together, the memory of which I would cherish forever. All Reever had to offer were one-syllable answers. I need a lot more than that.

"You refuse." His hand began to withdraw.

Feeling distinctly reckless, I decided it was time to ignore my pride and Reever's lack of human emotion. I needed him. Certainly that was more important than pride now. In fact, it was all I could think about.

I snatched his hand with mine, and forced my fingers back through his. "Tell me exactly what you want."

The words came from him, with great difficulty. I could almost hear them being dragged out, kicking and screaming not to be uttered. "I want you to be with me, to share your experiences. I want to know you, to talk to you. I want to touch you. I want to link with you. I want—"

"Okay." I wanted some of the same things. Especially that touching part. "Good enough."

His fingers tightened between mine. "You will spend time with me?"

That was one way to put it. Could he sense the way I was burning up inside? Was that sweat beading above his lip? "Sure."

The cold eyes warmed a degree or two. "Thank you."

"You're welcome." I felt shaky, but there was no backing out now. Every nerve ending in my body was demanding some attention. What a relief not to have to think about it. I slipped my hand from his and rose from the table.

"When can I see you again?" he asked me as he stood.

He needed an appointment? Unmanageable demands surged inside me, overriding what was left of my usual caution. "Come back to my quarters with me. Now."

I don't know who was more shocked. Reever, who had admitted he wanted me, or me, the amateur seductress. I tried not to ruin my suave moment by taking back my offer the moment it left my lips.

Duncan looked like I just kicked him where it hurts Terran males the most. His pupils enlarged. When he got the words out, they were raspy. "You are sure?"

Did I really have that kind of effect on him? "No." I held out my hand. I thought that was better than shrugging off a corner of my tunic and fluttering my eyelashes. "Come on."

We walked back to level nine and stopped at my quarters. Before I could open the door panel, he took my shoulders and turned me around. I stared at the collar of his tunic, and bit into my lower lip.

"Cherijo. Don't be afraid of me."

Did I want to have sex with him? Yes. Did I want him to play the protective male calming the hysterical, near-virginal female? No. I had *some* pride left. Somewhere. Not to mention enough heat streaking through my vessels to melt an infuser tube.

"I'm not afraid of you." I hauled him by the arm into my rooms. Jenner greeted us with a casual yowl as he scampered out into the corridor. I adjusted the lighting, then leaned against the wall panel for a moment, dizzy with need.

This was wrong. *Wrong.* I needed a distraction. A delay tactic. My head examined. Why was I doing this? It was him, definitely him. Every time Reever came near me, every nerve ending went on full alert. What could I do to keep him away until my head cleared . . . ? My prep unit! "Would you like something to eat? Drink?"

"We just had a meal."

Okay, maybe my disc collection would buy me some time until I got my libido back under control. "Do you like Terran historical music?"

He was right behind me. "I have no preferences," he replied, and moved closer.

"What about archaic jazz?"

"I've never heard any." Each word puffed a breath against the nape of my neck.

I swallowed a groan. "Sit down. Jazz is the only audio art form ever produced on Terra." I selected a disc. "We'll start with Miles Davis. He played the trumpet like an angel."

He didn't sit down. He started touching my hair. "Angels are characters in religious mythology."

I let myself enjoy the feeling of his fingers against my scalp. "Wait until you hear Miles. You might change your mind." Davis's subtle syncopation colored the air with cool, dark sound. Reever's hand gripped my waist. No, don't do this, I thought, and swiftly turned to my prep console. "Would you like a drink?"

"No"—he started coming at me again—"thank you."

"Well, I could use a server of tea." He knew I was stalling and knew I knew he knew. My thought patterns were beginning to degrade. Fast. "Did you know on Joren they brew some varieties of saltwater vegetation and—"

"Cherijo." His hands touched me again. This close, I could smell him. Clean, masculine, familiar. Human. "Calm yourself."

There wasn't a system in my body that was functioning normally. "I'm calm."

"I am not," he said. I could feel his heartbeat accelerating just above my left shoulder blade.

"You, Reever?" Humor was my last resort. Panting ruined the effect, though. "You'll ruin your reputation."

Too late. His hands bracketed my wrists. "Link with me."

"Are you sure about the drink?" Frantic to prolong the inevitable, I began babbling. "You haven't tried my Terran blend. Do you like rosehips and camomile?" I felt the intimate sensation of his mind reach out to me, and closed my eyes. "Maybe some coffee—"

"Joey." His thoughts flowed over the edge of my consciousness. "Let me in."

I had never liked this telepathic thing. Reever somehow completely incapacitated my will as he connected my mind to his. He took me in his arms, and swept me into a waltz as Miles Davis's trumpet played like angels crying.

He was making me dance. *You can't waltz to jazz,* I thought.

Why not? His voice spoke inside my head. *It is music, is it not?*

It wasn't like I had a choice. *Okay, maybe we can.* I moved closer to the warmth of his body. *Why did you want to link with me first?*

Duncan pressed his cheek against the top of my head. *Your thoughts were turbulent. I thought it would calm you.*

I lifted my gaze. *You can read me without a link?*

His lips briefly collided with mine. Shock made me stumble. Reever boosted me over his feet with a fancy twirling motion. *Just dance with me, Cherijo.*

We danced for some time, while Reever did something to settle my thoughts. What thoughts I let him have a peek at. I had learned early on to block him from the parts of my mind I didn't want him snooping around in. I'd only reached into his mind voluntarily once during the epidemic on K-2. I wondered if I would ever get the nerve to do it again.

The jazz recording came to an end. Duncan twirled me one last time down the length of his arm and back, until our bodies pressed together.

I want to be with you. His hand stroked my hair. *In all ways.*

I could think of one particular way. *End the link, Duncan.*

Of course.

We stood in the center of my quarters, locked in a close embrace. For the first time I wondered how much control Reever's mind had over mine. Had we really spent the last hour just *waltzing*?

We'd been doing something. I was perspiring freely. My respiration was rapid and shallow. He showed similar signs of arousal. His arms tightened around me. I felt his heart hammering against the swelling mound of my breast.

"Thank you." His breath warmed my mouth. My thighs clenched against the subsequent inner throb. He broke off the airy kiss and let go of me. "I will leave—"

Leave? I grabbed him and pulled him back to me. "I don't think so." My fingers tangled in his light hair and brought his head down to my level. My mouth did the rest.

A Terran kiss was a curious thing. I could understand why some offworlders found it extremely disgusting. When Reever kissed me, however, revulsion wasn't an issue. Neither was any other coherent thought. Our lips, like our bodies, matched perfectly. I wanted more. So much more.

Beneath my fingers, his hair felt silky and alive. I pushed one palm over his chest, irritated by the garments that kept our skins from touching. His kiss deepened until my throat arched. My fingernails dug into his shoulder. His arms pressed in, removing the last small spaces between us.

"Cherijo." He wrenched his mouth from mine.

Oh, no, I thought, grabbing his head and pulling him back down. We were created for this. Male, female. The two sides of wanting. And I needed my other half. Now.

Something bizarre and ferocious instantly ignited between us. I heard fabric tearing. Felt the coolness of air on my exposed skin. Then his hands. Oh, God, his hands.

"Duncan." I clutched at him, dizzy, desperate. "Please."

He dragged me to my sleeping platform. Maybe I dragged him. I didn't know. Didn't care. We got there. Now

I wanted his body over mine. Needed it. More than I needed to breathe.

"Joey." He didn't appear indifferent anymore. He looked ravenous. Hard hands shoved me back on the mattress. He stood over me as his narrow blue gaze burned down the length of my body.

"Come here." I held out my arms.

He moved so fast I didn't have time to blink. Reever's weight suddenly forced me down, down into the slowly adjusting mattress. His hands were on my breasts, then his mouth. The rigid length of his confined erection pressed between my thighs. Yes, yes, that was what I needed. What I wanted more than anything. The way he felt, moving against me. He reached, pulled my face up to his. Sounds spilled from my throat, hummed against his mouth.

"Cherijo."

I shook my head, caressing him with my lips. "Don't . . . don't say anything." I didn't need a cargo hold of words now. I was more than willing.

His head lifted. His long frame went rigid.

"What?" I was breathless, still moving under him. "What is it?"

Now he shook his head, as if to clear it. "No, Cherijo."

I couldn't have heard that right. "No what?"

His hands hurt me. "No more mindless seductions."

Mindless? Seductions? My overloaded nerve cells made it hard to put the words together. They made no sense.

Then they did. He was referring to the only time we'd had sex. When the Core (by rendering him mindless) had forced him to take me. To rape me, however reluctantly. My lungs expelled a ragged breath. Reever was comparing this to *that*?

"Have you lost your mind?"

"Is this all you want? To have intercourse with me?" His voice was absolutely frozen. So were his eyes. I must have hallucinated all that heat before. Maybe he'd spiked my chicken noodle soup when I wasn't looking.

Wanton desire became cold-blooded fury. "Right now? Of course not, Reever. I thought we could discuss the League negotiations in the Tuyhui Quadrant. What the hell do you think?"

"What sort of stimulant did you program into the prep unit?"

I stared at him, aghast. He thought I'd spiked *his* soup. "None!"

"Then you merely want to have sex?"

Ah, I got it. *He* needed a bunch of words. "Yeah, I do."

"Do you expect to find satisfaction in this?"

"Do you expect to be breathing in another five minutes?" I struggled. "Get off me!"

He kept me pinned beneath him. "Why me, Cherijo?"

"Good question!"

"Why not one of the Torins?"

"Take your damn hands off me." When his grip loosened, I shoved him away and rolled off the mattress. "God, Reever, you know how to choose your moments."

I stalked over the viewport and stared at the stars. I was trembling. Duncan Reever had me trembling.

"Why don't we do this another time?" Never again. Ever. I'd commit suicide first. No, I'd kill him, *then* I'd commit suicide.

"What is wrong with you?" he said. "You are never like this."

"How would you know?" I got snide. "The only time you had sex with me, an alien life-form had to take over your *brain* first!"

"I could do this." He sounded cruel; another first. "I could touch you, take what you offer. I could use your body, Cherijo, until you couldn't move from that bed from exhaustion."

I glanced over my shoulder. Saw behind the mask of his face. All that passion simmering. Waiting. He denied me that.

I jerked my head back toward the viewport. Made my voice as nasty as his. "Promises, promises."

"Cherijo. Look at me." When I didn't, he came up behind me and spun me around. "I could do all those things, but that is not why I came here."

"Oh, really? Funny, I thought that was the whole idea. Why *are* you here?"

He only shook his head. "I won't be used as a substitute."

"As a substitute for *what*?" I pushed him away from me, and flung my hand toward the sleeping platform. "Do you see anyone there, Reever? *No.* Heard of me sleeping with anyone else? For your information, *I'm not.*"

"The Jorenian males remind you too much of Kao Torin."

"Oh, for God's sake!" I pushed a handful of loose hair back. "Jorenians bond for life, remember? No wedding, no sex. I get involved with someone, next thing you know, I'll be picking out names for our kids!"

"A Torin would expect you to bond with him."

Was he deaf? "Yes. Yes!"

"So to avoid commitment, you chose to take me as a lover instead."

That wasn't the case at all. So why did my jaw drop open? *Had* I chosen Reever because I'd feel no obligation? Because he was human, not Jorenian? No. He was twisting my emotions to suit his perceptions. Obviously this was the wrong approach. Maybe reason would work better than screeching.

"Look, Reever, we're adults. We can make this work—"

"Based on what?" Reever folded his arms. "You have no feelings for me."

I could have lied, but I didn't. "I—care about you."

"You don't *know* me." He walked to the door panel, then paused. "Notify me when you are interested in more than my physical convenience."

It was a great exit line. Out he went.

I was unexpectedly, absolutely enraged. An empty server flew at the door panel, but it had already closed. I picked up another server and tossed it anyway. The crashing sounds they made were music to my ears.

I wanted to tear something apart. I wanted to hammer something into dust. I wanted to—

Sit down and figure out why the hell I had completely lost it.

I reached for my scanner, sat on the edge of my sleeping platform, and ran an initial series on myself. My heart, pulse, and respiratory levels registered well over normal range. I was angry; it could be due to the sympathoadrenal response.

Or maybe I *had* been drugged.

The prudent thing to do would be to go down to Medical and run a blood series on myself. Only the Omorr would immediately stick his nose in what I was doing and want to know why. No, forget that. I'd run the series when he went off shift.

Why would anyone want to drug me, anyway? The Jorenians had adopted me, welcomed me, practically smothered me in friendship.

I fell back on the mattress and thought about Reever. This had to be another of his telepathic manipulations. Only he didn't want me without the words. Why hadn't he just *made* me say them?

Eventually I calmed down. Memorized the swirly patterns on the upper deck. Closed my eyes.

I floated in a sea of warm, black fluid. An intricate web held my body suspended. I liked it here. It was warm and safe. Much better than how Reever had left me.

Unexpected light pierced that eternal night. I closed my eyes against it. Pain shimmered through my curled limbs as one of the strands pulsated, and something entered my body. I felt myself changing, emerging from the safety of the darkness. My mind formed its very first conscious thought.

This is wrong.

As if in response to my thoughts, more strands flexed, and agonizing jolts bombarded my small bones.

Small. I was so small. Helpless. The pain I felt, it was shaping me. I would fight it. Defeat it.

Another chamber. Here the dim glow to the air was soft gold. I was myself again, and breathed in relief. What a nightmare.

What was that?

I wasn't alone. I couldn't see the presence in the dream with me, but I knew it was there. The nightmare hadn't ended, but had somehow . . . shifted.

"Here. I am here."

The low voice whispered, offering comfort to me. I inched toward the sound. Was it Reever, come to taunt me here as well as on the other side? Let him try to link with me. I'd knock a hole through that enigmatic brain of his.

"I can help you."

The sound of that voice was determined. Dangerous.

The words swirled around me as it chanted my name, over and over. I should have been lulled into acquiescence. The first nightmare was too fresh, though, so I remained on guard.

Hands reached out, touched me—

I jerked out of sleep with a shriek. Sweat made dark patches all over my undershirt. Dread curled in my stomach. Throwing up had enormous appeal at that moment. I rubbed my eyes and breathed deeply. Reever had to stop doing this to me.

No. It wasn't Reever. I remembered now.

The hands in my dream had been six-fingered.

CHAPTER THREE

HouseClan Call

I threw myself into my work after the confrontation with Reever. Even ran a series of blood tests the following morning, but nothing unusual showed up. Which proved nothing except that I hadn't been drugged with any identifiable chemical substance.

Reever avoided me. Whenever I saw him, I merely turned and walked into an available gyrlift. We were being very civilized. It was a big ship. Both of us had plenty of responsibilities in our respective positions. We could do this all the way to Joren.

"Priority direct relay for you, Healer Cherijo."

I walked over to the main display and acknowledged the signal. "Forward it through to the Senior Healer's office for me, please."

I grabbed a server of tea from the ward prep unit on the way in, closed the door, then activated Tonetka's display. The vid screen glowed and coalesced into an image of a sleek, well-groomed blond woman. "Ana?"

"Hello, Dr. Grey Veil!" K-2's Administrator smiled as she scrutinized me thoroughly. "You're looking very well for an escaped League criminal with an outrageous amount of credits on your head."

I laughed with delight. "Ana Hansen, how in the universe did you manage to make a direct relay to the *Sunlace*?"

"Commander Norash owed me a favor, and the Jorenians were happy to help. We arranged a signal rendezvous before you left orbit. So tell me, how are you?"

I quickly related some of the events since my rescue from K-2, leaving out the latest clash with Reever.

She was astonished to learn I had been adopted by HouseClan Torin. "This makes you Dr. Cherijo *Torin*?"

"Among other things," I said, and took a sip from the server. "Namely, ClanDaughter, ClanCousin, Clan-Niece. . . ."

She beamed with pleasure. "Just what you needed. One big family." I could debate that, I thought, but decided instead to tell her about replacing Tonetka once we reached Joren. "Quite an honor," was her reaction.

I winced. "Please, don't say that word. The first week I was on board, I said something about what an honor it was to be working with the crew. Apparently my wording translated to a licentious proposal to three different males standing nearby."

"Did any of them hold you to it?"

"Happily, no."

"Too bad," she said. "Speaking of males, how is Duncan?"

I tried to find out, I thought sourly, but he got cold feet on me. Irritation made me flush, and I tugged at my collar. "He's working as the ship's linguist."

"Any . . . progress between you two?"

"No." Time to change the subject. To anything but Reever. "How are things at your end of the galaxy?"

"The League cruisers pulled out of orbit some weeks ago, when it finally became apparent you weren't coming back."

Idiots. "Takes them awhile to catch on, doesn't it?"

She nodded. "Your old nemesis Phorap Rogan was dismissed at the same time. Rumor has it he returned to his homeworld."

"The patients declare a colonial holiday?" I finished my tea and set the server aside.

"Some wanted to." Ana tried to look official, but the grin spoiled the effect. "Dr. Mayer sends you his regards. He asked me to say that should the League's decision ever be reversed in your case, he will allow you to be Chief of Staff while he spends a few years on Caszaria's Moon."

I laughed. I couldn't imagine the taciturn surgeon ever relaxing on K-2, much less a resort planet. "How are the colonists? Has everyone settled down?"

One of Ana's slim hands rubbed her brow for a moment. "Those who are left, yes. We've had a general exodus. More than half the population transferred out as soon as Pmoc Quadrant lifted the last travel restrictions."

That was a shame. "Colonial Admin had to figure that was going to happen." Surreptitiously I rubbed my damp palms on my trousers, and wondered if Squilyp had been fooling with the environmental controls again.

"We planned for it, but the need for key staffing has become critical. We now need construction workers as much as medical personnel. No one, naturally, wants to transfer in. We hope, with time, the panic will fade." She grew serious. "What about your situation, Joey? Will you be all right with the Jorenians? Are you happy?"

"I'm satisfied with my position. Happy . . ." I grimaced. "Who wants to look over their shoulder forever?"

"Keep your chin up," she said. "If you need help, remember you still have friends here. Whether you return to Pmoc Quadrant or not."

We didn't say it. We both knew this might be the last time we had direct contact with each other.

"Thanks, Ana. I'll try to stay in touch."

"Thank you. Tell Dhreen and Alunthri I send my greetings. Oh, and give Jenner a hug for me." Tears sparkled in her eyes. "God bless and safe journey, Cherijo. I will be thinking of you, always."

The traditional Jorenian farewell seemed appropriate. "Walk within beauty, Ana."

I terminated the relay. Before I turned from the console, a signal from Operational came in. Ndo's image appeared on the screen, his broad features etched with tension.

"Alert status," he said. "Medical, prepare for emergency transition. Assemble medevac teams, report to level eighteen, launch control."

A couple of the nurses came over as I acknowledged the signal. "What is it, Ndo?"

"NessNevat has been attacked by raiders. Make haste." Ndo's relay abruptly terminated.

Getting the patients prepped took time. Residents,

nurses, and the Senior Healer appeared in rapid succession. I looked up from Fasala's suspension cradle. Tonetka seemed worried.

"We've got to get the berth harnesses in place," I said, sweeping my hand toward the last of the unsecured patients.

The Omorr resident bumped into me as he bounced by. "Doctor! Didn't you hear the announcement? We have to hurry and make preparations!"

"Don't get your gildrells in a knot, Squilyp." I felt like smacking him with something hard and heavy. "This is why we have all those endless drills, remember?"

We managed to strap all the patients in protective harnesses just before the ship's transitional thrusters fired. I turned to locate a spare harness. Squilyp, who was already strapped in, gave me a derisive glare. What a little paragon of caution he was.

"See? Nothing to worry about. I bet that had to be a record—" I found myself flat on my face, watching the deck below me ripple and reshape itself. "Forget what I said." I groaned, and pushed myself up on my elbows as the *Sunlace* transitioned.

Through the distortion of reality, the Omorr looked like a big blob of white corkscrews. Corkscrews that were jiggling with laughter.

"You can get up now, Healer." Tonetka was too polite to laugh at me, once the transition was over. "Perhaps I will *increase* the number of drills we perform."

"The Doctor could apply some off-duty time to remedial training," Squilyp said. Always the helpful resident.

I'd like to apply something flat, wide, and adhesive to his gildrells, I thought. I held my head and stood up carefully. "I'll never complain again. Long as I live." Which I hoped would be until I was a little old grey-haired genetic construct.

"Remain still, Cherijo," the Senior Healer said, and performed a brief scan. She frowned slightly. "Your vitals are registering above normal parameters. Norepinephrine levels are also unusually elevated."

"It's just the sympathoadrenal response, Tonetka." I straightened my tunic. "Terrans exposed to sudden, unexpected stress generally enter a hypermetabolic state."

"As you say, Cherijo." She didn't look entirely convinced, but we had other things to do. "Come, we must perform rounds." To the residents, she said, "Prepare the field packs. Allow enough supplies for possible heavy casualties."

The Senior Healer made sure we had enough staffers to cover the ward, then she and I performed quick rounds. Squilyp and another resident sorted what equipment we would need. The supplies were divided among the medevac team. I shouldered my heavy pack with a grimace. The Omorr must have put an extra fifty kilos in mine.

"Caution," the Medical Bay display announced. "Medevac launch will depart *Sunlace* in ten minutes."

We took the gyrlift down eleven levels, where one of the launches was waiting for us. Other teams were still loading their shuttles with relief supplies and equipment.

"Have you received reports from the surface?" Tonetka asked once she was inside the launch. I stowed my pack before shrugging into a harness rig. The pilot turned around, and the interior light revealed a thatch of orange hair with two small, red hornlike protrusions. It was my Oenrallian friend, Dhreen.

"No signal from the colonists," Dhreen replied, and punched in the initiation codes. The launch engines hummed into life.

Squilyp leaned forward. "What about the raiders?"

The Oenrallian, who had long ago transported me from Terra to K-2, shrugged. "A trader reported that ships were attacking the colony," Dhreen said. "Probably a passing route jaunter who saw them firing on the planet from orbit."

The Omorr looked pained. "A trader? Surely more reputable sources could have provided information."

"Nothing wrong with traders," Dhreen said.

"They're the worst sort of opportunists." Squilyp's gildrells bristled. "Always looking to profit from the suffering of others. Why, once I knew this—"

"Uh, Squil?" I interrupted him. "Want to guess what Dhreen was before he joined the crew?" The Omorr's eyes widened as he glanced from the unsmiling Oenrallian to me. "Exactly. So . . . you were saying?"

"Nothing," he mumbled.

Dhreen winked at me. I felt much better.

The launch shot out of the flight bay and into open space. Below us the looming sphere of the planet swelled into view. It was a placid-looking world. Land masses solidly paved the outer surface in a myriad pattern of green and brown topography. Small blue circles indicated water sources, probably former sites of ancient meteor collisions.

I noticed that Dhreen was scanning the immediate sector continuously. Slipping from my harness, I went to the helm and quietly asked him about it.

"Standard procedure after raider attacks," he said, his oddly pitched voice equally low. "Loot haulers sometimes hide close by, wait for rescue to come in, jump them as well."

"According to the reports, this species is principally involved in agricultural trade," Tonetka said behind us. "Who would attack such a world?"

Dhreen's cheerful voice iced over with contempt. "Scum looking for easy takings."

It took only minutes to descend through the upper atmosphere, and clear the last distance to dock. En route we used the time to check our equipment and review medevac protocols.

"Triage must give priority to *salvageable* cases," Tonetka made the grim reminder. "Remember to enlist the aid of any native healers whenever possible. We come to assist, not to offend."

I thought I was tough, that I'd seen the worst. I'd been a surgeon on Terra for nearly nine years, and after that had survived a planetary epidemic on K-2. I discovered I hadn't. After we landed, one glance through the viewport made my stomach turn.

NessNevat's Central Transport had been completely razed. The smoldering ruins of a dozen vessels surrounded our launch. Craters pitted the docking pads, like the footprints of a rampaging titan. No one responded to Dhreen's request for landing clearance. The Oenrallian pilot still performed standard decon procedures before he permitted us to disembark.

"I'm jaunting back up to the ship to ferry another team," he said when I passed by the helm. His spatulate fingers pressed mine briefly. "You owe me another round of whump-ball, you know. Have a care, Doc."

I squeezed back. "You too, pal."

When the outer hull doors parted, the stench of death and destruction welcomed us. Among other things.

"Mother of All Houses," one of the staffers muttered.

"Monstrous." The Omorr choked out the word. "Monstrous."

For once I agreed with him. "You're right, Squilyp. There were definitely monsters here."

Motionless, mutilated bodies littered the ground, dismembered body parts flung around them like parts of broken toys. Blood gleamed dark and wet. It was everywhere. Pooled under the bodies. Splashed over ruined equipment. Blended with the spilled fuel that oozed past our footgear. Blood that was red, like mine.

There were no rescue efforts being made by the natives. No signs of life. Nothing moved but drifting smoke on a warm, fetid breeze. That came from the fires burning both around Transport and in the distance. A lone warning claxon echoed an eerie wail.

I shifted my pack as I scanned the horrified faces of the medical team, then caught the boss's eye. We often had moments of perfect empathy. This was one of them.

Time to get busy.

"Okay, people, we've got work to do," I said. "Let's go over the plan one more time."

My announcement drew the team's attention away from the massacre and jolted them out of their initial shock. Faces cleared. Backs straightened. Eyes sharpened. The Senior Healer took it from there.

"We will set up our triage station where we find the highest concentration of survivors. I will see to the use of existing facilities. The Engineers will build a temporary hospital if necessary." She turned to me. "Cherijo, your first priority is getting an area secured for the surgical cases. Squilyp, supervise triage until we can set up sterile fields. Let us make haste."

Whoever did this had no concept of mercy or surrender. All around us were the scorched scars left from heavy pulse fire and displacer blasts. What wasn't burned was blown to rubble. I was so mesmerized by the widespread destruction that I stumbled over one of the bodies.

Looking down, I bit my lip to keep from groaning.

Up close, the inhabitants of this world were even more pitiful. Red-blooded mammalians, from the look of their furry bodies. They were smaller than me. Benign faces. Little muscular development.

I remembered what Dhreen said. *Easy takings.* The butchers.

"Over there," Tonetka said, and pointed.

Several small, fearful faces peeked at us from the shadows of a partially collapsed structure. As we walked, we kept our hands open to show we carried no weapons.

"Where the hell is Reever?" I said under my breath.

"He's on the next shuttle. Keep a pleasant expression," Tonetka said. "Smile, nod, beckon to them. It will ease their fear."

The survivors slowly crept out of hiding to get a better look. We stopped and stood still as they drew close. Tonetka spoke softly to them as her graceful hands moved in soothing patterns.

"Come, we are friends, here to help you. Come, we have medicines, we will bind your wounds, we will comfort you." She kept smiling as her eyes met mine. "Cherijo. You are closest in size to these beings. Approach one of them, very slowly, please."

I moved cautiously toward the largest one, who was only half my height. These survivors were a lot smaller than the other victims we'd seen.

"Hi, there. My name is Cherijo. We're here to help you." I kept smiling. "Come on, I won't bite. I promise."

This one displayed an apprehensive smile and moved within inches of me. One small paw tentatively touched my blue tunic. I didn't try to touch it, afraid it might scamper off. It turned its head and spoke to the others. Their native tongue was a rapid, uneven stream of throaty mutters and yips.

"They sound like they're growling," Squilyp said.

"No, look at their eyes," Tonetka said, her voice still entreating and gentle. "They're simply afraid."

The little paw trembled as it curled around my fingers. I caressed the silky fur.

"So soft," I said, then it dawned on me. "Tonetka. These are the children." This one had a bad burn across the shoulders. "He's wounded." I took a scanner from my pack, very slowly, and let the child hold it to see that it wouldn't hurt him. I made a quick scan, and my mouth tightened to a flat line. "Someone shot him with a pulse rifle."

Tonetka approached now. The little one curled up next to me and squinted up at the huge Jorenian. She made soothing sounds as she examined the child's wound. The other survivors lost their fear and gathered around us. All of them had suffered nearly identical wounds. Tonetka used her hands to point to all the burns, then to show we didn't understand how they had been hurt.

All but one of the children stretched out on the ground, paws behind their heads. The one left standing pantomimed shooting them in the back by sweeping an imaginary weapon from right to left. The ones on the ground rolled over and writhed, then went still.

"The raider who shot them didn't realize he missed the back of their heads," I said. "They faked him out."

We were grim as we helped the children back up. The Omorr suggested treating this group, but Tonetka shook her head.

"Not here. Look. They want to take us to the others."

The largest was pointing to one of the few buildings left standing just outside Main Transport. Other shuttles had landed by now. I saw Reever sprinting across the docks with his team to catch up with us.

About time.

"Senior Healer," he greeted Tonetka, then turned to me. "Doctor."

"Linguist Reever." My boss smiled with relief. "I am very glad to see you."

In order for our vocollars to work outside the confines of the *Sunlace*, a portable terminal was normally brought from the ship and set up on the planet. However, since the Jorenians had made no previous contact with this species, it was useless.

Reever was going to be a very busy guy.

The children led us to the other survivors. It was slow going, because we had to stop along the way to check the bodies. There were plenty of stops. They were all dead. The kids began whining miserably as they apparently recognized some of the corpses.

Here in what had been a city, there was no breeze to take away the smell of death. Sweat beaded my brow as the temperature continued to rise. I hoped the climate on this world wasn't too warm. The odor would be the least of our problems.

The airless interior of what had once been a storage facility was crowded with the injured. Many, I saw, were already dead or dying. The living coughed and growled their pleas through raw throats as they had for days. We found no power, water, or food supplies. Puddles of blood and waste were everywhere. The stench was as thick as the bodies.

It soon became apparent there were no medical professionals among the survivors. What supplies they had before the attack were evidently gone or destroyed. The wounded themselves were terrified of us, and fought when we tried to examine them.

"Linguist Reever." Tonetka's hands made a gesture of frustration. "We must relay our intentions. Will you interpret for us?"

"Of course." Reever listened as the Senior Healer quickly outlined the emergency aid plan. He then approached one of those still ambulatory and made a gesture known throughout the system as one of peace and friendship. He reached, took one small paw. The small creature gazed up at him.

They remained locked in a still, silent regard for some time. Then Reever growled. The survivor did, too. That went back and forth for a minute. At last Reever released the creature's paw and went directly to the Senior Healer.

"I have informed him of our intentions. Their computer core was damaged during the assault on the colony. This one believes enough information remains to download their linguistic files into our database."

"We also need access to medical data, if possible," I said.

The Omorr, who had been hopping between the puddles of filth, got indignant. "Why must we access native data? They are warm-blooded, mammalian life forms. Even you, Doctor, can surely handle—"

"Squilyp?" The Senior Healer's sharp voice cut off the Omorr's sneering. "Shut up."

I managed—only just—not to applaud.

"I will transfer the data personally," Reever said.

"Good idea," I said, knowing Reever had the expertise to handle the task. "Did the NessNevat tell you what the city's population level was before the attack?"

"Several hundred thousand," Reever replied.

"Not so good." I looked around and made a swift estimate. "There are only about five hundred here. Where are the others?"

"These represent the only survivors on the planet."

Everyone stopped what they were doing to stare at Reever. Even Squilyp, which ruined his grand thumping exit.

"This is all that remain?" Squilyp's gildrells arched in surprise. "The trader indicated—"

"The trader was wrong," Reever interrupted him. "The native population has been exterminated."

"How can you be so sure?" I wanted to know.

"I have seen such assaults in the past. All of the colonists were herded to this immediate area, then systematically massacred."

"That's preposterous!" Tonetka said. "Anyone knows that raiders only take what they can trade!"

"This wasn't a raid," he replied. "It was an assault by the Hsktskt Faction."

Four hours later, as I was preparing for my eleventh surgical case, the Jorenian database finally accepted the Ness-Nevat linguistic download. We knew because our vocollars began translating the sounds our patients were making into words.

Under my hands, the adolescent with severe cranial fractures got particularly eloquent.

"Mother . . . Mother . . . take me back . . . to your . . . womb. . . . End . . . this. . . . Mother . . . do not . . . leave . . . me. . . ."

"I liked the growling better," I muttered under my mask. The nurse next to me repositioned the instrument tray so she could stroke a gentle gloved hand over the boy's furry brow.

"I am here," she lied to him. He couldn't understand

her, but the sound of her soft voice calmed him. "I will make the pain go away."

My thought exactly. "Put him under."

Squilyp and the other surgical resident were set up a few meters away from us. Engineering had installed remote generators which created two large sterile fields and powered the portable laser rigs. Through the containment static, I heard the Omorr swear now and then. Tonetka appeared regularly, monitoring both of us. A nurse told me the Senior Healer was coordinating all the relief efforts while simultaneously treating the minor surgical cases.

I had refused her offer to replace me and only requested the nurses be rotated every five cases. I told Squilyp to do the same, which he didn't like. He had an unpleasant tendency to view nurses the same way he did a lascalpel: You only replaced it when it couldn't function any longer.

The NessNevats' voices drifted from the open area beyond our temporary surgery, mourning the dead, crying out from pain. I knew many would die. Tonetka, Squilyp, and I were the only surgeons, and there were simply too many critical cases.

Reever's cool voice kept echoing inside my head. *This wasn't a raid. It was an assault by the Hsktskt Faction.*

That kept me cutting as fast as my hands could move.

Hours crawled by. I worked. Nurses came and went like the patients. I learned the rather limited extent of the Omorr's repertoire of curses. Sweat made my gear cling to every inch of my skin. The lascalpel hissed. The odor of singed fur and cauterized tissue filled my head.

The same stench the Hsktskt had smelled, as they fired upon the colonists.

Much later, after I'd finished closing the center incision on a NessNevat with internal injuries, the Senior Healer appeared. I noticed her standing across the table from me in a fresh mask and gloves. Over my shoulder, I saw Squilyp and the other resident were already gone.

I pulled the laser up and out of the way. "Checking up on my work, boss?"

Her white eyes were tired, her once-immaculate tunic ruined. "I am replacing you, Healer. Stop and rest for an interval."

The Hsktskt hadn't rested while they were here. "I'm fine."

"You've been performing surgery for seventeen hours without ceasing."

"Is that right?" My nurse nodded. I started the post-op scans. "I'm up for another seventeen more. Go on, Tonetka, take a rest yourself."

"It is not a matter of discussion, Cherijo. Until I retire, you remain my subordinate," she said, and plucked the scanner from my hand. "Go. You may not have another opportunity for some time."

With a helpful push from the nurse, I stepped away from the table. "Okay. Thanks."

My legs were numb from standing in one place for so long. I hobbled out from surgery into the general hospital area. Several of the nurses stopped me to consult on post-op cases. So far my patients were stable or improving. Once I was satisfied, I slipped out of the building into the ruins of what had been the NessNevats' largest settlement.

Until the Hsktskt showed up.

The nurses had brought me bits and pieces of information while I operated. The death toll stood at approximately two hundred thousand. Search teams were still sweeping through the formerly populated areas, but evidently Reever's theory was right, they hadn't found anyone still alive. A special construction crew had been sent down from the *Sunlace* to excavate the mass graves that would be needed.

An estimated ten thousand more natives had been taken from the planet. Slaver goods, if they survived the Hsktskt preference for raw flesh, and the jaunt to Faction-occupied space.

The survivors numbered only eight hundred fifty-two. Most of those were children who had evidently hidden in nooks and crannies during the assault. It was theorized that their weaker life signs hadn't registered on the Faction's proximity scanners.

Or perhaps, I thought, the bastards couldn't be bothered and had just left them here to die.

I sat down on a battered section of wall.

It wasn't a wall anymore. Not since the Hsktskt had stopped by.

A year ago I'd delivered five Hsktskt infants during a hostile visit by two of the Faction to the FreeClinic on K-2. At the time, I'd gone so far as to help the reptilian warriors leave the planet without violence. In gratitude, the female had promised to name one of the young after me— the equivalent of being made a Hsktskt godmother.

Godmother to the Hsktskt. Godmother to the butchers who had done this.

Somehow I didn't think the NessNevat would appreciate my dubious honor. Had the pair I'd helped taken part in this?

"Cherijo."

Reever walked up behind me. I glanced at him without enthusiasm. "Hello, Duncan. Pull up a chunk of rubble. I'm taking a break."

"You have been busy."

"Yeah, I have." I stared at the dust and rings of sweat on his black garments. "You, too."

He brushed at his trousers with a half-hearted swipe. "We began to dig out the lower level of a collapsed learning facility. As scans revealed all the children within were deceased, we discontinued the effort." He said all of it without inflection. I was too numb myself to react to his usual prosaic manner. "You called me Duncan."

I raised my gaze to his. "That's still your name, right?"

"You never call me Duncan."

This seemed like a really stupid conversation to be having. "Sure I do. Just not very often. I'll go back to Reever, if you want."

"I have no preference."

"Maybe I should. The last time I called you Duncan, you kicked me out of bed." I toed a bit of scorched rock around. "So, what else would you like to talk about? The weather? Seems nice down here for summer, if you ignore the smell of the decomposing bodies and the smoke from those fires they haven't put out yet. What do you think of the natives? Not that there are a whole lot left. Their kids are pretty good at fooling executioners. How about the view? Once the crew finishes digging those graves, they could pull down a few of these building remnants, maybe—" I jammed my fists against my eyes. *"God."*

"Don't blame yourself for this."

"Don't waste a perfect opportunity to say *I Told You So.*" My hands dropped away. I had no tears, not even for myself. "Remember? I brought five Hsktskt into existence. Five future Hsktskt butchers. Mayer was right. I should have killed them, and their parents."

"That would make you as callous and indifferent to life as the Faction," he said.

"Maybe. Then again, maybe I might be able to look at these kids and not feel like a co-conspirator to this massacre." I studied my hands. There was a fine, dry residue of powder on them from my gloves. No blood. At least not the kind I could see. "I don't know how to handle this, Reever."

He moved closer. "Call me Duncan."

I had no choice. I had to laugh. The sound erupted, raw and wild. I choked it back as soon as I could. It seemed obscene, especially here, among these ruins.

"Your anger and self-recrimination will not change what has happened here," Reever said.

"I'm not angry." I was a authority on the subject. It didn't feel like this. "You've seen me angry."

"Yes."

"You had every right to turn me down." I had put this off long enough. "I *was* using you." I stared back at the fragments of stone below my footgear. "I'm sorry about that. You deserve better."

I chanced another look at him. He was a block of stone himself, staring back at me. In spite of my black mood, my lips twisted. "This is where you gracefully *accept* my apology, Reever."

"You do not—" He halted, muttered something in an obscure language I couldn't decipher, then added, "I will never completely understand human females."

"I'm not exactly a role model," I said, and jumped down from the wall. "Want to take a walk? I should stretch my legs before I head back."

We picked our way through the vestiges of the thoroughfare. Avoided the broken bodies being stacked for burial. We reached a small clearing where the supplies were being coordinated and sorted for the survivors. The rescue team had everything under control—Jorenian efficiency was phenomenal during times of crisis. I looked over some medical gear as we walked around it.

"They're going to need more than medicines and food," I said. "Most of their adult generation is gone. They won't be able to rebuild—" Reever's hand pulled me to a stop. "What?"

The mask hadn't cracked, but something showed through it. "I would like to hold you."

Far be it from me to argue. "Sure."

We were both dirty, sweaty, and smelly, so we cancelled each other out. The feel of his body soothed me. His scarred hands rubbed in circles over my back. It was a nice feeling. The first I'd had since landing on this devastated world.

"What are you thinking about?" he asked against the top of my head.

"All these children, left orphaned. Stranded. Alone." I heard the hitch in my voice and shuddered against him. "I keep pushing myself past it. And I go right back again. Want to hear something awful? I wish you'd never updated the linguistic core. They keep calling for their parents. Praying. Begging their dead mothers to wake up. And all I can do is repair their bodies."

He was inside my mind before I said another word. I expected to find myself paralyzed again, but this time he let me retain control over my limbs. Or maybe he was too tired to make me into a statue. Our thoughts entwined. Reever's cool, white soul cloaked me against the horrors I'd seen.

For a moment, I let myself snuggle against him, body and mind. I needed this. *I wish I could be like you. Disconnect myself from all these emotions.*

They are part of you. He was remembering when we had been this close, back on the ship.

Maybe you should let me go. The last time we did this, we nearly started fistfighting.

We can be friends.

I was dubious. *Friends?*

We can try. I know what you shared with Kao Torin is beyond us. Yet—

I cut him off. *Try your luck with one of the Jorenian women. I've got to get back.*

The link ended. When I would have stepped back, Reever's arms held me in place. His mouth brushed over my brow. Tenderness, from *Reever*. What would be next? Smiling and laughing? And what was I doing, letting him get this close to me?

"Joey." No change to the flat set of his countenance, I saw. "When this is over, will you spend time with me again?"

"Sure." As soon as I had a complete psych-eval.

He released me. "I will walk back with you."

I went back and had one of the nurses drag Tonetka out of my surgery (we referred to it as assisting the Senior Healer). I watched my boss strip off her protective gear as I sterilized for the next case. Weariness made purplish shadows beneath the Jorenian woman's eyes. It wasn't good for a woman her age to work like this. I didn't tell her that. I liked my head where it was attached.

"Your color is better," Tonetka said once she had inspected me. "I want you to take regular rest intervals of at least ten minutes between cases."

"Sure I will. The same way you have, right?" I snapped my mask up over my face. "Go do your rounds, boss."

My next patient was a diminutive girl with a mangled lower limb. The regenerators couldn't locate a viable vessel in the crushed leg. Gangrene had set in, causing extensive tissue necrosis. I was forced to amputate. While I performed the hideous necessity, the nurse sponged sweat from my eyes. Okay. A few tears, too.

"How old is she?" I asked, after I sealed the stump with the laser.

"Two and a half revolutions," the nurse replied.

"Damn it." I stripped off my gloves and threw them down. Beneath outrage, guilt quietly gnawed at me. The nurse called for the next case. They kept coming. Terrible burns. Broken bones. Compression damage. Massive internal trauma. Three more amputations.

One of the children with grievous head injuries died on my table before I ever touched her. I had just sterilized and turned around to find the nurse gently closing the wide, blind eyes. It shook me down to my heels.

She'd made it this far, only to die?

The damage was too extensive, an inner voice argued.

No one could have survived four days of waiting for treatment. Not in her condition.

No one else had died on my table. I'd been able to save them. Had my former patients come here and wiped out these people? Destroyed hundreds of thousands of lives? Shot this little girl in the head?

How was I going to live with it, if they had?

The Omorr passed by, stopped, and studied the dead child. "What happened here, Doctor?"

"If you need me to tell you, go back to medtech!" I tore the mask from my face, and threw it across the table at him.

Squilyp seemed piqued. "There is no reason to attack me. I'm only trying to offer—"

I reached across the child's body. Grabbed two handfuls of his protective gear. Hauled him over until our brows nearly touched.

"What? Some more of that superior expertise? Is that what you're offering, Squid Lips?"

"Release me," he said, his coloring darkening from pink to puce. "And my name is Squilyp."

I shook him once, hard enough to make him fling out his three arm-limbs so he wouldn't fall on the corpse. Just so I had his attention.

"Listen to me very carefully, *Squid Lips*," I said. "You want to be Senior Healer? No problem. Talk to Pnor, tell him how wonderful you are. You want to impress Tonetka with your surgical skill? Be my guest. God knows you have enough of it. But never, I repeat, *never*, get in my face about a patient I've just lost. Got it?"

He nodded slowly. I let go.

"Good boy." I smoothed out the wrinkles I'd made in his tunic, then gave his chest a shove. "Now, get away from me."

Squilyp stalked over to his table. My nurse had disappeared. I spent a few precious moments cleaning some of the dried blood from the dead child's face. She'd been a pretty little thing. Just before I pulled the linen over the body, I bent down over and kissed the tiny cool forehead.

"I'm so sorry, sweetheart."

I donned fresh gear. Shouted for a nurse. Watched as the diminutive corpse was removed for burial. Sterilized the table and my hands. Took the next patient.

It went on through the night and into the next morning. Someone kept bringing me water laced with saline and fed it to me through a tube stuck in the side of my mask.

I kept going. Horror and shame were great motivators.

In the afternoon heat of the second day, I paused long enough to inject myself with stimulants. No one objected. I would have torn their heads off if they had. Another twelve hours passed before I left the table. The only way that happened was by Tonetka yelling, grabbing the front of my tunic, and shoving me away from the laser rig.

One of the nurses pushed me out into the central complex. I couldn't summon enough energy to walk. I slid down against a broken pillar and closed my eyes against the coming dawn.

The medevac team didn't notice, or they were too scared to touch me. Didn't matter. I slept.

The surgical resident assisting Squilyp shook me awake so I could relieve Tonetka. I paused long enough to remove my filthy tunic. The protective gear could only take so much saturation before fluids seeped through to the garment beneath. I didn't wash the blood off, just put clean gear on top of it.

Three days later, we cleared the last of the surgical cases. The medevac team had worked straight through, halting only to drop, sleep, then get up and continue. I took the bulk of the critical surgical cases. Squilyp and Tonetka shared the balance.

Two hundred of the survivors died anyway.

Tonetka and Squilyp were hauled off by some equally exhausted nurses. I only brushed them aside when they tried to do the same thing to me. Although the surgical cases had been covered, there were more problems that needed attention. Dressings that needed replacement. Suture sites requiring irrigation. A voice crying out for comfort.

So many voices, hands, eyes. All needing me. Nearly as much as I needed to make amends.

In the end Pnor sent Dhreen to take me back to the ship. Jorenians were too polite to *kidnap* someone. Former Oenrallian traders weren't as tactful.

One moment I was adjusting a dialisyzer. The next I was

being pulled from the equipment by strong, yellow spoon-fingers.

"Dhreen!" My voice was hoarse after days of snapping out orders. "What do you think you're doing?"

He tugged the scanner from my numb hand. "Time to go, Doc."

"I can't. This patient—"

"No, Doc." He put an arm around my waist.

"Don't be ridiculous. I have to—"

"Let's go, Doc." He dragged me away from the cot.

"You don't understand, there's a—"

"Now, Doc."

When I didn't budge, he stooped, bent, and slung me over his shoulder.

I argued upside-down the whole way from the hospital to Transport. I had no idea Oenrallians were that stubborn. By the time we reached his launch, I was feeling very much put upon. And light-headed. It showed. His thin lips twisted as he rigged me into the harness the way he would a dis-obedient child.

"Don't grimace at me that way," he said, looking back from the helm before he fired the engines. "I'm just follow-ing Captain Pnor's orders."

"Uh-huh." I stared at the viewport as the chilled interior air made me shiver. My eyes widened as I saw the ghostly reflection of my image on the plas. I looked down. My tunic was gone, my undershirt stiff and soiled. I couldn't recall the last time I sat, ate, or slept. A snarl of hair hung around my cheeks, limp and filthy. I smelled of sterilizer solution. Dried sweat. NessNevat blood.

"One of the neighboring ally worlds sent replacement relief teams. They're arriving today. The rest of our people will return to the ship when they land."

"I should have stayed," I felt I had to point out.

"Doc, you're extinct on your appendages."

"I am not dead on my feet," I corrected him with great dignity. The change in temperature was making me tired, that was all. A yawn divided my face in half. "Okay. Wake me . . . when we . . . ge . . . ."

I woke up in the launch bay as we reached the *Sunlace*. My body went on strike when I tried to get up from the seat. Dhreen had to lift me out of the rigging and carry me to the gyrlift. He got me to my quarters, then turned me over to a nurse already waiting there.

Things became blurry after that. My garments had to be peeled off my sluggish limbs. My cleanser unit pounded the filth from my flesh. Something warm and bland was urged to my lips. The world went from vertical to horizontal. Someone put on one of my jazz discs. A lonely sax spilled a cascade of abstract notes. The weight of a soft coverlet was drawn over my aching body.

I slept, but badly. My dreams were filled with the hiss of a lascalpel against torn flesh. The pitiful cries of wounded children. The dead eyes of a little girl.

CHAPTER FOUR

Particular Deaths

Sometime during my extended rest interval, the *Sunlace* transitioned out of orbit away from NessNevat and continued the jaunt along its convoluted route to Joren.

My experiences left me beyond exhaustion. The first time I woke up, I rose only to take care of my immediate needs, then staggered back to the sleeping platform. The second time I tried to stay conscious. My mind and body conspired against me, and I fell asleep sitting up, with Jenner curled in my lap.

It was the kink in my neck that roused me the third time. Yawning, I tried to rub out the cramped muscles while I checked my display.

"Forty hours!"

I signaled the Medical Bay, and demanded to know who sedated me.

"No sedation was required," one of the nurses said. "Your labors on the planet were most adequate, Healer Cherijo." She told me most of the sojourn medical team, including Tonetka, were still confined to quarters. Pnor's orders.

I grinned. The Senior Healer would hate that. "What's your status?"

"All cases currently list good or better condition, Healer," my nurse replied. She looked tired, too. "I will confess we would appreciate your presence, however, if you are rested." The ship's skeleton medical staff had been working double and triple shifts since the teams had left on sojourn.

"I'm on my way."

I grabbed a quick meal before I left. Since I'd been drinking my meals over the last week, my shrunken stomach nearly balked at the solid food. As I gulped down a server of tea, I told my belly to shut up and be grateful I wasn't looking for another syrinpress full of stimulant.

When I arrived at Medical Bay, I relieved most of the staff and put the remainder on half-shifts. The residents had been spelling each other for nearly a week now, covering for the sojourn and the subsequent, much-needed rest the planet team had enjoyed. Everyone was beat.

Everyone except the Omorr, who had revived enough to prepare the latest shift schedules for the nurses. I read over what Squilyp had posted, swore, then deleted them. The hours were so long they bordered on abuse.

I worked out a temporary replacement roster, posted it, and sent Squilyp a copy. If he didn't like it, I'd be glad to explain it to him. The same way I had the last time we chatted.

I made rounds, ending with Fasala, whose condition had improved dramatically. After a quick examination confirming that, I turned and nearly collided with the Omorr, who had hopped up behind me.

"Squilyp." I made to go around him.

"I would speak to you, Doctor." His gildrells were stiff as icicles. So was his tone.

Guess he'd gotten my schedule revision.

We retreated from the ward to Tonetka's office in silence. I watched as he hopped around her desk and plopped down in her chair. Like he owned it. His three arm-limbs folded neatly before him.

I get it, I thought. He wants to play Senior Healer. Put me in my place. Tell me the way it's going to be. Everyone has their limits. Did Squilyp know he just pushed past mine?

"Doctor, I received what appears to be a temporary roster of shifts for the nurses. Half-shifts, I should say. I was told you deleted my schedules and replaced them with this."

I love it when I'm right. "Yes." I crossed my arms and

leaned back against a wall panel. Perspiration dampened the back of my tunic. Not surprising, given the amount of hot air I was being subjected to.

"Scheduling the nurses is my responsibility."

"Scheduling, yes. Working them to death, no."

He produced a dermal probe and placed it on the desk. "I found this in my personal display. It was lodged in a keypad seam. Perhaps you can explain that?"

I picked up the probe. "Toñetka has a habit of doing that when she's in a rush to access the database. She drops what she's holding and it ends up jammed somewhere. Hadn't you noticed? Oh, I forgot, you're usually tied up fawning and simpering over her."

His gildrells flared. Muscles tensed. Eyes glittered. The epitome of Omorr outrage. Guess I was supposed to be afraid.

I yawned.

"When I attempted to assist you during the sojourn, you physically attacked and threatened me," he said. "Your behavior directly violated Healer protocol."

"Uh-huh." I picked up a chart and fanned myself with it while I made a rotating gesture with my other hand: Let's hear the rest of it.

He drew himself up with dignity. "You made a disgusting parody of my name."

I remembered calling him Squid Lips. The Omorr must have accessed the Terran database to find out what it meant. I smiled. I do have my moments.

He rose from the chair and leaned forward over the desk. For a moment, his stance reminded me of William Mayer, the FreeClinic Chief of Staff back on K-2. Dr. Mayer had chewed me out like this often enough. My smile faded. I didn't need this kind of grief. Not from a conceited, callous jerk like Squilyp.

"Have you nothing to say in response?"

"Plenty," I said. "Sit down."

"I will not allow—"

"*Sit down*, Resident." Those limits of mine really needed some sort of warning beacon. "Or I will sit you down *myself*."

Squilyp sat down. I pushed away from the wall panel and walked to stand before the desk. I caressed the edge with one hand. It was a nice desk. Tonetka had everything arranged very neatly. Someday it was going to be *my* desk.

I shoved it forward, hard, pinning the Omorr and his chair against the plaspanel behind him. A foreign flare of satisfaction surged through my limbs as I saw shock round his eyes.

"I've had enough of this. *Enough.*" I held up a finger for each point I made. "Your schedule was unkind and unreasonable. Your so-called helpful assistance was offensive and vicious. Your name is not God. Your title is not Senior Healer. And you have absolutely no authority over me." I ran out of fingers.

He'd recovered by then, and shoved the desk right back at me. Had to admire him, he wasn't intimidated. The moron. "You have personal issues with me, Doctor."

"Oh, *knock it off*, Squilyp!" I said. "We're supposed to be professionals, not two kids arguing over who gets the biggest toy!" The door panel behind me slid open, but I was too furious to deal with whoever was barging in.

"I am not playing with you," he said. Omorr sneers were remarkably similar to the kind humans make. The gildrells spoiled the full effect, though.

"Doctor." Behind me, Reever's voice carried a distinct warning note to it.

As if I cared.

"Really?" I leaned in now. "I disagree, pal. You've been itching to do this since Tonetka announced my appointment. We're going to settle this. Once and for all."

"You wish to permanently resolve this matter?" he asked.

I should have picked up on the wording he used, but I was too angry. "Hell, yes."

Reever got loud. "No, Cherijo!"

Squilyp beamed at me. Like I'd given him a present. "I accept your solicitation."

"Accept my—" I was lost. "What are you babbling about now?"

"You have physically threatened me, and expressed your desire for a permanent resolution. That constitutes a solicitation." The Omorr stood. "I accept, and will allow you the usual period of preparation—one standard week."

Reever came to stand beside me, and I looked from him to Squilyp in complete bafflement. "What?"

"Consult the database, should you have further questions. Good day, Doctor." Squilyp regally bounced out of the office.

I sat down, staring at the empty chair behind the desk. "What the hell is a solicitation?"

"The Omorr refers to his species' traditional manner of settling disputes. The challenge to a physical confrontation is called solicitation."

On Squilyp's world, problems were settled by challenging one's opponent to physical combat. Which was, apparently, exactly what I'd just done. "Wonderful."

"Joey—"

"Stay out of this." I got to my feet, pushed past Reever, and went back to work.

As soon as I went off duty, I signaled Xonea from my quarters, filled him in on the latest development, and asked him to help me.

My ClanBrother wasn't exactly pleased. "Did you sustain a head injury while on NessNevat?"

"Very funny." I glowered at the display. "Well? Are you going to help me train for this fight, or not? Or do you want to beat him up for me?"

"As it was *you* who made the threat against the Omorr, I cannot," Xonea said. "Very well, I will teach you Clan-Spar. Meet me in the environome on level nine."

Before I could get out of there, Reever signaled me, and offered some gruesome statistics.

"I don't care how many Omorr die every year in challenges," I said when he was done. I was changing into an old tunic and trousers. Jorenian blood might not stain, but mine did.

Duncan Reever's voice crackled over the audio. "Squilyp is an experienced competitor. He has advised me that he currently possesses the record for highest number of wins in his homeworld province."

"So he's a jerk *and* he brags. Big deal." I braided my hair tightly. No need for it to be flying in my face. I'd have enough problems. Like trying to keep Xonea from breaking my neck while we did this ClanSpar thing.

"You are a physician with no combat experience." He was shaking his head, like that was a bad thing. "I will assist you in training."

"There's no need. Xonea already agreed to help me." It was rather insulting, all these males, offering to protect me. I wasn't helpless. "And don't tell Pnor or Tonetka, either." The last thing I needed was upper management getting involved in this mess.

He muttered something in a strange language, then abruptly terminated the signal.

I hated to admit it, but Reever had a point. Physical brawls weren't in my job description. What sort of doctor inflicted pain and suffering instead of alleviating it?

A doctor who had been pushed too damn far, a hostile inner voice replied.

I met my ClanBrother at the environome programmed for warrior training on level nine. Xonea initiated the program, and indicated I precede him into the simulator.

"So, what do I do first?" I glanced around. The practice area was a flat three-meter square of shorn yiborra grass.

Xonea pointed to the center of the square. "Stand there, Healer." As I took position, he reached out and encircled my waist with his hands. "Breathe."

I breathed.

"No, from here." He tapped my diaphragm. I expanded it. Xonea eyed my torso, shook his head, then let go of me. "Lift your arms above your head." I did. "Now extend this leg." As I did that, he made a distinctly unmusical sound.

"What?"

"You have less reach than our children." Xonea walked around me. "No significant mass. Severely limited muscular development." He picked up one of my hands. "No claws."

"I can look really, really mean," I said, demonstrating.

"It is a miracle your kind evolved." Xonea made a double-handed gesture of extreme exasperation. "By the Mother, even jaspforran would do nothing to aid you."

My brows rose. "What's jaspforran?"

"An herb, taken by warriors before combat. It dampens nerve endings, focuses the mind, and enhances aggression."

Lovely. No telling what it would do to a Terran. "So show me what to do, minus the jaspforran."

He made me stretch virtually every muscle in my body.

When I complained, he warned me that we would be doing this limbering stuff every half hour, to keep my body flexible. After that, Xonea walked up to me and took hold of my arms. The next thing I knew, I was on my back, with Xonea straddling me.

"You are dead."

"That was fast." I groaned as he helped me to my feet.

I also learned that there was nothing esoteric about hand-to-hand fighting. There were no body parts that could be used as deadly weapons, no mystical nerve-pinches I could employ to win.

"In ClanSpar, one strikes to ground the opponent. Lack of body mass is your single greatest disadvantage. Thus, you must not allow me to strike you."

I learned to dance backward as Xonea advanced, then counter his attacks with simple evasive movements. I still landed on my backside. A lot.

"When do I get to hit *you*?" I said as I rubbed my abused posterior.

"Your profession requires you not resort to using your hands to strike. Your Terran physiology limits you to short-range strikes." Xonea studied me for a moment. "You will use your knees and elbows whenever possible."

"Where do I hit him?"

Xonea went to the room display and pulled up the database on the Omorr species. "Since Omorr genitals are extruded only when in the throes of passion—"

"Obviously, not around me."

"—you cannot strike to that area. These are the other unprotected sites." Xonea pointed to specific areas displayed.

He made me stretch again. Then we sparred.

"You learn quickly, Healer," Xonea said an hour later.

"You think so?" I pushed a handful of tangled, sweat-soaked hair out of my face. My body was bruised in places I didn't even know I had. "Let's hope I heal just as fast."

Alunthri paid me an unexpected visit when I came off shift the next day. I had a pretty good idea of why the Chakacat had showed up.

"Big Mouth spilled the beans, didn't he?" I asked.

"Big mouth?" The bullet-shaped silvery head cocked to one side. "Beans?"

I kept forgetting the vocollars translated idioms literally. "Reever told you about the fight."

Alunthri nodded. "He related the situation between you and the Omorr resident, and suggested I discuss it with you."

"It figures." I stepped back and waved a hand. "Come on in, I'll tell you all about it."

Alunthri had adopted a minimal amber garment that allowed it the most freedom of movement. Its silvery pelt shone with health, the sensitive ears were erect and proud. Only months before, the Chakacat had been forced by its owner to wear a collar and sleep on a rug on the floor. I had taken it in. We nonsentients had to stick together.

I smiled as colorless eyes regarded me with grave concern. "I haven't gone crazy, if that's what you're worried about." Quickly I related the details of the confrontations with Squilyp, and how they had escalated over time. "It was probably inevitable."

"But he manipulated you into making the solicitation!" Alunthri said. Near-invisible whiskers trembled as it added, "I am certain that if you explain this to Captain Pnor, he will force the Omorr to nullify the challenge."

I toyed with the idea for a moment, then shook my head. "No. Won't work. Squilyp thinks if he wins, it'll prove to Tonetka that he's the better candidate for her job. On his world, that's how it's done." The Chakacat's distress over the idea of the fight was pretty obvious. "Don't worry, I'll be fine."

"If you say so, Cherijo. Ah, here is my friend Jenner, come to visit with me." Alunthri held out welcoming arms as my cat leapt up into its lap. "Have you come to offer greetings, small sibling?"

"Your little brother smelled the food," I said. "Guard your plate."

His Royal Highness glared at me. *That's enough out of you, impudent serving wench.*

"We will share." Alunthri offered a crust to Jenner, who delicately sampled, then wolfed it down. "I heard of your efforts during the relief mission for the NessNevat."

"Some effort." I rose to my feet as I recalled all the orphans left behind. "Nothing I did will bring back their dead."

"Once lost, those still exist in memory." The Chakacat was obviously thinking about its parent and litter siblings, which had been killed outright for their pelts on Chakara.

I hurried to change the topic, and asked what it was currently involved in. The Chakacat had been busy, too. I listened as it related some details from its intense study of Jorenian weaving.

Hard to believe the intelligent, articulate Chakacat had been considered nothing more than a *pet* back on K-2.

"The last time I saw you, you mentioned you had some big decision to make," I said. "Have you decided to switch your studies from art to something else?"

"I've made my decision, and no, it is not in regard to my studies." Alunthri put Jenner down and went to my display. "May I access from here?" I nodded, and its claws swept over the touchpad, bringing up the navigational data charts with rapid ease. "There is an interspecies artists' colony that has been established . . . here." It used a talon to indicated the region. "It is called Garnot."

"Are we planning a sojourn there?" I asked as I examined the screen. It wasn't that far away.

"I made a special request of Captain Pnor." Alunthri touched my arm with a gentle paw. "Cherijo, I have decided to immigrate to Garnot."

I was startled. "Will the colonists recognize you as a sentient?"

Alunthri nodded. "I have signaled the colonial rulers. As they are not League members, I meet immigration requirements, both for resident status and sentience. They believe I have a great deal to offer with the scope of my studies."

"That's wonderful." No, it wasn't. I smiled sadly. "I'm going to miss you."

"And I you. If not for your help, I would still be enslaved to the Chakarans. I do not wish to leave my friends aboard the *Sunlace*, but . . . " Its colorless eyes moved to the screen. The longing was unmistakable. "Garnot is where I belong."

"How long before we reach the colony?" I asked.

"Some weeks."

"Good. I'll juggle my shift schedule. We can spend some time together before we get there." I made a face. "If I'm not confined to a berth in Medical, that is."

A priority signal came over my console, and I frowned as I switched screens. "Yes?"

"Healer." Xonea looked solemn and happy at the same time, and a cold chill inched down my back. I remembered the last time I'd seen that expression. "You are needed here in Medical," he said. "A path has been diverted."

That meant someone was dead. My throat tightened as I thought of the current patient roster. "Fasala?"

"No. Roelm Torin."

Since all the gyrlifts were in use, I ran the two levels up to Medical. I cursed Jorenian engineers and their stupid ideas of construction every step of the way, too.

Spiral bores into dimensional barriers be damned, I thought. An internal elevator or hover lift would have been really convenient once in a while. Like now.

Tonetka was halfway out of the bay when I got there. It took me a moment to catch my breath. "What happened?"

"Come." She hauled me over to the berth, where members of the medical staff were disconnecting monitors and removing life-support equipment. The techs stepped out of the way as I reached over and drew the sheet back.

Shocked, I took a half-step back. "My God."

Roelm's cheerful face was grotesquely distorted. Eyes swollen shut. Features bloated. Upper torso bruised from resuscitative efforts. His abdomen was so severely distended that dark striae scarred his flesh with jagged purple streaks.

"Ascites?" I'd never seen a case this bad before. Any form of edema sometimes caused excess fluid to accumulate in other parts of the body—especially the abdomen—but not like this. Not so fast. I pulled on a pair of gloves before I touched him. "What happened?"

"Roelm left the Medical Bay and went to check the engines. Xonea found him in the eleventh level corridor," the Senior Healer said. "By the time he was brought here, airways had constricted. Full respiratory and cardiac arrest occurred moments later."

"Brain scan?" I asked, carefully palpitating the lower torso. The tissues were so flooded that my fingers left dents in his flesh.

"Clear. No hemorrhaging. It must be anaphylactic shock."

"Not like any case I've ever seen." I checked the rest of the body, then stripped off my gloves. There was nothing more I could do until the postmortem.

An autopsy would be performed, but not for a rotation. Jorenian custom prohibited disturbing the body during the time when they considered the "shreds of the soul" might remain within. Personally? I thought it was stupid. Dead was dead.

"You're running full toxicologies?" I asked.

"Yes." Tonetka gently touched Roelm's cheek. "He made me his Speaker yesterday, Cherijo. It was as if he knew."

That meant Roelm had confided his last request to Tonetka. It was a heavy responsibility. One she was obviously not taking well, I discovered over the next hour, as she dropped instruments, misplaced several charts, and snarled at anyone who spoke to her. Eventually I talked Tonetka into going off duty and had one of the nurses escort her to her quarters.

I reported to Ndo and requested he make the announcement to the crew. Arrangements for the death ceremony would be scheduled by the Captain. I reviewed the current ward status and made rounds. Every patient except Fasala had witnessed Roelm's tragic end. No one had much to say. The nurses were unusually solemn. Even Squilyp seemed subdued, for a change.

My youngest patient was still sleeping when I reached her berth. Darea sat beside her, her expression still stiff with shock.

"I take it you were here, too," I said, and the Jorenian woman nodded. No matter how much they celebrated the death of a HouseClan member, watching someone die wasn't easy. Especially as violent an end as Roelm had come to. "I'm sorry. I liked him very much."

"I honored him as well." She glanced at Roelm's body, which was being prepared for removal to the morgue. "How fares Tonetka?"

"She'll be all right." I deliberately changed the subject. "I see Fasala's vitals read near normal levels now. That's a good sign."

"She remains on the path." Darea's eyes were haunted.

I could see this ClanMother wouldn't celebrate her own child's death. "Thank the Mother."

"The Mother should thank *you*," was my observation. "Fasala senses you're here. That security promotes healing faster than anything I can do."

"You are kind, Healer Cherijo." She watched as Squilyp hopped past us, and her expression hardened. "Unlike that one with the mouth."

I updated Fasala's chart and went back to Roelm's berth once the postmortem prep of the body was completed. I repeated the non-intrusive exams, and came to an immediate conclusion.

If the man had died of anaphylactic shock, I was an Omorr.

Roelm's lymphedema had been a minor annoyance. I checked the pharmaceutical logs. The diuretics Tonetka used were standard. I accessed his medical history and found he had been prescribed the very same medication only a year before.

It was true that certain allergies could manifest themselves in the body at any time. True or not, I was suspicious. Protocol demanded our entire supply of the drug be removed for contamination analysis, so I pulled the stores to be tested and had a fresh batch synthesized.

That was when I noticed my smallest patient's agitation. Darea had disappeared, probably off to get a meal tray from the galley.

"Fasala?" I went to her berth and gazed down at her. She'd been restlessly tossing and turning. "Is something bothering you?"

The white eyes widened. "Oh, no. I feel very well, Healer Cherijo. All my injuries have healed. There is no pain."

I smiled. "I forget my phrasing is never as precise and correct as yours. What I meant was, are you troubled about something?" She nodded. "Is it about your accident?" Another nod. I sat down on the edge of the berth and took her hand in mine. "Want to talk about it?"

She bit her lip, and glanced over at an empty berth near hers. "Healer, my ClanMother told me that Roelm Torin embraced the stars."

"Yes." I wondered just how *much* Darea had told her child.

She finally blurted it out. "Was it my fault his path was diverted?"

"Of course not, Fasala. Roelm was . . . " How did I explain this? I knew all about guilt, but not how to get rid of it. I considered signaling her ClanParents, then plunged on. "Fasala, someone else diverted Roelm's path. Whoever did this will be punished. But it's not your fault."

"I was in the restricted area," she said. Her lips trembled. "It was wrong to be there. When I saw the ring of light, I should have run away. Roelm spoke to me about it, then he became angry and left his berth."

What was that all about? "Fasala, you aren't responsible for what happened." The ring of light—wasn't that what she had been muttering in her sleep? "Tell me what you told Roelm."

"He wanted to know what it looked like. It was so pretty, like a rainbow. I told him there was a terrible sound . . . " Tears filled her eyes. "And then it hurt me."

"I know, sweetheart. It's okay." I put my arms around her as she wept. I thought of the little girl I'd been unable to save back on NessNevat. Closed my eyes and rocked Fasala gently. This one was alive. I had to hold on to that.

One of the nurses came up and quietly offered to signal Darea. I nodded my approval over the small dark head.

At last the child's sobs slowed. I blinked away my tears, then lifted her face and wiped hers away with my thumbs. "There now. I always have a good cry when I feel bad. Your ClanMother will be here soon, honey."

Fasala sniffed as she looked up at me. "What is 'honey'?"

"A sweet, delicious floral extract on Terra," I explained. "And what Terrans call very brave, very honest little girls."

"I am HouseClan Torin," she said with pride, her tears forgotten. "We are the bravest of all Houses."

"We sure are." I tucked her sheet in around her small body, and saw Darea hurry in the Bay. "Here's your Clan-Mother. Try to rest now." I pressed a kiss against her brow. "I'll be back to check on you soon."

Adaola Torin, the senior nurse on duty, asked to speak with me in Tonetka's office soon after that. We left the ward and once inside, she closed the door panel.

"This must be serious," I said, hoping it wasn't. My emotions were on the shaky side already.

The tall, perpetually cheerful woman wasn't smiling now. "Healer Cherijo, I— I would know if I am responsible for diverting Roelm's path."

She wanted to know if she'd killed him, too? What was going around, some kind of guilt virus? "Why do you think you're responsible?"

"I myself administered the diuretic just before Roelm left Medical. It was suggested . . . " Her six fingers convulsed on the edge of the desk. Plasboard splintered. "Forgive me." She jerked her hand away.

I wasn't going to reprimand her. Ever. "It's okay."

She smiled faintly at the Terran idiom. "Okay" roughly translated to "smooth path" in Jorenian, which everyone but me thought was very funny. "I was confident I used the correct dose," she said. "Could I have been in error?"

Even the best nurses made mistakes. "Tell me what you did just before you administered the drug."

"I scrubbed, gloved, and consulted the patient's chart. After that, I calibrated and checked the syrinpress twice, as always." She spread her hands. "Yet I was the only one who touched Roelm. What else could have diverted his path?"

"Plenty." Splinters speckled in one of her palms. I'd have to get busy with a dermal probe right after our chat. "Acute allergen/histamine reaction. Contaminated drugs. Septic shock. We don't know the whole story yet. A good nurse doesn't jump to conclusions."

Adaola's chin lifted a little at that last part. "Indeed."

"We've drawn fluid samples for toxicological analysis. If you made a mistake in dosage, the excess will show up in the lab reports." I tacked on my own opinion. "You are a good nurse, Adaola. One of the best I've ever worked with. The tests will be negative for overdose."

"The Omorr resident believes differently."

"The Omorr resident can go jump into the stardrive," I said.

Some of the indecision cleared from her eyes. "My presumption was based on opinion, not fact," she said, and bowed to me. "Your pardon, Healer Cherijo."

"None required." I made the traditional response, stifling

a sigh. Jorenians could be so ceremonious. I was going to strangle that damned Squilyp. "Now, let's go take care of these splinters."

"Splinters?" She became aware of the damage for the first time and examined her hand. "Oh. Yes. Of course."

"After that, why don't you ask Darea and Salo to take a break, maybe have a meal together. Offer to monitor Fasala while they do. It will reassure them to know you're watching her." And give Adaola time to pull herself together, as well.

It took a few minutes to remove the slivers of plasboard from the nurse's palm. After that, Darea and Salo reluctantly let her relieve them. One problem solved.

I wrote up my shift summary for Tonetka's review, adding a note about the merits of permanently gagging the Omorr. For the nurses' benefit *and* his own continued existence.

I left the Medical Bay after shift change. All I wanted was a cup of tea. Some hot food. Maybe a game of toss the yarn ball with His Majesty, if he was in the mood. Anything to keep from thinking about the dead.

None of that helped. The image of the lost NessNevat child stayed with me, and followed me into my dreams.

The next day I found out I'd personally be doing the autopsy on Roelm Torin. The Senior Healer insisted. I didn't protest. Tonetka wouldn't have asked unless she was literally incapable of handling it herself.

"Sure. No problem." I went to put on my gear.

Tonetka touched my arm. "You appear fatigued, Cherijo."

"I didn't sleep much last night." I wasn't going to tell her why. I had to find a way to deal with the guilt on my own.

After we prepped for the procedure, Roelm's body was wheeled in. The nurse manning the gurney quickly left. No one liked postmortem exams. Including me.

"A moment," Tonetka said when I would have activated the recording drone. She placed her gloved hands on either side of Roelm's distorted face, and bent close. "Old friend, forgive me. I cannot rejoice in your new journey. I cannot."

She was starting to worry me. "Senior Healer?"

Her hands fell away and her expression cleared. "You may begin, Cherijo."

I'd bluffed enough times to know when someone was doing it to me. She didn't have it in her to watch me cut open a man she obviously cared deeply for. "Why don't I get one of the nurses in here to assist, while you—"

She gave me that Jorenian *you're-seriously-beginning-to-annoy-me* glare. "He was my friend, Cherijo. My Clan-Uncle. He would want me here."

Nodding, I set the drone to record. "If you change your mind, let me know."

"Proceed."

After squelching a sigh, I began to recite the facts for the record: "Postmortem examination of Roelm Torin, Jorenian male, fifty-one years in age. Body is 210.5 centimeters in length. Weight 173.5 kilograms upon admission." I checked the exam pad monitor. "Distention of body is consistent with acute ascites."

Tonetka made the necessary dermal scans. I adjusted my lascalpel and made the incision from throat to pelvis. I glanced at my boss from the edge of my mask. Her brows made a single dark slash above haunted white eyes. The scanner shook a little in her fingers.

"Abdominal cavity is distinctly enlarged, with marked dermal striae." I selected my clamps. Counted the number of injection sites where Tonetka had administered a battery of drugs. "Seven dermal breaches, consistent with application of syrinpress nozzles. Four circular bruises on upper torso, consistent with anti-mortem application of stimulator pads."

The Jorenian woman made a bitter gesture.

I switched off the recorder. "Tonetka. Come on. You can't keep blaming yourself for this."

She shook her head, reached over, and turned the recorder back on. Sure she could.

I clamped back the skin flaps while Tonetka prepared the rib-extension unit. I cut through the tough inner abdomen cavity lining. Fluid shimmered beneath the laser in a black pool. That was odd. Jorenian blood didn't turn black, even when it coagulated.

"I don't see his ribs," she muttered.

"Internal viscera and skeleton are obscured by what appears to be necrotic fluid." I took a sample. "Suction, please." Tonetka applied the extractor's tip and evacuated the fluid for what seemed like an hour.

The internal organs didn't appear. Neither did the bones. We exchanged a look, and she shut down the extractor's pump.

"Scanning to detect current position of internal organs." I ran the series, then handed the scanner to Tonetka and grabbed a surgical probe.

Her mouth grew tight as she read the display. "This data is in error."

"It better be." Even as I said that, the instrument in my hand indicated otherwise.

I discarded the probe and pushed the lascalpel rig to one side. The Senior Healer averted her gaze as I put my gloved hand into Roelm's body, and searched with my own fingers. The black fluid felt thick and cold.

"Tonetka. *Tonetka.*" She didn't want to hear this, but we had to include it in the data record. "His internal organs are missing. His ribs. Everything. They're *gone.*"

"Mother of All Houses." Tonetka pushed away from the exam table, and yanked off her mask. "This cannot be. I ran full organ scans immediately after death. All were intact, as was the skeletal structure."

That was yesterday's news. I wanted to know what had happened to this man's body *today.* I stripped off my ruined gloves and sterilized my hands before donning a fresh pair.

Something occurred to me, a thought that made me swallow my own bile. "Tell me you ran a biodecon scan."

"Several. All negative."

My nausea receded an inch or two. "Let's run another one."

During the epidemic on K-2, I'd watched thousands die from a contagion that had not only been undetectable, but sentient to boot. No matter how minute the possibility of a pathogen was, I'd learned my lesson.

Roelm's readings came up contagion-free again. However, every internal organ, along with all of the bone, muscles, and tissue in the Engineer's body had been destroyed. Only the tough subdermal cartilage sheath had kept the epidermis from dissolving from the inside out, but that was beginning to liquefy, too. A comparison with the organ series taken immediately after death confirmed Tonetka's statement. Roelm had died with his body intact.

Lymphedema didn't do this kind of damage. I couldn't stop thinking about the K2V1 epidemic, and scanned for the specialized white cells that engulfed viral particles when an immune response was triggered. The display reflected no macrophage trace. Lymphocytes were slightly elevated, but that could have been brought on any number of minor conditions

"No virus I know of could cause this kind of corrosive damage." I had an idea of what could. "I'll have to analyze the lymphocytes to be sure they weren't invaded."

"Have you examined the syrinpress Adaola used to administer the diuretic?" Tonetka asked while she drew several samples of the fluid.

I nodded and tugged down my mask. "I'll take another look at it later."

"What do you believe you will find?"

I stalled. "No allergy could have done this."

"Cherijo."

"All right." I placed my scanner on a side console and faced the Senior Healer. "I don't think Roelm was injected with a *diuretic* before he walked out of Medical."

CHAPTER FIVE

Soft Spots

Two days later we held a ceremony for Roelm. Before I left to attend, I discharged one educator and arranged to have the remaining patients monitor the service via their bedside terminals.

Tonetka signaled to remind me to get a move on. Her voice sounded strained.

"Are you going to make it through this?" I asked as soon as I saw her. She looked ready to embrace a few stars herself.

"I . . . will be well. Make haste, Cherijo, or you will be late."

I checked out and hurried to my quarters to put on my ceremonial robes. It was in one of the HouseClan shades of blue, a dark shade that matched the color of my eyes. I didn't like wearing it. Out of respect for Roelm, and because Tonetka needed support, I pulled the voluminous garment over my head.

My reflection made me sigh.

The other crew members would wear similarly shaded robes. They'd look like they always did: stately, regal, and much better than me. Only Tonetka would wear black, the color I associated with mourning from Terran customs. The color of the first life, as someone told me, was required to be worn in her role as Roelm's Speaker.

Dying didn't scare these people. On the contrary. In the Jorenian culture, deaths were celebrated as the beginning of another journey. It was a nice way to think about it, I suppose.

To me, death tended to be a personal insult.

Roelm's body would be placed in a special receptacle, the Jorenian version of a coffin, which during the ceremony was fired from the ship into the corona of the nearest star. When the Jorenians said they embraced the stars, they meant business.

I hurried down to level ten, where the ceremonial chamber was located. Captain Pnor must have put the *Sunlace* on auto-stardrive, from the size of the crowd. Most of the crew were assembled and waiting.

Roelm's ClanSiblings performed the traditional preparations of the body first. On the center dais, they formed a circle around the receptacle, and danced as they wove fine, silvery strands of yiborra grass to bind the outer panels.

As I watched the receptacle shroud taking form, I recalled how Roelm had been so embarrassed to admit he'd been studying Jorenian weaving. I'd go down and access his environome program later. That would be my way of saying good-bye.

The rest of the assembly chanted a harmony that I felt throb deep in my bones. Their voices were so solemn, yet joyous. No one wept. HouseClan Torin honored their dead with smiles and happiness.

I didn't try to fake a smile. I wasn't happy.

Once a complex web of silver encased Roelm's receptacle, the song dwindled away. In silence, the ClanSiblings bowed to an oversized vid screen that had been lowered from an upper deck. I watched as Roelm's bondmate offered her blessing for his new journey via direct relay from Joren.

I had done this, for Kao. Worn the same iridescent "journey" robe. Said the same words.

The anguish I'd thought had begun to pass twisted like a fresh blade inside me.

Kao, killed by my own blood.

The NessNevat girl, dead before I could touch her.

Dra Torin's voice shook as she repeated the ancient words. "From your bondmate, your heart, can only come what is bright and beautiful and honorable. You and I will never lose each other . . . "

As Dra continued with the ritual blessing, Roelm's receptacle slid into the ejection tube. As the receptacle was fired into space, I closed my eyes.

Roelm was gone.

Tonetka mounted the dais to address the assembly. Her face looked terribly strained. New, thicker streaks of purple had appeared in her dark hair.

My God, I thought. She's *trembling*. What had Roelm told her that could be *that* bad?

"I speak for the son of this House, Roelm Torin. His words were given to me, to be brought to those he honored. I bring them with joy."

No, she didn't. Everyone could see that.

Duncan Reever had said those same words weeks before, for Kao. Distracted by the memory, I scanned the assembly for him. Was he here or had he decided to skip—

There. A few yards away, Reever looked back at me. Was that sympathy in his eyes? Sure enough. I snapped my head around, rigid and furious. He had no right to feel sorry for me. It required a heart. He didn't have one.

The Senior Healer's skilled hands bunched at her sides as she delivered the traditional farewell. As she did, her white eyes scanned the assembly, alighting on Captain Pnor. The man in charge of the *Sunlace* must have sensed the same thing I had, for he began to approach the dais. Tonetka shook her head slightly, and Pnor halted. Her voice rose, loud and strong.

"I charge the HouseClan Torin with my last request: Find the one who has sabotaged the *Sunlace*."

I'd never thought six hundred people could jump out of their footgear simultaneously. I was wrong. There was a collective gasp. Some startled exclamations. Not a single eye moved from the dais.

"One who is not one of us has deliberately damaged this vessel. My warning must be heeded, or more paths will be diverted. Find the traitor and invoke the right of ClanKill. Farewell and safe journey. I embrace the stars."

All hell broke loose.

Hands made savage gestures I'd never seen before. Faces reflected undiluted fury. Hard voices demanded something be done. Tonetka descended from the dais, looking ancient and exhausted. Captain Pnor rushed to her side.

No wonder my boss had dreaded this ceremony. Who wanted to enrage six hundred or more Jorenians? Against each other, for that matter?

I remembered Darea and Salo's reaction to Squilyp's verbal indiscretion, and multiplied that by three hundred. Maybe it was time for me to get out of here. I'd lock myself in my quarters until the Torins calmed down. Say a few weeks.

Someone seized my arm, and I nearly jumped out of *my* footgear.

My ClanBrother loomed over me. "Come with me, Healer."

Xonea swiftly guided me from the ceremonial chamber. I didn't pay attention to where we were headed. I was too relieved to be out of there, and still pondering exactly what had just happened.

Find the one who has sabotaged the Sunlace. A saboteur, on board the ship? What would make him believe such a thing? There were those engine problems just before he'd died. But what made Roelm go from worrying over malfunctioning transductors to accusations of sabotage?

My warning must be heeded, or more paths will be diverted. If Roelm was right, certainly lives were at stake. *Find the traitor and invoke the right of ClanKill.* What did that part mean? Was he asking the entire HouseClan to kill whoever was doing this?

And what exactly had he meant by *one who is not one of us*?

I was so wrapped up in my thoughts, I didn't notice the door panel that closed behind me. Xonea's voice finally got through my preoccupation.

"Healer."

Reality snapped back into focus. I looked around, and discovered we were alone, in his quarters. The very *last* place on the ship I wanted to be alone with Xonea.

At once I chided myself. Xonea was my ClanBrother. I was as safe here as I was in, say, Squilyp's quarters. As long as Xonea didn't think *I* was the culprit. If he did, my life wasn't worth a vocollar franchise on Terra.

"Nice place," I said while prudently hovering near the only exit.

His rooms were arranged with the harmonious elegance

I'd come to expect from the Jorenians. Furnishings uphol-
stered with countless shades of HouseClan Torin blue. Xonea's weapons collection was seriously impressive, judging
from the amount he had displayed on the walls. That, or
his quarters doubled as this level's armory.

Besides the guns, knives, and other virulent-looking
items, there were mementos of alien cultures. I caressed a
dense cluster of transparent nodules and snatched my hand
back as alien music spilled into the air.

"Hey! What's this?"

"A singing prism from Udarc," Xonea said.

I saw the look on his face and took an automatic step
back toward the door panel. "Um, why don't we do this
another time?"

"No, it must be now."

"I just remembered I have to—"

"Cherijo." He pointed to a large divan. "Sit. I will
explain."

An enraged Jorenian never offered to chat, so I relaxed
and sat down. He offered refreshment. I politely accepted
a server of jaspkerry tea. He paced over to the viewport
and stared out at the stars for a long time. I sipped my tea,
and tried not to wrinkle my nose at the overly sweet taste.
Ugh, how did he stomach this stuff day in, day out? And
why was he being so quiet now?

"Xonea." He turned around. "What's wrong? Besides
Tonetka's Speaking, that is?"

He crossed the room and sat down beside me. What little
space there was on the divan abruptly vanished. This close
to him, I felt as small as Jenner. His hand rested over mine.
Another point in my favor. Jorenians did not hold hands
with someone they intended to pound into the decking.

"Do you know we were once a nonverbal race?" Xonea
asked.

I thought for a moment. "Kao said something about it
once, how you evolved from a more primitive life-form.
Most species do."

"The first humanoids on Joren were highly skilled preda-
tors," Xonea said. "At first solitary, then banding together
in small familial groups for cooperative hunting. Over time
they settled into territorial tribes, and a complex social
structure developed. The first House was born."

I tugged at the collar of my robe. "Was that when your people developed language?"

"Not in the beginning. Our ancestors had no need to verbally communicate. Nor had they ever known territorial boundaries." He went to his prep unit and made his own server of tea. Too bad, I would have happily given him the rest of mine. It was like drinking straight sucrose. "HouseClans began clashing over land, resources, and hunting rights. They had no method of negotiation, other than acts of violence."

"So they threw rocks at each other instead of chatting," I said, rearranging my skirts. Maybe I should ask him to adjust the room temperature. My ceremonial robe was making me sweat.

His brows drew together. "Wars are not fought with the throwing of rocks, Cherijo. Hundreds of thousands of our people died in the subsequent decades of conflict."

Now was not the time to mention Terran history. "Sorry."

"Over time, our people realized the only way to achieve lasting peace between the HouseClans was to develop specific disciplines regarding conflict. For that, we needed language. Joren became a united world, and never again suffered civil war. Those disciplines have never been forgotten."

"But you still have warrior-training," I said.

"We train as warriors, yes." His hand tightened around his server. "Yet there is only one reason warfare is permitted—to defend the HouseClan."

"I'm with you so far."

He didn't want to tell me the rest. I could sense that much. He emptied his server with two swallows and put it aside.

"Cherijo, you must understand, we were a savage, ruthless species. Hunters without parallel. It is this part of our past that lives on in us today, when we protect the HouseClan."

"Most species have similar practices," I said, and lifted my braid off the back of my neck. "Terrans have a number of cultural methods of self-defense." So what was the big deal?

"Do you know what an invocation of ClanKill entails?"

I'd read a little about it; what there was in the database

wasn't all that specific. "If I remember correctly, when you say that to someone, you intend to kill them."

"Do you know the conditions under which it can be declared?" I shook my head. He sat down next to me again. "If an individual makes a threat against a member of the HouseClan, in the presence of the HouseClan, a warrior may declare the outsider as ClanKill. Roelm stated someone has threatened HouseClan Torin. He has charged everyone with what he could not do himself. We will take action on his behalf."

Not good. "Action against who?"

"It could not be a Jorenian." He looked away from me. "There are not many others left. Pilot Dhreen. Linguist Reever. The Omorr. The Chakacat. And *you*."

So that was it.

"Xonea, I assure you, I haven't threatened anybody. Dhreen, Reever, and Alunthri wouldn't do anything to sabotage the ship. Squilyp is a resident physician, sworn to do no harm." I wasn't going to mention the incident with Salo and Darea. I didn't hate the Omorr *that* much. "Why couldn't it be one of the Jorenians?"

"You heard Roelm's Speaker," he said. "Tonetka stated it was 'one who is not one of us.'"

"Roelm was so paranoid about the engines he frightened a little girl, then walked out of Medical without clearance." I felt I had to point this out. "I don't know if I want to take his word on this."

"ClanKill is not invoked upon a whim, Cherijo. Not when it means one of us will have to eviscerate another being while they still breathe."

I got to my feet at once. "You're joking."

"No." He scowled at me. "Kao did not tell you of our traditional response to our enemies?"

"He never said anything about disemboweling people!" Disgusted, I regarded a display of swords with new eyes, then glanced back at him. "These what you use to do it?"

"No." Xonea extended his hand, and flexed it. Six very sharp-looking claws suddenly shot out of his fingertips. "We use these."

"How convenient," I said. The claws retracted. Kao hadn't shown me *that* little surprise, either. I forced my lungs to slow down, and swiped at a trickle of sweat running down the side of my face. "You do give them a trial first, right?"

"No."

"So how do you know they're guilty?"

"The threat must be repeated in the presence of a HouseClan member."

"That's it?" I turned around. "That's *all*?"

"It is more than enough to justify invocation."

"I see." I wanted to slap him. "Someone says the wrong thing, and you eviscerate them. Perfectly normal behavior. What was I thinking?"

"Cherijo." Xonea rose to his feet, came toward me, and seized my hand. His grip was hard enough to make me gasp. "You must tell me if you know of whom Roelm spoke. At once."

"I don't." I jerked my fingers away. If he didn't cut it out, I might end up a ClanKill candidate myself. "I don't know anything, Xonea."

Something strange gleamed behind his pale eyes. "I saw your expression when Tonetka Spoke for Roelm."

"What's that supposed to mean?" I flung out my arms. "Sure, I was upset. I knew what she said wasn't going to make everyone applaud!"

Now his hands descended on my shoulders. Not gently. "Cherijo, you must not conceal knowledge of the traitor from us."

My teeth clenched. "I'm not concealing anything. Take your hands off me."

He didn't. "You were too eager to leave the ceremony."

"*You* dragged me out of there, remember? Besides, why would I want to hang around six hundred upset Jorenians? Someone might have taken a swing at me."

"No one would have dared touch you!" He shook me, hard. "Unprovoked assault has been banned for centuries!"

"Really? What do you call what you're doing now?" I yelled back. "Energetic hugging?"

Xonea's hands dropped away from me as though scalded. He took several deep, controlled breaths, then said, "I never meant to harm you." When I rubbed my bruised flesh, he averted his gaze. "Your pardon, Healer."

"Yeah, well, you're not forgiven." I was doing some deep

breathing of my own. "How would you like being accused of sabotage? Did you kill Roelm, ClanBrother?"

That really shocked him. Seven-and-a-half feet of solid Jorenian went absolutely still. Color drained from his face, leaving it a chalky pale blue.

"Never would I betray my HouseClan thus. *Never.*"

"No?" To even things up, I decided to press the point. "You *do* know a lot about this buffer that supposedly never shatters. Then you haul me in here, hand me a bunch of attitude, and accuse me of conspiracy. Just what are *you* trying to cover up?"

His hands worked convulsively at his sides. "I did not divert Roelm's path. I brought you here out of concern for your safety." He reached out, and I automatically took another step away. "Do not fear me."

This, from a guy who had nearly shaken my teeth out of my skull. "You think what you're doing is making me *trust* you?"

"I am . . . anxious." A weary hand pressed against his eyes for a moment. "I never meant to frighten you, Healer. Please, your pardon."

Although I was still mad enough to deck him, I'd take that on face value. For now. "Okay. You're pardoned."

"I would never betray my HouseClan, or force myself on another's path."

"Right." I mopped my face with my sleeve again. I'd better finish this and get out of here; the stifling atmosphere was unbearable. "Forget about it."

Xonea didn't stop. "I cannot begin to express—"

Damn Jorenian formality. "I got it, Xonea. You're innocent. *I believe you.*" Good thing *I* didn't go around eviscerating people who gave me a hard time. "This unprovoked assault thing—that ties in with ClanKill, right?"

"No Jorenian would threaten another life-form, unless after invocation of ClanKill. It is—" What he said was untranslatable. It was that bad.

"Okay, I get the picture."

"Our people are incapable of such deviant behavior," he said, looking very righteous.

"But you think *I* might be capable of it. Or Reever. Or Alunthri." I planted my hands on my hips. "*Alunthri*, for God's sake, who never even raises its voice in anger."

He had the grace to look ashamed. "You are not born to us. Our traditions are unknown to you."

"It wasn't any of the non-Jorenians, Xonea," I said.

"It will be determined." He made a noncommittal gesture. "If you discover who has done this, Cherijo, you must inform me. At once."

"Okay, let's say I find out, and tell you. What happens then?"

"Our ways are very specific," he replied. "The traitor will confess before the entire House. Outsider or Torin, ClanKill will be declared. If the traitor chooses the cowardice of silence, then a sentence of banishment is imposed."

I'd read about banishment while studying HouseClan protocols. For a Jorenian, it meant being thrown out of the HouseClan. Forbidden to return to the homeworld. Shunned by all Jorenians. Forever.

"Why would someone risk so much?" Something suddenly clicked. "Hold on. Are non-Jorenians subject to the same law?"

"Yes." He thrust a hand through the hair above his furrowed brow. "I must speak with Captain Pnor about the others."

The others and I were in trouble. Automatically I thought of Duncan Reever, who always seemed to appear whenever that happened. Too bad he couldn't pop in here now. Reever could—*Reever!*

"Wait. I can't prove I'm not the saboteur, but Duncan Reever might be able to. He can access my memories—"

"No." Xonea went to one of his weapons racks. His strong blue hand moved lovingly over a six-bladed knife with an ornate hilt. "I believe you, Cherijo. Linguist Reever need not be involved."

"That's very generous of you," I said. "But if I can prove my innocence, why would you want to stop me?"

His fingers curled over the gleaming metal. "I accept your account. You have no reason to ask this of Reever."

"Xonea, he's done it before—"

"No! It is a violation!" Xonea's hand flexed, and greenish blood instantly streamed down his long arm. He hissed and pulled his fingers away from one of the blades. A deep gash bisected his palm.

"Oh, great," I said, and hurried over to him. He was

dripping all over the deck. I cradled his hand in mine and applied pressure to stop the flow of blood. It was going to need sutures. "Nice work. Feel better now?" I reached down and tore a strip of fabric from the hem of my robe. So much for my ceremonial outfit. "Let's go to Medical and take care of this."

Xonea said nothing as he walked into the gyrlift. I came in behind him. His back was as uncompromising as his silence. Once we arrived at the Bay, it took a few minutes to repair the damage to his hand. Out of curiosity, I scanned the tips of his fingers.

"These claws of yours are actually the tips of the distal phalanges," I said, then carefully manipulated a finger and watched the thin bony blade emerged from beneath the overlying dark blue nail.

Xonea gazed around from the exam table while I finished dressing the sutures. "It is very quiet here today."

"It is. We miss Roelm. He really knew how to liven things up." I thought about the startling postmortem exam, then Roelm's mysterious accusations. "Xonea, has anyone told you about how Roelm died?"

"No. Captain Pnor desired the matter be kept confidential."

Pnor. No wonder he had tried to climb the dais and stop Tonetka from dropping Roelm's bombshell. He must have guessed it was something bad, and how the crew would react.

"Tonetka and I performed an autopsy on Roelm." If there was a saboteur on board, he may have done more than mess with the stardrive. "He was probably right about the sabotage. It looks like he was murdered."

Anger over Tonetka's Speaking subsided, but things were never the same after that. Captain Pnor made a very brief announcement that Roelm's death and his accusations would be investigated. Most of the crew seemed restless and unnaturally quiet. Cheerful attitudes disappeared, and everyone appeared worried or withdrawn.

Some of the Jorenians occasionally gave me odd looks, or stopped talking when I walked by them in the corridor. It didn't take a genius to figure out why. *One who is not one of us.*

My problem with Squilyp didn't allow me a lot of time

to brood over it. When I wasn't on duty, I was training with Xonea. My ClanBrother continued to harass me about withdrawing the solicitation, but I was adamant. Bad enough I had to learn how to deliberately inflict pain. No way was I going to be a coward and back out of a fight.

There were other problems, too.

"Oomph!" I landed flat on my back for the ninth time that session, and opened my eyes. Over me, Xonea stood in the classic death-strike position. I sighed. "Okay, you win. Again."

"Indeed." I saw him tug at the warrior's knot at his nape, then shake his head. Thick black hair, as long as my own, spilled down his back. He had removed his uniform tunic a while ago, and was now wearing only a pair of loose-fitting trousers. His respiration was accelerated, and sweat glistened over bulging blue muscles. White eyes stared down at me as he extended one big hand. "Get up."

I was tired of getting knocked on my backside. With my hand, I grabbed his, then lashed out with my legs and knocked him off his feet. With a hard jerk I managed to yank him down on the mat beside me. He rolled over, but by that time I was straddling him, and thumped my hand against his sternum.

"Gotcha." I grinned as he reflexively grabbed my wrist. "Too late, pal. Your path is history."

He scowled at me. "That was not honorable."

"So I cheated. It worked, didn't it?" I began to climb off him.

"No." He curled an arm around me to hold me in place. That was when I realized how intimate my position was. I was sitting right on top of his— "The Omorr's pectoral bones render his chest invulnerable," he said. "Show me where you would strike him."

"Xonea." New heat flooded my face as I tried to shift my weight. "Let me go."

Instead of releasing me, Xonea made a quick move. A heartbeat later I was flat on *my* back and he was straddling me. "And if he pins you, thus?"

"I haven't a clue." My new position made it even more difficult to act nonchalant. "You win, Xonea. Let me up."

"Cherijo." His hands tightened, and I felt the tips of his claws extrude and lightly scratch my skin. I'd learned that only happened when a Jorenian was really, *really* angry. "You are too small, too frail."

I stared into his narrow white eyes. "For what?"

One huge blue hand moved down the side of my body, and rested on my hip. His thumb rubbed a circle around my navel. "One direct strike here, and the Omorr will divert your path."

That wasn't all that was diverting me. I arched my back, trying to dislodge his hand, but that only made the situation much, much worse. "Um, Xonea—"

My ClanBrother's voice lowered to a growl. "I will gut him if he harms you."

"Hey." Now he was scaring me. "Let go."

He got to his feet, and I wobbled a little as I did the same. We looked at each other for a long moment.

I cleared my throat. "That's enough for today." Then I simply turned and ran.

Back in my quarters, I spent a long, soothing interval in my cleansing unit while I reflected on what had happened. I could have sworn Xonea meant to do more than show me where Squilyp might punch me. No. Xonea was my ClanBrother. I was imagining things. But that rage of his— what was that all about?

After that session, I was careful to be as impersonal as possible with Xonea. It never happened again, nor did he refer to the incident; he simply treated me the same way he would a younger, exasperating sibling. Which was okay with me.

There was also the problem of keeping the fight a secret. Tonetka was the first to notice how stiffly I was moving while I was on duty.

"What ails you, Healer?"

I grimaced. "Overdid things during my recreation interval yesterday." I rubbed an aching thigh. "I think I'll try basket weaving next time."

Her sharp eyes inspected me closely. "What manner of recreation did you indulge in?"

"Oh, you know"—I made a vague gesture—"stretching and that sort of thing." That sort of thing being me getting knocked on my backside thirty or forty times per session.

The Senior Healer gave me a suspicious frown, but before she could start questioning me, a nurse interrupted.

As far as I knew, Xonea hadn't told anyone, nor had Squilyp, Reever, or Alunthri. Apparently it was up to me to spread the news. Well, I wasn't going to invite half the ship to watch the Omorr wipe up the deck with me. According to the cultural database, I was allowed a "second," someone who would throw in the towel if I was too badly hurt to surrender.

How reassuring.

Under the circumstances, I couldn't ask Xonea. So I went to Reever and requested his assistance. He didn't say "yes" right away. He had to give me a hard time about it first. Of course.

At last the day of reckoning arrived.

Squilyp was already warming up when I entered the environome at the appointed hour. He had discarded his resident's tunic and wore only a brief, one-legged garment. His limbs were longer than I remembered. His frame bigger. His muscles larger.

Behind me, the environome's entrance panel parted again. Duncan Reever, Xonea, and about twenty Jorenians filed in. I knew Alunthri wouldn't be there, I'd asked it to stay with Jenner for me. The Chakacat was far too sensitive to sit and watch two beings beat the daylights out of each other.

Xonea had already promised to keep quiet about the challenge. I glared at the ship's Linguist.

"You've got a big mouth," I said as Reever strode past me.

"It is minuscule compared to your temper."

"I *told* you not to tell anyone!"

"You said you did not wish the Captain or the Senior Healer to learn of this debacle," Reever said. "I did not tell *them.*"

He walked past me and went directly over to the Omorr, and engaged him in a terse, inaudible exchange.

Xonea programmed gallery seating for the spectators before he came to me. He eyed my opponent, too. "This is insanity, Healer."

"Some coach you are." I did a few stretching exercises, trying to look tough. Okay, and maybe a little taller. "If you thought this was crazy, why teach me to fight?"

My ClanBrother turned on me. He was not a happy Jorenian. "You did not tell me the Omorr was a champion on his homeworld."

Obviously someone else had. And I didn't need three guesses as to who: Reever, the busy little bee.

"So?"

"I should have never agreed to this madness," Xonea said, his fists as tight as his jaw. "He will divert your path."

I was sick and tired of everyone telling me how wonderful Squid Lips was. "Maybe not." I bent and placed both my palms on the floor before I straightened. Only a week ago, I couldn't have done that. "If I win, do you think I'll get his title?"

Xonea hauled me close to him by grabbing the back of my neck and flexing half a muscle. "Do not do this, Cherijo."

I knocked his hand away. "What's the matter with you? This is what you've been training me for."

"I am your ClanBrother." Now he grabbed my upper arm. "I cannot permit harm to come to you."

"This is my fight, big brother." I clenched my teeth to keep from grinding them. "And just for the record, I don't need your permission."

"If he harms you, I—"

I pried his hand off. "Will do absolutely nothing, pal." He had that *never-touch-my-kin-or-you-die* look on his face. I jabbed my finger against his chest to emphasize my next words. *"Not . . . a . . . thing."*

Xonea swore, then stalked off to the gallery. Reever had a word with him. They both glanced back at me, and appeared ready to challenge me themselves. Nice to know my friends were worried. Everyone settled into their seats. Reever took his position a few feet away from me.

I waited while Squilyp completed the final programming sequence for the challenge. The dimensional imagers hummed, and the environome's simulators shifted around us.

This had to be a chunk of the Omorr homeworld. Hills of cobalt rock rose around us. Clear, feathery plant life sprang up in thin bunches. Overhead, birdlike creatures circled, their pink-feathered wings sweeping through the cold air. The scavengers had beady black eyes, and large, sharp beaks fringed with short gildrells.

Family members, maybe?

Another Omorr hopped between us, startling me for a moment. This one was draped in ceremonial vestments. Very realistic for a programed simulation. Right down to the Omorr sneer I got as the rules were decreed.

"A solicitation has been made," the computer-generated Omorr said. "To Squilyp of Maftuda, by the Terran Cherijo Grey Veil. Our beloved son has accepted. All Maftuda praises Squilyp, who has never been defeated, who has—"

"Enough ego to fill a cargo hold," I said. "Can we get on with it?"

The simulated Omorr's gildrells stiffened in simulated outrage. "No weapons are to be used. No outside aid is to be enlisted. Failure to adhere to the restrictions will result in automatic forfeit. The challenge is met when one of the combatants capitulates, becomes incapacitated, or dies."

Squilyp rubbed his membranes together as he stared at me. No doubt he was savoring the thought of my Terran blood all over his nice program.

"Does the solicitor wish to withdraw?" the Omorr simulation asked. I shook my head. He turned to Squilyp. "Does the solicited wish to withdraw?" My opponent made a quick, negative gesture. The Omorr simulation bowed to both of us. "Take your places. At my signal, you may begin."

I moved to my mark. Squilyp hopped to his a few yards away. That put me directly in front of the gallery. I saw that Reever had his arms crossed over his chest, and looked a little pale. My big brother Xonea was poised on the edge of his seat.

All this confidence in me was overwhelming.

On a whim, I faced the gallery and held up a clenched fist. *"Morituri te salutamus." We who are about to die salute you.*

Reever now looked pale *and* faintly disgusted.

"What does that mean?" Squilyp called out. His vocollar wouldn't translate—antediluvian Terran Latin wasn't in the ship's linguistic database.

"It means I'm going to enjoy this," I yelled back.

A high, fluted sound vibrated through the air. I stepped forward. Squilyp began hopping toward me.

We met in the center, faster than I'd expected. I ducked

as one of his long limbs swung over my head, and spun around to find him almost on top of me. I crouched and drove my right elbow into his thorax. Too high. I caught the bottom half of his pectoral bone, which was like hitting a plasteel wall.

I felt a breeze as another limb barely missed my face, then lashed back and caught me with a solid blow. My right cheekbone exploded with pain. I fell, rolled with the impact, and came up on the balls of my feet.

That *hurt*. My right eye began to tear. A bad sign. If it swelled shut, it was going to cut my range of peripheral vision in half. Not to mention ruin my pretty face for a few days. Maybe I should have gotten some of that jaspforran herb after all.

"You dance like hypoglycemic child," Squilyp said as he hopped after me. "Hold still and fight."

"You mean, give up and let you stomp on me?" I replied, circling to the left. "That how you win all your fights?"

"I win"—he grunted as he lashed out with two limbs, and I narrowly avoided the whiplike membranes—"because I am the best!"

"Better work on that insecurity complex of yours, Squid Lips," I said. Then I dropped. Somersaulted out of his reach. Landed on my feet.

Squilyp was right there, in my face. I danced backward.

The Omorr grabbed a membraneful of my tunic, and ripped part of my sleeve before I wrenched away. He stared at the ragged swatch of fabric he held, and that was when I turned and kicked him in the jointed midsection of his single leg. He began to lose his balance, then righted himself.

"Is that the best you can do?" he said, pretending it didn't hurt as he started after me.

My face felt gigantic, and profoundly ached. I whirled away and came around him, eyeing a section on his back. Had to be there. Swiftly I moved in, lifted my leg and drove my knee into his spine. Two of his limbs smashed into me before I could avoid them. I was tossed through the air to land painfully on my side some three feet away.

"Joey!"

That had to be Duncan. No one else called me that.

He'd knocked the wind out of me. I heard the Omorr's hopping step and rolled away. Voices were starting to rise. I looked over at the gallery. Reever still stood on the sidelines. So did Xonea. They were arguing while Reever held Xonea's upper arms. Holding him *back*.

Men. They made a lousy cheering section.

"Stop . . . and I will . . . spare you," Squilyp wheezed, drawing my attention back to the fight.

Spare me? Oh, sure, and then he'd give me a big kiss and say all was forgiven. Had to get up and get moving.

My arms shook as I pushed myself off the floor. I squinted at the Omorr as my vision doubled for a moment. Two muscular frames glistened with sweat. A whole roomful of gildrells quivered with labored breath. One more shot, I thought as I stood. If my knees would hold.

"Spare me?" I said as I backed away. "Mercy from . . . the grand champion . . . of Omorr?"

"Terran fool." He gasped for air as he pursued me. "You have lost!"

If he hit me one more time, I agreed silently. I'd struck two of the few places he was vulnerable. I'd have to risk a final attempt. I watched him, saw how he was tiring. The Omorr don't usually move much when they fight. They just stood together and pounded on each other until one of them fell or died. Like two statues—

That was it!

I stopped, assuming an aggressive, stationary stance the way one of his people would. He looked startled, then eagerly hopped closer. This was his style of fighting. He'd demolish me in no time. Just another meter, then—

It was a suicidal leap, but it worked. I collided with the Omorr in mid-hop, knocking him off-balance. At the same time, my right fist plowed into his gildrells. I put all the force I could muster behind that punch. He waved his limbs wildly, but it was too late. He fell with me on top of him. The back of his head slammed into the simulated stone beneath us. I rolled off and out of reach. He half rose, then collapsed and went still.

My right hand was lacerated, and numb from the jolt. I couldn't see clearly out of my right eye. Still, I bent down over him and put my hand on the pulse point in his upper thorax. Rapid but steady Omorr rhythms beat in the organ that served as his heart and liver. Some of his gildrells had ruptured and were oozing white-pink streaked blood.

Suddenly I was yanked back by a powerful arm. Xonea's big hands reached for Squilyp. His extended claws indicated he was ready to find each and every soft spot the Omorr possessed. And remove them.

I grabbed the closest wrist. "No, Xonea!"

"You are bleeding," the Jorenian said with a hiss. *"Bleeding!"*

"So is he!"

"I will divert his path!"

"If I wanted it diverted," I said as I lunged in front of my ClanBrother, protecting the Omorr with my own body, "I'd have done it myself. Now back off. Back off!"

Reever was suddenly there, putting himself between us, murmuring something low and musical. I sat back and watched as he somehow calmly convinced the big pilot not to disembowel my unconscious opponent. Xonea stalked off. The ship's Linguist turned to me. "Are you all right?"

"Been better," I said. I couldn't smile. My face hurt too much. "Signal Medical for me, will you? Let them know we're bringing a patient." I touched my cheek gingerly. Looked at the blood on my fingertips. "Make that . . . two . . ."

Good thing he grabbed me. Didn't need another head injury, I thought, and passed out.

PART TWO:

Explorer

CHAPTER SIX

Hired Guns

After the challenge, Squilyp spent the next four days in a medical berth. He sulked, but otherwise behaved himself.

I spent a day stuck in a berth myself. Despite a fractured cheekbone, facial lacerations, assorted bruises, and a splendid black eye, the damage healed in record time. Genetically enhanced immune systems had their uses. My rapid recovery gave the Omorr one more thing to brood about.

None of the crew had much to say to either one of us about what had happened. Not all the Jorenians refrained from commenting, however.

When Squilyp and I were brought in, the Senior Healer regarded us both with astonished disbelief. Her arched brows and open mouth were the first things I saw as I regained consciousness. The Omorr, I was pleased to see through the only eye that worked, was still out for the count.

"What say you?" she was saying to Reever. "This was *deliberate*? They *inflicted* these injuries on each other?"

Tonetka was, well, *furious*. When she decided to speak to me again, it was to inform me that if I ever repeated this stunt, she'd personally divert my path. Gave me all the gruesome details about how she'd do it, too. Then she followed that up with scalding opinions on my lack of restraint, supervisory skills, and common sense.

I could have told her Squilyp had tricked me into the challenge. I didn't. It was as much my fault as his, so I silently accepted the reprimand.

Reever came back to check on me the first day. I thought that was rather sweet. For about two minutes.

"You are far too reckless," he said. He went on to tell me all the reasons why I shouldn't have won the challenge.

"But I did win, Reever. My warrior training paid off."

"You need more training in personnel relations," he said.

"Your mouth needs a few sutures!"

Xonea never showed up. Dhreen stopped by and mumbled something about a whump-table and the surprising capacity for flight it had in the hands of a Jorenian in full rage.

I went directly to my quarters after I was released from Medical. Jenner greeted me at the door panel with distinct suspicion.

"Don't you recognize me?" I asked. "I'm the one who feeds you."

Jenner's fur rose as he peered up at my swollen, bruised face. *Maybe*, he seemed to say before he turned and stalked off, tail held high. When I would have stroked his back, he darted out of reach. *Then again, maybe not.*

"Do I look that awful?" I asked as I closed the door panel.

Large blue eyes blinked at me. *You have no idea, stranger.*

I checked my console, then sat down and watched the stars through my viewport for a while. Eventually Jenner decided I wasn't an imposter in a bad mask, and jumped up on my lap.

So it is you. He sniffed at me. *Where have you been, anyway?*

"Making a major mistake," I said.

His whiskers twitched. *This is news?*

To his credit, His Majesty allowed me to cuddle and stroke him and never once objected to the tears that made damp circles on his soft fur. I held him for a long time, and came to the conclusion that the worst thing about regret was it never came *before* you did something really stupid.

The next morning I reported for duty. The exhaustive relief efforts on NessNevat had created a considerable backlog in the patient schedule and adminwork, and we spent the next week getting Medical back in shape. Routine cases of minor injuries or illnesses came and went. Tonetka thawed enough to argue over patients with me again. Even Squilyp was his old, obnoxious self, although he pointedly avoided me now.

The only difference I noticed was a marked change in the nurses. Before the fight with Squilyp, they had practically tripped over themselves to be helpful and friendly. Their attitudes now ranged from puzzlement to skepticism. They watched me when they thought I wasn't looking. A couple of them openly avoided me altogether.

I knew what they were thinking. A physician was supposed to repair damage—not inflict it. Someone who deliberately administered a beating might have no problem, say, sabotaging the stardrive. Or murdering the man who'd uncovered it. For the moment, there was nothing I could do but hope Pnor would find the saboteur. Soon.

Not everyone was avoiding me. Alunthri and I spent more time together as the ship got closer to Garnot. We were having tea one afternoon when my door panel chimed. I opened it to find Fasala and her educator Ktarka waiting to pay me a visit.

"Come in," I said, waving my hand. "Alunthri is here. Hey, maybe we should have a party."

Ktarka and her pupil greeted the Chakacat and sat down with us. The child was disappointed when Jenner decided he'd had enough and fled to hide under my sleeping platform. I called him silly names until her smile reappeared. I was glad to see the healthy appetite she displayed when she spied the morningbreads and tea.

"If it won't spoil your next meal interval, help yourself," I said. Turning to Ktarka, I asked what kind of beverage she preferred. The Jorenian woman was watching Fasala plow into the goodies. I had to repeat my question before she made a startled sound.

"Forgive me." Her hands danced apologetically as she gave me a rueful smile and nodded toward the little girl. "I find no end to my astonishment that Fasala has made such a quick recovery."

"Educator Ktarka came to see me every day in Medical Bay." Fasala beamed at her teacher. The woman made a modest gesture and accepted my offer to try some Terran herbal tea Dhreen had smuggled off K-2 for me.

"Very interesting blend," she said. "On Joren, we—"
The cup in her hand dropped and smashed on the deck as
the *Sunlace* suddenly, violently destabilized.

"Get down!" I stumbled, but managed to catch Fasala
before she hit the decking. I rolled with her and held on
until the ship's stabilizers restored balance. Ktarka took her
from me and I hurried to my com panel.

I pounded the display, to no avail. My signal to Ship's
Operational wouldn't go through. I rerouted to Medical
Bay, and one of the nurses responded. I could hear To-
netka shouting in the background.

"What happened?" I demanded

"We're under attack. Mercenary vessels. Several levels
have been compromised. Healer—"

The League had found us. Dear God. "I'll be there in
two minutes."

I flung an apology over my shoulder and ran out of my
quarters. Halfway to Medical, the ship pitched violently
once more, which tossed me into one of the wall panels.

I didn't have time to feel the pain. I ran. Along the way
I stopped twice to check on crew members sprawled in the
corridor. One had only some minor lacerations and bruises.
The other, a helm officer, had a dislocated shoulder. I
swore under my breath as I realized it was Hado Torin.

"I thought you wouldn't be cluttering up Medical anymore," I said as I checked him over. His repaired heart
was functioning normally, but it certainly didn't need the
additional strain.

"Your pardon, Healer," Hado replied. "It was not my
intention to return, I assure you."

No, he'd just had the bad luck to be on the same ship
as me. "Do you know what's happening?"

"There are five mercenary vessels currently engaging the
ship. Levels one, two and three have been seriously compromised. Secondary command has been transferred to
level nine."

Five of them firing on us. Three levels rendered useless
already. They wouldn't stop until they got me. Joseph Grey
Veil had predicted as much.

*Any planet that gives you sanctuary will be invaded. Any
ship you travel on will be targeted. Anyone who helps you*

will be considered an accomplice and eliminated. You will
be hunted down like an animal until you are apprehended.

I should have stayed on K-2. Or gotten off the ship as
soon as we'd escaped the League. Why had I thought I
could outrun them?

"Healer?"

I looked down at Hado's pain-etched face, and cursed.
Now was not the time to do this.

"Hold on." I braced my feet and took hold of his limp
arm. "This is going to hurt."

The navigator flinched as I quickly manipulated the joint
back in place. I would have hauled him along with me, but
he refused.

"Go, Healer, there are more badly wounded. I will make
my way shortly."

I got to Medical. There were bloodstained bodies everywhere. Nurses running scans, applying dressings, calling for
assistance. The main display politely announced more injured were on the way. And the facility was half-filled with
bodies already.

How many more would be carried in? How much more
suffering on my account? I moved forward, and something
made me slip. I caught myself before I looked down at the
floor. It was slick with something green.

I froze. Stared at the Jorenian blood on my footgear. It
was all over the decking. Everywhere.

Tonetka hurried past me, her hands inside the chest
wound of a big Jorenian male, performing open heart massage. The gurney he was on was being pushed into surgery.
"Cherijo. Thank the Mother."

Her voice snapped me out of my trance, and I caught up
to her. Though she must have seen the horror and shock
on my face, Tonetka didn't mince words. "Adaola has triage. Scrub."

I prepped and ran into surgery. The Senior Healer
stepped back as I took over for her and continued the
cardiac massage. She didn't wait to observe me, but returned to the ward. By the time the team had their equipment on line around me, the patient's heart was beating on
its own.

"Initiate sterile field," I said. My hands were steady—

the only part of me that wasn't trembling. "Get the setup over here."

One nurse took position next to me with an instrument tray, while a second went to the other side of the table.

"Stats," I demanded, and performed the visual. His chest was a mess. How many crew members would end up like this? On this table? Someone gave me his readings. "Scanner."

I passed the instrument over my patient and saw the heart was intact. The two-sided liver Jorenians possessed, however, was in bad shape. If I didn't get into his chest right away, we were going to lose him. I yanked the charred shreds of his tunic aside.

"Speaker," the patient was muttering. "Bring my . . . Speaker."

"Put him out!" I said, positioning the lascalpel at the chest wound's lower edge.

Incredibly, both nurses stepped back from the table. One bowed her head and started praying out loud. The other shut off the field generator.

"What are you doing?" Outraged, I looked from one to the other. "Reinstate that field! You, get over here and help me!"

One obeyed. The other stared at me without comprehension. I couldn't believe she just stood there.

"That means you, too!"

The white eyes widened innocently. "He asks for eternity, Healer." She actually turned and began to walk out again. "I will get—"

"Get your *ass* back over here!" The appalled nurse reluctantly returned to the table. I activated the sterile field myself. "Assist me." I elbowed the instrument tray toward her. "Clamp!"

It took some fast, fancy cutting, but I located and stopped the hemorrhaging vessel. All that was left was to put the liver back together as fast as my hands could patch. The next case was wheeled in before I closed.

"Not yet!" I positioned the lascalpel. Squilyp pulled it from my hand. We looked at each other for a moment. The surgical suite was dead silent.

A perfect time for him to sneer at me. He'd be more than justified, this time.

"Go," he said, stepping up to the table. "I'll close for you."

Astonished, I nodded and stripped off my bloody gloves. Then I turned on the mutinous nurse. She seemed dazed as she looked from me to the patient she had tried to walk out on.

"You." I pointed to her, then jabbed my thumb toward the door panel. "Out."

She gave me a reproachful frown. "Healer, I meant no disrespect."

"You froze up on me," I said. "I don't need that in here. Go help with triage." As she started to hand me some kind of Jorenian philosophical nonsense, I shook my head. "Forget it. Get out."

Another series of blasts rocked the ship. Then the main display announced we were going into transition. At once.

"Hold on!" I shouted to the Omorr, who thrust the laser aside and pinned the patient with his three limbs. I braced myself over mine and felt a sickening drop as the *Sunlace* bored into another dimension.

A day later, I was in Tonetka's office. Neither of the surgical patients who had been on the table during transition showed any ill effects from the dangerous dimensional shift. Nor had any of the other thirty casualties suffered repercussions. That wasn't what I was pacing back and forth about. The Senior Healer trudged in and gave me a disgruntled frown.

"I ordered you off duty." She rounded the desk and dropped into her chair. Her tunic was still splattered with green blood.

"We need to talk." I came to a halt in front of her desk. "Five patients died yesterday, Tonetka." I knew every one of their names. I'd examined each body. Knew I'd never forget their faces.

"I know."

I picked up a chart. Thumped it down in front of her. "This one didn't have to."

Tonetka sat back in her chair and sighed before she studied the chart display. "Bola Torin, abdominal injuries, multiple fractures, Speaker requested." She gazed blandly back at me. "I see no issue here."

"Didn't you hear me? He didn't have to die. Bola bled to death." She nodded. I couldn't believe it. "He bled to death *here*! In a berth! No one touched him! He was left to die!"

"He died because he chose to."

I reared back. "What?"

"Bola refused all aid. He requested only his Speaker."

"Bola refused—" Confused, I sat down. "The *patient* refused treatment?"

"It was his right." At my blank look, Tonetka explained. "In our culture the path is predetermined solely by the one who travels it."

So it was some kind of religious thing. Great. "You're telling me suicide is okay with you people."

The Senior Healer nodded. "It is our custom, Cherijo. Should that decision be to embrace eternity, we cannot bar the path."

Religion was one thing, but this man's life could have easily been saved. "How could Bola be relied upon to make a rational decision? He was in shock!"

"We do not judge such decisions, Cherijo, we merely respect them."

"So you respect an injured man's desire to bleed to death." I leaned forward. "Tell me, what other charming customs do you have that I don't know about? I already know the one about disemboweling an enemy while they're still alive. Do you ritually sacrifice children to some deity every now and then? Torture someone if they get sick of the color blue?"

"Of course not." She sounded exasperated. "Cherijo, why are you so angry?"

"Five people are dead, Tonetka. Thirty more injured. All because I'm on this ship. I'm not Jorenian, so don't expect me to sing and dance about it."

"You belong to HouseClan Torin, Cherijo," Tonetka said. "You must respect our customs." Her voice gentled. "You must not hold yourself accountable for this incident, either."

I'd hold myself accountable for whatever I damn well felt like. But that wasn't the issue. "Your custom violates everything I believe in as a physician. We're trained to provide care and *save* lives. Whatever it takes."

The Senior Healer frowned. "Your Terran philosophies do not nullify one hundred thousand years of Jorenian tradition."

We'd just see about that. "Tell me something, Tonetka. When I'm Senior Healer, will I have to respect the wishes of these suicidal patients?"

A flicker of something crossed her face. "You may try to persuade them to embrace life."

I recalled the long discussions Tonetka once had with Hado Torin before we performed his surgery. How frantic she had been to keep him from dying. Her reaction to Roelm's death.

"You feel the same way I do," I said. "You try to talk them out of it, don't you? That's what you did with Hado."

"If I can." She rubbed her eyes. "Sometimes I do not hear their requests. I am traveled, my tympanic nerves are aged."

I stared at the chart. "Except yesterday." I looked up and through my pain saw her own. "You didn't know about Bola until it was too late, did you?" She made an eloquent gesture. "The nurses did this. One of them tried to do the same thing in surgery."

"Did you prevent her from getting a patient's Speaker?"

"Prevent her? I practically decked her!"

"Then you will be officially reprimanded by me for violating Jorenian custom. Consider it done." The Senior Healer rose and indicated the door. "Now go to your quarters and get some rest."

I left Tonetka's office, but rest was out of the question. At least until I decided what I was going to do.

I could stay on the ship, but if the mercenaries had found us once, they'd find us again. My presence directly endangered the crew. I could find a non-League planet, get off the ship, and hide there—but my presence would endanger those people.

Any planet will be invaded. Any ship will be targeted. Anyone who helps you will be eliminated.

There was only one choice, after all.

I spotted Ktarka Torin through the viewer of one of the isolation rooms, and went to see what she was doing. On the berth inside the room was a Terran male.

"Who is this?" I asked.

"One of the mercenaries," Ktarka replied. "He was attempting to board the ship when the *Sunlace* transitioned. They found him on level two, unconscious, with minor injuries."

He was lucky to be alive. I noted the tough, sinewy body and the shaggy mane of dirty hair. His relaxed features retained harsh, brutal lines of experience. A hunter. One of the many who had been coming after me.

"Has he regained consciousness?"

"No." Ktarka indicated the locking restraints that held the mercenary pinned to the berth. "When he does, Captain Pnor wishes to interrogate him. Do you know him?"

Jorenians assumed everyone in a species was either related or acquainted with each other, as they were. "No, I don't." I picked up his chart and made a note to be informed when he regained consciousness. I wanted to know just how many more ships the League had sent after me. "He looks mean." I looked at the Jorenian's weary face and touched her shoulder. "So why are you here?"

"My co-workers and I volunteered to assist with the injured," Ktarka said. "Adaola asked me to monitor this one. The nurses are very busy, and no one wishes . . ." She made a diplomatic gesture.

Nobody wanted to help those responsible for the deaths of five Torins. I could understand that. I wondered why no one had done the same to me, since I was one of the responsible parties.

A nurse passed by the isolation room. Her angry gaze bounced from the unconscious man's face to mine. I decided to call her in to relieve Ktarka, but before I could speak, the woman abruptly turned away.

Well, that answered my question, and hurt, more than I cared to admit. "I have to get out of here before the boss chases me out, Ktarka. Thanks for your help."

From my quarters, I signaled the temporary command level and inquired after the condition of the ship. It wasn't good. Displacer fire had rendered the upper three levels of the ship unfit for use. Level one was nearly completely destroyed. Half the gyrlifts were nonoperational. We were all going to be walking a lot for the next few days.

In return, I reported the death toll, complete casualty numbers, and details on the patients in serious condition.

Every name created new weight on top of the five already crushing my heart. By the time I was done, I knew what I had to do.

"May I to speak to the Captain?" I asked the duty officer, and was told he was unavailable. "Please ask him to signal me as soon as possible." I recalled the injured Terran. "What are you planning to do about this mercenary we've got over in Medical?" The Jorenian only smiled and flexed his hands. "Never mind. I don't want to know."

Jenner jumped up and snuggled next to me as I curled up on my sleeping platform's soft pillows. His cool nose nuzzled my hand. I stroked him absently.

"Hey, pal. You hungry? I'll be . . ."

I fell asleep instead. My dreams were immediate and ugly. Filled with faceless demons pursuing me wherever I ran, finding me wherever I hid. Their hands snatched at me, tearing my tunic, pulling at my hair. Rough, frightening voices called my name, laughed at me. I ran until I tripped and fell. Then they crowded all around me, their sharp teeth glittering.

"No escape, lab meat." One of the hideous things leaned close. *"You'll never get away. Now get up. Get up—"*

"Get up."

I opened my eyes. A Terran stared back at me over the edge of a surgical mask. The rim of a pulse rifle barrel sat on the bridge of my nose.

"Get up now." It was the mercenary Ktarka had been monitoring. Somehow he had gotten into full surgical gear and walked out of Medical. "Slow and easy."

I moved carefully, sliding off my sleeping platform to stand up. I was only wearing an undershirt and briefs. He pulled off the head gear and mask while he took a long look.

"Well, well, well. You're going to earn me a tidy little bounty, Dr. Grey Veil."

There was probably no chance of me taking him off-guard, as I had Squilyp. That rifle he held trained on me an inch never twitched an inch. My display was too far away to reach and signal for help. If I tried to use voice commands, I suspected he'd knock me out.

My shoulders sagged. I could go quietly, I thought, and be done with this.

"Very nice." He moved closer, reached out and grabbed my breast. I concealed my revulsion with indifference. "Pity I don't have time now. Maybe when we get back to my ship."

No. I wasn't going quietly. Not with this animal. "Don't get your hopes up."

Brutal fingers squeezed until the pain made me inhale sharply. "That's right, Doctor. I'm in charge. Remember that." He let his hand fall away. "Get some clothes on."

I pulled on the first garments that came to hand. Jenner was nowhere in sight. Had he done something to my cat? I couldn't ask. If Jenner was hiding, he was safe.

"Where are we going?" I asked.

"Shut up and get over here."

I tugged on my footgear and approached him slowly. When I got within a foot, he grabbed my braid and used it to pull me up against him. The pulse rifle pressed against the back of my head. There was Jorenian blood on him; I could smell it. Who had he hurt or killed to get out of Medical?

Ktarka.

"Maybe I do have enough time," he said, and ground his hips against mine. "The old man doesn't care what shape you're in. Only that he gets you back on Terra."

It took every ounce of strength to remain motionless as he jammed his mouth over mine. His thick tongue squirming against my clenched teeth made me want to vomit. He groped my breasts with bruising greed. I kept still and didn't fight him. He raised his head at last, plainly disappointed.

"Have to work on you," he said. "You've been with these blue-skinned freaks too long." One calloused hand forced my thighs apart, and he rubbed his fingers back and forth in a grotesque caress. "Forget how it feels to have one of your own kind between your legs?"

Honesty is the best policy. "I'd rather mate with a Hsktskt."

He backhanded me across the face with his fist, then grabbed the front of my tunic to keep me upright. Blood began to trickle down my chin. My teeth must have cut into my lip when my head snapped back.

I met his gaze, then deliberately spat bloody saliva at his feet. "Two Hsktskts."

"Come on, you stupid bitch." He shoved me in front of him. "We're leaving." I walked through the door panel and turned to enter the gyrlift, but he yanked me back. That was when I saw Ktarka, huddled against the corridor wall. Blood and lacerations masked her features. Before I could go to her, the barrel of his rifle jammed into my side. "No." The Terran yanked the educator to her feet. "She can still walk."

He must have used her as a hostage. "They'll kill you," I said.

"Not if it means the two of you die first."

As we moved down the empty corridor, my heart pounded in my ears. I could only hope no one would cross our path. The crew would react to the threat, and he in turn would shoot them where they stood. Come to think of it, why was the corridor so deserted? With half the gyrlifts down, we should have been wading through Jorenians.

"How did you get loose?" I asked him.

"I had some help," the mercenary said, then chuckled.

Who would have helped him? The saboteur? I tried once more to turn back to Ktarka, but his weapon prodded me again. "Did you have to beat her?"

"I should have killed her, but I was in a hurry."

He was a dead man. "What's your name?"

"Did I forget to introduce myself?" He chortled again. "Call me Leo."

"Leo, listen to me. You don't have a prayer of getting a launch off this ship."

"I got on it, didn't I?"

"Let me go. I'll negotiate for you."

"Shut up."

We reached level eighteen. Still no sign of the crew. Leo was openly suspicious as he shoved me through the launch bay entrance. Inside, there were a dozen empty vessels, but not another soul.

"Where are they hiding? In the launches? Behind the cargo bins?" He swung around, eyes frantic, reacting to the echo of his own voice.

"If you leave Ktarka behind, they'll let you go," I lied. After the Jorenians found out he'd attacked one of their own, they'd jaunt across the universe to get their claws on him.

"Get in that one." He pointed to the launch nearest the huge pressure-lock doors, and followed me, dragging a semiconscious Ktarka with him. We were almost to the boarding ramp when Duncan Reever stepped out from behind the thrusters. His empty hands were held open to show he carried no weapon.

"Mercenary."

Leo targeted Reever at once. "Tell the rest of them to come out!" he said. Sweat trickled down the sides of his face as he shoved me forward with a hard hand. "Get in the launch!"

I looked past Reever and saw a figure behind one of the launches. Another shadow appeared between the launch and the hull. I quickly averted my eyes.

"There is no one else here," Reever said. "I will escort you from the ship."

"I don't need you!" Leo shouted. "Just her!"

"Who will pilot the launch?" Reever asked.

"She will!"

"I don't know how to fly one of these things," I said at once. "And Ktarka is in no shape to do it."

"If you take the helm, she'll try to incapacitate you," Reever said. "Leave the injured woman behind. Take me with you. I'll serve as pilot."

"Get in the launch with them." He thrust the now-sagging body of the educator at Reever. "No tricks." He aimed the rifle at my head. "Or I blow her brains into space."

I reached out to Reever with my mind. Silently, he completed the connection.

Are you crazy? I demanded. *Get out of here!*

Remember the Dervling? Reever moved to stand next to me.

You're going to get us all killed, you idiot. I let down the barriers that kept Reever from complete access. Felt him draw on the strength of our combined minds. Saw the false image he projected directly into the mercenary's thoughts.

Leo's eyes widened. Reever's mental projection made him think the three of us had disappeared into thin air. He hurried right past us and climbed into the vessel.

"Where are you?" With a roar of fury, the mercenary jumped out of the empty launch.

Reever thrust Ktarka's limp body into my arms. What

he did then I could never describe with words. It wasn't like anything Xonea had ever taught me, either. It was better. Faster. *Scarier.* He whirled in some kind of supple, inhuman roll. His hands moved faster than my eye could follow. There was a brief flicker of light, and Leo's rifle was in Duncan's hands. The mercenary collapsed, writhing in pain.

Two Jorenians appeared a moment later. Hado, his arm still in a sling, his face contorted with rage. Beside him was Adaola, trying to hold him back.

"Stay away, both of you." I carefully eased the educator down and made a quick examination. She'd been beaten badly, but she'd live. I went to the mercenary, then glanced up at Reever. "Where did you hit him?"

Reever kept the weapon in his hands trained on the fallen man's head. "I didn't."

I pressed my fingers to Leo's straining throat and put one palm over his heart. His blood pressure was dropping fast. Pulse rate fluttered erratically.

"Get a medical team down here." I pushed the Terran into a prone position. His abdomen was so rigid that my palm couldn't compress it. "Relax, I'm not going to—"

Leo's eyes bulged. He let out a long, agonized scream. I watched in disbelief as his abdomen swelled out several inches in as many seconds. His breath caught in a horrible gurgle. His chest fell under my palm and didn't rise again.

"By the Mother of All Houses, I mark this mercenary as my ClanKill," Hado said, and started toward us. My eyes widened as I saw him rip the sling from his injured arm. The navigator's claws sprang from his fingertips.

I couldn't let Hado gut the man. What had Xonea said about this? I protected the mercenary with my body, and faced the enraged Jorenian.

"No, Navigator Torin. I shield this one."

Deep confusion replaced the murderous mask. "Why, Healer?"

"We'll chat about it later. Reever, put down that rifle and get over here."

I showed him how to lock his hands and do the compressions. Then I covered Leo's mouth with mine.

We continued cardiopulmonary resuscitation. It didn't

help. By the time the team arrived, the mercenary was dead.

Reever helped me to my feet after I finished checking Ktarka. She had cracked ribs, severe facial contusions, and almost certainly a bad concussion. Hado was disappointed when I wouldn't allow him to make the mercenary into something he called ClanSign.

"What's he talking about?" I asked the nurse as we transferred the educator onto a gurney.

"It is what is done with the body after ClanKill," Adaola replied, her voice low and cold. "Ritually displayed, as a warning to those who would likewise threaten the HouseClan."

"Right. Well, you're going to have to wait, Hado. I need the body for an autopsy." I picked up the discarded sling and rewrapped the navigator's arm. "After I'm done, you can do whatever you like with him."

Hado regarded the dead man with seething pleasure. "My thanks, Healer."

I went down to Medical with Ktarka's gurney while Reever arranged to have the mercenary's body removed. Once I had her stabilized and resting as comfortably as could be expected, I left Adaola to monitor her and reported to Command. Reever caught up with me in the corridor along the way.

"You are making your report to the Captain?"

"I'm not sure what to tell Pnor," I said, not counting what I'd planned to propose about ending the League's pursuit. "Reever, are you positive you didn't hit him?"

"I merely disarmed him."

Right. That was like saying I was good with knives.

Pnor remained unavailable, so I reported the incident to the S.O., who recorded my statement in a hurry. When that was done, Ndo said something about the engines and disappeared. Reever had vanished sometime during my interview.

I'd forgotten to thank him, I realized. Again. I'd have to signal him later; I had to get to Medical and get some answers.

Because the mercenary wasn't Jorenian, Tonetka could perform the autopsy immediately. I assisted.

"Internal organs are even now beginning to liquefy." My boss stripped off her gloves and passed her hands under the sterilizer. "It is the same as it was with Roelm."

I insisted on running full pathogenic scans, which came up negative across the board. As they had with Roelm. It didn't make sense. I'd been there, watched him go down. Nothing had touched him, except Reever, and he couldn't have inflicted this kind of damage. If Hado wanted to use the body, he'd better work fast.

Then it occurred to me that whatever killed Leo may have been administered prior to his attempted abduction. "Who was the last nurse to make a chart notation?" I asked.

Tonetka checked. "Adaola. She took his vitals a few minutes before he escaped."

She had also been the last person to touch Roelm before he died. That was an unhappy coincidence. "Did anyone see anything suspicious?"

"Not to my knowledge." The Senior Healer studied the lab results. "Hematology shows no trace of toxin. I cannot think of a compound that could do this kind of damage, and yet not show on our scans."

I'd learned my lesson about physical evidence on K-2 from a pathogen that mimicked the tissue it inhabited in order to escape detection. "Perhaps it resembles digestive acid."

"The enzyme levels would be escalated."

"True." I thought about it for a moment. "Maybe it isn't something the men were injected with."

Tonetka raised her head. "What else could it be? Any external force would leave massive epidermal damage."

"Let me check something." I went over to access the database. She finished cleaning up and joined me at the console.

"You are comparing tissue scans from Roelm and the mercenary. Why?"

"There has to be a common denominator."

"It will take time to determine it. One is Jorenian, the other human. Even the blood chemistries are completely different." She reached past me and switched off the terminal. "That is quite enough, Healer. Go and rest. It has been an eventful day for you."

That it had.

I went back to my quarters, and spent a half hour under my cleanser. It didn't remove the memory of Leo's touch, or the beating Ktarka had suffered on my behalf, but it kept me busy. Once I was dressed, I signaled Reever.

He seemed surprised by my relay. "Yes, Doctor?"

"I'm sorry, Reever. I forgot to thank you for what you did today." I pushed my damp hair off my brow. "I'm very glad you showed up when you did."

"I was happy to be of assistance." He seemed to be more interested in watching my fingers as I fastened my tunic.

I should tell him what I'd decided to do, I thought. Yet the words didn't come out that way. "Where did you learn to do that thing you did to disable the mercenary?"

His gaze rose to meet mine. "You don't want to know."

Before I could reply, Reever terminated the signal.

Hado did something with Leo's body; I didn't try to find out the particulars. I'd overheard a conversation between two nurses about various methods of ClanSign, and that was enough for me. I kept busy attending to the crew members injured in the attack.

Leo's brutality had one positive effect. The crew's animosity toward me disappeared, and they began treating me like one of the family again. The change was a relief, but it didn't make me forget about my decision. When the Captain returned my signal, I politely made my request. With equal courtesy he refused to grant it.

"I cannot allow you to do this, Healer. Not until matters currently under investigation are resolved."

I pressed him for a commitment. "And when they are resolved? What about then?"

Pnor reluctantly nodded.

To expedite matters, I immersed myself in analyzing all the available data on the two dead men. Someone on board the ship had killed the engineer and the mercenary. How they'd been murdered was still unknown. Over the following weeks, I ran every test I could think of, and every comparative analysis possible between the two men's medical records. I came to the conclusion that whatever killed them wasn't a known viral, bacterial, chemical, or organic agent.

That trimmed the possibilities down to a weapon. But what sort of weapon turned a living body into slush? That and thoughts of the future kept me pacing the deck far into the night.

Determination became obsession. I forgot to take meal intervals. Weight I didn't need to lose melted off me. The lack of sleep made me look haggard, too. Still I kept at it, and mainly ignored the renewed, sympathetic concern from the crew.

One afternoon, while I was completing some chart notations, the Senior Healer appeared early to relieve me. She put one of the residents in charge of the ward and took my arm.

"Come," she said. "I have something I wish to show you."

Grumbling a little about not finishing rounds, I followed Tonetka out of the Medical Bay. We took the gyrlift down to level nine. Outside the environome, she activated the panel viewer.

Inside, a dozen children were making the finishing touches on a huge tower of intricately shaped celebration breads. Beside them a half dozen educators were preparing tables and seating for a large group.

"What's the occasion?" I asked.

"I accessed your personnel data file," Tonetka said. "On Terra, today is the fourteenth of July."

"It isn't." My heart sank, and I groaned. "You didn't."

She keyed open the panel and pushed me inside with a gentle shove. "I will join you later, after rounds."

As soon as they saw me, the children shouted, "Happy Birthday, Healer Cherijo!"

The kids led me to the place of honor at the head of the table. Ktarka Torin stood there, arranging servers and smiling at me. There was still a slight stiffness to the way she held herself, and some faded bruises on her face.

"How are you feeling?"

She ducked her head and made a graceful sweep of one hand. "It is nothing."

After what she'd been through, I didn't blame her for not wanting to discuss it. Especially with the person who'd caused the whole mess. I glanced around me, not quite sure how to handle this sudden outpouring of benevolent kindness. Running and hiding was pretty tempting. "To-netka talk you into doing this?"

"On Joren we do not celebrate the beginning of this path as humans do," the other woman said, misunderstanding me. "However, as you have accommodated our customs, so we wished to do the same." Everyone gathered around us. "We wish you a joyous day of birth, Healer Cherijo."

"Yes, joyous birthday, Healer!" one of the kids said.

"Happiness always!" another called. Then more voices chimed in, until I gave up, rolled my eyes, and held out my arms.

"Okay, okay." I laughed and hugged as many children as I could hold at once.

"We have made the wax sticks you light with flame for the breads," one of Fasala's classmates told me. "Do all Terrans set their food on fire before they eat it?"

The thought of that strange custom produced a great deal of giggling.

"No, that isn't right!" an older child said. "They only set fire to the round baked thing they call a cake!"

"We are sorry we do not have a cake, Healer," Ktarka said. "There was no program on the database for such."

"This is perfect." I spied the pile of gaily wrapped packages by my seat with some dismay. "Presents, too?"

From behind the crowd of kids I saw Xonea, Dhreen, and Alunthri enter the environome.

"Everyone is here now, Healer, can we begin?"

"Sure." Maybe I could sneak out at some point.

I sat down, and eyed the formidable tower of breads. Ktarka carefully lit the small candles, which flickered and glowed as the environome darkened.

The children's voices swelled into a classic rendition of "Happy Birthday." I had to blink back tears as they finished.

"Extinguish the fires, Healer!"

"No, impatient one, she must entreat her gods first!"

"Yes, yes, entreat your gods, Healer Cherijo!"

I closed my eyes, and wished the Captain would grant my request, today. Then I leaned over, and with a show of much huffing and puffing, blew out all twenty-nine candles.

There was a burst of Terran-style applause. I saw Xonea watching me, and tried out a tentative smile on him. He returned it. That was a pretty nice birthday gift in itself. We'd been avoiding each other since the challenge.

Where is Reever? that traitorous inner voice asked. I told it to shut up.

Everyone took their places as Ktarka and I portioned out the beautifully made breads. Dhreen cheerfully passed around fruit beverages for the children, but insisted I sample the vintage Terran spicewine he had brought as his gift to me.

"It will produce bristles on your bosom," he said.

After a profusion of joking and laughing, and eating every delicious morsel, the kids pressed me to open my gifts. One by one I was solemnly presented with delightful handmade articles. Ornaments for my hair. Beautifully woven baskets. An extensive disc collection of Jorenian poetry from the educators. A special blend of floral tea from Ktarka. Even a whimsical plassfiber sculpture of Jenner.

Alunthri gave me a tiny dimensional imager, which I held in my hand and examined, puzzled. The Chakacat activated a tiny switch on the bottom, and a small projection of a NessNevat child appeared. This one was happy, healthy, and smiled at me.

"Remember there is no great misfortune, Cherijo, without some small benefit," Alunthri said. "The NessNevat will thrive again."

I had no idea what the small benefit was, but I hugged my friend, and the big cat didn't say a word about the wet patch my cheek left on its fur.

Adaola and the other nurses on duty had sent a gorgeous yiborra grass basket they had all worked on. It was filled with real flowers that, according to Xonea, Adaola grew in her quarters as a hobby. Xonea's gift, the alien prismatic nodules I'd admired in his quarters, trilled a lovely handful of notes as soon as I opened the package.

One present had no label, but when I opened it I knew who had sent it.

"Is that to aid cleansing, Healer?" one of the kids asked.

"No," I said, and put the elegant brush and comb set aside. "It's to keep my hair tidy."

When Tonetka joined us a short time later, she handed me a metallic cylinder.

"For you, with my wish that your path continues in beauty," she said.

I opened the tubular case. Inside was an actual *paper* scroll. I carefully unrolled it. The smooth surface was filled with the beautiful but incomprehensible pictographs of Jorenian written language.

"I hope these are not my marching orders," I said.

Ktarka leaned over my shoulder to see, then shook her head.

"No, Healer." Her cheek brushed against mine for a moment as she gave me a quick hug. "It is a deed of naturalization. You are now a citizen of Joren."

My jaw dropped into my lap. My boss looked smug.

"I assured the Ruling Houses you would bring honor to us," she said, and made an airy gesture. "As you say, no big deal."

On the contrary. "I'm Jorenian now?"

"As much as if you were born Torin," Tonetka said. She laughed. "May the Mother of All Houses help us."

CHAPTER SEVEN

Art and Soul

My birthday would have been perfect, if I hadn't accessed my relays after the party. When I returned to my quarters, I made myself a server of Ktarka's tea, then accessed my display. After the surprise party, I'd expected a few signals.

A few? My intership file was packed.

Some of the crew had a good idea of what a birthday was. *"Greetings on the anniversary of your nativity—"*

Others stuck with conventional blessings. *"May the Mother of All Houses grant you prosperity—"*

A few seemed to think I'd given birth myself. *"Healer! Joyous time of delivery—"*

Then there was the good old standby, journey philosophy. *"We wish your path commencement commemoration to be smooth and trouble free—"*

I had a good time until I found one relay originally routed to Ship's Operational. I checked the file, but there was no tag. Odd. Probably a mix-up, I thought, and signaled the S.O.

"Ndo, I think I've received one of your relays by mistake." I transferred the relay to his terminal.

The second in command made an embarrassed gesture and transferred it back to me.

"Your pardon, Healer Cherijo. I did not label it as I meant to contact you first. Since the attack, however, we have been busy." Operating Command from the lower level while crews worked to repair the badly damaged upper levels had kept everyone on double shifts. "This relay was originally meant for you."

"Where did it originate?" I asked.

"It was transmitted by one of the mercenary ships," Ndo said. "From your parent, Healer."

I toyed with the idea of destroying the relay without ever accessing it. "Thank you, Ndo."   I terminated the signal and sat at the display for a while.

My *parent.* Well, that was one word for him.

Dr. Joseph Grey Veil began his career as a brilliant surgeon, then went into research, developing new and better techniques in thoracic surgery. Over the years, his work (mainly creating cloned, disease-free organs for transplant patients) had saved millions of lives.

For years I had believed my "father" had dedicated himself to the preservation of life. He had. Just as long as they were *human* lives.

Joseph Grey Veil had organized a group of fellow rabid xenophobes and had the Genetic Exclusivity Act passed as World Law. Through his efforts, nonhuman immigrants were forever prohibited from settling on Terra.

His place in history secured, Joseph decided to apply his genius to one more project. He wanted to create the perfect human. The ultimate physician.

That's where I came in.

Joseph Grey Veil created me by cloning his own cells. I wasn't the first of his prototypes, but so far the only successful one. Nine other clones had been created before me. None of my "brothers" had developed properly in Joseph's experimental embryonic chamber.

That was a shame. I'd hated being an only child.

My creator had extensively refined my DNA, changing my gender and fine tuning just about everything else. Nine months later he became daddy to a seven-and-a-half pound bouncing baby girl. He even named me with the project's acronym: Comprehensive Human Enhancement Research ID: J Organism—C.H.E.R.I.J.O.

That was twenty-nine years ago, today.

I took a deep breath and pulled up the relay. An austere face appeared on my display. Joseph Grey Veil was an attractive, if somewhat remote, Terran male. His silver-black hair (like mine) was kept short and perfectly groomed (unlike mine). He didn't like his slight stature (like me), because he worked hard to maintain his over-developed physique (unlike me).

Women were initially drawn to him. Some even lasted a few minutes in his company. My creator limited himself to two topics of conversation: *What a Genius I Am,* and *My Future Brilliant Plans.* No wonder he had resorted to test tubes for procreative purposes.

Curiosity proves lethal to many life-forms. Jenner had enough sense to scamper out of sight when I played back the message.

"I send this message for the nonsentient designated Cherijo Grey Veil." Joseph's attitude hadn't changed. By claiming I was nothing more than an experiment, he had convinced the Allied League of Worlds to help him recover his "property." "I am informed many among the crew of the *Sunlace* were injured during the recent recovery attempt by League loyalists."

"Recovery attempt? League loyalists?" I scoffed. "Is that what they're calling *unprovoked attacks* by *bounty-hungry thugs* now?"

He didn't respond to that. It was a prerecorded relay— he couldn't. "You must realize the risk you present to the Jorenians," he said. "Your oath as a physician directs you to do no harm. Surrender to any Allied League world. I will personally negotiate on your behalf."

"I'd enjoy that. About as much as Anteberran Orifice Disease." I studied the image. He looked remarkably calm and unruffled. Not a sign of weakness. But something . . .

I stepped closer to the display. Something wasn't right. His eyes seemed strange. I expected the usual "I'm God, you're clay" sneer. But my creator had changed. *This* Joseph Grey Veil looked almost . . . *feverish.*

His message continued. "Your willing surrender would ensure the League's magnanimity. As long as my field trials continue, you may expect to be lavishly rewarded."

"What I want won't fit in a culture dish," I said. Okay, so he couldn't hear me. I couldn't help myself.

"Your cooperation would guarantee you virtually limitless compensation."

"There you go," I said. "When in doubt, fling credits."

He paused for a moment. Ah, there was that superior

smirk I hated more than anything in existence. I'd almost missed it.

"Twenty-nine years ago I took you from an embryonic chamber. You owe me your life."

"Joe, you remembered my birthday. I'm touched."

The feverish glitter in his eyes intensified. "Come back to me, my dear child."

My jaw sagged. The man I once considered my father had never called me *my dear* anything. Never. He was either drugged, or losing his mind. I didn't know which to root for.

"Disembark on any League world. Your allies will not be prosecuted. I will allow—"

Allow? God, he loved that word, didn't he? I terminated the relay and keyed my console to erase the message. That was progress. His last message had made me so mad I'd destroyed an entire console.

Before I moved away, a general announcement was made. The *Sunlace* was preparing to transition, and begin orbit around the planet Garnot. Alunthri's new home, I recalled. We were there already?

I waited out the transition, and subsequent brief disorientation. All at once I felt exhausted, drained of all emotion, and barely made it my sleeping platform.

"Comprehensive Human Enhancement Research ID: J Organism," my creator's voice hissed.

I was thrust into blinding light. Through a fluid, distorting wall, I looked at a slightly younger version of Joseph Grey Veil.

"My finest achievement."

I knew this place. I looked around the huge bubble I was floating in. Everything seemed perfect normal. I lived here. This was the place of new beginnings, something told me. The passage to . . .

Suddenly the fluid began to drain rapidly from the capsule. I felt myself clawing at my face, unable to breathe in the liquid that kept me alive. Hard hands pulled my tiny body into cold emptiness. My eyes were scalded by merciless light. A tube was roughly inserted into my tender mouth. Cold, metallic-tasting air filled my lungs. I pushed it out at once.

"Yes, yes," a voice said. "Breathe."

"Give her to me."

The woman's voice penetrated my terror. I felt myself moving. Through blurred eyes I saw a familiar set of features. Wonderfully gentle hands cradled me against a yielding breast. The tube was adjusted, supported.

"Cherijo," she whispered. A finger caressed my face. "Yes, little one, you are safe. You made the passage."

"Put it down on the table so I may begin the examination."

"Her, Joseph." The woman sounded angry. "She's a little girl."

"It's a clone," he said. "Until we know it will survive, it is foolish to form an emotional attachment."

I managed to open my eyes. I looked from the woman's taut, unhappy face to the cold visage and large hands of the man reaching for me. The tube was removed. I open my tiny mouth. Drew my first voluntary breath. Used it to scream.

The dream twisted, changed abruptly. I was dragged from the terrifying lab to another familiar place. I was in the benign and comfortable chamber again. The light was dim and the air soft against my skin. Something warm seemed to draw me forward, leading me into the shadows.

"Outcast," a beautiful voice said. Hands stroked my hair and face. "Belonging to no one."

I felt the pain of my loneliness and isolation at once multiplied tenfold. My tears were smoothed away by a soft caress.

"I don't want to be alone," I said.

"That is what brought us together. I will kill anyone who tries to hurt you. Nothing will ever harm you again." Lips touched mine. When I would have jerked back, the hands held me fast. "No, let me show you the path."

The hands became more insistent as they moved down my body. The alien touch didn't arouse me. I felt my skin crawl, and pushed the hands away.

Fingers curled into fists. "You dare?"

Something slammed into me, over and over and over—

"Stop it!"

I was sitting up in bed, shouting.

Jenner peered at me from under "our" favorite chair. *Stop screaming already!* His eyes were huge and frightened. *I got out of it!*

The vivid quality of the nightmare shook me. Made me nauseous. I scrambled off the bed, hunched over with the memory of the pain. I had to get clean again. Wash away the nightmare. Ignoring the bruised sensations, I stumbled to my cleanser unit and proceeded to scrub myself thoroughly.

My door panel chime rang repeatedly, forcing me to leave the stall. I dried off quickly and pulled on a robe.

Xonea stood outside. "Cherijo."

I knotted the belt of my robe securely and checked to make sure nothing was on display. "What are you—"

"You were heard crying out."

"Oh. Sorry. I had a nightmare."

"May I come in?"

"Of course." I stepped aside. I was shocked to see Captain Pnor following him. "Captain?" What was he doing here? I confronted the two Jorenians uneasily. Xonea kept staring at my wet hair and state of undress. He seemed almost *revolted.*

I started with Pnor. "Sir? Is there a problem?"

"Healer," Pnor said, his expression stern. "You know I would never violate your privacy."

My privacy?

"We were coming to speak with you, and encountered Hado Torin. He reported while passing your quarters he heard you cry out, several times." The Captain looked around, as if trying to spot someone else.

"I'm fine." No, I wasn't.

"Pnor, you see how she is," Xonea said. Fierce white eyes peered down at me. "You felt defiled, did you not? That was what compelled you upon waking to cleanse yourself?"

"Yes, but . . ." I stared at my bare toes. I don't know why I felt so ashamed. It wasn't as if taking a shower was illegal. This wasn't making any sense. Why couldn't I focus?

My ClanBrother didn't let up. "In this nightmare you spoke of, Cherijo, what happened to you?"

"I don't know, exactly. I could feel six fingers—"

"Mother of All Houses." Pnor turned away from me. "It cannot be."

Xonea hissed something my vocollar decided not to translate. Pnor faced him. They looked ready to start swinging at each other. Which made even less sense.

"Someone want to tell me what's going on?" When neither man answered or broke their deadlock stare, I rubbed my eyes. "Look, it was just a bad dream—"

"Someone violated her." Xonea's huge hands became even bigger fists. "Of our House, Pnor."

The Captain only shook his head.

I stared at Xonea. "Violated who?"

He glanced at me. "Hurt you while you were unconscious."

"Wait a minute." I noticed his rigid shoulders, then the way Pnor had his fists clenched. To keep the claws from emerging, I guessed. What the hell was going on here? "Hurt *me*? How?"

"There will be physical signs," the Captain said. "Perhaps an infuser mark, if drugs were administered."

I turned my back on both men and jerked at my robe. Sure enough, there were several big bruises already darkening on my breasts and thighs. A yank at my sleeve revealed I'd also been injected in the forearm with something very recently. There were no indications I'd been raped, but I'd still have to have an exam to be sure. I wrapped my robe tightly and belted it again.

"Someone broke into my quarters, drugged me, then assaulted me, didn't they?" Pnor didn't respond. *"Didn't they?"*

Xonea rubbed his hand against the back of his neck. "Yes."

I started pacing. I'd just gotten out of the cleanser, and I wanted to go straight back in. And stay there. For a week.

Someone had come into my quarters. Come in here. Drugged me. *Violated* me. My skin crawled. I began compulsively rubbing my palms against my arms. A horrible iciness descended over me.

Whoever had done this was going to pay.

Pnor never stopped watching me. Xonea, on the other hand, went to the viewport, as if he couldn't bear the sight of me. Xonea's collection. Yes, that was what I needed.

Something that would inflict a great deal of pain. Slowly. "I want a weapon."

Xonea turned around. "I will attend to your defense." As he said that, the Captain made a strange gesture I'd never seen before. Xonea returned it with another odd motion.

"I can defend myself." My body shook as I wrapped my arms tightly around my abdomen. "What now?"

"There is little data we have on such an—aberration," Pnor said. "You will need a physical examination, and counseling, Healer."

"Space counseling. I want some answers." Brave words. My legs gave out and I sat down. "How could anyone do this to me?"

In a strained voice, Pnor told me the rest. How during the nonverbal period in their long history, Jorenians used fear as a weapon. Especially to subjugate captives.

"Male captives were often tortured," Pnor said. "For females, however, it was much worse. No greater dishonor could be imposed on a Jorenian female than to force her to mate with her captor."

When I didn't say anything, Pnor made a suggestion. "Perhaps you would feel more at ease speaking with one of our females—"

"No!" For some reason, I didn't want any of the women on board to know about this. I tugged the lapels of my robe together under my chin. It was completely irrational, yet I was adamant. "No," I said in a more controlled tone. "I'll have Tonetka perform an exam, then I'll talk to Reever."

Xonea went back to staring out the viewport. Pnor frowned at his back before he addressed me again.

"Healer, while we respect your outrage and pain, we must put an end to this quickly. A deviant who assaults an unconscious female is a highly disturbed individual. One who presents a danger to the entire HouseClan."

"Has this happened to anyone else?" I asked.

All at once the Captain wouldn't meet my gaze. "Not to our knowledge."

"I'm confused now. Why were you coming to talk to me?"

"Healer, there has been some discussion of your involvement with the death of Roelm Torin and the mercenary."

"Some discussion?" I glanced at Xonea. "What sort of involvement, Captain?"

"You had direct contact with both victims. As a healer, you possess both knowledge and opportunity to inflict such injuries. You performed both autopsies, during which evidence as to cause of death could have been overlooked or eliminated."

"You think I killed them?"

"It is possible." The bald truth didn't do wonders for my ego. Pnor went on. "Your behavior of late has been . . . erratic. Many crew members have witnessed you display extreme aggression. Your challenge to the Omorr is one example."

My emotions *had* been on a roller coaster lately, I thought, and cringed a little. Still, that didn't merit this kind of accusation. "Having a bad temper doesn't automatically make me a killer, Pnor."

Now the Captain looked at me. "You will have to be questioned further, Healer."

"I understand." The hell I did. "Am I permitted to continue working in Medical, or are you going to restrict me to quarters?"

"Cherijo," Xonea said, with a note of warning.

"I have no direct evidence against you, Healer, however"—Pnor frowned—"your activities will be closely monitored until this matter is resolved."

At least he hadn't taken my work away from me. Yet.

"There is another procedure that must be followed now," the Captain said. "Xonea will . . . help you with what must be done."

"What if *he* was the one who did this?" I asked.

Xonea looked as though I'd punched him in the mouth. He spoke like it, too. "I am not the one who assaulted you!"

Pnor seemed even more uncomfortable. "Allow Xonea to . . . explain our custom. Perhaps, in time, you will remember something about the identity of your attacker."

I'd been drugged, I reminded myself. "What if I can't remember who it was?"

"Aberrant behavior such as this is rarely confined to one

case." The Captain made a disgusted gesture. "The deviant will repeat this act again, in time."

"Thanks," I couldn't help saying. "That'll help me sleep nights."

Pnor left, his shoulders hunched.

"Okay." I looked up at Xonea. "What's this custom thing? Is it as much fun as transitional training?"

Xonea sat next to me and took my cold hands between his. "I would rather endure a thousand diversions to my path than harm you, Cherijo."

"I know that." I watched him rubbing my fingers with his. "What's wrong? You look a little pale."

His hands tightened. "I am disturbed over what has occurred." He smiled a little. "What do you always say? Relax." He did something with his hands, inverting his palms so that his fingertips rested on my inner arms.

I could relax later. No one was going to break into my quarters and drug me for their sick pleasure. "Tell me what we're doing here, Xonea."

Big blue hands covered mine. "You honor me, Cherijo."

I shuddered. Kao had said the same thing, the first and only time we had made love. I remembered Kao touching me. His skin, like damp azure silk, smooth and resilient under my hands.

Xonea lifted my hand. The same odd, textured HouseClan symbol was hidden beneath his black hair, just below the left ear. It was shaped like a dark, soaring bird. I had once had one, when Kao Chose me. It had faded—

The large hand guided my fingers to my throat.

"My HouseClan symbol," I said as I felt it. Absently I smiled. "I told him . . . it looks like . . ."

"Come, Cherijo. *Etarra nek t'nili.*" He said it again. "Come with me to the eternity we share."

I snapped out of the trance. This was *wrong.* This wasn't some kind of game plan to catch a rapist. HouseClan symbols didn't just regenerate for no reason.

Xonea was *Choosing* me!

"No." I jerked my hands from his. "What have you done?"

"I have Chosen," Xonea said. He was there, pulling me into his arms.

"No, Xonea!" I struggled to free myself. "Take it back!"

"Hear me," he said, and shook me once. I stared up into the hard white gaze. "This was the only way. I could make no other Choice."

"The hell you couldn't!" I yelled. "How could you do this? For God's sake, I'm supposed to be your *sister*! Damn it, let go of me!"

Xonea released me. The shift made me sway on my feet. His hands shot out to steady me. I pushed him away.

While working as a Trauma physician on K-2, I'd been Chosen by Kao. It was something all Jorenians were supposed to do when they attained emotional and physical maturity. Some bizarre internal time clock went off, and they Chose a bondmate.

But this had nothing to do with that. It was all wrong.

"I refuse. No, wait." Their laws were pretty complicated. "What happens if I refuse?" He didn't answer me. "Tell me!"

"I am obliged to break the Choice. My life is forfeit."

I stared at him. "Are you telling me you have to kill yourself?"

"Yes."

Now I saw why the Captain had selected his words so carefully. "Pnor knew this, didn't he? You both knew. This was what those strange gestures were about."

"You have been violated. By Choosing, I can protect you, and be ClanFather to your child."

Oh, my God. If I'd been raped as well as beaten, I could be pregnant. I shoved the thought aside. One disaster at a time.

"You knew I wouldn't let you kill yourself," I said. "Everyone knows how I feel about the ritual suicide you Jorenians seem to love so damned much. I'd cut my own throat first!"

He didn't say anything. He didn't have to. I'd guessed it all.

"Get out of my quarters."

The next day, I stood at the launch bay doors with Reever, Alunthri, and a group of Jorenians. Xonea had elected to remain on board the *Sunlace*. I'd told him earlier that I'd either go along with this shotgun wedding, or shoot him in the head. My decision was pending.

I don't think my ClanBrother was worried about getting together with his Speaker.

We had landed on Garnot and were waiting for the last of the biodecon scans to be completed. I hadn't mentioned to anyone that I was now, in Terran terms, engaged to be married. Or the fact it was because someone had beaten me (I hadn't been raped, I'd learned, after Tonetka performed a thorough exam). Only Xonea, Pnor, and my boss knew.

"No bugs detected. You're clear to disembark," Dhreen called from the helm.

A large reception party of many different species was waiting to greet us at the bottom of the docking ramp. Most dressed in the flamboyant garments artists seemed to love.

The Jorenians dispersed, giving out their traditional kiss of welcome. Reever and I lagged behind. Alunthri disappeared at once into the group, re-emerging only to look back at us.

"We'll follow you!" I called out. The Chakacat waved. The next moment it was exchanging views with a menacing-looking creature that resembled a gigantic snake.

"Well, what do you think, Reever?" I asked.

"I am not an artist," he said.

"Me, neither." I glanced at him. "By the way, thank you for my birthday gift."

He eyed my smooth hair. "You're welcome."

The planet Garnot itself wasn't very impressive. The vista seemed almost bland—all beige soil, indifferent vegetation, and drab skies. The very neutrality of the place worried me, until I saw the sprawling Main Transport complex. Constructed of a silver-white stone chiseled to throw off a million tiny flashes of light, the structure was dazzling. And that was just the first of many.

We followed the crowd to the main settlement, where more unique buildings lined the glidepaths and walkways. All of them were astonishing, as though the most beautiful structures from a thousand worlds had been transplanted here.

The crowd poured into a central towering stone edifice. Inside the ornately carved doors, a bewildering collection of art covered virtually every inch of available surface:

paintings and pictographs. Sculptures. Dimensional imagers. Even light and sound creations that appeared seemingly out of thin air.

Once inside, the Garnotans crowded around Alunthri as a beautiful chime sounded, and they all bowed to the Chakacat.

"We welcome our newest colonist, Alunthri of Chakara," the snakelike being said. "Garnot rejoices in you!"

For the next hour we circulated among the colonists. Alunthri eventually found me and Reever watching an immense sculpture reform itself at the mental command of its creator.

"Cherijo, have you seen—" It paused as it saw my indulgent smile. "Forgive me. This must seem most frivolous to you both."

"Nonsense," I said. "I may take up telepathic sculpting myself. If Reever ever teaches me some of his brain tricks." Reever made a sound that underlined his disbelief in my attainment of such a goal. I ignored him. "Well, what do you think of this place, Alunthri?"

"I have no words." The colorless eyes scanned the hall with emotion too overwhelming to be categorized. "Only that without your friendship, I could never have come here."

I ruffled its brow fur affectionately. "Be happy, pal."

Darea and Salo joined us. They admired the towering crystal sculpture, then the sculptor made them an unusual offer.

"The crystal is partially sentient," he said. He was a stout, benign-looking humanoid with three metallic ornaments piercing one angle of his wedge-shaped face. "It only allows itself to be shaped by a compatible mind."

"A picky crystal," I said.

"Would you care to try to impress your thoughts upon it?"

"Not me." I didn't want to scare the colonists.

He made the same offer to the Jorenians. Salo and Darea conferred quietly for a moment, then accepted. They mounted the platform with the artist as a small crowd began to gather.

"Join your hands thus." He moved Salo into place, then showed Darea how to stand opposite. "Concentrate on

each other, and the crystal. Allow it to see your inner
vision."

We watched. At first the two Jorenians seemed self-
conscious, then something marvelous happened. The huge
colonnade began to undulate. Elongating shoots stretched
out, swirling around the Jorenians. They remained silent,
only their hands touching, eyes closed, faces serene.

"Look," I said to Alunthri. "It's forming something."

One portion of the crystal began to weave a beautiful,
complex net that formed a spherical dome. Inside it, transparent matter swelled into larger, more bulky shapes that
refined themselves into statues. I recognized Fasala playing
with other Jorenian children. Birds flew around them. Yiborra grass sprang up under their feet. Flowers appeared.

In the center, the crystal formed an exact copy of Salo
and Darea. His hands cupped her face. Her arms were
twined around his waist.

Guess they didn't need the word *love* after all.

"Glorious." The sculptor breathed the single word in
awe.

Salo and Darea opened their eyes, and glanced around
them in blank astonishment. The crystal had obligingly left
an aperture for them to duck out of, and allowed others to
walk in and admire the new sculpture.

The artist was so delighted he insisted the couple take a
piece of the sculpture back to the *Sunlace*. A blushing
Darea chose the statue of Fasala. Salo seemed a little embarrassed as he joined us.

I nudged him with my elbow. "Nice going, big guy."

"I did not know it would do all . . . all . . ." He gestured
helplessly. *"That."*

When the couple were drawn into conversation with another admiring colonist, I looked at Reever. "Want to take
a walk?"

"Yes."

We slipped out and down the main glidecar path to an
open field, where several artists demonstrated their skills
on a myriad of projects. Smiling faces greeted us along
the way.

"I see why they chose this world for their colony," I said.
"It's perfect: one big, blank canvas for them to paint on."

"It can hardly detract from their efforts."

I waited until we had left the artists behind us, and were walking through a woods of some rather insipid-looking trees before I spoke again. "I need to tell you something, Duncan."

He pointed to a fallen trunk, and we sat down. I was careful to keep a space between us, unsure of what his reaction would be. I never knew with Reever.

"Something happened to me yesterday." Briefly I filled him in on the assault. His expression never changed, but his eyes darkened as I related the part about Pnor's suspicions, and how I'd been drugged and beaten. "I wanted you to know. You of all people would understand." When he put an arm around me, I stood up at once. "There's more."

Reever got up, too. "It is not your fault, Joey."

"What happened while I was drugged, no. What happened when Pnor left and Xonea . . ." I made a seesaw motion with one hand. "I should have realized—the way he was acting—but I was still pretty shaken up, and—"

"Cherijo." He put a finger on my lips. "Just tell me."

"Xonea Chose me."

His hand fell away, and he stepped back. I remembered the last time he looked like this. I'd knocked him on his backside in a gnorra grove on K-2. He turned away.

"Reever, I didn't ask him to do it. He thinks he can defend me this way, or something."

"I understand." He sounded uninterested.

"The only way Choice can be broken is if Xonea commits suicide."

"I know." Not very sympathetic.

"I can't let a man die because he wanted to protect me!"

"Of course not." Didn't he feel anything?

"Duncan!" I grabbed him, made him turn around and face me. His features were in the usual blank mask. "Talk to me!"

Carefully he removed my hands from his tunic. Then he walked back toward the colony.

I sat down on the tree trunk. So much for explaining things to Reever. Dull, crumpled leaves fell around me.

I knew just how they felt.

The balance of our sojourn on Garnot went smoothly, although Reever avoided me like a virulent contagion.

Dhreen noticed all the tension, but thankfully for once didn't comment. Before we boarded the launch to return to the *Sunlace*, Alunthri took me aside and pressed something in my hands.

"To remember me," the Chakacat said, and added a neatly wrapped ball of string. "For my little brother."

I hugged Alunthri, smoothed a hand over the back of its silvery head, then ran to the launch. Reever, I noted, had seated himself as far away from me as possible, next to some trader who had arranged passage to the next system. Reever never once met my eyes as Dhreen piloted the launch back to the ship.

I didn't know why he was so furious. *I* was the one being forced into marriage, not him.

The lump in my tunic pocket brushed against my forearm, and I withdrew the small object Alunthri had given me. It was a pouch, with a garment pin inside. It had been designed to represent two faces: mine and Alunthri's. When I turned it over in my hand, I saw it had been fashioned from the license and inoculant chips the Chakacat had once been forced to wear.

I tightened my hand around the beautiful symbol of our friendship. Sniffed a lot. Tried not to burst into tears.

Once we were back on the *Sunlace*, I disembarked quickly, not waiting for the others. I couldn't face spending the entire day in my quarters, either. I needed something to do, so I took the gyrlift to Medical.

Most of the cases acquired in the aftermath of the mercenary attack were ready to be released or were already discharged. I made rounds with Adaola, reviewing cases I had already memorized. The Omorr resident was sterilizing a batch of instruments, and nodded to me as I walked by.

Pnor was right; I'd been too aggressive on more than one occasion. I thought about all the bridges I had burned in the last day. Maybe it was time to mend one.

"Squilyp?" He looked up from the biodecon unit. "Got a minute?"

He hopped along with me to Tonetka's office. Once inside, I pulled out a chair in front of the Senior Healer's desk. I was gratified to see he did the same. Maybe this would work.

"You aren't scheduled for duty today," Squilyp said.

"No. I was restless and needed something to do." I glanced back at the ward through the viewer. "You probably feel the same way when you start sterilizing everything in sight."

He made the equivalent of a Terran shrug. He wasn't going to help me, but then, it wasn't his job.

"Squilyp, I owe you an apology." That got his attention. "I've said some things to you I regret. Done some things, too. Like the fight."

"You won the solicitation fairly."

"It shouldn't have happened." I got up, thrust my hands in my tunic pockets. This sort of thing was hard for me. "I'm a physician, sworn to heal. By hurting you, I violated my oath."

"I provoked you into making the solicitation."

I swung around and faced him. "I didn't have to accept, Squilyp. I could have called the whole thing off."

"You have your pride."

"And you have yours. What I'm trying to say is, I'm sorry. I'd like to start over with you. Clean slate."

He cocked his head to one side. I guessed *clean slate* didn't exactly translate into Omorr, from the puzzled look.

"Forget the past," I said. "You and I are colleagues. Let's start acting like we are."

"I see." The Omorr hopped up, approached me slowly. "So you expect me to disregard the hostility between us?"

"Yes." Was he going to take a swing at me? There was nowhere for me to go now. I was in the perfect position for him to regain his title.

"You consider me a colleague? An equal?"

"Squilyp, I've never worked with a more gifted resident. There are doctors who would sacrifice a limb to have your abilities. Your work is flawless." I watched as he extended one of *his* limbs toward me. "However, if you don't think it's possible—"

"On your world," he said, "is it done like this?"

He was picking up my hand with his membrane, curling it gently around my fingers. "What?"

"A gesture of friendship?"

"Oh. Yes. This is how it's done." We shook our respective "hands." "Thanks, Squilyp. I really do appreciate this."

"I don't understand Terran ways," he said, his gildrells

undulating slightly. Up close like this, they weren't too terrible. Actually, they gave his face a sort of elegant beauty, like a flowing white beard. "Yet I know sincerity when I see it, Healer."

He'd called me *Healer*. Relief had me grinning. "You can still call me 'Doctor,' if you like."

"And you—you may call me . . . Squid Lips . . . if you care to." His strained expression indicated the enormity of the concession he was making.

"When I do, it will only be because you're driving me crazy," I said, and patted his shoulder. "I'd like your opinion on one of the patients. I'm seeing more drainage than I like from his chest wound. Want to take a look?"

"Of course. There is something I wish to ask you, first."

"Sure."

"When you have some off-duty time, will you accompany me to an environome?"

I was confused. Here I'd thought we'd settled things. "Why?"

"I would like to practice challenge moves with you. That last assault you made—" He shook his head. "Who taught you to fight like that?"

I thought of Xonea, and my lips flattened. "My Chosen."

Squilyp gaped. "*You* are to be bonded?"

"Not if I have anything to say about it." I shook my head when he would have asked more. "Long story. Let's go examine that patient."

I spent a surprisingly successful shift working with the Omorr. We disagreed on a few cases, but now it was more like the arguments Tonetka and I had. A sense of mutual respect went well with the bickering.

I could really like Squilyp, I thought, as I trudged into my quarters. Jenner was waiting for me, and scented Alunthri on the ball of twine I tossed him. He even ignored his food dish for a full five minutes to pat the ball around.

Once my pet abandoned me for a nap, I made myself a server of tea, then went to my console to access the cultural database. Pnor's investigation, as far as I knew, had yielded no new information on the killer. Maybe I could turn something up.

The very rare cases of murder in modern Jorenian history had usually been committed by offworlders. Every killer had been caught and nearly all of them declared ClanKill. Three suspects on record who'd refused to confess to their acts had been banished from Joren forever. One of them, a native Jorenian, had killed himself as soon as the sentence had been handed down. I downloaded the case file so I could study it further.

The Jorenian involved had apparently returned to the homeworld after several years of imprisonment on an alien world for some unspecified transgression. From the time of his release and subsequent reunion with his HouseClan, he displayed violent and irrational behavior that indicated a state of severe psychosis. When he learned his bondmate had petitioned the Council to have their bond dissolved and him committed, he killed her. Later, he refused to admit to the crime. Since there had been no witnesses, a sentence of banishment had been decreed.

A few moments later, the mentally ill male had committed suicide in front of the Ruling Council.

I could see why Xonea found it hard to believe a Torin had killed Roelm and the mercenary, when the only case involved a deranged psychotic. Still, it was proof that a Jorenian was capable of murder. And psychotics could successfully conceal their illnesses, sometimes for years.

The question was, which Jorenian? Why would one of the crew kill Roelm, an engineer, and Leo, a Terran mercenary? There didn't seem to be any connection, other than the fact that both had been confined to Medical shortly before they were murdered.

I'd have to give it more thought.

As I scanned through the available data on their judicial process, I also learned Pnor could have put me off the ship, just by simply suspecting I was involved in the murders. So why hadn't he done that? Then I came across a very interesting paragraph.

Suspected offenders Chosen by a member of the victim's HouseClan after the offense has been committed may be thus shielded from judicial action until such time as the case can be presented before the Ruling Council on Joren.

So Xonea had another reason for making his Choice. Anger swelled inside me. Why hadn't he mentioned this little clause? I got up to adjust the envirocontrols, then went back to check the rest of his story.

Offworlders had also been responsible for every recorded case of rape. Pnor's disbelief was justified then. Unbonded victims had been Chosen within hours of the assault. Pregnancies as a result of rape were even more rare, the records indicated only seven. It was my guess that the children were never told.

I didn't need Xonea to protect me, not from murder charges or a rapist. Just what would it take to break this Choice?

There was no divorce, and no case of a Chosen breaking the Choice due to unwilling participation. Given the Jorenian attitudes toward sex, I thought as I deactivated the console, their monogamy wasn't surprising.

I couldn't seem to relax, so I secured the door panel and injected myself with a mild barbiturate. Just as I prepared to drop on the sleeping platform, my display panel chimed.

"What is it?" I asked, fighting the artificially induced cocoon of sleep.

"Message from Ship's Operational."

I dragged myself over to my display and accepted the signal. It was S.O. Ndo.

"Healer. Forgive me for disturbing you."

"No problem." I yawned behind my hand. "What's the problem?" Boy, that sounded bright, I thought sluggishly. Nothing destroys your vocabulary faster than a good dose of drugs.

"I am preparing my formal report on the mercenary attack," Ndo said. "I need to clarify some aspects of your statement with you."

"Can we do this tomorrow, S.O.? I'm beat."

He nodded.

Good. I'd had quite enough for one day.

I scheduled a time to meet with him and programmed an appropriate alarm signal. Jenner was waiting on the mattress for me when I fell into it.

I thought of Xonea, Reever, Alunthri, and Squilyp. Results were evenly divided. I'd like to throttle Xonea, I thought. Reever probably wanted to do the same to me. I'd said good-bye to Alunthri, my old friend. Now I had a potential friendship with Squilyp.

A small, rough tongue rasped against my cheek, and I fell asleep.

CHAPTER EIGHT

For the Children

"Let's review your report one more time."

S.O. Ndo was methodical, precise, and unaware I had a massive headache. A large, horrible instrument of torture pounded at the back of my skull, from the inside. Barbiturates had that effect on me. Not even two scalding-hot servers of floral tea had helped.

Morning-afters. Universally to be avoided.

"Of course." I carefully recounted everything I could remember from the moment I woke to find the mercenary Leo standing over my bed.

I was at the point of "Reever managed to disarm him, there was a flash of light, and then—" when Ndo interrupted.

"A flash of light? That was not in your report."

I frowned. I hadn't put it in my report. The only lights I ever concerned myself with were medical optic scanners, and the ones that made it possible to walk around my quarters without banging into things.

"Sorry. Yes, there was a light or something that flashed, just for a moment. I thought it was from an internal scanner." Even as I said that, I realized how silly it sounded. Jorenian scanners didn't produce light. "I really didn't think about it."

"Describe how it appeared to you."

I concentrated. "Reever had linked with me to project a false image. The projection fooled the mercenary into believing we were inside the launch already. When he came back out, Reever took his rifle and stepped back. Then there was this bright flash of . . ." I halted. "Not a flash. Something else." I shook my head, frustrated. "Why can't I remember?"

"It is understandable. You were under extreme duress." Ndo appeared sympathetic, but I heard the same frustration in his tone.

"Why are you concerned about the light? Do you think it had anything to do with—" My eyes widened as I remembered. "Fasala saw some kind of light, too. Just before her accident in the cargo bay. A *ring* of light!"

"That is what you saw?"

"Yes! It *wasn't* a flash, but a perfect circle." I was excited as the image finally sifted to the top of my sluggish memory. "Large, perfectly circular, about two meters in diameter. White with a prismatic edge. It couldn't have lasted more than a tenth of a second."

"Two meters?" Ndo seized on that. "You're certain of the dimensions?"

"Of course. Why?"

"The damage to the buffer was calculated to be the same area, given the amount of alloy recovered from the injured."

"You're kidding." I sat back in my chair. "It could have been the same thing Fasala saw, then."

Ndo nodded as he keyed the information on his data pad.

I speculated out loud. "So what do we have on the ship that creates a two-meter circle of light, slices through adaptable sonic alloy, and dissolves living bone and tissue?"

"Nothing," Ndo said as he continued entering the data.

While I waited, I went over the shift when Fasala had been brought in. Squilyp and I had argued over how to detect the buffer shards. Roelm had said something. . . .

"The Engineer described equipment used to fit the buffers on ships. He said the technology was based on sound."

"Harmonicutters."

"Do you have any those laying around somewhere?"

Ndo shook his head. "They are too large. The vessels they are used on must be docked in specially designed bays in a specific region on our homeworld."

"There is no such thing as a *portable* harmonicutter?"

"Not to my knowledge."

That wasn't exactly a *no.* "How does a harmonicutter

work?" Ndo gave me a slightly exasperated look. "Please, it's important."

"It produces continuous, high-intensity energy, Healer. Rather like your surgical lasers, only a harmonicutter uses sound instead of light. Its sonic beam converts raw alloy material into the dimensions required on the particular vessel being fitted."

"This sonic beam, is it composed entirely of sound waves?"

"Yes."

In the past, extracorporeal shock-wave lithotripsy, or ultrasonic waves, had been used to break up kidney and upper ureteral stones on Terra. The primitive procedure often caused mild to moderate cellular damage at the entry and exit points.

This harmonicutter was obviously much more powerful. If used on a living being, would such focused sonic energy have a more lethal effect? It would explain the absence of any toxin and why their insides had been turned into liquid, too.

"Roelm and the mercenary could have been murdered using a sonic beam of that intensity," I explained my theory to Ndo.

"A harmonicutter is not as focused as a laser, as the energy it generates is utilized on immense areas. A harmonicutter used as you describe would destroy everything within at least a ten-meter radius. You and Linguist Reever would not have survived."

Okay, so my theory had some holes in it.

"Tell me something. Who on board the *Sunlace* would know how to operate a harmonicutter?"

He looked thoughtful. "Most of our engineers and senior helm staff. Roelm, of course. Xonea, Captain Pnor, and myself as well."

No help there, that was about a hundred people. Too many to make a viable list of suspects. I pushed a tired hand through my hair.

"S.O., may I continue this discussion with you after I've had time to think about it?" I was feeling distinctly ridiculous, fighting off a continuous wave of yawns. Surely I hadn't overdosed myself. Had I?

"Of course." He rose and offered his hand as I struggled from my seat. "Are you feeling ill, Healer?"

"I've had better days, Ndo. Thank you for your patience."

I trudged off to the gyrlift and took it up to my quarters. Dhreen was waiting for me just outside my door panel. He tried to talk me into a game of whump-ball. I yawned in his face.

"Too tired," I waved my hand. "Later."

"Does this have anything to do with the fact you and Reever aren't speaking to each other? Again?" Dhreen's guileless eyes glinted.

"None of your business." I barely had enough energy to key myself in. The door panel closed behind me. I was in trouble, I thought. My sluggish brain finally processed the fact that this was not a natural weariness.

Nothing could make me *this* tired. I'd been drugged again.

I reached up and hit the comm panel with an awkward swipe.

"Xonea . . ." I fell back and slid down the wall. "Alert . . . Xon—"

He was hurting me again. The man with the hard hands, who relentlessly probed my body. I screamed and writhed until I thought my lungs would burst.

"Resistance test gamma-fourteen negative," he said. "No signs of contagion."

"Shall I prepare the next series, Doctor?"

The dark blue eyes looked down at me. "Give me the nasal probe. I want to check the sinuses."

"If she sounds snotty, it's because she's been crying for an hour, Joseph!"

The woman pushed him out of the way and took me in her arms. She wrapped my naked body in something soft and warm while she glared at the man.

"Margaret, put her down."

"You're hurting her."

"She will not remember any of this."

"You hope she won't." The woman cradled me close, and my shrill screams died as I nuzzled instinctively at her breast. "When was the last time you fed her?"

"We must keep her stomach empty until the trial is complete." The man made a curt sound. *"It will not harm her to go without nourishment for a twenty-four-hour period."*

"Give me a bottle."

"Put her down and leave, Margaret."

"And if I don't?" she demanded. *"What are you going to do, Joseph? Starve me, too?"*

"Put her down!"

My body was wrenched from the woman's arms, and I heard her scream blend with mine.

Take control of the dream, Cherijo.

Take control.

Take take take—

I was standing in a chamber, my breath burning in my chest. The presence hovered there in the depths of the shadows, just out of reach. I tried to take control, to leave that place.

"You think you can control me, little one? Me!" The laughter was chilling. *"I could crush you with a thought."*

"Then do it." I centered my consciousness and drew strength from the sense of power it gave me. *"Get it over with."*

"You know nothing of power. Watch and learn."

Before my eyes a window appeared, one that displayed the level where I had just been interviewed by Ndo. He was still there, looking over my report, frowning and making notes on a touchpad.

"He resents his place in the succession, but would never reveal it to Pnor."

"Leave him alone!"

"Look at him. Ever loyal, steadfast Ndo, who has yet to Choose, yet to make a child. He thinks he knows something, but his arrogance blocks insight." The voice lowered, became almost gleeful. *"Let me show him the true inner path."*

I saw a ring of light form in mid-air behind the S.O. He jerked back, falling from his chair as the light shattered over his body.

"Stop it!" I shouted.

"It is done. Now he will know the emptiness I feel."

*I watched in horror as Ndo collapsed in convulsions.
He was dead in minutes.*

*"You killed Roelm and that mercenary, didn't you?
You bastard!"*

*The presence turned on me. Smashed into my mind. I
couldn't shield myself from the pounding fists. The shrill
voice shrieked disjointed accusations, punctuated by
more blows.*

"You let him . . . believed you . . . killed for you . . ."

*Another presence was there. Something vague, far be-
yond the battering hands. The other spoke to me.*

Cherijo. Wake up. You must wake up.

*". . . make you wish . . . never born . . ." the first one
was screaming. I couldn't take much more. I reached out,
desperate to escape.*

Cherijo. Wake up. Wake up!

"Cherijo!"

Someone slapped me, hard.

"Wake up!"

I fell out of the dream, and found myself in a convulsive
state. Pain clutched at me. I curled up in a fetal position,
automatically trying to protect my injuries. Literally every
single inch of my flesh throbbed in agony. My eyes fluttered
open when six-fingered hands touched me.

Xonea rolled me onto my back. I was on the deck. Then
the world went black.

The next thing I knew the big pilot was running, carrying
me in his arms. I fought to keep my eyes open.

"Ndo?" Strong hands kept me from getting loose. "Ndo!
He's in trouble!"

"Be calm, Cherijo. You are injured."

I fell unconscious again, and woke up on an exam table.
The Senior Healer was leaning over me.

"Tonetka? Ndo!" I tried to hurl myself off the table.
Xonea's face appeared on the other side. Now his hands
held me down. "I have to—"

"Remain still, Healer." Tonetka opened my tunic and
performed a brisk, thorough examination. Xonea averted
his eyes, while I glanced down. Saw more bruises forming
on my pale skin. A lot more.

"Tonetka." She met my gaze. "What the hell happened?"

"You were beaten," Xonea said, his voice low and filled with dangerous menace. Now he looked, memorizing each mark.

I sagged back on the exam pad. "Then it's too late."

"Too late?" Tonetka echoed.

"Ndo. He's dead. Whoever did this killed him."

I was confined to a berth in Medical Bay. Again.

"Anaphylactoid purpura," Tonetka said a day later. "Severe ecchymoses and petechiae. Three reasons you will stay in that berth, Healer, until I advise you differently."

"We've done this before, remember?" I said. "I won last time."

She clutched a scanner and passed it over me. "The last time you were my patient, you did not have ruptured blood vessels over virtually every centimeter of your epidermis!"

"No, I had a stroke and two heart attacks. That was a lot worse than a couple of bruises."

Tonetka muttered something that the nurse next to her overheard. The younger Jorenian woman's eyes rounded. "Senior Healer!"

"She'll never do it," I told the nurse. "And if she tries, I'll thump her."

"I would be greatly entertained by such an attempt!" Tonetka said.

A resident came over, brave enough to enter the fray. "Senior Healer. Healer Cherijo. You are disturbing the other patients."

"See?" I glared at her. "You're disturbing the other patients. Now give me my clothes, so I can get up and strangle you myself."

"I should have induced a coma!" Tonetka said. Was that gesture she made a nonverbal obscenity? "Divert your path with your Terran stupidity. I will *dance* at your death ceremony." She stalked off to her next patient.

The news confirming Ndo's death had left both Tonetka and me with frayed tempers, I thought, and sighed.

"Pig-headed old witch." I shrugged at the wide-eyed nurse. "What's worse is she's probably right."

Later, one of the residents offered me an analgesic for my bruises, but I refused. My mind was muddled enough.

I didn't want to take a chance and slip into another unprotected sleep.

The next time I might not wake up.

The crew heard, of course, and many stopped by to visit me. The Senior Healer spent more time that day chasing HouseClan Torin out of Medical than she did examining the patients. The only thing I was allowed to receive was a package.

"What's this?" I turned the slim box over in my hands.

"Our passenger from Garnot sent it for you," the Senior Healer said. "Dhreen related the nature of your injuries to him, and he wished you to have this."

I opened the lid, and removed a thin, golden cuff. "Wow. Nice bauble."

"One he claims will heal the body and soothe the soul."

"If it does, you'll be out of a job," I said, admiring the pretty thing. I slipped it over my hand, but it was a little too big for my wrist.

"Traders will say anything to peddle their wares," Tonetka said as she examined me, then instructed one of the residents to cover the ward until the Omorr reported for his shift.

"Hey, where are you going?"

"I have a class today with the primary students." Tonetka often scheduled time to teach the Jorenian children. She was an expert in a number of subjects, including (of course) journey philosophy. She held up an old, wicked-looking blade. "Today I am presenting facts for the children about prehistoric medical practices and instruments."

"Ugh. That looks sharp. I wouldn't pass it around. Here." I removed the bracelet and placed it around her wrist. "You like? You wear. It doesn't fit me, and I'll just lose it or something."

Once Tonetka had departed, I managed to talk one of the nurses into procuring a terminal for my use by making a solemn and soon-to-be-broken promise to access it for no more than an hour or two.

"The Senior Healer will be most upset if she finds you at work when she returns," the nurse said. "Then you will begin insulting each other and disrupting the ward—again."

"Don't worry." I winked at her. "I'll take all the blame *and* the insults."

I retrieved all pertinent records pertaining to Fasala's injuries, the mercenary attack, and the deaths of Roelm, the Terran Leo, and Ndo.

The facts would begin to correlate, I thought, if I kept shuffling them around. Roelm, Leo, and Ndo had each died of identical symptoms from as of yet unidentified causes. Fasala and the two educators had been injured, not killed. The only thing the dead victims had in common was that they were male. Fasala and the educators weren't, and their wounds were completely different, too.

I was comparing medical histories when Xonea appeared and sat down beside my berth.

"Healer, you are looking well."

"I thought Jorenians didn't lie." I looked terrible, and he knew it. "Any progress?"

"The Captain has discovered no evidence connecting the attack on you and Ndo's death," he said, and glanced at the data on my terminal. "You are comparing medical charts?"

"I had hoped to find some similarity in their profiles." I removed the charts on Fasala and the two educators and concentrated on the dead men. "Roelm and Ndo were Jorenian, approximately the same age. Yet Roelm was much heavier than Ndo. The Terran mercenary was older than both, but weighed much less. They were killed in different parts of the ship. Roelm and Leo were surrounded by different people. Ndo died alone. He was murdered at his Command display, wasn't he?"

"Hado found his body exactly where you said it would be," Xonea said. Absently, he rubbed one hand across his abdomen. "Do you recall anything else?"

"Only that I have no idea why I wasn't killed, too." I switched off the terminal and put my head back. "Tonetka believes whatever killed the men couldn't have caused my injuries." Xonea was staring oddly at me. Again. "What?"

"It has been suggested that your injuries prove you were involved with Ndo's murder," he said. "That Ndo inflicted them upon you in self-defense."

"Just who is spewing this waste?" I demanded.

"Captain Pnor will not say. There is more I may do to prove your innocence, with your . . . cooperation."

I'd heard this kind of proposal before. Last time it got me engaged. "Define *cooperation*."

"The one who assaulted you will try again. Allow me to guard you."

"Guard me?" An image of Xonea dogging my heels made me frown. "I don't see you following me around all day."

"You can be monitored while you are on duty. I will watch over you by sharing your quarters."

"You mean, move in with me? I thought you needed to bond with someone for that."

"Full bonding is not required. It is the only way I can protect you."

I sat up straight again. "I told you before, I don't need a baby-sitter."

That didn't make him happy. "You must do this, Cherijo." He stood. "You are my Chosen."

There was nothing that equaled Jorenian arrogance. Except me. "That doesn't make me your property, fly boy."

"Under HouseClan law, you must obey me."

I'd never heard *that* before. "Space your HouseClan law!" I slammed my hand onto the terminal keypad, scrambling the data.

"It is our path, Cherijo," he said, then grimaced and pressed his hand against his stomach again.

"Your path is giving me a headache, and you an ulcer!"

Before Xonea could reply, an explosion rocked the *Sunlace*. This one was much more violent than the tremors caused by the mercenary attack. I was flung from my berth onto the floor. Xonea covered me with his body. His massive weight forced the breath out of my lungs.

"Alert," the display panel announced. "Hull breach on levels five, six, eighteen, and twenty-eight. Internal buffers compromised. Levels will be secured. Evacuation must commence."

"The League must have tracked us from Garnot." Xonea pulled me up with him.

I stripped the monitor ports from my arms and called for the staff. Everyone in Medical mobilized around us.

"I want all senior residents to stay put," I said. "Squilyp, you're in charge." The Omorr nodded. "Set up for heavy casualties. You four emergency teams, take the gyrlifts to the nearest level you can get to the compromised areas.

Xonea, which level has the greatest concentration of crew members?"

"Level six. The sub-executive bays and educational facilities are located there."

"No." I paled. "Tonetka. The *kids*."

After dividing up the teams, we grabbed our emergency packs and raced out. More turbulence rocked the ship. I stumbled several times along to the way to the level above Medical. Xonea always managed to grab me before I hit the deck.

Xonea and I entered level six ahead of the team. Heat and a sudden, dense cloud of noxious smoke enveloped us. From the emergency kit I carried I pulled out two breathers and handed one to Xonea. I looked over my shoulder to assure the nurses were masking as well.

"Keep your hand on my arm!" Xonea's voice was muffled by the mask. I nodded and grabbed onto his sleeve. He led me through the blinding fumes to the first of the children's classrooms. The door panel was jammed. When Xonea started to force it open, a burst of flames made him snatch his hands away.

"Look!" I shouted, pointing through the open gap. Over the fiery wall we saw a group of small bodies huddled in a tight mound. Two educators were shielding the children from the fire with their own bodies. One of them was Ktarka Torin.

Evacuation units kicked in at last. They removed enough smoke from the level corridor to let us take off our breathers.

"Emergency controls are operational," Xonea said. He keyed the exterior deck panel. I wiped the filthy sweat from my face on my sleeve and saw a square aperture open in the upper deck just inside the classroom door panel. "This will extinguish the flames."

Thick streams of chemical foam cascaded from the slot. It worked—the flames were smothered at once. That left smoke, which was as deadly as fire.

"We've got to clear the air," I told him.

"I am purging the room through the exchange dampers," he said as he rewired the panel controls. I didn't wait to watch him, but strapped on my breather. After I grabbed my pack, I kicked aside some smoldering debris, and stepped inside.

The children had to be checked first. All of them were coughing heavily. I handed out breathers as I made a quick scan of each child for lung damage and burns. The educators were calm and kept reassuring the children. I would have never guessed both women had second-degree burns on their backs, a fact I discovered right after I'd dealt with the kids.

Ktarka's eyes were still filled with panic as she tried to hold the singed shreds of her tunic over her breasts. I patted the part of her shoulder that wasn't injured as I passed my scanner over her.

"Hold on, lady," I said. She gave me a confused stare. Shock was starting to set in. "You'll be just fine." One of the nurses appeared beside me, a syrinpress in her hand. I injected Ktarka with pentazalcine and helped the nurse get the educator to her feet.

"Healer—" Ktarka began, then coughed violently.

We both stumbled against each other when the *Sunlace*'s hull was battered with a fresh wave of displacer fire. The nurse supported Ktarka from the opposite side as she sagged. It took a few minutes to maneuver her limp body out the door panel and gently down on the deck. We went back for the other educator and the kids.

Once the classroom was evacuated, I turned to the nurse.

"Have the women taken to Medical." I pointed to the children who were in respiratory distress. "These four, too." I went to the only functional corridor display, and routed a signal to Medical.

Squilyp's face appeared. Behind him, I saw the staff trotting in different directions. "Doctor?"

The ship rocked wildly again. I grabbed the sides of the console and held on. "I'm sending you two adults, both with second-degree burns. Four kids on oxygen. Gyrlifts are down, so they'll be on gurneys. Check everyone for inhalation exposure and toxins. Set up for more burn patients." I felt the transitional thrusters many decks below throb into life. "What's your status?"

"The ward is full. Three serious, one critical. I'm prepping for surgery." The Omorr looked over his shoulder and yelled at a nurse, "Move those low priorities out in the corridor!" He looked back at me. "Adaola is taking triage—"

"Caution," the display interrupted. "Emergency transition."

"Get those patients prepped. Don't be exemplary today, Squil," I said. "Be quick. Go!"

He nodded, and I terminated the signal.

"Cherijo?"

At Xonea's call, I left the nurse to take care of the patients. The rest of the classrooms we could access were empty, he told me when I caught up with him. The Jorenian stood before an insurmountable pile of rubble blocking off the corridor leading up to level five.

Transition into another dimension began without warning. Once reality untwisted, I found myself on the deck, sprawled next to Xonea. I rubbed a hand over the new bruises on my hip.

"Nothing I love more than emergency transition in the morning," I said.

"Launch bay has been destroyed," Xonea told me as he helped me up. He nearly doubled over before he propped himself against one wall panel.

"What is it? Are you hurt?"

"No, I am just winded. Here." In his hand was a scanner. The display showed a concentration of some fifty life-forms behind the blockage.

"Can you raise anyone on level five?"

"No response. We must find a way through this. Heat levels are rising on the other side of the obstruction."

I knew the gyrlift was useless. "What about the emergency controls?"

"The panel has been badly damaged."

I spotted a gap in the debris level with the upper deck. It was too small for Xonea. One skinny human might make it, though.

"Can you lift me up there?" I pointed.

He shook his head. "It is too dangerous."

"Then I'll climb."

"You cannot do this. Cherijo!" He took my arm to hold me back.

"Let me go," I said, and shook myself loose. Both our faces were coated with blackened sweat. Every bruise on my body throbbed. The stench from the lingering fumes made me dizzy, so I kept my breathing light and shallow. Then I saw a group of crew members entering the corridor. They were wearing envirosuits.

"You!" I yelled at the smallest one, and waved him over. "Take that off and give it to me."

As the crew member obligingly stripped out of the suit, Xonea fumed.

"This is madness!"

"You can try and stop me." I tugged the oxygen unit from the back of suit. There was no way I could fit through the gap with it on, and even if I did, the fire would probably cause it to explode. With no air supply, I'd have to make it a quick climb. "Or you could work on what's left of the emergency controls while I climb over through there."

His mouth was a hard, colorless line. "Your hands will be burned."

I discarded the gloves—they were so big I'd never get a handhold while wearing them—and fastened the over-large suit as tightly as possible. "Don't worry, I'll live."

"What about oxygen?"

"I'll hold my breath."

He yanked me into his arms, and held me for a moment. My face barely reached the lower vault of his chest.

"Come back to me, Cherijo," he said.

I nodded, then donned the head covering. At my thumbs-up, big hands encircled my waist, and Xonea lifted me over his head. Wish I had that kind of strength. Surly patients would no longer be a problem.

I thrust my body forward into the gap. The skin on my fingers and palms split as I grabbed torn metal.

"Ahhh!"

As my body fell against the rubble, hot spots seared through the suit, burning me. I clenched my teeth against another cry. Had to keep moving. I ducked my head in and bent my elbows, my shoulders scraping the sides of the gap. I heard a ripping sound, and felt the back of the suit tear from my neck to my waist. So much for the envirosuit. With a grunt, I hoisted myself through.

Smoke. Flames. The stench of destruction. The sound of children crying made me claw my way forward. Something

hot and jagged pierced the suit and stabbed my right thigh.
I jerked my leg away, felt the blood pulsing from the
wound. Artery?

"Help us!" a familiar voice shouted.

I squinted and tried to see where they were. Black, bil-
lowing smoke made the air into a thick fog. Above me,
ruined deck plates had burst, spilling deadly lengths of live,
writhing component wiring. All around me crimson and orange flames crackled and flared, creating a deadly barrier.
One I had to get through. Now.

There. Fifty yards away, Tonetka was herding the children back from the danger zone. Painfully I crawled down
the steep debris pile, until a solid wall of flame barred
my path.

"Go back!" Tonetka shouted.

After ruining a perfectly good envirosuit? Not a chance.
I tucked my hands under my arms, curled up, and pushed
myself into a tumbling roll. Incredible heat burned through
the suit and seared my flesh as I hurtled through the fire.

When I landed on the deck below, my suit was burning.
The children screamed in terror. Tonetka quickly beat out
the flames and pulled the smoldering material from my
body.

"Your path could have been diverted!" the Senior
Healer shouted as she yanked me to my feet.

I coughed convulsively. "You okay?" I asked, when I
could breathe again.

The children were in good shape. Some had minor burns,
but the majority were simply scared. My boss hadn't fared
as well. Tonetka was covered with lacerations. Dust greyed
her hair, and her usually immaculate tunic was a tattered
rag. She'd torn up most of it to bind the children's wounds.
Dark splotches marred the smooth blue skin of her face.

"What happened to you?" I demanded.

"The corridor panels collapsed on me." She pointed back
to the debris pile. "The children were able to pull me out
before the fire started."

I turned my head, trying to locate a way out. Then I saw
it, and gasped. "Mother of All Houses."

Behind the Senior Healer, an entire section of the hull
had been blown out into space. The invisible buffer was all
that stood between us and the killing vacuum.

"We have to get them back through that gap." I pointed where I had come from. Tonetka was already busy binding my leg with a strip of her tunic. She straightened to gauge the opening. At the same time, a disjointed com signal announced that the section buffer field was weakening. As if we needed more problems. "Let's get the flames out first."

Tonetka shook her head. "The extinguishing equipment won't work. I have tried manual override, but the backup panel malfunctioned."

I looked around for something we could use. I spied the classroom equipment. "That," I pointed to a large plastic tub.

"It is too small, and will melt," Tonetka said.

I nudged the lid up and pushed it aside, revealing the hundred pounds of clean, sterile sand inside. I knew it would be there. After all, *I* was the one who had explained the Terran concept of a sandbox to these kids.

"We can pour it on the flames," I said. "It will extinguish even the chemical fires. Get some of the bigger students to help us."

We passed out containers to the older children and formed a Terran bucket brigade. Tonetka and I took up positions by the fires. The kids passed full containers of sand down to us. We emptied them on the flames and passed them back. In a few minutes, all that was left was smoldering components and a heap of sand-covered debris.

"That's it," I said. "Let's get them out of here!"

Tonetka nodded, and gestured to the children. "Listen carefully now. Wrap your hands with strips of your clothing. Do not touch anything for very long. Move as quickly as you can."

She tried to examine my ruined hands, but I yanked them away.

"Later. We've got to move, *now.*" I turned toward the opening and shouted, "Xonea! We're sending the kids through! Get ready!"

"Ready!" a distant, muffled voice called back.

It took both of us to boost each child up to the gap. As their weight fell against my burned, broken hands, I said some words I hoped the kids would forget. We kept hoisting them up. Ten. Twenty. Thirty. Finally we pushed the last child through.

I turned to Tonetka. "Let's see how well you can climb, old woman."

She eyed the gap. "Piece of bread."

"*Cake.* Piece of *cake.*" It hurt to laugh. "Wait till you get to the top. Come on, let's go."

"You must go first, Cherijo."

"Age before beauty."

"You won't be able to climb with your hands. I will have to lift you."

I looked down. So much for my surgical career. "You'd better not drop me."

Tonetka cradled my face with her hands, and gazed into my eyes. "I bless the Mother for the day you became our ClanDaughter." She even kissed my forehead.

I scowled up at her. "Yeah, I honor you, too, you stubborn old battle-axe. Now give me a boost."

I was the same size and weight as most of the kids, but Tonetka had to push me up by herself. With a string of curses my vocollar ignored, she thrust me up to the gap.

Large hands were waiting to pull me through—Xonea's and Hado's. I made it without bruising my already abused body too much. Xonea saw my hands and leg, and cursed. As soon as my feet touched the lower deck, I turned and called out to Tonetka.

"Come on, Senior Healer!"

Hado put a hand on my shoulder. "Healer Cherijo. You must come away from this area, now."

A strange sound and subsequent vibration shuddered through the level. Had the mercenaries somehow followed us? The huge pile of rubble shifted, as if it was sliding over, away from us.

It was collapsing. On top of the Senior Healer.

"Tonetka!" I screamed, but Xonea was helping Hado pull me away. "Hurry—we've got to—" My hands wouldn't work right, I couldn't get them off me. "What are you doing? Help her!"

Hado looked at the opening with a sad expression. "She cannot fit through the gap."

"I'll make her fit!"

"Cherijo!" Xonea shook me. "You must see to the children!"

Small cries of pain finally penetrated my fury. I grabbed the front of my Chosen's tunic as best I could, and thrust my face close to his. "Listen! I don't care how you do it, get her out of there!"

Xonea nodded. I let go. He went back to working on the panel with Hado.

One of the nurses sprayed my wounds with skinseal, against what she told me was her better judgment. I ignored her. I gloved while I bit back a shriek of pain, then went to treat the wounded. Four entire classes of children had been rescued. Most were suffering from shock, minor burns, and smoke inhalation.

More injured were brought out from a collapsed section. They were educators who had been in a planning session when the attack occurred. Two were dead. Three more died on the deck as we tried to keep them breathing. Their bodies weren't just burned, they were *charred*.

Crew members from all over the ship assisted in removing the critical cases on litters. When those ran out, the injured were simply carried off in strong Jorenian arms. I had just stabilized one of the children for the move when an ominous rumble shook the deck. The sound of tearing alloys ripped through the air. I glanced toward the obstruction, saw it shaking, and ran.

"Tonetka!"

Xonea and Hado stood a few feet from the pile of rubble, still fiddling with the emergency controls.

"Get her out of there!" I screamed at them.

"We cannot. The buffers are too weak." Xonea caught my arms. "They have already begun to reform. She has chosen her path!"

"The hell she has!"

Another vibration shook the level, then the rubble collapsed and disappeared out into space. All that was left was a huge, empty hole.

"No!" I shoved Xonea away from me and ran up to the buffer. Debris floated just beyond the gap in the hull. I pounded on the invisible wall, making my gloves split, leaving bloody splotches hanging in mid-air.

A strong arm hauled me away. "She is gone, Cherijo."

"No!" I looked over at the navigator, who was closing the access panel. He shook his head. I wrenched myself around until I faced Xonea. "Why didn't you get her out?"

"I tried." He lifted his hand toward my face.

"Don't touch me!" I pushed him away.

Hado spoke up then. "She begins a new journey, Healer."

That made me snarl, "Oh, shut up!"

The navigator inclined his head. "I regret your pain."

"And you." I turned on Xonea and thumped a bloody fist against his broad chest. "You'll just plan another big party, won't you?" Snarling had become ranting. I didn't care. "Maybe her body will get pulled into a star, and you can save yourself a grass shroud!"

"Doc." Dhreen put himself between us. His spoon-shaped fingers settled on my shoulders. Troubled amber eyes peered into mine. "Don't do this."

I pushed Dhreen to one side, and advanced on Xonea. Once I got close enough, I pulled back my arm, and let it fly. My shredded glove made the slap sound louder than it was. My bloody handprint glowed against his blue face.

"I'll *never* forgive you for this," I said. *"Never."*

Then I walked away.

CHAPTER NINE

A Matter of Honor

Dhreen kept Xonea away from me. That extended his life expectancy. It was nice for me, too. I wasn't sure how much more punishment my hands could take, and my hands were needed elsewhere.

Someone brought up fluidators and foam cradles. We used them for the worst of the burn victims. Nurses kept coming at me, babbling about my injuries. I shoved them away. Yelled when that didn't work.

Others weren't so concerned.

"What have you done?" A furious ClanMother who'd just arrived on the scene pulled me away from one of the children I was treating and backed me up against a panel. "Have not enough been harmed? Now you cause our children to suffer?"

"I'm sorry. I never meant anyone to get hurt."

"Show your contrition." She gave me a shove. "Leave us." Then she picked up the child and carried him away.

Someone touched my arm, and asked if I was all right. I wasn't. But I needed the pain. Wanted it. God, I *deserved* it.

I coordinated moving the last of the injured from level six down to Medical, then followed. Patients overflowed into the outer corridors. The least-seriously wounded sat on the deck, patiently waiting to be seen. A few got to their feet when they saw me. I told them to sit back down, waded through the labyrinth of bodies, and limped into the Bay.

What should have been chaos was simply a busy, crowded triage. Squilyp was one hell of a manager. The patient roster was the first thing I checked. My injuries weren't bothering me that much. The envirocontrols simply needed adjustment.

I read the names that had been entered. So far we had nearly a hundred casualties. I read each name, felt each one burn into my mind. *I'd* done this. *I* was accountable for every single entry.

Duncan Reever's name wasn't among the wounded. I told myself it didn't matter. When I looked up and saw him standing in the entrance to Medical, my eyes closed briefly.

Of course it didn't matter. Not now that I could breathe again.

"Cherijo?"

His eyes were green, I decided. Not blue. Not happy, either. He came across the busy ward toward me. The tunic he wore was filthy. He'd probably been helping with the evacuation. His hands were a mess, the old scars latticed with dozens of new wounds. I'd done that, too.

How was I going to tell him what I'd only just figured out?

"Reever." His hands didn't feel *that* wonderful as he took hold of me. I didn't breathe in *just* to smell his scent. "Better have one of the nurses look at you."

"What have you done to yourself?"

He was yelling. Reever *never* yelled.

"I've been busy."

"Nurse!"

The pain was making it hard to concentrate. Why was he gripping me so tightly? "I have patients to see to," I told him. "So take your messy hands off me, if you would, please." I couldn't claim he was soiling my tunic. All the smoke and blood hadn't left it very sanitary.

He released me, and my knees decided to get cute. The thigh wound I'd forgotten about was throbbing so hard I nearly moaned out loud. No, I had to keep moving, that was all. I limped over toward the sterilizer array. After a disaster like this, the surgical cases would be endless.

"Healer Cherijo?" someone said.

I thrust my hands under a sterilizer. *So I was glad Reever was alive.* The bloody wounds and skinseal had glued the gloves to my flesh. *Hadn't I saved his life back on K-2?* I activated the unit with my knee. *I had a vested interest in his survival.* The sterilizer spray stripped the glove and skinseal material from my fingers. *If I couldn't imagine life without Duncan Reever around, it was no big tragedy.* A million hot needles of pain flashed up my arms.

Behind me, Adaola screeched, "What are you *doing,* Healer?"

"Scrub . . . bing . . . " I looked down, saw the gleam of white shining through blackened, tattered flesh. My hands were in shreds. The ends of splintered finger bones were sticking out here and there. "Oh." Stupid me. Should have expected they would be this bad. Where was the damn skinseal?

The nurse grabbed my wrists and jerked my hands away from the unit. "Iolna! Here, with me!" she called over her shoulder.

I tried to tug free, but it was useless. Adaola could have squashed me like a bug with one finger. Not to mention the fact the agony of my hands increased a thousandfold with every passing second. I'd better find some skinseal *and* a syrinpress.

"Let go me, please." I tried to be polite. Sweat ran freely down my face. Why couldn't I find a nurse who would follow orders?

"Healer, we must treat your wounds."

Reever hovered on the other side of me now. They guided me over to an exam table, then Duncan lifted me like a little kid. Honestly, the stuff I had to put up with, just because I was short. He spotted the binding Tonetka had wrapped around my thigh, and touched it gingerly.

"Her leg," he said. Why did he sound so upset? It was just a little jab. I tried to sit up. "Don't move, Joey."

The other nurse appeared, her eyes wide as she looked at my hands, then my leg. I felt blood start to pulse from the wound again as they cut away my trousers. I peered down my body. The fabric, stiff with dried blood, had temporarily sealed the wound.

"Artery plug!" Adaola said.

"If you'd left it alone you wouldn't need one," I told her. "Just seal it and let me up."

Neither of them listened. They were fiddling with me,

scanning me, being a general nuisance. Here I'd thought Jorenian nurses so efficient. Now the hole in my leg became a new well of torment. This was going to make standing in surgery a little difficult. Well, I'd just use a stool or something.

"I'm all right. Seal the damn wound and get me another pair of gloves." I glowered first at the nurses, then Reever. "Aren't you people listening to me? Move!"

"Of course, Healer," Adaola said.

She had the smallest set of bonesetters in her hands.

Just what was she planning to do with those?

"Now, Adaola!"

I found out Jorenians *do* lie. Before I could defend myself, the other nurse had a syrinpress in her large blue hand and pushed it against my throat. The sedative went to work instantly. I stared helplessly up at Reever.

"The patients . . . Have to . . . help . . . the . . . "

"I know." His hand touched my brow. "I know."

Blackness.

I woke up briefly while they were prepping me for surgery. Felt the pain, though it was distant and nonthreatening. Adaola's eyes narrowed over the edge of her mask as she bent down to me.

I had to know. "How . . . bad?"

The mask rippled as she replied. "The femoral artery in your leg is completed severed. You have second- and third-degree burns on both hands, as well as severe lacerations and tissue damage. There are twelve separate fractures of the phalanges and metacarpals; three are compound."

"Squilyp . . . operating?"

"Yes, Healer."

I got out two last words before I went under again.

"No . . . amputations."

Post-op Jorenian nurses were efficient, competent, and dedicated individuals. They didn't take any nonsense from their patients. Even those who usually *gave* the orders.

"Healer, will you lie down!" Iolna said from her position at the vitals display. For the tenth time. She forgot to say "please," too.

I sank back on the pillow. My lips were as thin as my patience. I had been out of surgery for more than six hours.

Most of my meds had worn off. I was conscious, rational, and in a considerable amount of pain. Now all I wanted to know was *exactly* what that Omorr had done to me.

"Signal Squilyp," I said. For the tenth time.

"By the Mother." Iolna didn't normally use Jorenian swear words, but I could see it was becoming a temptation. "Resident Squilyp is taking a rest interval."

He could sleep later. "Signal him anyway."

"Healer. *Please.*" The reproachful tone was worse than the all the "by the Mothers" she kept scolding me with.

"Oh, all right." I sulked, then brightened. "Time to change my dressings?"

"No."

"There could be signs of infection." I was hopeful. "Let's check."

She cursed softly. "You have *antibacterial* dressings on both hands."

"I think I can feel some serious keloids forming."

"Healer Cherijo." The nurse thrust aside my chart and came to the berth. "I know you are distressed, but you cannot remove the dressings. You cannot check for infection. There has not been *time* for scars to form."

"I'll think of something," I muttered.

She heard. "I have checked the human database. There *is* nothing you have not thought of. Please."

I could pull rank. After all, Squilyp worked for *me* now. The reason for that made my temper abruptly evaporate. "Sorry."

Another six hours passed before I saw Squilyp's handiwork. By the time the big moment arrived, I was so impatient I would have cut the dressings off myself. I would have done it, too, if I didn't have nearly every finger in a bonesetter. Adaola, the replacement post-op nurse, gently unwrapped my hands. Iolna had already gone off duty, muttering to herself as she left about gags and sedatives.

The Omorr, who looked almost as bad as he had after our fight, bent over me and performed a visual scan. He made a non-committal sound that puffed out his gildrells.

"Well?" I was flat on my back and couldn't see a damn thing.

"Scanner," he said to Adaola. She placed it in his membrane. "Status?"

He was ignoring me. Typical doctor-patient arrogance. I should have known. I was an authority. Just not on this side of it.

"Extremely ill-tempered, demanding, and prone to frequent outbursts," the nurse said. "Otherwise she's making an excellent recovery."

Ill-tempered? *Demanding?* I tried to pick my hands up to check them myself, and found Adaola had strapped my arms with berth restraints. Outrage made me jerk against them.

"Remain still, Doctor," Squilyp said. He was examining my right hand while making multiple passes with the scanner.

"If someone doesn't start talking to me," I told the group at large, "I'll make the worst patient you've ever treated seem like a recreational interval!"

"You *are* the worst patient I've ever treated," the Omorr told me.

"That's right. Go ahead and insult me, now that I can't smack you," I said. "I won't be stuck in this berth forever, Squid Lips."

Squilyp moved from the right hand to the left. The scanner hummed. My nerves frayed. The nurses were giving each other these weird, troubled looks.

"How is she?" I heard Duncan Reever ask.

I lifted my head and peered eagerly past the green and blue tunics. "Reever!" I forgot we weren't speaking to each other anymore. "You're human, you have to be on my side. Do something. Challenge Squilyp!"

He came to stand next to Squilyp. They exchanged a completely masculine look. It pushed me to the about-to-scream level in my frustration.

"Is she becoming difficult?" Reever asked while he gazed at me. The same way he would a slide smear under a 'scope.

"Becoming?" The Omorr let out one sour chuckle. *"Becoming?"*

The ship's linguist nodded. "Her temper is swift to flare."

"Swift?" My voice squeaked. "I'll have you know, Duncan Reever, I am being *restrained*!"

"That's because you won't hold still," Squilyp said. I muttered something they didn't teach you in Medtech. He glanced from me to Reever. "Has she always been this rude?"

"Since the moment I met her," Reever said.

"That's it." I still had legs that worked. Basically. "Unstrap me. Now."

To my complete astonishment, Squilyp nodded to Adaola, who released the arm restraints. Despite my previous impatience, I didn't lift my hands up. I couldn't.

"You did get my message about *not* cutting off my hands, right?" I asked the Omorr. He didn't reply as he made a chart notation.

I closed my eyes. Tried to control my breathing. I wasn't afraid. I was just going to wait a little while before I looked. A decade or two.

Reever reached over, grasped my wrist, and lifted my hand. "Open your eyes, Cherijo."

I did. I saw my hand. My swollen, burned, sutured, splinted, but undeniably *whole* hand.

It looked bad. Awful. Revolting. I'd never seen anything so beautiful in my life. Bonesetters ensured I couldn't move my fingers. Who cared? They were still intact. Still *attached*.

The burns appeared to be the most serious damage. Deep red and promising a wealth of pain, once the rest of the meds wore off. I turned my hand, then raised the other.

"I thought I had third-degree burns," I said. I saw nothing to indicate Squilyp had performed any skin grafts.

"You did," Adaola said. "Twelve hours ago."

The Omorr handed her my chart. "Remarkable. I've never seen anything like it."

There was a lot more he'd never seen decorating my DNA. Now was not the time to update him on that.

"What about the fractures?"

Squilyp held up his scanner so I could see the display. It showed three transverse breaks, and innumerable hairline fractures. No bone chips. No tissue missing. Ligaments and tendons all accounted for. He pointed to the most severe site.

"I pushed this proximal phalanx *back* into your finger." He pointed to another area. "This metacarpal as well." He went on to describe the areas where third-degree burns had eaten away sizeable chunks of flexor and extensor muscle tissue. He scanned my hands once more. "Even your keratin flaps—"

"Fingernails."

"—your fingernails have begun to grow back. I removed all of them, Doctor."

I checked. Small half-crescents were sprouting at the ragged end of each finger. Humans rarely regenerated a nail once it had been surgically removed. To achieve this would have taken a miracle—plus about three weeks of healing—times ten fingers.

Squilyp dismissed the nurses, then regarded me thoughtfully. "I would appreciate your telling me exactly *what* you are, Doctor Torin."

Uh-oh. I stared at my hands. "Apparently, very lucky."

"But not human. Or not like any human I've ever treated."

Reever and I exchanged a glance. Although everyone knew I was being hunted by the League, the facts behind my creator's genetic tinkering were known only to the Captain, Tonetka, and Reever.

"It's a long story," I told the Omorr. "One I'd like to tell you someday. For right now . . ." I lifted a shoulder. "Let's skip that."

"I see." He completed his chart notations with no sign of visible irritation. "I'll be back to check on you during my next rounds. Stay in the berth."

"Yes, sir." I managed a clumsy salute. He nodded and went on to the next patient.

Reever was the only one left. He looked exhausted. The color of his skin had a grey cast to it. Both eyes were slightly sunken and rimmed with red.

The words spilled out of me. "I thought you were mad at me."

"I was. I am."

He wasn't going to give an inch. As usual. Not that I warranted any better. "Then why are you here?"

The fair head tilted to one side. "I am trying to imagine you as the mother of Xonea's children. I find I cannot do that."

That should have made me lose my temper, but it didn't. "Me, too." I thought of all the Jorenians wounded in this last attack, and became even more dejected. "I have got to get out of here."

He misunderstood me. "Tonetka is gone. These people need you more than ever." He cast an uncertain glance at my hands.

"Yeah, I've been thinking the same thing," I said. "Not much future for a surgeon who can't hold a lascalpel, is there?"

"You will heal."

My injuries would. I had serious doubts about my soul. "What about you?"

He studied my berth panel. "I've requested that Captain Pnor allow me to disembark on the next non-League world we reach."

"What?" I jerked, causing fresh needles of pain to radiate from my hands. Then I sat back and closed my eyes. "You don't have to do that, Reever."

"It is the wisest course of action."

"I know," I said. When I opened my eyes, Reever was gone. Which saved me from telling him I planned to surrender to the League as soon as Pnor would let me off the ship.

It took a week to convince Squilyp to release me, and then only by using some fairly dire threats. He refused to permit me to work, and made a few threats of his own when I tried to insist.

"I'll be back in the morning," I said as I headed for the corridor.

"I'll notify Security," the Omorr called after me.

As it happened, Ktarka Torin was being discharged at the same time, and we walked out together. Most of the gyrlifts remained inoperable, but I welcomed the chance to stretch my legs.

"I don't know about you," I said to the educator as we walked down the corridor, "but I was beginning to hate that berth!"

"I feel the same . . . relief." She made a tentative movement of her shoulders, and winced. "Such inactivity is almost as unpleasant as the burns were." She glanced at my bandaged hands. "Have your wounds mended, Healer?"

"Not yet, but I'm getting there." I wasn't going to complain about my bandaged fingers. Not when so many had suffered much worse. We arrived at my quarters. "Would you like to come in for a server of tea, Educator?"

An hour later, we were on our third server of Terran chamomile, Ktarka listening as I related some of the highlights of my year as a colonial trauma physician.

"You did not," Ktarka said after I'd described the tense encounter with Rogan and a mob of rioters during the K2VI epidemic.

"I did." I smiled. "You should have seen how fast that room cleared out."

"Surely you did not open the containment barrier?"

I shook my head. "Just the sound of releasing that first latch was enough."

"You are so . . . composed, Cherijo," she said with a shade of envy. "No matter what the crisis."

"Composed? *Me*?" I snorted. "I'm usually yelling at everyone." I put down my server, and watched Jenner as he curled up next to my guest. "You've got yourself a slave for life now."

Ktarka stroked his pelt. "He is a gentle creature." Jenner raised his head so she could scratch under his chin, then eyed me. *Keep this one around, will you?* "What are your plans for the future, Healer?"

"I'm not sure." I lied. "How about you? Will you be staying on board the *Sunlace*, or getting off at Joren?" I asked.

Her hand froze. The beautiful face went absolutely still.

"Sorry," I said. "I don't mean to pry."

"My Chosen remains on Joren," Ktarka said. "I cannot return."

"Your *Chosen*?" Once bonded, young Jorenian couples were practically inseparable. "Don't you want to be with him?"

"You do not know my history." I shook my head. She placed her server down carefully. "No Torin would speak of it. My dishonor shames them."

Dishonor? Now there was a bad word among the Jorenians. Majorly bad. "Ktarka, if it's none of my business, say so."

"No, I will tell you." She made a bleak gesture. "When my time to Choose arrived, I was in Marine Province, among HouseClan Torin. As it was an honorable House, I remained to make my Choice."

I didn't understand all the who-got-Chosen-by-who complexities of Jorenian culture, but nodded anyway.

"I knew I had found my Choice when I met Konal Torin." She rose gracefully to her feet and stepped around the sofa to head for the viewport.

Funny how when Jorenians got upset, they automatically went for the view. "Konal must have been a special guy."

"Konal was my Choice," she said. "I was young, and wished to surprise my new family, so I told no one of my decision. Not even Konal."

"What happened?"

"There was a celebration. I stood and spoke of my heart." Her voice dropped to a bare whisper. "I Chose Konal."

I was with her so far. Which made it even more confusing. "Ktarka?"

She turned around. Raw suffering drew tiny lines around her mouth and eyes. "Some days before I made my Choice, Konal had Chosen another."

"Oh, no. Didn't anyone tell you?"

"The Choice banns were not given to me."

"Choice banns?"

"They announce the Choice, and the time of the bonding ceremony."

"That's it?" She was exiled from the homeworld because someone screwed up the wedding invitations? "Excuse me for being blunt, but why are you still alive?"

"I attempted to divert my path, and failed. My dishonor and my cowardice shamed my ClanParents." She rested her hands on the back of the sofa. "HouseClan Torin adopted me, and Captain Pnor offered me a position so I could leave Joren. I have been content here."

"Do you still have to honor your Choice?"

"Until Konal dies, or I do, yes."

"But you don't have to kill yourself, right?" She nodded. I began imagining how many ways I could inflict pain on Xonea Torin. As a physician, I knew where all the best nerve endings were located. There were a lot, too.

"This is absolute nonsense."

"I Chose." Ktarka said it the way the other Jorenians did, with that hushed reverence.

"Just when I think I'm beginning to understand your people, Ktarka, I find out I don't." I stood up, went to her, and gave her an awkward pat on the shoulder. "I'm sorry. The whole business stinks."

One dark eyebrow arched. "Why say you this? I made the Choice, and brought dishonor on my name."

"Why didn't they make Konal go?" I asked. "After all, it was partially his fault. He didn't tell you about his Chosen."

She looked shocked. "I did not know you would understand."

"Believe me, I know all about inauspicious Choices." I went on to tell Ktarka about what Xonea had done to protect me.

"Without your consent? How can you remain so calm? I would divert his path!" she said, then made an embarrassed gesture.

I smiled. "Don't worry. I have no intention of giving in to him. Xonea is going to find out, up close and personal, just how stubborn Terran females can be."

Medical leave, I decided, was a subtle form of torture. And that was only on the second day after my release. Squilyp had signaled me to report for my first physical therapy session. An hour later, I decided the Omorr wasn't trying to take my place, only drive me insane.

"Squeeze the spheres, Healer," Adaola said.

We were sitting in the therapeutic room. I held a soft plas ball in each palm. I curled my fingers, then uncurled them.

"Again."

I'd had about enough of this. "How many *agains* am I looking at here, nurse?"

She pursed her lips and consulted my chart. "One hundred repetitions for each hand."

I squeezed. Pretended one was Xonea's head. The other Squilyp's. Something popped.

"Healer." Adaola took the deflated remains of each ball from my hand, and studied them for a moment. "Perhaps we should try weaving."

There were more death ceremonies to get through. Seven crew members had died during the attack. Six Jorenians, including Tonetka. We'd lost the trader from Garnot, too. He had been taking a tour of the *Sunlace* just before the mercenaries struck. He and his guide had been blown out into space with most of level five.

I appeared at each death ceremony. Watched the ritual binding. Listened to the Speakers. I couldn't be happy they were dead. Not when I was to blame for each and every one of them. When it came time to honor Tonetka, however, I locked myself in my quarters. Not even Dhreen could coax me out.

It was spineless of me, but I couldn't celebrate the fact that she was gone.

The power grids on level five were gone, destroyed by displacer blasts. The mercenaries had attacked and damaged four more levels. It was believed they were trying to disable the ship. Most of the areas they fired on were usually unoccupied. All except level six.

Although I tried to avoid him, Xonea eventually cornered me one morning on my way to therapy.

"Senior Healer." He wouldn't stop calling me that.

I wasn't quite as polite. "What?"

"Captain Pnor has requested your presence."

Since the first four levels of the *Sunlace* were inaccessible, Pnor had been relocated, too. The Captain's command and Ship's Operational were now working out of level twenty-one, in the middle of Engineering.

The few functional gyrlifts were occupied, so walking down eleven levels took some time. Xonea didn't make conversation, for which I was grateful. Adaola wouldn't be happy if I destroyed all her physical therapy while dislocating my ClanBrother's jaw.

We found Captain Pnor in the center of the crowded level, discussing hull tolerances with one of the structural engineers. He looked up and nodded at us.

"Good. Come with me, if you would, please."

We followed him to the Senior Engineer's office. Xonea closed the door as I sat down. Pnor had that same grim look I'd seen the last time these two had made decisions concerning me.

I'd wait, see what he had to say. If I liked it, no problem. If I didn't, Squilyp could be Senior Healer a little sooner than I'd planned.

"Thank you for coming." He was courteous, as always. "How are your hands?"

"Better." I eyed Xonea. He knew what this was all about. I could feel it.

"Senior Healer, new evidence has been brought forth about the murders of Roelm, the mercenary, and Ndo."

"What evidence?" I asked.

Pnor inclined his head to Xonea, who produced a tiny object from his tunic pocket. He handed it to me. It was about the same size as my thumbnail.

"Cherijo, have you ever seen this before?"

I studied it, then shook my head. The design was something like a wristcom, but much smaller. I handed it back to my ClanBrother. "What is it?"

"A transdimensional beacon," Xonea said. "Calibrated to transmit encoded signals."

I glanced from him to the Captain. "Where did you find it?"

Pnor folded his hands on his desk. "On level six, near the site where you rescued the children. In the" —he consulted a data pad—"sandbox you made for the primary class."

What?

"This was also discovered." Pnor handed me another data pad. The screen displayed a statement about the attempt to abduct me, written in my own words.

"Ndo used this during my interview," I said as I handed it back. "He was working on it when he was killed. Was this with the beacon?"

"No. Whoever killed him must have removed it." He gave me a measuring look. "The data pad was found in your quarters."

For a moment, all I could do was gape. Then I focused on what the Captain had said. "Whoever? Don't you mean me?"

"I searched your quarters after you were assaulted," Xonea said. "The data pad was placed there after the search, but before your release from Medical."

I stared at the dead man's instrument. "Put there to frame me."

Xonea nodded. "Both items, I believe, were placed thus to implicate you as a traitor and murderer."

"I can see why someone would want to frame me for the murders, but what reason would I have to signal the League?"

"Perhaps the saboteur has formed an alliance with the League," Pnor said. "Your affection for our children is well-known. Perhaps he planned the attack on them, suspecting you would insist on leaving the ship afterward."

"It worked," was all I could say.

"Whoever has done this is *insane*," Xonea said.

Yeah. That was my diagnosis, too.

Pnor wasn't finished. "I do not believe you guilty of sabotage or murder, Senior Healer. Yet I cannot ignore an opportunity to reveal the one who is." He made an eloquent gesture. "You will allow Xonea to . . . share your quarters."

This baby-sitting business again. "I don't need a guard, Captain."

"If you refuse, I must make it a direct order." Pnor sounded strained to his limits. "There is no alternative."

"I disagree." I regarded Xonea. "You didn't tell him about Reever's telepathic abilities, did you?"

"No." One big blue hand made a cutting gesture. "I will not allow it."

"I don't recall needing your permission." I turned to Pnor. "Duncan Reever is a telepathic linguist, Captain. He can access my memory and determine if I retained any subconscious impressions of my assailant."

"No," Xonea said. One big blue hand wrapped around my arm. "I will not permit you to be violated again."

"It's not a violation." Why was he acting like such a jerk? Didn't he want my name cleared? Why wouldn't he want Duncan to uncover the truth? "It's a solution."

My ClanBrother wasn't listening. "Captain Pnor gave you an order. I will occupy your quarters and protect you."

I eyed the Captain. "I'm not refusing his order. I'm offering a viable option."

"HouseClan law is explicit," Xonea said, his voice losing its musical lilt. "You must—"

My temper blew.

"I don't have to do a *damn thing*, pal." I pried his hand from my arm and got up. "I refuse your Choice." Xonea made a furious sound that didn't translate. "Your second-in-command needs a refresher course in courtesy, Captain. That, or a muzzle."

"Enough!" Xonea shouted, folding his arms over his abdomen. "You will comply or I will embrace the stars!"

"Oh, no, you won't." I sprang the trap. "Guess what I found out? You don't *have* to kill yourself if your Chosen refuses. Why didn't you tell me that?"

"You know nothing about Choice!" He sounded furious and, wonder of wonders, suddenly couldn't look me in the eye.

"Really?" I wondered if he'd been counting on that. "Ktarka Torin would disagree with you. She filled me in quite a bit about the subject."

Pnor gaped for a split second before recovering his composure. "Cherijo, Ktarka is an exceptional case."

"Oh? And I'm not?"

Xonea thrust himself away from me and slammed out of the office. Pnor and I watched him go.

"My ClanNephew honors you, Senior Healer."

"Your ClanNephew can't have it his way, so he's throwing a tantrum." Or was it something more menacing than that? I wondered. I caught Pnor's pained expression and sighed. "Believe me, this is the only logical solution."

"It would be much simpler if—" The Captain searched for the right words.

I beat him to it. "If I just shut up and played the good little Jorenian wife-to-be?" My foot tapped the floor. "Sorry to spoil your plans. I have no intention of further jeopardizing the safety of the crew, simply to act as bait for a killer. Nor will I let Xonea commit suicide when he doesn't have to. Let's make this simple, Captain. Grant my request. Put me off the ship so I can surrender to the League."

"I cannot." Pnor looked regretful. "You are the only connection we have to the traitor."

After a second, confidential conference, this one with Duncan Reever and Captain Pnor (minus Xonea), we decided to conduct the link immediately. Pnor worried that my "fiancé" might storm in and start inflicting bodily harm on Reever. In deference to my condition, the Captain insisted that we perform the link in Medical.

I agreed. Reever didn't react. Squilyp simply thought it was a bad idea.

"Cortical coupling?" The Omorr looked askance. "I wasn't aware humans were capable of such functions."

"We aren't," I said. "Normally. Reever and I are . . . exceptional."

"A dangerous method of investigation." The Omorr accessed the database from his display. "Reever must project his RAS impulses directly to your brain stem." He tapped an appendage on the side panel.

"Assuming that's how he does this *link* thing, my brain stem will be fine. I've suffered no ill effects from previous encounters."

"What is RAS?" Reever asked.

"An acronym for the reticular activating system," Squilyp replied. "The RAS is made up of conductors in the brain stem reticular formation. They receive sensory neuron impulses from the periphery and relay them to the thalamus. The thalamus sends them all to all parts of the cerebral cortex."

"In other words, if you stub your toe, the RAS tells your brain it hurts," I said.

The Omorr gave me a dirty look.

"I see." Reever leaned forward and examined the display. A dimensional schematic of the human cerebral cortex rotated slowly as Squilyp studied the data. "I did not realize it was so complex."

"It is not simply *entering* the brain. For you to access Doctor Torin's mnemonic accumulation, you must identify and use the specific neuronal chains involved. If you can locate them in the subconscious mind." Squilyp keyed something on the touchpad. "Here." He highlighted a section of the display. "I believe the specific memories may be located in or near the hypothalamus."

I sat down next to the Omorr. "I see why you don't want us to do it."

"Exactly." Squilyp peered at the display. "If you do, I must closely monitor both of you."

Reever cleared his throat. "Could one of you explain? In less technical terms, perhaps?"

I translated for him. "Reever, a part of the human brain serves as a connection between the psyche, or mind, and the soma, or body. It's called the hypothalamus. Certain parts of that work as reward centers for primary drives, like drinking or eating. It is also responsible for maintaining emotions and keeping the body in a waking state."

"Where is the danger in accessing this hypothalamus?"

"By accessing the hypothalamus, you may stimulate cholinergic and adreneric fibers, which release NE, or norepinephrine and ACh, or acetylcholine. They're two of the chemical transmitters that regulate the central nervous system. Too much of either one could kill me." I consulted the display again. "Access the limbic system, Squilyp. I want to see something."

When the display enlarged a sagittal view of the brain, I highlighted the five vital areas.

"Here's where I want you to oversee the link. Calibrate the neurotracer to monitor at the cingulate gyrus, isthmus, hippocampal gyrus, uncus, and hippocampus. Watch for fluctuations in neuron activity. Scan continuous vitals on both of us, too."

"I still believe it is an unsafe procedure." The Omorr's gildrells fluttered with exasperation. "How can I break this coupling between you?"

"Direct cortical electristim." I waved my hand as Squilyp began to protest. "I know, I know, it's dangerous. It's also the only way you can interrupt the link if one of us loses control."

"Cherijo?"

Again I gave the short version to Reever. "Squilyp is going to be monitoring us by tracing the activity in my 'emotional brain.' If my levels spike on the neurotracer, he'll know I'm in trouble. He'll use low-voltage stimulation to disrupt my brain waves. That should break the connection, and prevent my NE or ACh levels from killing me."

Reever's mouth compressed. "Shock treatment?"

"Not exactly, but close enough." I got up and called for a nurse. "Let's get started. I want to get this over with."

CHAPTER TEN

No House Divided

The Omorr and two nurses spent several minutes hooking me up to a neurotracer, monitor portals, and everything else Squilyp could think of. Reever got a vitals band wrapped around his wrist. That was it. Didn't seem very fair.

We reclined on two exam tables, me on my back because of all the hookups, Reever on his side facing me. I looked over at him. His hair was getting long, I thought. It fell past his shoulders now, thick and light. My fingers itched as I recalled how soft it felt. Vivid blue eyes swept over me as Duncan made his own scrutiny.

"What?"

"You are still too thin," he said.

"Oh, really? Well, you need a haircut." Squilyp bent over me and checked everything for the fiftieth time. I pushed his membranes away. "Quit fussing, Squil. Get on with it."

"Doctor . . ." The most confident surgical resident on the ship actually hesitated. "Are you sure you want to do this?"

"Positive. You don't want to know what the alternative is."

"Very well." The Omorr gave a terse series of instructions to the nurse by the monitoring equipment, then turned to Reever. "You may begin."

My eyes closed as I settled back. I heard the hum of the monitors, the quiet voices of the nurses in the background. A plopping sound, as Squilyp hopped over to the neurotracer. A sense of being paralyzed, then—

Cherijo.

It was Reever. Inside my head. Just beyond the barriers I had unconsciously erected.

You're getting very good at this, I thought. *Too good.*

Yield to me.

Now came the hardest part for me. I had to yield my mind to him. Complete and total surrender. I'd only done it twice before.

Yield to me, Cherijo. We must hurry.

With a mental kick, I knocked down the wall between us. Duncan flooded me like a sweeping, white-fringed ocean wave. He sank into my mind, farther than before, until I almost lost the tangible thought-connection between us.

Duncan?

Yes. I am here. Try to remember the first time the presence came to you.

A gold-glowing, silent chamber swallowed me. I wasn't alone. Couldn't see who else was there, but I felt it.

Yes. You are in the first dream state. Turn around. Look for the presence.

Shifting. Pivoting. Searching.

"Cherijo . . ."

Low, beseeching voice.

You know this person, Reever thought.

I ignored him and floated toward the sound.

You thought it was me. Became angry. Wanted to . . . He made a strange sound. *Knock a hole through my brain?*

I didn't respond. I couldn't. My heart slammed against my ribs as the nightmare sank over me.

". . . help you."

The presence swirled around me. Wanted me. Wanted to get inside me. I'd felt that same kind of desperate, irrational desire before. But from who?

Reever, I finally sent out a desperate plea. *Get me out of here.*

I see hands reaching for you. Jorenian hands.

Yes. Whatever. Get me out of here, now!

Duncan came up all around me. His arms enclosed me, cradled me, protected me against the hands. Those horrible hands that had beaten me, over and over. So much anger.

It's all right, Joey. Hold on to me.

Duncan? I felt him leading me from the chamber into another.

I will stay with you. Experience it with you.

My perception of the chamber changed. Here the familiar, benign light seemed cold and chilling. The air that I once thought so soft was smothering. Warmth flooded the chamber. I felt as though I were being immersed in a vat of congealing blood.

"Outcast . . ."

It was crooning to me. Stroking my skin with its fingers. I shuddered violently; even being battered was better than this.

There is love, Duncan thought, his arms still around me. *Love that has been denied. The love you refused.*

The only person I'd refused lately was . . . Xonea.

Belonging to no one . . . weeping for an end to the loneliness . . . was that me, or the presence? Or both of us?

Reever! I turned my face from the seeking lips, reaching for the pure, white light that came from Duncan.

You must face your attacker, Cherijo.

The hands held me in place. I was squirming, trying to free myself. Something about me being little, and being shown the path. Low, amused laughter.

Look, Cherijo. See the face of who violates you.

I couldn't look. I had to get out of here—

A powerful surge of energy blasted me out of the link.

"Doctor!"

Squilyp held me down on the exam table. I could feel my body heaving and twisting, and couldn't control it. Just as suddenly as I was jerked out of the link, the seizure ended. I collapsed on the table, trying to catch my breath.

"Give me her stats!" Squilyp yelled at a nurse.

"BP 225 over 97, Heart rate 140."

No wonder my head was buzzing. If my vitals didn't level out, I'd have a stroke. How much electristim had the Omorr administered?

"Norepinephrine in the red range," the nurse said. "Epinephrine also elevated."

"Fifty ccs valeumine!"

I felt the syrinpress at my throat, then the immediate, soothing effect of the tranquilizer. My heart rate slowed, my muscles went lax, my blood pressure dropped. The feelings of extreme anxiety and shame seemed to be evaporating, too.

Drowsy from the drugs, I opened my eyes and saw Duncan next to me. He was holding my hand.

"Hey."

"She's conscious," he said over his shoulder, before turning back to me. "Squilyp would like to know how you feel, Doctor Torin."

"Tired. Glad it's over." I tried to keep my eyes open. "Find out who it was, Duncan?" He shook his head. "We will. Next . . . time."

The Omorr's face appeared. "Doctor?"

"Report." I tried to sound like a Senior Healer. Ruined it when I added, "Please."

"We traced the beta wave patterns to the hypothalamus. Two separate sets swept from the precentral gyrus of the cerebrum's frontal lobe."

"He means you were in my brain," I said to Reever in a stage whisper. The meds were making me goofy.

"Activity in the hypothalamus rose dramatically. You began relaying impulses back and forth. Axon terminals at synapses and neuroaffector junctions subsequently increased production by a factor of ten. Acetylcholine, norepinephrine, and gamma-aminobutyric levels went immediately into red range."

"You found the memories just where Squilyp said they'd be," I said. "Triggering the memories released too many chemical transmitters. My central nervous system overloaded."

"Why is she not in a coma?" Reever asked the Omorr.

"I don't know," he replied as he shone an optic light in my eyes. I scowled and tried not to blink. "Perhaps because there were synthetic amounts of both AChE and COMT bombarding the hypothalamus."

"What?" That cleared some of the valeumine fog from my brain. "You shot me up with artificial enzymes?"

Squilyp snapped off the light and helped me sit up. "No, Doctor, I did not. Linguist Reever is not the only person interested in stimulating your synapses. The enzymes were released shortly after Reever initiated the cortical coupling. I located two dormant pockets of the same in your upper digestive tract."

"Time-released neurotransmitters." I held my now-aching head with both hands. "This gets more weird by the minute."

"What does that mean?" Reever demanded.

I gave him a weary smile. "It means someone dosed me with enzymes that artificially stimulate my brain." Which explained all the unexpected mood changes I'd been experiencing. No wonder I'd been so hot and edgy all the time. "I want them neutralized, Squilyp."

The resident nodded. "I will run a full hematological series, then administer the proper counteragent."

Reever helped me down from the exam table. That was when Xonea burst into the Medical Bay, thrusting staffers out of his way as he headed straight for us.

Xonea, who'd wanted to protect me. Who'd Chosen me. I'd refused him. Angered him.

Just as I'd refused and angered the one in my dreams.

"Duncan?" I pulled half a dozen hookups from my head. Adrenalin surged in my veins, counteracting the tranquilizer. "Go out through the emergency panel. Now." I grabbed his hand and pulled him around the platform.

"Cherijo!" The commanding tone halted us both in our tracks.

I turned around slowly. "Xonea."

"You allowed him to violate you." My ClanBrother's black hair streamed wildly down his back. He carried one of the multibladed swords from the display in his quarters in one of his huge fists. From the look on his face, he meant to use it.

"Reever." I didn't take my eyes off the enraged Jorenian. "Get out of here. Find some help."

Only one person could stop two-hundred kilos of rampaging, homicidal Jorenian male. His Chosen. Unfortunately, that was me.

The Omorr hopped between me and the huge Jorenian pilot. Squilyp faced slow death by dismemberment, just to shield me and give Reever time to escape. I'd have to give him a raise, if any of us survived this.

My resident appeared very calm. "May I help you, Pilot Torin?"

"Yes." He raised the fan-shaped blades and leveled the tips at the Omorr's thorax. "Remove yourself from my path."

I glanced behind me to make sure Reever was gone. He was. "Get out of the way, Squilyp." The Omorr looked back at me. His gildrells were stiff and bristling. "It's okay. Call Ship's Operational. Ask them to send someone up here." Not that they'd be able to do much. Maybe assist in scraping up my remains off the deck.

"She's been badly injured and is still recovering," Squilyp said to Xonea. "If you even attempt to harm her, I will challenge you, here and now."

Xonea nodded once. The Omorr reluctantly hopped out of the way. Now I faced the consequences. I never expected it would be carrying a sword with seven—no, eight—blades on it.

"Problem, ClanBrother?" I asked.

Xonea looked around me. The lines around his nose tightened. "So the coward has fled." A flicker of pain crossed his face for a mere second, then was gone.

"I assume you're referring to Linguist Reever. Yes, he's gone. What's this for?" I waved a hand at the sword. "You want to hack *me* up with that thing?"

"I defend my ClanSister," Xonea said with a distinct snarl.

"Reever wasn't hurting me, Xonea," I said. The meds kicked in unexpectedly, and a thick fog muddled my senses. What timing. "Uh, before you kill me . . . would you mind . . . "

"Cherijo!" The sword dropped from his hand and clattered on the deck. I stumbled back against the exam table. Strong blue hands caught me, lifted me.

Squilyp was there in an instant. He began another vitals scan. "BP and heart rate are too low. Doctor, you must rest now." He gave Xonea a look that said this was all *his* fault.

"Good idea." My fingers curled under Xonea's. I was too tired to fight him anymore. Let him do whatever he wanted to me. I'd sleep through the whole unpleasant experience.

"Once the drug wears off—" the Omorr began to say, and Xonea cut him off with a growl.

"She has been drugged? Again?"

I listened as the Omorr explained the aftereffects of the

link. Everything seemed to be dwindling down into a long, dark tunnel.

"Did he touch her? Did he harm her?"

"I would never harm her." That was Reever.

My eyelids agreed to open one last time. Duncan and Dhreen were at the door panel behind Xonea. So were about twenty of the crew. Reever had brought the whole cavalry. Captain Pnor stepped up beside Duncan when Xonea swiveled.

"Xonea?" He studied his ClanNephew's face. "Explain how you knew the Senior Healer and Linguist Reever were here performing this cerebral connection. Why you came here armed."

Pnor was trying to make him repeat the threat, I realized, so ClanKill could be declared. Xonea's sword was kicked somewhere out of the way; I heard it slide across the deck.

"No. I will not explain." Xonea released my hand and stepped toward Pnor. "That is a matter of honor."

Pnor seemed deeply disgusted. "I dislike being manipulated." He turned and made an efficient gesture. Three huge Jorenians approached Xonea, took positions on either side and behind him. No one touched anyone else. Jorenians were like that. Without another word the four exited the Medical Bay.

The Captain came to me. "Senior Healer, I regret this."

"Talk to him, Pnor," I said, my voice slurred. I couldn't stop yawning. "Something is wrong with this. With him."

"Linguist Reever tells me you could not identify the killer."

I shook my head. "Tried. Couldn't . . ."

The Captain pulled a coverlet over me and tucked me in like a child. "Rest. We will talk soon." He disappeared.

"Squilyp?"

The surgical resident came to my berth. "Yes, Doctor?"

"Administer . . . stimulate . . . four hours."

"But, Doctor—"

"Just . . . do it . . . Squid Lips." I smiled, and fell asleep.

I didn't dream—the drugs prevented that—but simply slept the deep, serene slumber of childhood. It was wonderful. My over-taxed body and confused mind were happy to shut up and leave me alone.

I woke up when the Omorr dutifully administered an amphetamine. Artificial vitality sizzled in my veins as I sat up and threw aside the cover. Squilyp made a disapproving noise as he began to strip the monitor portals from me.

"I dislike stimulating your norepinephrine levels," he said. "Especially after the incident during the cortical coupling."

"You have another cure for complete exhaustion?" I rubbed the back of my neck. "Did you determine how much was introduced to my system?"

"Enough to kill you several times over, had it not been separated and encapsulized. I neutralized both while you were unconscious."

"Good, then I can get out of here, right?"

He ignored the question and began scanning me. "Any anxiety?"

"Just the normal amount," I replied. Actually, I was worried about Xonea. Something about the confrontation with him didn't make sense. He'd seemed out of control, completely irrational. *I defend my ClanSister,* he'd said. Could he have been following instinct, rather than reason? Acting exactly like any other, rather overprotective Jorenian big brother kicked into overdrive?

"Delusions?"

"Of grandeur? Probably. Otherwise, no."

The Omorr persisted. "Hallucinations? Tremors?"

"No, Mommy," I said. "Can I go and play now?"

Squilyp put down his scanner with a decided thump. "I'd like to be your parent. I'd restrict you to your quarters for another month." He removed the last of the hookups and helped me down from the exam table. "Xonea has been placed in detention."

"Has Pnor formally charged him with anything?"

"I don't know."

I'd have to speak with the Captain, but that could wait. "Where is Reever?"

"Linguist Reever left two hours ago, but did not indicate his destination." The Omorr fussed over me, straightening my tunic, checking my eyes again. "You seem to have recovered. If you experience sudden mood changes, dizziness, or any other odd sensations, report back here at once."

"Yes, sir." I touched his membranes. "Thanks, Squilyp."

"For enticing me to commit malpractice? Save your gratitude, Doctor." He sounded brusque and embarrassed,
which made me want to hug him. "Go now, before I am
tempted to confine you to a berth."

I left Medical and went looking for Reever.

The best method of determining the location of a crew
member on the *Sunlace* was by accessing the vocollar transmitter. Each device had an autonomous frequency. By
tracking that particular signal, you could pinpoint someone's whereabouts.

The problem was Reever wouldn't *wear* a vocollar. A
man who spoke a ka-zillion languages didn't have to. I
started at his quarters and worked from there. It took some
time. Most of the crew tried to be helpful. Many of them
wanted to thank me for my efforts during the last attack.
One of them, the ClanMother who had attacked me on
level six, actually apologized.

"Your pardon, Senior Healer." She made a gesture of
supreme embarrassment. "I saw only my ClanSon's injuries.
Only later was I told how you saved him and the other
children from sharing Tonetka's path. I thank the Mother
that you came to us."

"Your ClanSon should have never been hurt in the first
place," I said. "That was my fault."

She gave me an odd look. "And if it were mine? What
say you if these mercenaries pursued not you, but me? Or
my bondmate? Would you wish us to leave the ship?"

I frowned. "Of course not."

"You would protect us, would you not?" She smiled.
"As you protected the children. As we will protect you,
ClanCousin. No one may divide the House."

That gave me something to think about for the next
eleven levels.

Eventually someone told me they'd seen Reever heading
into environome six. When I got there, the entrance was
secured. There was a program in progress, I saw, and
frowned. It wasn't as if I could knock, I thought, and accessed the door panel circuits. My inept fiddling quickly
shorted out the locking mechanism, and the door panel
slid open.

Just wait until someone gave me a hard time about my
lack of tech ability next time, I thought, and walked in.

I was standing in a Trauma Assessment center. There were dozens of patients waiting to be seen. Behind the main display, a towering, vermillion, insectile form sorted through charts and rapped furiously on a touchpad.

"T'Nliqinara?"

I stepped back until my shoulders hit the simulated wall of the FreeClinic on Kevarzangia Two. Two humans strolled past me and never noticed. One of them was Duncan Reever.

The other one was *me*.

"Another altercation with Dr. Mayer?" Reever asked my duplicate.

"You could call it that," she replied. She looked grumpy. Sounded grumpy. *I didn't act like that. Did I?* Her exotic eyes narrowed as she glanced at him. "Were you listening at the door?"

"It wasn't necessary. Both of your voices carry quite well." Reever halted. "Pause reenactment sequence." The environome's imaging systems stopped the simulation. Everyone froze. "Return to last inquiry by Doctor Grey Veil." The program ran backward for a moment, then restarted.

"You could call it that," the other Cherijo repeated. Same tone, same sideways glance. I studied her. *My nose wasn't that beaky looking. Was it?* "Were you listening at the door?"

"No," Reever said. "I needed to speak with you. May I—"

My twin ignored him and walked away to speak to T'Nliqinara at the Assessment desk. Reever stood there, looking as frustrated as I'd ever seen him.

So this was when he showed emotions. When my back was turned.

My double returned at last. "Okay, Chief Linguist, I can give you exactly one minute," she said as she picked up a stack of charts. *Oh, give me a break. What was he using to project this? A pompous ass imager?* "What do you want?"

"Yes, Chief Linguist," I said. "Just what exactly do you want?"

Reever whirled around. His usual bland mask cracked as his jaw sprang open in stunned disbelief. My arms crossed as I stared back at him.

"Terminate program," he said. The other Cherijo and the K-2 FreeClinic vanished. "I secured that door panel."

"I overrode your security code," I lied. Well, I had, sort of. "Mind telling me what this is all about, Reever?"

"It is an exercise to practice human behavior."

"Uh-huh." I walked over and made a circle around him. "You look pretty human to me."

"Your invasion of my privacy is inappropriate."

"I'm not feeling too fond of you myself right now, either." I planted myself in front of him. "Why the simulation, Reever? After all, you've got the living, breathing version of Doctor Grey Veil on this ship. God knows you're not the sentimental type."

"As I told you, practice." He went to the display, tapped a few keys. "Access Reenactment Sequence R-1." I saw a vid of the Trading Center on K-2. I was walking with Ana Hansen. Reever was sitting just outside Cafe Lisette.

"That's the first time we met."

He nodded. "I have successfully resolved the conflict during this encounter. Instead of questioning you about your genetic heritage, I make general, nonintrusive comments and offered you a welcome to the colony. Your simulated reaction was much more favorable."

"Nice to know it worked out for you."

"Access Reenactment Sequence R-2." Now a vid of my encounter with Reever outside William Mayer's office was displayed. "Here you were quite upset after arguing with the Chief of Staff. Rather than making what you may have considered at the time provocative remarks, I offered my services as a sympathetic confidant."

"Let me guess—my simulation cried all over your shoulder."

"Actually, we shared a brief meal interval and had a pleasant conversation. Later, after Karas died, you came to my quarters."

"Right." I reached over and terminated the access. I didn't want to know what else he had been doing with my simulation. Especially in his quarters. "Reever, do you know why I left Terra?"

"You discovered the illegal activities Joseph Grey Veil was involved with—"

"And I didn't want to be an experiment anymore." I swung a hand at the imager console. "Sound familiar?"

He had the good sense to look faintly guilty.

I took pity on him. "You can't go back and fix the past, Reever. You have to live with your mistakes, and move on." A painful lesson I'd only just learned myself.

"As I have indicated, I am merely practicing methods of successful conflict resolution."

He had a lot to learn about his own species, but this wasn't the way to do it. "Duncan, being human means *making* mistakes. There is no *perfect* encounter, no *ideal* conversation. We don't get to practice. Part of the process is messing up and learning from that." I eyed the display. "Have you programmed a reenactment of every interactive problem in your past?"

"No. Only those encounters which involved you."

I never got to ask why—the environome display emitted an emergency signal.

"Senior Healer, Linguist Reever. Report to launch bay, level eighteen. Disabled Furinac transport vessel is being retrieved. Expect casualties."

"Good thing we're close," I said as we hurried out of the environome. I grabbed his sleeve. "This conversation isn't finished, Duncan."

"I did not expect it would be."

Our path intersected with the medical team on the way to the retrieval. I ripped off my bandages and took one of the emergency packs.

Iolna looked startled. "Senior Healer, are you certain—"

I waved my mostly healed hand at her. "See? It's a miracle. Let's move."

The launch bay on level eighteen was still being repaired from damages acquired during the last attack. In spite of this, Ship's Operational had managed to send out two launches. They were now towing the crippled transport in to the landing pad. Hundreds of tiny craters scored the Furinac vessel's hull plates.

"Displacer fire?" I wondered out loud as we waited for clearance to approach. Engineers in protective gear were already crawling over the ship, scanning for dangerous radiation leakage. Had the League taken a shot at the Furinac, too?

"Meteor swarm," someone said. "Must have flown directly into it."

The Furinac had barely made it out alive, from the look of the transport. I counted three cracks in the hull that looked deep enough to compromise the internal compartments. One of the engines was so badly battered it was literally hanging on by component wiring alone. A gaping hole between the thrusters was all that remained of the stardrive. Cracked viewports also indicated the interior pressure may have been breached.

"How many on board?" I asked one of the waiting evac team.

"Four that we scanned as alive."

"The flightshield generator has been ejected," one of the engineers said as he removed his helmet. "No radiation present."

While the evac team worked to get the damaged hatch open, I set up a triage area and got our equipment ready. With a hissing screech, the damaged vessel's hull doors parted at the center seam. A yellow hand thrust through the gap.

"Help! Help me!"

The voice sounded familiar. I approached the transport with the rest of the medics. Reever gave me an enigmatic glance.

"Friend of yours?" I asked him.

The engineers forced the door panels to open wider. At last a corpulent humanoid stumbled out and fell down, face-forward on the docking ramp. His garments were filthy. The stench of his body drifted over to us within seconds.

I knew that smell. It couldn't be. Fate wasn't that cruel.

As the medical team entered the transport, I bent down next to the injured being on the ramp. It took a minute and substantial effort to get him turned right-side up.

He stared at me, his lidless eyes bulging at the sight of my face. Around the two orbs, deeply scored parallel grooves held thousands of miniature, grey, writhing polyps. His skin was bright jaundiced yellow. He smelled a lot like a Terran skunk.

"You!" he shrieked. His four lips gaped over pegged teeth, making his sparse mustache separate.

"Hello, Phorap," I said.

PART THREE:

Disclosure

CHAPTER ELEVEN

Aiding and Abetting

"Phorap Rogan, M.D.," Squilyp read out loud as he joined me at Rogan's berth a few hours later. He looked down at my unconscious nemesis and wrinkled the derma around his nostrils. "He needs cleansing."

"Among other things," I said. Once I'd finished making my notations, I handed the chart to the Omorr. "You're his primary. My condolences."

"I thought we were friends now." Squilyp sounded testy.

"We are. Doctor Rogan has refused to allow me to treat him," I said, pointing out the patient's emphatic statement listed at the bottom of the chart. "We have an unpleasant history."

"I see."

I studied Rogan's polyp-pocked face. What were the odds that a transport carrying one of my worst enemies would become critically damaged just as it came within range of the *Sunlace*? No, it couldn't be a coincidence.

"Come into the office." I still couldn't call it *mine*. "I need to review this mess with you before I go off shift."

We went through the charts as I summarized what my old nemesis had told the Jorenians before he'd passed out.

"Dr. Rogan and the four other patients were en route to the Furinac homeworld when the pilot lost power. The flightshield became unstable, so they dropped out of light speed and found themselves in a meteor swarm."

Squilyp skimmed the outline of my report. "What happened to the fifth occupant?"

"The pilot was killed by what appears to be a power surge from the helm controls. The Furinac passengers were injured while presumably guiding the transport out of the meteors."

"Presumably?"

"We've downloaded the transport's database, which included all medical data for the species, but the linguistic files were damaged. Reever's working on it." I didn't like having to rely on Rogan's word for anything, but until Reever repaired the problem, we had no way to communicate with the others. I handed the Omorr one chart and added, "Keep close monitor on this one. He's the oldest of the group, and won't take much more systemic stress."

Squilyp nodded and reviewed the patient's chart display. "No sign of internal bleeding."

"Keep him on oxygen feed, just as a precaution." The Furinac had no lungs. Their species breathed through spiracles, small holes on either side of their exoskeletons.

Squilyp switched off the chart and regarded me. "This Rogan—he's going to be a problem, isn't he?"

If he was working for the League, that was a given. I nodded. "He was discharged from his position back on K-2. Phorap has a bit of a God complex." I refrained from commenting how well Squilyp might relate to that personality quirk. "He's also incompetent, irresponsible, overbearing, and last but not least, extremely *fragrant.*"

"Not for long," Squilyp said. "I will personally supervise his daily cleansing regime."

"Just don't underestimate him. And let me know if anyone stops by to visit him." Though I doubted our killer would be that stupid, I thought, and winced as I flexed my throbbing fingers.

"How are they?" The Omorr leaned over and curled his membranes around my wrists.

"Stiff. Too bad I can't borrow someone else's hands for a few days." I may have healed in an amazingly short time—something I really didn't want to think about—but my normal range of motion was slow to return. I also had recurring periods of temporary numbness. I demonstrated my lack of dexterity for him and added, "You'll be the only one manning the lascalpel for a while."

He manipulated my joints and checked each finger. "Not

for long. The regenerative properties of your metabolism are nothing short of miraculous."

"Yeah, well, that won't help if we need to start cutting on one of those Furinacs," I said. "Study the database. See if there are any miraculous qualities to *their* physiologies."

He gave me one of his old, lofty glares. "I already have."

"I should have known." I grinned. "Mr. Wonderful."

We made rounds before I finished out my shift. Adaola reported that despite the language barrier, the Furinac patients were being cooperative. Rogan was still unconscious. I left the Omorr to run the ward, and went to my quarters.

My console practically hummed with relays. I muted the audio and ignored it in favor of a lengthy cleansing, a quick meal, and an hour with Jenner.

You're certainly in a good mood. My cat surveyed me as he lost interest in pawing at the strip of fabric I dangled for him.

"Guess who we rescued today?" I asked him as I got up and accessed my display.

His Majesty's head raised for a moment. *The big one who looks like me?*

"Nope. Dr. Phorap Rogan."

His blue eyes closed. *Oh. Him.*

A direct relay waited at the top of my com file. I didn't recognize the tag, and made a quick wish that it wasn't Pnor waiting to talk to me about Xonea. I reactivated the audio and tapped in an inquiry.

"Direct relay through transdimensional transmitter, signaling on all frequencies."

Bad news. Whoever was sending this was not on the *Sunlace.* I sent a quick signal to Communications.

"Yes, Senior Healer?" Salo Torin was on duty. I explained the odd relay. "I can monitor your console while you accept the signal," he told me. "Do you suspect the League?"

We'd rescued a suspiciously stranded Rogan, and now someone wanted to chat with me. It had to be the League. "Yes, I do. Can the signal be used to locate the *Sunlace* if I do?"

"Possibly." Salo took a moment to check his equipment. "It is being transmitted on a scattered dimensional pulse. I will ensure our return signal matches their transmission. It will read as an echo, nothing more."

I thanked him and then accessed the relay.

Joseph Grey Veil's face appeared on the screen.

"Cherijo."

I was astonished, and verified the signal once more. It was being transmitted direct relay from wherever Joseph Grey Veil was currently located. "How long have you been relaying this signal?"

"I have kept an open channel since the last attempt to retrieve you from the Jorenian vessel."

"Hear that, Salo?" I asked, knowing the Jorenian was listening in from his console. "Take a good look at this monster. He's the one who killed our people and burned our kids."

"I have killed no one," my creator said.

"Did you send Rogan after me?"

"I do not know anyone named Rogan."

This was a waste of oxygen. "What do you want?"

"How many children have to die before you surrender, Cherijo?" He was a master of delivering guilt. I should have known, I'd been swallowing it most of my life.

No one may divide the House. "How many more do you plan to murder?" I shot back.

"My dear—"

He was *dearing* me again.

"I am not 'your dear.' I am your clone. Your creation. God, your sister, but not your *dear anything*!"

He tried the dignified approach. "You are my dream for humanity."

"Yeah?" Despite the guilt I felt, at that moment I knew I could never surrender to him. He'd use what he learned from me to destroy humanity's natural progress. And Terra would let him. "Well, it's about time you woke up."

"We can exchange insults, or we can reconcile this intolerable situation. The future safety of your colleagues depends on it. The League has found the *Sunlace* on several previous occasions. We will find you again."

"Salo, are you still monitoring?"

"Yes, Senior Healer."

"Good. Tell Dr. Grey Veil what Jorenian warriors do to

those who threaten members of their HouseClans." I smiled at my creator. "Be *specific.*"

Salo was happy to oblige. At length. For a quiet man, Salo was an experienced, *creative* warrior. One who truly enjoyed protecting and avenging his HouseClan.

Eventually, after a few abortive attempts to interrupt, a much paler Joseph Grey Veil terminated the direct relay.

Salo broke off his ghastly litany at once and addressed me. "Was I specific enough?"

"Yep." I was a little shaken myself. I had no idea a Jorenian warrior could do that many things with the viscera they tore out of a living being. With their claws. "Thank you, Salo."

"My pleasure, Senior Healer."

I asked him to copy the relay record to the Captain. I sent Pnor my own signal detailing my suspicions about Rogan and his possible connection with the murderer. The rest of my relays were mostly expressions of gratitude from the crew members who hadn't personally thanked me after the last assault. There were also relays from Reever, Xonea, and Dhreen. I sighed and accessed each one.

Dhreen challenged me to a game of whump-ball and promised to spot me ten points, seeing as I was "handicapped." Reever wanted to see me; Xonea requested the same from detainment. The two plagues of my existence could wait. I changed and went to find the Oenrallian.

Although most of level ten was currently being used as a temporary school, the games area remained available for use. I found Dhreen there, finishing a game with one of the other pilots.

"Doc!" He tossed a whump-glove in my direction. "I was beginning to think you'd never get out of Medical."

The other pilot and I smiled at each other.

"How many credits has he hustled you for?" I asked.

"Doc!" Dhreen said, looking wounded.

"Too many," the pilot told me as he stripped off his glove and hung it on a dry-rack. "Pilot Dhreen has all the Gods of Luck in his hands."

"That, and those devious little spoon-fingers," I said.

The pilot departed and I began to set up for a new game. Dhreen circled the table, pretending to eye the angles while he really looked me over. "How are your hands?"

"Terrible." I flexed my digits, miming pain and stiffness I didn't feel. "Spot me fifteen points."

"Doc, that would be *giving* it away."

"I thought you were my friend."

Dhreen shook his head. "Not for fifteen points."

"Fourteen."

"Twelve."

"Done." I pulled on the whump-glove and chalked the contacts. The game required skill and strategy in order to direct thirty-three small, brightly colored globes into a series of geometrically aligned pockets. I was getting pretty good at it, too. "Darks or lights?"

"Darks," Dhreen said.

I set up my first shot. The light-colored globe spun out, banked twice and sank into appropriate pocket. "Dhreen, do you plan on staying with the *Sunlace*?"

He considered my question while I sank my second globe. "For now."

"But not forever. Damn." I missed a vital angle and the bank on the third globe sent it hurling into the others, scattering the table. "Your shot."

Dhreen tugged on his glove and took position opposite mine. The dark globe he selected banked perfectly and sank at once. "Once we reach Varallan, I thought I'd see what sort of transport they build out there." He made his second shot even faster than the first. "I miss the *Bestshot*."

Dhreen's vessel, the *Bestshot,* had been destroyed after he'd been infected with the Core, had tried to leave K-2, and crashed. I didn't have the same fond memories. It was a miracle that refuse heap had ever maintained a stable flightshield.

I watched him sink globes three, four, and five. "If you keep this up, I may finance the transport personally." I waited until he was set to make the sixth shot. "Would you take me with you?"

"What?" His globe skittered across the table, missed the pocket, and nearly bounced off onto the deck. Dhreen straightened and stared at me. "Did I hear you accurately?"

"Yeah." Two light globes were in an excellent position for a double-drop. I took careful aim and executed the intricate shot. Both globes sank.

Dhreen groaned. "You've been practicing."

"For weeks," I said. "Well? Will you?"

The Oenrallian frowned as he watched me chalk my contacts again. "I thought you liked being the ship's Doc."

"I do." I sank another globe. "And I don't."

"Females." Dhreen ran his fingers through his bright orange hair, scratching around his horn-shaped almost-ears. "You never give a linear answer to a direct inquiry."

My fifth shot was not as precise, but a whump-ball table allows for minor deviations. It teetered on the rim of the pocket, then slipped over it.

"You want a straight answer? Okay." My sixth globe tore across the table and slammed into the pocket. "I'm tired of people I like risking their lives and dying for me." I missed the seventh globe.

"Is that factual? And what am I?" Dhreen repeated his sixth shot. This time the globe found the pocket. "A Larian Flatworm?"

"Of course not. I'm not asking you to bond for life, just give me a ride." I looked through the viewport at the distant pinpoints of the stars. Although what that ClanMother had said to me made me feel better, I knew I couldn't stay on the *Sunlace*, or Joren. It was simply too dangerous. If an idiot like Rogan could find me, other, smarter beings would. "There has to be a place where they won't find me."

A dark globe made a triple bank, ruined my potential seventh shot, and sank. He *was* insulted.

"Running won't resolve anything," Dhreen said.

"Yeah, but think of all the fun we could have."

The display put out an audio signal. "Caution. Personnel emergency. Senior Healer, report to Medical."

"Wonderful." I tossed my glove on the dry-rack and went to the panel. "Confirmed. I'll be there shortly." I turned to Dhreen. "Your game, my friend."

"One more shot," Dhreen said. "I sink mine first, you stay on board the *Sunlace*. You sink yours first, I'll transport you. No charge."

I eyed the remaining globes and pulled my glove back on. "I see myself staying on board the *Sunlace*."

"Maybe not." Dhreen grinned. "You said you've been practicing."

We set up quickly, aimed and shot. Dhreen's dark globe careened rapidly across the table. Mine banked once and intercepted his, knocking it out of alignment before the light globe fell into a pocket.

"That's an auto-penalty!"

"No, that's how you sink a globe before your opponent can," I corrected him, and slapped his glove with mine. "Thanks for the game and the free jaunt. I'll get back to you about the arrangements."

Dhreen glared. "I should have left you in that tavern back on Terra."

I took the gyrlift up to Medical, where the nurses were waiting for me. One had Phorap Rogan in restraints. Another was holding an optic scanner over Squilyp's bleeding, swollen face. The rest of the ward was in an uproar.

"Quiet!" I took the scanner from the nurse and examined the Omorr myself. "What happened?"

"Need to talk to you." Squilyp's voice was thready with pain. "About the Furinac."

"The Furinac can wait. Hold still." There were crescent-shaped wounds all over his brow, cheeks, and eyelids. The display reflected traces of a chemical compound that was particular corrosive to unprotected Omorr flesh. "How the hell did you get a face full of dermal sanitizer, Squilyp?"

"Your friend Rogan doesn't like me, either," he said.

I sucked in a quick breath. The curved wounds suddenly made sense—they were the same size and shape as a spray nozzle. His eyes were a mess. Tiny ulcers were already forming on the damaged corneal plates. Blood in the aqueous humor obstructed most of the retina. I doubted he could see an inch past his gildrells.

"How many times did he hit you with the topical applicator?"

"I lost count." Squilyp winced as I tilted his head for a different angle on the injuries.

"What was he doing with the instrument in the first place?"

"He grabbed it out of my hand," the Omorr said. "One minute I had initiated his cleansing, the next he had an arm around my neck and started hammering on me. He's stronger than he looks."

"What is that *thing* doing here?" I heard Rogan shriek.

"Excuse me for a moment. Nurse!" I flapped my hand

at the nurse restraining Rogan and got her attention. "Sedate that man."

"You cannot prescribe for me!" Rogan screamed. "I refuse treatment! You are not a sentient!" The nurse jammed a syrinpress against his thick neck. "No! No! She's trying . . . to kill . . . meee. . . . "

"Thank you, nurse." I went back to examining my resident. "What did he think you were scrubbing him down with? Acid?" I put the scanner aside and tilted the Omorr's head up. I peered at the blistered flesh intently. Contact burns made his derma look bloated and raw. "Tell me someone flushed your eyes out immediately."

"They did." One of his membranes brushed my arm. "I will recover. That is not the problem."

"Resident, Senior Healer." A nurse appeared on the other side of the table. "The Furinac's condition has begun to deteriorate."

I looked from Squilyp to the nurse. "Which Furinac? The old one?" She nodded. Great. Just great. Rogan had just blinded the only competent surgeon on the ship. "Get me the chart." I turned back to the Omorr. "This the problem you were talking about?"

"Yes. The Furinac's monitor went off the same time Rogan did."

"How bad?"

"Bad enough. You may have to operate."

The elderly Furinac displayed signs of moderate abdominal pain. I couldn't interview him; the linguistic database had not been completely updated. Reever needed to put in some overtime.

"Get the Ship's Linguist down here," I said. "Tell him to run. And notify Security. I want Rogan moved to detainment."

I rescanned the patient. His abdominal wall had gone into spasm. Palpitating it was impossible—his exoskeleton was hard as plasteel. I read no evidence of peristalsis, which meant his intestinal muscles had stopped working. That *was* bad. The Furinac's thick peritoneum was badly inflamed. I calibrated the scanner and ran an organs sequence. When I saw the results displayed, I nearly dropped the scanner.

"Nurse!"

Two of his stomachs and part of his intestinal tract were

perforated. Digestive acid, bacteria, and unprocessed food had been slowly seeping into his abdominal cavity for hours. I stripped off my gloves once Adaola appeared. She took the scanner from me and gasped at the display.

"Prep him," I said. "Fast." I turned and raised my voice to a near-bellow. "Surgical team! Two minutes!"

I checked on Squilyp once more before I scrubbed. The dermal neutralizer was working, but it would take the regenerators a few days to heal the damage to his eyes.

"The Furinac?" he asked me.

"Peritonitis," I replied. "He needs a double gastrectomy and a partial colectomy, minimum. I've got to get into his belly and take a look." At his frown, I added, "He's got four stomachs. Don't worry. He'll make it."

"I'm not concerned about the number of stomachs, Doctor," the Omorr said. "Your hands."

Well, there was that, too.

"I won't drop the lascalpel, I promise." I finished my scan and leaned closer. My voice dropped to a whisper. "If I do, you can have the big desk."

"I don't want it."

"That's a first," I said. It was still so easy to get his gildrells bristling. "Okay, okay. Rest now. I'll have a nurse bring you regular updates."

"Patch my berth terminal into surgery, if you would," he asked. "I can't observe, but I can listen in."

Reever appeared as I was sterilizing for the procedure.

"Did you receive my relay?"

"Not now." I didn't have time to have a conversation. I thrust his hands under the sterilizer. "Stop squirming. When you're clean, gear up."

"I beg your pardon?"

"Put one of those on"—I nodded to the racks of surgical gowns—"and a mask and gloves." One of his eyebrows arched. "You're going into surgery with me."

"For what reason?"

I nudged the sterilizer with my knee and shook off my hands. "Furinac physiology is a bit unusual. We can't put this species under sedation." I gloved and masked. "I need you to translate for me while I operate."

Reever reluctantly donned the surgical gear. I directed

my team to their positions while a nurse wheeled the patient in.

Furinacs were long-limbed, thick-torsoed humanoids with dark, plated exoskeletons. I suspected if one crossed a horse with a giant beetle, something like a Furinac would result. The patient, whose proboscis was quivering with pain, looked at me with large, multifaceted eyes.

"How are you feeling?" I asked. Reever translated, his voice taking on a distinct insectile buzz.

Furinac language reminded me of Dr. Dloh, an arachnid colleague I'd worked with on K-2. The patient hummed something in a weak reply.

"The Patriarch is experiencing considerable pain and some anxiety," Reever said. "He would appreciate an explanation as to why you want to access his thorax."

"Tell him we have to operate." I explained the threat of peritonitis and what I planned to do to circumvent it. Reever relayed the information. The Furinac nodded his fuzzy, silvered head. "I know I can't sedate you completely, nor can I access your gastric compartments without your help. We'll be doing this together, Patriarch."

Once this was translated, the elderly being relaxed and made an affirmative gesture with one of his limbs.

"Sterile field," I said. A bioelectric curtain surrounded us. "Administer the neuroparalyzer." I couldn't sedate him, but I could make sure he didn't feel any more pain. "Keep his spiracles oxygenated." I pulled down the lascalpel and glanced at Reever. "Ask the Patriarch to release his abdominal hinge-plates."

The Furinac extended the twin sides of his exoskeleton, which I draped and secured out of the way. The soft, vulnerable underbelly gleamed white in the stark light. I gripped the lascalpel, my fingers feeling like sticks.

I can do this, I thought.

"Suction."

I made the first incision. The Furinacs have almost no abdominal muscle sheathing, so I penetrated the fat layer quickly.

"Clamp."

Beneath it, the inflamed peritoneum stretched, bulging and purple. A sickly odor rose from the exposed tissue.

"Tell the Patriarch I am beginning the gastropic inspection."

After I breached the peritoneal layer, the Furinac contracted an internal plate of cartilage, allowing me to inspect what served as his digestive system. Two of the quartet of greyish organs were ruptured in a dozen places. A small portion of the large intestine was also punctured. I described what I saw as I suctioned out the dangerous fluids and matter that had accumulated in the compartmental cavity.

There was a profusion of buzzed humming from the Furinac once Reever was through interpreting.

"The Patriarch would like to know if the organs can be saved," Reever asked me. "Proper consumption of his native diet requires the preservation of all four stomachs. He says he is old and has few pleasures left."

I surveyed the organs, then shook my head. "Can't do it. I'll try to clone the damaged organs, and replace them at a later time. Best I can do."

The elderly Furinac sighed just like a human once he heard this translated.

"A change in diet beats dying," I said.

The Patriarch indicated through Reever that I should proceed. My right hand slipped on the lascalpel as I lifted it. I couldn't feel it anymore.

"Damn." I flexed my left fingers, they weren't much better. I had been trained to operate ambidextrously, but that wasn't going to help. I looked at Reever. "We have a bit of a problem, Duncan."

"What is it?"

"I don't have enough sensation in my hands to perform this procedure."

Everyone within the sterile field stopped what they were doing for a full five seconds.

"Calm down," I said to the room at large. "We'll find a way."

Reever looked at the team. "What about one of them? Can they take your place?"

Tonetka, Squilyp, and I constituted the full staff of surgeons for the *Sunlace*. A few of the more experienced residents were doing some simple procedures, but none had graduated to the level of cutting required for this kind of work.

On the other hand, if we didn't do this now, the Furinac

would die. I turned my face toward the display panel just beyond the sterile field.

"Squilyp, can you hear me?"

His reply was low but audible beyond the field static.

"Yes, Doctor."

"If you have any bright ideas, now's the time." I thought for a moment. "If I guide you with my voice, could you do the procedure by touch?"

"An interesting proposition," the Omorr said. "I have a better one."

"Don't be shy."

"You made a comment about borrowing someone's hands. Could Linguist Reever lend you his while you share a cortical coupling?"

A radical idea. A great one, too. I looked at Reever. "Can we do that? Operate on the Patriarch using my mind and your hands?"

Reever's eyes went from me to the open thorax and exposed organs, then to his own hands. He swallowed hard before he said, "Yes."

Why, he's *squeamish,* I thought. How cute.

"Just think of it as helping the handicapped." I turned my head toward the console. "Squilyp, I'm giving you a raise in compensation. Major credits. You can have the desk, too."

I explained what we were doing to my team members while Reever translated my proposed solution to the Patriarch. I had no idea how he explained that the Furinac's surgeon couldn't use her own hands, but somehow he got the message through. The Patriarch agreed. Reever turned to me. His eyes were dull green above the edge of his mask.

"Whenever you're ready, Doctor."

"Remember to let me do my job while we're linked. I need full control of your hands." I crinkled my eyes in a surgical-room smile. "Relax, Duncan. I know what I'm—you're—doing."

We linked. I raced into Reever's thoughts impatiently. He was feeling nauseous, which made me nauseous.

Cut it out. Now is not the time to decide you don't like touching squishy things. I reached out with my mental hands, and felt him guide me to his. Through my eyes, I watched as I lifted Duncan's hand to the lascalpel. His fingers shook a little. *Get a grip. Can't do that when you're in someone's abdomen, you'll cut out something important. Just relax and enjoy yourself.*

You enjoy doing this? Reever seemed crabby.

We grasped the lascalpel and angled it over the Furinac. *It's the great love of my life. Now, we're going to make the first incision. I have to give instructions to the team, so just let me use your hands and stay out of the way.*

Once the surgical team adjusted to the idea, they were only too happy to slap instruments into Reever's gloves. He jumped at the feel of metal striking his palm the first time.

Steady, Duncan. I leaned closer to the first stomach, clamped off and ready for removal. *Here we go. Whatever you do, don't jerk the lascalpel.*

The operation went on for three more hours. I had to work slowly. Reever's untrained hands were capable but unaccustomed to the fine manipulation required. I felt his muscles cramping as we completed the last of the excisions.

Tell the Patriarch to release his internal plate. I pushed the lascalpel away with Duncan's hand, and asked one of the team to close for us. *That's it. You can end the link—*

The world tilted, disappeared. I was in a dark, silent place. The sounds of a child crying made me whirl around. *Reever?*

I saw an image of a little boy, dressed in nothing more than a filthy rag twisted around his hips. His pathetically thin body rocked back and forth. A mass of scabbed, infected gashes covered the back of the child's hands. *Duncan?*

The image dissolved, reshaped itself. A taller, older version of the boy got to his feet. He was wearing a surgical gown. Furinac blood stained his gloves.

No. I didn't mean to remind you of this. Duncan, I'm sorry.

Cherijo, I'm glad I was useful to you. I didn't want the Patriarch to die. But don't do this to me again.

We were back in the surgical suite, staring at each other. Reever excused himself as soon as I deactivated the sterile field.

"Doctor?" It was the Omorr, sounding anxious. I gave him a summary of the operation as I cleaned up. When I came out in main Medical, Adaola was waiting for me.

"Security cannot move Dr. Rogan to detainment for the moment, Senior Healer," she said. "Captain Pnor wishes Xonea to remain in isolation."

With all the uproar over Rogan, the Furinac and Squilyp, I'd forgotten about Xonea. "What for?" The nurse made an I-don't-know gesture. "All right. But I want him kept in restraints at all times."

Adaola nodded. "May I ask what happened to Linguist Reever?"

"It's complicated," I said. I looked around, but didn't see Reever anywhere. "Where is he?"

"He departed. I offered an antiemetic to him, but he refused."

"An antiemetic?"

"Why, yes, Senior Healer. I thought it would be helpful, considering the way he vomited when he came out of surgery."

I monitored the Furinac for a few hours, then left him in the capable hands of Adaola so I could catch a sleep interval. There would be very few of them for me from now on. I'd be the only physician on duty until Squilyp recovered from Rogan's attack.

I programmed an alarm for four hours and dropped on my sleeping platform. Four seconds later, the alarm went off. Well, it felt like four seconds.

I dragged my lethargic body off the mattress and into the cleanser. Of course my display's emergency signal chose that moment to activate. I muttered dire threats against Jorenian tech as I left a trail of wet footprints across the deck.

I punched the keypad. "What?"

Salo's image appeared. "Senior Healer, Xonea has requested your presence. Captain Pnor will permit a supervised interview."

Pnor could go talk to him. I had patients to see to. "Tell him I'm busy."

"Healer." Salo tried to sound stern. "This is the only opportunity you will be given to speak to Xonea."

"Why?"

"Xonea will explain." Before I could say anything, Salo

leaned forward and lowered his voice. "It is important, Cherijo."

"I can't do this over a channel?" Salo shook his head. "Okay. I'm on the way." My brows drew together. "Just exactly where *is* detainment, Salo?"

"Level twenty-seven."

Twenty levels down. Most of the gyrlifts were still out of operation. This had better be good.

Some time later, my tired legs stopped at level twenty-seven's barricaded entryway. Two very large, armed crew members stood guard. No congenial kidding around here, I discovered as I was permitted access. Those pulse rifles meant business.

Xonea's cell was a large, empty area, probably used for cargo storage most of the time. There weren't a lot of reasons to detain a Jorenian. When there were, it wasn't for the long term.

I strode up to the mesh barrier and halted where he could see me. "You rang?"

Xonea rose from the bunk he was lying on and approached the barrier. He looked terrible.

"Aren't they feeding you?" I asked.

"Cherijo, thank you for coming." He began to reach through the barrier, then saw my face and dropped his hand. "Before I go, I would express my regret over what I have done. You were correct. You never invited my Choice, and did everything to discourage it. Your pardon would mean much to me."

"You're forgiven," I said. "Before you go where?"

"Captain Pnor has informed me of his ruling." Xonea pressed one huge hand against his flat belly, and winced with a spasm of pain. "I am banished."

"Banished?" My jaw dropped. "For what?"

"Pnor believes I intend to divert your path. That I would have, when I confronted you in Medical." Another spasm made him take a quick breath.

"What's wrong with your stomach?" I demanded, automatically looking around for a first aid kit. "And don't say it's nothing. That's the third or fourth time I've seen you grab it like that."

"It does not matter. Whatever is wrong will soon be of no consequence. I am banished."

"So apologize and promise you'll never do it again."

"It makes no difference, Cherijo. It is decided."

"This is crazy." Xonea Choosing me was bad enough, but banishing him because the Captain *thought* he was trying to kill me? "Pnor's wrong. I'll tell him he's wrong."

"He will not reverse his ruling."

"Don't you people have due process?" At that, Xonea looked mystified. "Never mind. I won't let him do this. Not without some kind of trial. Can't I . . ." I recalled how I'd felt under the same circumstances. Saw the glimmer of expectancy in his white eyes. "What?"

"Pnor cannot banish me if I am shielded."

I recalled the clause from the database. *Suspected offenders Chosen by a member of the victim's HouseClan after the offense has been committed may be thus shielded from judicial action . . .*

"Let me get this straight. You want me to go to Pnor. Tell him I Choose you. Then you're shielded until we reach Joren. Have I covered the *entire* plan?"

He turned away from the mesh. I felt a little ashamed of myself. Xonea had done the same thing to protect me, when Pnor had suspected I was involved in the murders.

"Look, Xonea, I—" Oh, the hell with it. "I'll go and see Pnor now."

His shoulders tensed. "You will?" He pivoted, hope erasing the etched despair on his face.

I held up a hand. "There are conditions. No bonding chambers, no vows, no kids. When we reach your homeworld, we go our separate ways." Before he could start giving me his opinion, I shook my head. "I don't care what the rules are. I'll go along with this until we get to Joren. Then it's over."

He obviously didn't like it, but nodded. "Agreed."

I found the Captain after a brief search of Engineering and made my request. Pnor took me back to his office and at once tried to talk me out of it. For an hour, he talked about HouseClan traditions and deviant behavior and a hundred other reasons to throw my ClanBrother off the *Sunlace*.

"He will expect to claim his Choice," the Captain added, just for good measure.

We'd just see about that part, I thought, and shrugged.

"Once free, he could easily kill you."

"Captain, Xonea shielded me when you thought I was the killer." I stood up. "He deserves the benefit of the doubt, just for that."

Pnor was bitterly convinced he had made the right decision. "He meant to divert your path, Cherijo. Xonea deserves banishment."

"In your opinion," I said. "On my homeworld, we believe people to be innocent until *proven* guilty."

"A naive concept," someone else said.

I turned around to find Duncan Reever standing behind me.

"Did our voices carry well enough for you to hear everything this time?" Reever nodded. I glanced back to the Captain. "I checked the judicial database. You can't stop me."

"Xonea will be restricted to quarters," Pnor said. "If you Choose, that will be *your* quarters, Senior Healer."

Oh joy. Maybe I'd sleep in Medical for a few weeks. "Thank you, Captain." I grasped Reever's arm and tugged him out of the office with me. "I need to talk to you."

I found a deserted alcove and pulled him into it with me. It was small and we had to stand close together. The warmth of his body met the chilled surface of my skin.

"Duncan, we've had this conversation before."

"Yes." His eyes turned wintry grey, gleaming like a frozen Terran lake. I couldn't get through that cold remoteness now. Maybe it was a form of protection. Maybe Reever *needed* to feel nothing for me. Fine.

"Reever, I—"

All of a sudden he grabbed my tunic and jerked. Our bodies collided. My arms came up around him in reflex. He muttered something, then cradled my face between his scarred hands. Our mouths jolted together, off-center, but he fixed that.

Reever did feel something, after all.

We didn't speak when our lips parted. There wasn't anything left to say. I stepped out of the alcove, turned and walked away. I didn't look back to see if Reever was watching me go. I already knew he was.

CHAPTER TWELVE

She Who Preserves

I checked in with Medical, made my rounds, and spoke to Squilyp and Adaola. Explaining things was impossible. It didn't matter. From the sympathetic looks I got, it already appeared to be public knowledge. I asked Squilyp to assist the nurses until I got back. He was polite and pretended to believe my invented excuse.

I went to my quarters. Signaled the Captain. Made a few final preparations.

This time I caught a functioning gyrlift and returned to level twenty-seven. The two guards were conspicuously absent. Instructions had been left on the outer display on how to let myself into the detainment area.

Xonea was still standing in the same place I'd left him. His eyes widened as he saw me walk in. I guessed he had counted on me not coming back. He was in for a few more surprises.

"Cherijo."

"Xonea." I pressed a few keys on the display panel, which deactivated the barrier-locking mechanism. "Are you ready to do this?"

He smiled as I entered the cell and secured the barrier once more. "You speak as though preparing to perform a medical procedure."

"Surgery is a lot more fun."

"Perhaps." He walked toward me. Two enormous hands descended to rest lightly on my shoulders. "Perhaps not."

He bent forward and brushed his lips against the top of my head. "I am honored."

"Uh-huh." I didn't want to do this. It made me remember when Kao had Chosen me. Aka the happiest day of my life. "How's your stomach?"

He ignored that and stroked my hair. "I will not hurt you, Cherijo."

"Your ClanBrother said the same thing to me." A single tear spilled from my lashes. Oh, for God's sake, I didn't want to start crying now. I wanted to be clinical. Detached. On another vessel a thousand light years from the *Sunlace*. "All right." I took a deep breath. "Xonea Torin, I Choose you."

"Cherijo." His thumb rubbed away the small droplet. "Look at me."

I did. His fingers released the clasp on my vocollar, and lifted it from my neck. He did the same with his, and dropped them to the deck.

"Bad move," I said. "How are you going to understand what I'm saying when I tell you I'm not going to have sex with you?"

"Sher-ee-shoh," Xonea said, carefully wrapping his fluid Jorenian palate around the guttural syllables. *He was speaking Terran*. "Ahyee lahv hyoo." He touched my lips with his fingers. "Ahyee-huv ol-hways lahvduh hyoo."

He'd learned enough of my own language to tell me this. Because there was no word for "love" in Jorenian.

My first sexual experience had been with Kao, immediately after he'd Chosen me. Since that night, I hadn't been intimate with anyone except Duncan Reever, and that had been under duress. Now I had Chosen Xonea, who was expecting a wedding night.

I needed to work on my relationships with men.

Something cool and metallic encircled my neck. Xonea was replacing our vocollars. His fingers went on to work my braid loose, then released the warrior's knot in his hair. A thick swath of black spilled over his shoulders.

"Did I say it correctly?" he asked me.

"Very smooth," I said. How could I put my refusal into words without hurting his pride? I stalled for time. "How long did it take you to learn how to say it in Terran?"

His lips twitched. "A week."

Pleading a sudden migraine wouldn't work. "I'm impressed."

"So little you are." He took me in his arms and lifted me up. "I fear I will hurt you."

Fear was good, I thought. Maybe I could use that. By then he was nuzzling the side of my neck. "Um . . . Xonea, I need to talk to you about this."

"Your skin is very delicate," he said. That faint touch of his fingertip skimming my lips made me swallow and close my eyes. "Terrans must bruise easily."

Good point. I opened one eye. "Exactly. Which is why—"

"I will be careful with you." Using just that one finger, Xonea traced a lot more of me. The hollows of my throat. The curves of both breasts. The line of my sternum. The slight convexity of my abdomen. The outer swell of my thigh.

"My Chosen." Silky black hair fell around me, a dark waterfall. His arms drew me in. "Mine."

Time to put a stop to this. Right now. "Xonea?"

He held me in that close embrace, his lips moving over my face.

"Xonea. Stop." I shivered as he buried his mouth against my throat. "I can't have sex with you."

He lifted his head. "It is the way of Choice." Xonea took my hands and pressed them against his chest. "You are shy."

"I'm not shy." I tried to tug free. "I'm simply not . . . um, interested."

"I want to see your eyes." His fingers sank into my hair as he tilted my face. "You are still afraid of me?"

"I did this to shield you," I said, and slowly backed out of his embrace. "Not to become your lover." I turned toward the barrier. "Captain Pnor."

"I am here, Senior Healer." Pnor's voice came from the display channel I'd activated and left open before entering the detainment cell.

Xonea simply stared at me.

"I've Chosen Xonea." I watched my lover's mouth flatten to a grim line. "I shield Xonea Torin from banishment."

"As you wish, Cherijo." The Captain sighed.

Xonea took a step toward me.

"Guards?" I called out. The two armed Jorenians had

returned once I'd reactivated the locking mechanism. They now stood just beyond the cell, their backs discreetly toward us. "You guys hear that?"

"Yes, Senior Healer," one said. They both left without turning around.

I reached up and flipped up a link cover on my vocollar. "Record terminate." The tiny recording drone deactivated on my voice command. I closed the cover.

"Why, Cherijo?"

"To protect you." I went over and disengaged the lock. "I needed the recording to present to the Ruling Council. Pnor insisted on the guards coming back. He's still worried you might try to kill me." I glanced over my shoulder. "I have to go to work now."

He stood there, seven-and-a-half-feet of highly upset male. "Come here."

I didn't think he wanted to give me a hug or kiss good-bye. Still, I wasn't going to let him intimidate me. He owed me his life, didn't he? I went to him, my chin up, the situation completely under control.

For maybe two seconds.

Huge blue hands seized me and lifted me up. I hung there suspended, my feet dangling. My pale face was a mere inch from his.

Okay. I was intimidated.

"There will be no more open display channels when we are together," Xonea said.

"Um, sure."

"Nor will there be a need for guards or recording devices."

I nodded quickly. Anything to get me back on the deck in one piece.

"Has Pnor restricted me to your quarters?"

Which reminded me. "Yes, but I never said—"

"There is much you did not say." Xonea put me back down. "On this subject, you have no choice. Now go, or I will claim mine."

I stomped out of there. No gyrlift to be had this time, so I walked up all eighteen levels to my quarters, changed into my physician's tunic, and stomped back out. Up two more levels. My injured thigh throbbed. Another reason to be mad.

I paused outside the Medical Bay door panel. Smoothed my damp hair. Straightened my tunic. Walked in. My expression dared anyone in my path to make a comment. Any comment.

No one seemed to notice. Nurses smiled dreamily back at me. Patients gave me knowing looks. Only the Omorr acted normally.

"This berth's linens need to be replaced," Squilyp said.

I looked over the top of his chart. "Weren't they changed this morning?"

"Yes, but there is a soiled area"—he pointed to a tiny speck—"here."

"You're nearly blind, Squilyp, and you can still see that?" His gildrells flared. "Okay, okay. I'll get your berth sheets changed." I finished my notations. "Everyone behave themselves while I was gone?"

"Yes." The Omorr shifted uncomfortably. "One of the residents told me . . ." he peered at me and tried again. "Did you really have to . . ."

"That's my business." I wasn't going to get into this with Squilyp. "Don't look at me like that."

"I'm not looking at you. I can't see you," the Omorr said, all innocence.

Behind me, a nurse let out a startled yelp. I turned my head just in time to watch a scanner fly across the ward and smash into a hundred pieces against the plasteel wall panel.

"Get away from me!"

The nurse who had been scanning Phorap Rogan was backing away, holding his chart in front of her like a shield. His sedation had worn off, and he had worked one arm out of his restraints.

Ah, perfect. "Excuse me for a moment, Squilyp."

I marched over, taking Rogan's chart from the nurse as I passed. When I got to my former colleague's berth, I smiled. "Hello, Phorap. Feeling better?"

Oily lidless eyes stared at me with utter loathing. "You." He hissed. "Don't touch me!"

" 'Fraid I have to. You beat up the only other qualified practitioner on this ship yesterday. Want to explain why you did that?"

The noxious odor of his body intensified. "Of all the

ships in the universe, why did I have to board the one with *you* on it?"

"You took the words right out of my mouth." I put the chart aside and caught his arm. He was pretty strong, but physical therapy had fortified my hands and arms. "Did the League send you after me, Rogan? Who are you working with?"

He wasn't going to confess. "Release me!" We wrestled for a moment before I got him secured once more. "Remove these restraints at once!"

"Settle down, Rogan." My stomach rolled as I scanned him thoroughly. Maybe I should start wearing a breather around him, I thought. "Hold still, you're screwing up my readings."

"How dare you?" he shouted. "I'd rather be crippled than let you examine me!"

"That," I said, "can be arranged." I gestured to the horrified nurse. "Start cleaning him up. Don't unstrap him under any circumstances. Oh, and bring me his latest lab work. I want to review it before I sedate him."

Rogan continued to shriek at me. I looked around the ward, searching for something that would solve this problem. Spotted the physical therapy room. I went in, picked up the hand manipulators and returned to Rogan's berth. His curses were elevating in volume by the moment. When his four lips spread to their widest, I thrust a large therapy plasball in his mouth. As a gag, it functioned beautifully.

"Thank you, Senior Healer," the nurse said. She gazed at Rogan with visible distaste.

"You're welcome." I patted one of Rogan's straining shoulders. "Remember what I said, Phorap. Be a good boy. Let the nurse give you a bath. Think of it as your contribution to the health and welfare of the other patients."

The ball muffled his squeals of outrage. I'd have to make a database entry on alternative uses for physical therapy equipment. Too bad I hadn't thought of it while Rogan and I were back on K-2.

"Senior Healer?" One of the nurses hovered, and gave me a sweet smile.

I'd probably have to put up with this nonsense the whole way to Joren. "What?"

"The elderly Furinac patient wishes to speak with you."

Evidently Reever had finished programming the linguistic database, for my vocollar immediately translated the Patriarch's speech.

"Doctor Torin," he greeted me once I'd reached his berth. His color was better, but he looked tired. Major surgery was hard on elderly beings. Their immune systems took longer to accomplish the healing process. "My thanks for your skill in saving my life."

"My thanks for not panicking when things got weird." I scanned him. His organs sequence looked good, and the peritoneum was only slightly inflamed.

He inclined his head in Rogan's direction. "I see our passenger has proved to be much less cooperative."

"Your passenger is a pain in the posterior," I said. This was my chance to find out how the Furinac were involved with Rogan and the League. "How did he end up on your transport?"

"My pilot brought him on board at the last world we visited." Air puffed indignantly through his spiracles. "Had I some forewarning of his distaste for personal hygiene, I would have never permitted it."

I could just imagine having to put up with the stench in such a small vessel. "Rogan must have offered your pilot some hefty credits to take him on your jaunt."

"He paid the standard passage rate, I believe." The Patriarch's rainbow-jeweled eyes moved to the other Furinacs. "My people are recuperating?"

"They're all doing very well." I had already checked them during my rounds. I placed a hand on one of his upper appendages. "I have to tell you there was one casualty. Your pilot was killed just after you entered the meteor swarm. I'm sorry for your loss, Patriarch."

"Thank you." The Furinac made a slow, mournful buzz. "He was a good man."

Or had conspired with the League to find me. Only Rogan knew for sure. "When you're feeling better, our crew will be glad to make any ceremonial arrangements you would like."

"It is appreciated, Doctor." He examined me curiously. "I've never met a Terran before."

Fortunate man. "Not quite what you expected?"

"I was told your species has a habit of ejecting saliva

frequently. Yet I have not observed you indulging in this practice. Is it only done on your homeworld? A means of marking territory, perhaps?"

I laughed. Xenophobic Terrans had a habit of spitting whenever they ran into alien species. "That's one way to put it. Sorry to disappoint you. I'm not what you'd call . . . a model Terran."

"One can't select one's species," the Furinac said. He made a buzzing, chuckling sound. Laughter is almost universal. "I have one request, if it is possible."

"Sure. What do you need?"

"An opportunity to speak with your ship's commander. It is of vital importance that my people and I reach Furin as soon as possible."

"Is there some sort of emergency we need to know about, Patriarch?" I asked. Or some kind of League rendezvous?

He sighed. "I had hoped not to reveal myself, but timing is of the utmost importance. Furinac criterion for sovereignty requires I not be absent from our world longer than a certain period of time."

"Sovereignty?" I echoed. "You mean you're the—the—"

"Yes, my dear. I am the Patriarch *of* Furin."

"I see. Um, nice to meet you." All thoughts of League conspiracy went out the viewport. I tried to look like I did this regularly. "May I ask what you were doing on such a dinky little transport?"

"I sometimes travel using less conventional means." He seemed embarrassed. "One wearies of pomp and ceremony."

Speaking of ceremony. "Should I address you by a certain title?"

"Patriarch is acceptable, Doctor."

"Great." I smiled. Inside, I fumed.

Reever needed to work on his direct translations. The elderly Furinac wasn't just a nice old gentleman with pretty eyes and a pleasant demeanor.

He was the *ruler* of an entire world.

Captain Pnor agreed to transport the Patriarch and his group to their homeworld, and even proposed to do the same for Phorap Rogan. I had a few things to say about that, but no real evidence to offer the Captain about my archenemy's possible involvement with the League. I relayed the news to the elderly Furinac before my shift ended.

As I walked down the corridor to my quarters, I thought about our very important dignitary. To think, I had performed surgery on a being who governed the lives of millions. With Reever's hands, no less.

Good thing we hadn't dropped the lascalpel.

At my quarters, I opened the door panel, walked in, and nearly ran straight into my new roommate's chest. "Oh. Hello."

"Greetings, Cherijo." He looked pretty happy to see me. "How was your shift?"

"Long. Tiring. I need to get some sleep." I began stripping off my tunic, then froze. He was watching me *undress*. "Do you mind?"

"No." He gave me a guileless smile.

"Xonea."

A dark eyebrow arched. "We are Chosen, Cherijo."

I didn't have to be modest, I thought, I *am* a physician. Used to this sort of thing. So I turned my back when I stripped the rest of the way. It didn't mean I was overly modest. I just didn't want to give Xonea any ideas. Swiftly I pulled on a soft undershirt I liked to sleep in and looked back at my new roommate.

He wasn't even paying attention to me. Jenner sat in his lap, his neck arched as Xonea scratched under his chin.

Disgusted with the state of things in general, I thumped food and water down on the deck for His Majesty. Jenner leapt down at once and made a beeline for his server. Xonea chuckled.

It was all a little *too* domestic for me. I stomped over to my sleeping platform and yanked the coverlet back. I'd have to get a bigger one now. I didn't think this one was rated for a two-hundred-kilo Jorenian. My tired muscles sang their pleasure as I stretched out. I put one arm over my eyes. So much had happened. Now there was this big blue man in my quarters to stumble over.

I felt the other side of the mattress depress, felt hands drawing me back. Xonea's arms cradled me against him.

"Sleep," I said in a mumble.

"Yes, Cherijo." He stroked my hair. "Go to sleep."

*   *   *

Everything changed after that. I wasn't used to changes in my life. Well, the rare times I *had* a life outside of my work. The only constant companion I'd ever had after Maggie had died was Jenner. My cat didn't demand more than occasional stroking, some light conversation, and regular feedings. I suspected Xonea would want a lot more.

I had no idea.

"Xonea?"

I tripped over a container positioned directly inside the door panel to my quarters. I regained my balance and kicked it to one side. Absolutely the *stupidest* place to put something.

There were more containers. Masculine garments were tossed over the ends of my furnishings. Vid and audio discs were stacked all on the deck. I hated clutter more than I hated dirt. Dirt you could get rid of. Clutter liked to *breed*.

"Xonea!"

My new roommate appeared, fresh from the cleanser, briskly drying his hair with a towel. He wore only trousers. I'd discovered over the past week that Xonea enjoyed walking around half-naked. Especially when he knew I was coming off shift.

For once I was too annoyed to gawk at his glistening chest. I gestured at the mess. "Where did all this junk come from?"

"This *junk* is mine," he said as he jerked me into his arms and hauled me up against him. "I've missed you."

I wanted to kick him. "You just saw me this morning."

"That was hours ago." His lips began descending.

"Xonea, put me dow—" He kissed me, hard and quick. "Down. Now." I straightened my tunic as soon as my feet touched the deck. My blood simmered, but I ignored it for the moment. "*All* this stuff is yours?"

Some of the larger containers were in various stages of being unpacked. Then I noticed the walls.

"Oh, no. No!"

"Cherijo—"

"Absolutely not!"

Some of the humor cleared from his eyes. "I only wished to add to the decor."

I went over and flung my hand at an enormous display

of archaic energy pistols. "With *guns*? I have to live in rooms decorated with *guns*?"

"Not only guns." He got all dignified and Jorenian on me. "I haven't put up my bladed weapons yet."

"That's supposed to be *better*?"

"My collections are very old and valuable."

"To who?" I was getting shrill. "Mercenaries? Raiders? *The Hsktskt*?"

"Cherijo."

My foot started tapping. "Take them down."

His arms folded. "We must come to an amicable agreement as to the disposition of our living space."

So did mine. "This was my living space *first,* pal. Pack it up, or I'll throw them in a disposal unit myself." I didn't smile so much as bare my teeth. "With great pleasure."

He looked pained, sighed, then went over to one wall and began disassembling the ghastly collage. "You are a stubborn female."

"You have vile taste in interior decor." I went to the console and checked my relays. There were a million, as usual. "Another thing. Why don't you ever clear out some of these console relays?"

He made a huffy sound. "They are *your* relays."

"Oh, give me a break. You know they're just another couple hundred well wishes for our fruitful union, eternal honor, and all that other rubbish the HouseClan spouts whenever someone Chooses."

"That is unkind, Cherijo." He put down the large-barreled stun emitter he was holding with a thump. I winced. Did he keep them all charged? "They are happy for us."

I skimmed the list. "Deliriously happy, from the looks of this. Well, I am not in the mood." I switched off the display. My stomach demanded some attention. "Whose turn is it to make dinner?"

"Yours."

Jenner jumped up on the mattress and draped himself over Xonea. With lazy satisfaction, both males watched me prepare our meal.

"Pasta and seafood alfredo for me." I placed one dish on the table, then a much larger server beside it. "D'narral with safira spice for you." I checked the stores. "What goes with d'narral? A light or a dark tea?"

"Light," Xonea said.

That would be jaspkerry, his favorite. Which reminded me— "Hey, did you report to medical and have that internal-scan series performed, like I asked you to?"

"I will, soon." He pulled on a tunic and came to the table.

"Your stomach could be developing ulcers from the stress. It's nothing to mess around with, Xonea. Make an appointment, will you?" I sat down. "Would you mind getting the tea, please?"

He didn't mind. For a male, Xonea was quite domesticated. He did his part to prepare meals, sterilize our garments, and keep the equipment sanitary. I couldn't complain, I thought, then my gaze fell on his belongings cluttering up the deck. Oh, yes, I could.

He offered me a server of the light floral tea I was becoming addicted to, and sat down beside me. "What is pasta?"

"It's sort of like t'fer root. Only in small, shaped pieces." I held out a fork with a small portion, which he tasted. He chewed it slowly. "Well?"

"T'fer is not so insubstantial. The alfredo, that is the pink-and-white topping?"

I took a sip of tea before I answered. "Alfredo is a style of preparation—with a cream or white sauce. The pink things are the seafood part."

He shrugged and started on his d'narral, which he had already explained was the heart of a giant tree-flower-something on Joren.

"Too much safira?" The spice, I discovered, was very similar to Terran cinnamon. It had to be used in small amounts or it became overpowering.

"No, it is excellent." He ate with the same frank enjoyment he did everything else. Xonea, like most Jorenian males, consumed massive amounts of everything. It took a cargo hold of calories to fuel their massive bodies. I could never keep up with his appetite. When we finished the meal, he began to clear up. "You are weary, Cherijo. Go, lie down." He gave me another of those intimate smiles. The ones that made me really nervous. "I will join you shortly."

"I'm not so tired." I did *not* want to get into bed with

him. Not until he got that look off his face. "Why don't we listen to some jazz?"

One dark brow rose. "We listened to your music last night."

"Okay, then we'll play toss-the-yarn-ball with Jenner."

"Jenner is weary of that." He dropped the dishes into the sterilizer. Something broke. "If you do not wish to share your sleeping platform with me, say so."

"Xonea . . ." I watch him stalk off to the viewport. Damn it. He was becoming more irritable by the day. Well, being confined to quarters was enough to shorten anyone's fuse, I guessed. I could only hope what was left of Xonea's would last until we reached Joren.

The *Sunlace* transitioned and went into orbit above the Patriarch's world a few days later. I was scheduled to escort the ruler, along with a sojourn team, for a brief visit. Once I'd learned the Furinacs' shuttle logs supported the Patriarch's story, and no League ships had been spotted within a light year of the system, I actually looked forward to the trip. Captain Pnor also made a rare exception and joined the launch party.

The Omorr's eyes had healed and he was back on duty, so I left him in charge of the ward. Rogan had been discharged from Medical, but on my advice Pnor had confined him under guard in his quarters. Although I was sure the guards could handle the smelly little twerp, I told Squilyp to put Rogan into sleep suspension at the first sign of trouble.

I was the last to arrive at the launch bay (as usual) and came to a skidding halt when I saw the team assembled. Duncan Reever was quietly conferring with one of the Furinacs. He didn't look up as I approached.

We'd been avoiding each other since we said our good-byes. I recalled what he'd told me the first time it looked like I'd have to Choose Xonea. A dull ache knotted under my sternum. Was this the non-League world he'd asked Pnor to leave him on?

The Patriarch greeted me with a friendly buzz. "Doctor Torin! I'm glad to see you could join us."

"Punctual as ever," Dhreen said in a low voice as I entered the launch. I nudged him with my elbow and sat next to my distinguished patient.

"How are you feeling?"

"Very well now." He patted his abdomen. "The new organs are working perfectly."

By combining Terran know-how and Jorenian tech, I had cloned replacement organs from the cells of the damaged originals a few weeks after his initial surgery. Squilyp performed the double-transplant while I observed.

The Patriarch began describing an amusing incident that happened at his palace, which I gathered was roughly about the size of the *Sunlace*. My thoughts drifted as we launched and began the descent to the planet. The past few weeks had been quiet, a nice respite from the near-continuous chaos we'd endured on board the ship since leaving K-2.

The journey to Joren was nearly half over. Soon I'd have to talk to Dhreen again. Find a way to remind Xonea I had no intentions of spending the rest of my life with him. We'd made a bargain, and I planned to hold him to it.

Xonea had been really agitated lately. Maybe I could make that little announcement from Dhreen's new transport as we were leaving Joren.

"Senior Healer?"

We were already at Furin Main Transport, I realized, yanked out of my reverie. Captain Pnor was waiting for me at the launch doors. Everyone else was already out. That will teach me to daydream, I thought.

I got up and shouldered my medical pack. Time to go and meet the natives.

Outside the launch was an impressive docking ramp, carpeted with a rich, brilliantly worked tapestry. The Patriarch and his party were strolling down, being greeted by loud buzzing and cheering. I looked beyond the ramp and caught my breath.

There had to be a hundred thousand Furinacs there, standing, waving, and shouting to their ruler.

Beyond the incredible mass of people, the majestic city of Cuot rose to ponderous heights. The city's carefully landscaped terraces supported row after row of cylindrical structures, each topped with a gilded, pear-shaped dome.

The most striking feature of Cuot was the style of architecture. There wasn't an angle in the entire city, I thought as I walked down with Pnor. All structures curved in concave and convex lines, making the dwellings appear to be flowing up out of the lush, manicured botanicals.

Someone broke from the crowd and rushed up to the Patriarch. The Furinac dropped down and prostrated himself before his ruler, weeping. He was dressed in an elaborate, bejeweled garment and wore a number of gaudy rings around the base of his proboscis.

"Oh, He Who Is Above Us All! We were signaled of your injuries! We wept for your pain! We praise your strength in recovering! We bless your determination in returning to us!"

The Captain and I stopped next to the ruler, who made a graceful sweep of one appendage and bobbed his head in a potentate's regal manner.

"Who is that?" I looked down at the Furinac, who was still kissing the docking pad.

"My heir, First Scion." The Patriarch regarded the prostrate figure with paternal pride. "Most devoted, is he not?"

"Uh-huh." That was definitely devotion in my book.

The heir raised his head a mere inch from the pad. His face rings jingled. "He Who Is Our Life's Blood, Who Is the Center of All Joy, may this insignificant one ask a question of Your Magnificence?" The Patriarch's head bobbed again. "Is this She Who Saved Your Omnipotence by Her Skill?"

Oh, brother. If the Furinacs were going to call me that, I'd be standing here forever just listening to Junior say Hi.

"Yes, First Scion. I introduce to you She Who Preserves All Life, Dr. Cherijo Torin. It is Dr. Torin who assured I would live to see our people again." He made another sweeping gesture, and his heir got up from the ground. "Dr. Torin, this is my heir, He Who Has the Future to Rule, First Scion of Furin."

The First Scion threw himself at my feet. "I beg you! Allow me to espouse you! Of all I can give, only this is suitable for She Who Has Brought Our Beloved Patriarch Home!"

My eyes went from the Furinac at my feet to Captain Pnor to the Patriarch. "Sorry, what does he want?"

The Patriarch looked smugly satisfied. "He wants to marry you."

It was only a ceremonial proposal, I quickly discovered.

That was still enough to make me very nervous while any-where near the First Scion. During the subsequent ceremonial welcome and reception, I smiled a lot, said little, and stuck close to the sojourn team. Captain Pnor found the Furinacs' extremely formal reception fascinating. Jorenians loved pomp and ceremony.

We had to stand through everything. I found it made my feet hurt.

From the reception, we were taken into a huge chamber where a feast had been prepared. Feast? There was enough food weighing down the banquet platforms to feed half the planet. Of course, half the planet showed up for the feast, so that worked out well.

I was given a seat of honor, at the Patriarch's right hand. Not that I got to use it right away. We stood there while a prayer of Sanctification was made. A very long, flowery, repetitive prayer. By the time we sat down, the Patriarch was beginning to look tired. My footgear felt like lead casings. I glanced sideways at the being who ruled millions.

"May I ask you a personal question, Patriarch?"

He bent his head toward me. "Of course."

"Do you really like all this—this"—I waved my hand at the elaborate decorations, crowded room, and sumptuous mountains of food—"stuff?"

He buzzed a quiet chuckle, and shook his head. "No, I do not, Dr. Torin. However, when I was First Scion, and my Patriarch ruled Furin, the ceremonies lasted *twice* as long." His buzz became a soft whisper. "It is also why I enjoy traveling by much less conventional methods, and visiting other worlds with less—stuff."

I grinned at him. "So I won't be thrown in a Furinac dungeon for my less-than-formal attitude toward you, Your Magnificence?"

"Please, Doctor." He looked pained. "Your casual friendship has been an absolute joy for me!" He sighed. "I fear I am not anticipating the next month with pleasure."

"Why not?"

"It takes that long to go through all the ceremonial welcoming," he said.

A month of all this, every day? I had an idea. "Want your doctor to fix that?"

He beamed at me. "Would you?"

"I trust you'll keep me out of the dungeon if I mess this up," I said, and got to my feet. I clapped my hands, effectively silencing every voice in the room. "Good and loyal subjects of the Patriarch! I wish to address you regarding His Magnificence's health!"

You could have heard a pin drop after that.

"As you know, the Patriarch underwent two major surgeries during his journey with us," I said. "His recovery has been remarkable." I could see they wanted to cheer, so I held up my hand. "As His Magnificence's Surgeon, I must insist your ruler be allowed as much rest as possible. The healing process takes a great deal of strength, and he must conserve his now." I scanned the room and noted the rapt faces of the Furinacs, all fixed on their sovereign. They really did love the old guy. "My standing orders are for the Patriarch to remain resting, quiet, and most of all, *undisturbed.* Will you assure that my orders are carried out?"

The buzzing cries of joyous agreement nearly shorted out my vocollar. The Patriarch grasped my hand and tugged me down close to his proboscis.

"For this gift, my dear Doctor, I may marry you myself!"

I escorted the Patriarch almost immediately from the banquet to his City Palace a short distance away. We were accompanied by an armed honor guard of hundreds. The Royal Conveyance, a Furinac version of the glidecar, hummed through the air. Other Furinacs, who I was amazed to find were fully capable of sustained flight on their own, hovered in precise patterns around their sovereign's vehicle. Captain Pnor, Reever, and Dhreen came along in a second vehicle.

While the First Scion spouted an endless litany to the glory of my intelligence, compassion, and beauty, the Patriarch and I shared the view and exchanged brief conversation whenever his heir took a breath. When I saw the City Palace, I whistled.

"Nice house," I said to the ruler.

"Glad you like it," he replied. He was enjoying himself immensely, even (to the barely concealed horror of his heir) using my abbreviated forms of speech. "Wait until you see the Royal Chambers."

Royal they were. Half the interior of the palace was devoted to the Patriarch's quarters. But I didn't pay attention to all the luxurious surroundings at first. My elderly patient's strength was waning fast.

I helped him past all the staff (another thousand or so devoted subjects) and got him to his bed. Once he dismissed the First Scion, we had a few moments alone.

"You are a clever and innovative young female, Dr. Torin. I shall remain in your debt for the balance of my existence." He buzzed with relief as he sank back on his dais, equal in size to our launch. I climbed up, crawled across and knelt next to him so I could run a few scans.

"Your vitals are good, but not where they should be." I put the scanner aside and checked his abdomen. "Everything is healing well, and will continue to, if you listen to your doctor and rest."

"I suppose you would refuse to become my adopted Second Scion, too," he said. I pulled the immaculate linens over him. "Wouldn't you?"

"I've already been adopted by the Jorenians, Patriarch." I shuffled backward until I found the edge of the immense dais and got to my feet. "Thanks for asking, though. Get some sleep now. I'll stop in to check on you in a few hours."

"My eternal thanks, Doctor."

CHAPTER THIRTEEN

The Third Suicide

Outside the Royal Chamber, a few dozen guards and personal staff members were waiting, along with Pnor, Dhreen, and Reever. The Captain was deep in conversation with one of the Patriarch's attendants. Dhreen hovered near one of the thousands of bejeweled panels curving around the Patriarch's door, closely appraising the inlay.

Reever was waiting for me.

"Please see that the Patriarch is not disturbed," I told the guards, then strolled down the wide, endless corridor winding toward the back of the City Palace. Reever kept pace with me. When we were out of listening range, I glanced at him. "Are you staying?"

"I have considered it."

We passed several portraits of the Patriarch and his ancestors, each nearly twenty meters high and ten meters wide. The material used as paint had a faint metallic glitter to it. On closer examination, I realized precious stones had been ground up and used as individual pigments.

"That gives new meaning to the term *priceless.*"

Reever simply waited without comment. We walked on.

"The Patriarch could probably use a linguist on his staff. The accommodations are beyond luxurious." He wasn't saying anything. "They'd probably even give you your own palace to call home."

"I have no home."

We had reached a darkened portion of the corridor when Reever put a hand on my elbow and pulled me to a halt.

There was only one reason for that. Immediately I flattened a hand against his chest.

"I can't, Reever."

His hand hovered just above my hair. "Just this once."

I didn't fight the link, but I didn't help him, either. His hands came around me, spreading over my back to press me against him. I just stood there, my head tucked beneath his chin, wondering where the words were that would tell Duncan Reever how I felt about this whole mess.

I've missed you, Duncan. I didn't know why I thought that. It seemed to come out of nowhere.

You and Xonea will find happiness, Cherijo.

Hardly. I'm leaving him when we reach Joren. I felt him stiffen in shock. *I don't love him, Duncan. I only did this to keep him from being put off the ship. Did you really expect me to stick around and have his kids?*

I did not know your plans.

I'm leaving the Sunlace *when we reach their homeworld. Squilyp will be ready to take over as Senior Healer by then. Dhreen agreed to get a transport and take me wherever I want to go.*

Where?

Somewhere the League can't find me. I reached back and pressed my fingers to his cheek. *Want to come with us? With me?*

Cherijo. He turned me around. *I want to tell you . . .*

Something intruded on the connection we shared, and I frowned. *Duncan? Did you hear that?*

Yes. Someone is approaching us.

Our link faded away as we stepped back from each other. I heard a faint click and electronic hum. A guard? Reever stepped in front of me, shielding me with his larger form.

"Show yourself," he said.

The Patriarch's heir emerged from the shadows. "Step aside, Terran."

I stood on my toes and peeked over Reever's shoulder. The Furinac looked a lot different from the devoted heir who only hours before had begged me to marry him. Matrimony might not be a part of his agenda now. I wasn't sure why I felt that way. Maybe it was the large pulse rifle Junior held, aimed directly at Reever's skull.

Reever didn't flick an eyelash. "First Scion, may I help you?"

"Step aside!" The Furinac gestured with his weapon.

"I think not."

"Silence! Give the woman to me at once!"

I'd been a little too trusting of the Furinac. "I'm not his to give, First Scion." I stepped to the side and came around Reever. "Why do you want me?"

"Cherijo." He grabbed my arm. "He means to kill you."

That was my impression, too. The Furinac raised and sighted down the barrel of the rifle now pointed at my skull. I put out my hands, palm up, the universal gesture of friendship. It was definitely time to start making friends.

"First Scion, have I offended you in some way? Why are you doing this?" And how much was the League paying him?

"I'd like to know, too." Dhreen suddenly materialized out of nowhere, to the right of the heir. He wasn't armed, but his sudden appearance seemed to stun the Furinac. Dhreen gave me an exasperated look. "Doc, what is it with you and weapon-carrying assassins?"

"It's a gift, Dhreen," I said.

Reever frowned. "Perhaps the Patriarch's heir will be good enough to explain why he feels he must murder the physician who saved his parent's life."

"Yes! You saved him!" The heir flung the words at me.

That puzzled me. "Of course I did. What did you expect me to do? Let him die?"

"Why did you have to save him? You could have let him go with dignity!" He flicked the firing mechanism to ready. "Now all my plans were ruined!"

"Preserving life is my job, First Scion." I used the soothing tone I would have with a terrified patient. "Why don't you tell us about these plans of yours? Maybe we can help sort the whole thing out." And nail whoever was killing people on board the *Sunlace*.

"You already have the evidence, do you not?" The barrel of the weapon shook slightly. "It took months to convince him to leave Furin. Hire men to track his movements. Arrange the transport accident. All that work and time and investment—for nothing!"

It had nothing to do with the League, after all. Some

devoted heir he was. Maybe if I could prod him a little, Junior would get loud enough to attract some attention. Some of those ten thousand guards had to be hanging around here somewhere.

"He's your parent, First Scion, and obviously loves you very much," I said. "How could you even think of harming him?"

"He has outlasted his rule!" the Furinac screeched. "I should be Patriarch now! If I wait for him to die, I will be too old and sick to rule! As he is now!"

That was more like it. If Junior kept this decibel level up, the whole Palace staff would come running. I gave him my best confused look. "But why kill me? Why not go shoot him?"

"She Who Preserves All Life." The Furinac sneered. "When they find your body with that of my dead parent, they will call you Assassin Who Wore a Cloak of Lies."

"No, Scion. That is what *you* shall be called."

The Patriarch's heir gasped, his proboscis bobbling as he turned his head. Out of the shadows stepped the Patriarch himself, Captain Pnor, and a group of armed guards. No one looked very happy or welcoming now.

"Put down the weapon," one of the guards said.

First Scion made a sort of buzzing yelp of dismay. The weapon in his hands swung from me to the Patriarch to me again.

"Hi, Patriarch." I had to get the rifle away from this idiot before someone got a hole blown through them. "Thought I ordered you to stay in bed."

"Doctor Torin, Linguist Reever, Pilot Dhreen." The elderly Furinac didn't sound shaken at all. "I must apologize for my heir's discourteous manner and reckless behavior."

"Do not distress yourself, Patriarch," Reever replied. "No harm has been done."

"Distress yourself, Patriarch," I said. I wasn't as detached as Reever. "If you hadn't shown up, a lot of harm might have been done by Junior here." *Still* might be done.

"Yes. Doctor, I confess I am as much responsible for this as my heir. At the reception, I mentioned to several of my people that you and Linguist Reever had evidence as to the identity of an assassin." The old ruler was doing a great job of faking calm confidence. I could see his appendages trembling. All part of the job, I guessed. "I had my suspicions, but to discover the attempt on my life was orchestrated by my own child . . ." He stared at his heir and shook his head slowly.

First Scion looked ready to weep. Or shoot someone. Probably both.

"How did you know someone was trying to kill you, Patriarch?" I edged a step toward First Scion as he stared blindly at the old ruler.

"We examined the shuttle thoroughly after the accident," Reever said for him. He glanced at me. Saw what I had in mind. He turned back to the heir, and moved a step so that his body blocked the movement of mine. "You arranged to have the flightshield generator sabotaged, didn't you?"

"It should have destroyed the ship!" Junior said. What a prince.

"Apparently the pilot discovered the malfunction just prior to failure," Reever said. "He transitioned, ejected the generator before it reached critical mass, and deliberately flew into the meteor swarm."

"Too bad he perished," Dhreen said, watching me, too. "Sounds like my variety of jaunter."

Another few feet and I would be within reach of the weapon. If only the First Scion wouldn't remember he wanted to shoot me first.

"The pilot did so on my orders," the Patriarch said. "We did not know if the generator had genuinely failed, or had been deliberately sabotaged in order to render the ship vulnerable to attack, or kill me. In my position, I must assume the worst. I very much regret the sacrifice of his life."

"A dangerous way to camouflage a crippled vessel." Captain Pnor made an eloquent gesture, drawing First Scion's attention now. I loved it when men were supportive and worked together. Especially when I was trying to disarm someone. "A most effective method, as well."

"It does not matter!" The heir finally cracked. "Your rule is finished, Old One Who Should Be Enriching Our Soil! I will end it mys—"

Last chance. As the heir swung back in my direction, I threw myself forward. I hit the rifle just as he fired. Impact angled the barrel up toward the domed ceiling. A loud boom echoed as the energy pulse hit. Gilded masonry dust rained down on us in a glimmering shower. We wrestled the weapon between us.

"Let go!" I yelled.

I heard guards running toward us. Great. I was about to be squashed between the good guys and the bad guy.

"I will kill you!"

"You—had your—chance!" I hooked my leg around his lower appendages and threw myself forward. The rifle fired again. My face was so close to the beam I felt the heat sear my cheekbone. We went down together, both of us landing on our sides.

He lunged. I dodged, and narrowly avoided being stabbed in the throat by his sharp proboscis. So he didn't want to play fair. Fine.

I slammed my elbow into the crevice between his hinge-plating. Junior screamed, but didn't let go. The end of the rifle was between our faces. I jabbed him again, trying to avoid his digestive compartment. No way was I going to operate on this jerk.

"Give it up!" I said, rolling on top of him. I wasn't heavy enough to keep him pinned, but he was weaker now. His breath rasped through his spiracles with an audible whistle. I managed to press the weapon closer to his face than mine.

"The Doctor is correct, Once Scion," I heard the old ruler say. "Release your weapon."

"Once Scion?" The heir's tone buzzed with new horror.

"Daddy's upset with you, Junior," I said. I kept him down, but he had a death-clutch on the rifle. Guards swiftly formed a ring around us. No one tried to interfere. The business end of the weapon was still too close to our faces. "Do what he says, maybe you can be Prince again."

"I will be Patriarch," he said.

"No, pal," I said, jerking on the weapon. No effect. "If you want to get out of this one, think floor-kissing. Lots of floor-kissing."

"She Who Preserves All Life," the former heir said, then buzzed out a faint chuckle. "I will deny you this one." His appendage slipped down the rifle case. "And tomorrow you will be dead."

I couldn't take my hands off the rifle. I heard the triggering mechanism click.

"No!" I screamed.

The Patriarch's heir jammed the nozzle beneath his proboscis. As the weapon fired, I jerked my face away and squeezed my eyes shut.

His head exploded, an inch away from mine.

That night Reever put aside his squeamishness and helped me remove the dead heir's remains from my upper torso. He stayed with me, too. I suppose all the vomiting I did was the reason. Patiently I explained I wasn't the squeamish type. I just had a problem combing brain and exoskeletal matter out of my hair.

I was in good shape, considering I'd nearly had *my* head blown off. One proximity burn on my left cheekbone. An empty stomach. Nerves that were shattered. Otherwise, I was just peachy.

I fell asleep watching him watch me. When I woke the next morning, he still occupied the same chair beside my bed.

"Are you well?" he asked me, sounding tired. I nodded. He rose and left. Well, Reever never was one for a profusion of words.

We departed Furin that same day. It was a decidedly silent sojourn team that made our very brief farewells, minus all ceremony, and returned to the launch.

I was as quiet and blank-faced as Reever. Having someone's face blow up under your nose left a sobering impression. Pnor seemed more disturbed by the First Scion's muttering about my dying after him than anything else.

Even Dhreen didn't say much, until something slammed into the launch. Then he cursed. If we hadn't been wearing our rigging, the impact would have sent all of us flying across the cabin.

"*Sunlace,* sojourn launch is under attack!" Dhreen began weaving and dodging through multiple yellow-orange blast beams. "*Sunlace,* advise!"

"Dhreen, four additional mercenary vessels converging on your position!" Xonea's voice came over the helm console.

What was Xonea doing at the helm?

My ClanBrother snapped out more orders. "*Sunlace* will

intercept in three minutes—you must divert to emergency route now!''

"Execute crash-landing procedures!" Pnor said to the team as he released his rigging. He took position behind Dhreen, who was frantically compensating for the attacking ship and attempting to avoid the others closing in.

The rest of us prepped the launch by rigging anything that moved with extra restraints. The launch was rocking wildly now. We had to anchor ourselves to the overhead grips to keep our balance. Once geared up, we strapped ourselves back into the rigging.

Pnor was bending over the display, speaking in a low, urgent tone to Xonea.

"Reever?" I said. He had moved to sit next to me. "Lie to me. Tell me we're going to make it."

He dipped his head and murmured, "Don't worry, it will be quick."

"Lie to me anyway."

Displacer fire was getting heavier. Pnor had closed the viewports and was giving the Oenrallian navigation coordinates from the helm display. The launch shuddered violently when something slammed into the port-side hull panels. An automated warning rang out.

"Caution. Launch hull tolerance range has been exceeded. Caution. Launch hull tolerance range has been exceeded."

The hiss of our interior atmosphere escaping into space was immediate and loud. After a brief argument, Pnor switched places with Dhreen. The Oenrallian was swearing in his native language when he came back to don emergency gear.

"That stubborn old scrapper!" Dhreen said as he slid the pack straps over his shoulders. "Thinks he can outfly me!"

"He is the Captain," Reever said. "He can."

"Hull breach!" the display's audio blared. "Emergency measures! Hull breach! Emergency measures . . ."

"Put your breathers on!" I yelled over the audio loop to the others. I turned, hooked an arm around Reever's neck, and kissed him. His lips were cold against mine. Then I yanked his breather over his face. I turned to the helm. "Captain!"

He didn't respond. Pnor was too busy flying through the

mercenaries' salvos. He also wasn't wearing any emergency gear.

I released my rigging, grabbed a pack and stumbled toward him. At that moment, a heavy blast struck the launch squarely, throwing me into an interior component panel. The burn on my left cheek exploded with pain. Hot sparks rained down over me.

The starboard hull plate was slowly bulging out. I heard the Jorenian alloys screaming, connectors tearing. Had to get to him—had to—

"Pnor!" I screamed with my last breath.

The hull plate crumpled. The sudden change in pressure discharged the launch's artificial atmosphere into space. I would have been sucked through the gap myself, but someone grabbed my hair and the back of my tunic and hauled me back. My breather was shoved down over my face.

Pnor.

I looked at the helm display, and saw in horror that the Captain had harnessed himself to the seat. He was still guiding the launch, though his body was spasming violently.

Gravity was gone. My body floated weightless above the launch deck. When I turned my head, I saw Reever was holding on to me. He was the one who had pulled me back. Where there had just been a twenty-foot section of hull was now a jagged-edge hole. Through it, I saw the looming profile of the *Sunlace*.

Were we going to make it?

The launch careened against the bay portal, then slid over the threshold, skidding over the *Sunlace*'s deck. Gravity reinstated itself and I fell, hard.

Reever held me up. I had my breather off and was at the helm in another heartbeat.

Pnor had managed to guide us in just before decompression burst his lungs. Green blood streamed from every orifice. His hands were still clenched over the controls.

The Captain was dead.

There was no time to grieve, the ship was still under attack. Xonea had taken over command, operating from level twenty-one. He took the news about Pnor without a blink. I didn't have time to wait for a reaction, or find out why my confined-to-quarters ClanBrother was suddenly running the ship. After a quick scan to assure the sojourn team had suffered no ill-effects, I ran to Medical.

The bay was in a state of controlled bedlam. I found Squilyp, who stopped shouting out orders long enough to report.

"Casualties are coming in from all decks. They're not being particular about where they hit us this time. We should be transitioning right about—"

Reality twisted. We both found ourselves, along with a number of nurses, on the deck.

"—now," he said, and groaned.

"We better step up the practice drills," I said, and pushed myself up on my elbows.

"There is blood on your face." The Omorr nodded at my cheek.

The burn from the rifle blast had split open when I'd tried to get to Pnor. I swiped at it with my tunic sleeve. "Remind me to make you go on the next sojourn."

"Your team arrived without incident?"

"We made it. All but the Captain." My raw voice earned me a grimace of sympathy. "Come on." I helped him up. "How many have been brought in so far?"

"Twenty. There will be more." He indicated the serious cases that were separated from the minor injuries. "These four first." He grabbed my arm when I would have started for them. "One of them wants to die, Senior Healer."

Not on my ward. "Keep the nurses out of there for now."

Two of the four required surgery at once. I shouted for the teams to prepare and scanned the other two. They could wait. I sedated them and went to the first surgical patient.

Squilyp told me a feedback had created an explosion in the huge banks of tech that ran the ship's automatic functions. The data programmer's face and arms were horribly burned, and she had massive respiratory damage.

"This is Healer Cherijo," I said as I bent close to her ravaged face. "We're going to take you into surgery. Don't be afraid, we're going to help you. Blink once if you understand."

She blinked her scalded eyelids once. I administered sedation, then moved to the next patient.

He was groaning miserably. A terrible gash across his torso revealed half his internal organs. White eyes opened when I touched him.

"My . . . Speaker . . ."

"Is busy fighting mercenaries," I said. So this was the one who wanted to die. "What is your name, ClanCousin?"

"Yetlo . . ."

"Yetlo, I'm going to take care of you. You are not going to embrace so much as an optic light today. Got it?"

"My . . . right . . ."

"I have decided to render my assistance," a familiar voice said from behind me.

I closed my eyes briefly. "One second, Yetlo." I straightened and turned. "Get out of my Medical Bay. Now."

Rogan stood there, cleaner than I'd ever seen him. Not that it made a big improvement.

"You need help. Your resident can't keep up with the injured."

"The day I consider you help, Rogan, tell them to shoot me into a star, all right? *Leave.*"

"Doctor." Squilyp joined Rogan. "We could use the hands."

I eyed the Omorr. "Fine," I said. "Then he's your responsibility. He does not assess patients. Let him suture and dress wounds. Keep a nurse on him while you're in surgery to make sure he doesn't screw that up."

Rogan didn't like that, and opened his four lips to tell me so. The Omorr grabbed him and pulled him away.

"Thank you, Senior Healer," Squilyp called out over Rogan's protests.

"You're not welcome," I called back. I bent to Yetlo again. "As you can see, I have enough problems without you wanting to die on me, ClanCousin. What do you say?"

He looked stubborn. "I . . . want . . . my . . . Spe—" His head lolled to one side as he lost consciousness.

"Oops." Had I accidentally administered the sedation before he could tell me what he wanted? It seemed I had. What a shame. Perhaps Yetlo had been asking for a speech therapist. A nurse appeared beside me, already geared for surgery. "Prep him."

"He asked for Eternity, Senior Healer."

Another one. I drew myself up to my full height and did an imitation of Joseph Grey Veil.

"He didn't ask me, nurse. Prep him, now."

While I was scrubbing, Xonea sent an emergency signal to Medical and had one of the residents pull me out of prep. I trotted over to the display, already scowling. The strong, glowering face staring back at me didn't improve my mood.

"What?"

"Status report," Xonea said. I gave him a brief outline of the casualties and indicated I was going into surgery. "Your hands?"

"I'll be fine." I wasn't so sure, but I wasn't going to tell him that. "Next time you want status, talk to one of the nurses."

"I wanted to see you were unharmed." He smiled briefly. "Command out."

Surgery was a bit crowded. Squilyp and I operated simultaneously on the two critical patients, our tables side by side. We shared the scrub team between us, enabling more staffers to deal with the overcrowded ward outside.

I had to repair fissures in Yetlo's chest cavity and clean up shards from a half dozen broken ribs. After a quick scan, I found a sizeable bone shard lodged in the wall of his heart. This was not my lucky day.

"How are you doing?" I said to the Omorr.

"I've performed a lobectomy where her alveoli were scorched," he replied. "Her bronchus on the remaining side is compromised in three areas. The tracheostomy tube will have to be permanent."

"Trach's gone?"

"What's left isn't viable."

"Preserve tissue samples. We'll clone the fibrous and muscle tissue the same way we did those Furinac stomachs." I swore under my breath as I visually located the bone shard. As it was now, there was only a vestige of cardiac hemorrhaging. Removing it would be like taking a cork from a bottle. "Yetlo, you are really beginning to aggravate me."

Squilyp's dark eyes looked up over his mask at me. "Heart?"

"Yeah. He's got a chunk of rib bone stuck in the right

ventricle. I yank it out, he's going to rupture on me." I straightened and let the nurse blot the sweat from my eyes. "We're looking at another four hours here with the open-heart procedure." I turned and gave the team instructions to begin cooling Yetlo down. Once we put him on the heart/lung supplanter, I could work on the damaged ventricle.

"I can cover the ward," the Omorr said.

"I'm not worried about that." I flexed my hands painfully. "You may have to take over cutting for me."

Squilyp stared at my hands. "Can you leave your patient for a minute?"

"Yeah." I had finished repairing the damage internally, all but the heart. "Start reducing body temperature," I said to the scrub nurse, and stepped around the table.

The Omorr gave orders to the assistant beside him. She began suctioning blood from his patient's chest cavity. My eyebrows elevated when he stripped off his gloves and hopped over to me.

"Did I accidentally challenge you to a fight again, or something?" I asked.

"No." He looked amused. "Give me your hands."

I held up my bloody gloves. "My hands?"

"Yes. Remove the gloves first."

Puzzled, I did as he asked. His membranes took hold of my fingers. His flesh felt odd, almost hot as he touched me.

"Uh, Squilyp? What's going on?" I could see me making some kind of accidental betrothal here. I seemed to be an expert at that.

"Close your eyes. I'm going to heal you."

I scoffed out some air. "In your dreams."

"I mean it." He sounded peeved. "You know my people practice touch healing. Close your eyes."

Reluctantly I shut my eyelids. His touch was growing uncomfortably hot now. "This hurts," I said. "Don't you think I have enough problems?"

"Shut up." He said something my vocollar didn't translate. "Visualize your hands as they were before the injuries. Remember what you could do with them."

I pictured myself performing surgery on Hado Torin. Then my fingers had flown so fast I'd extracted and re-placed a cardiac valve in less than three minutes.

"Yes. There is the power. I can sense it," he murmured. I peeked through my lashes. His gildrells flared, and made snakelike undulations. "I enable you with your power."

"Squilyp—"

"Believe."

The word seemed to echo in my chest. *Believe. Believe.*

Okay. I believed. Only my hands were burning again. I sucked in a quick, sharp breath, and squeezed my eyes shut.

"The pain is the healing," he said. "Take the pain. Make it yours to command. Force it back where it came from."

I concentrated. The scrub teams were whispering, distracting me. "Quiet, people."

I saw my hands in Hado's chest. Saw his heart being repaired. I could have that again. I *had* to have it.

The burning sensation faded. Neuropraxic tingling remained in its wake. The tingling became a warm, pleasant flush. Squilyp released me. We opened our eyes and stared at each other.

My hands should have been numb, so I looked down and shook them, then flexed my fingers in dumbfounded shock.

"It worked." My head snapped up. "Squilyp, it *worked*!" To prove my claim, I reached over and picked up a clamp and twirled it through my fingers. The instrument became a smooth, blurred circle of movement.

He nodded and looked at his own membranes. "Belief is a power unto itself."

"If that's all it takes," I said, grinning, "then why did we bother going to medtech?"

"Beliefs require faith. Certification boards do not."

I laughed. Leaned over. Kissed him right smack on the gildrells. I never knew the Omorr could blush.

Thirty-six hours and ten operations later, I let the nurses chase me from Medical and stumbled down two levels to my quarters. My rooms were darkened when I opened the door panel. Cautiously I peeked in to see if Xonea had left a new gauntlet of obstacles for me to trip over.

Jenner padded over and gave me the once-over. *Late again?* He raised his chin to my tired fingers, and sniffed at me. *There's blood on your hands.* Big blue eyes regarded me solemnly. *Why don't you ever bring home your kills for me to share?*

I sat down in a chair, trying to work up enough ambition

to head for the cleanser. A nerve in my neck twitched, and I rubbed my hand over it. Everything seemed fuzzy. I should have turned on the lights.

A low whisper startled me. "Cherijo?"

"No, it's a half-ton Hsktskt killer. Got any weapons?" I was too weary to do more than stand and start peeling off my tunic. "Sorry. I didn't mean to wake you up."

Twelve warm blue fingers were suddenly undressing me. Xonea didn't adjust the lighting as he helped me out of my tunic.

"I can't see anything," I said as he dressed me in my favorite undershirt. Yawning became a chore.

Smooth lips gently touched my injured cheek as he placed me on the sleeping platform. His hands stroked down my back.

"I'm really tired," I said, hoping that would be enough to convince him to leave me alone.

"I know, little one," his low voice whispered. "I will do everything."

Little one? Xonea never called me that. Suddenly a hand was between my thighs. The other on my breast. Hot breath scalded my face.

"No." I struggled, and the caressing fingers became cruel and bruising. "No!"

A fist slammed into my face.

I was pitched out of the sleeping platform onto the floor. Everything went grey for a few seconds. I heard running steps. The door panel opened and closed. No, I couldn't let him get away, I thought, and pushed myself up on my elbows. The door panel opened and closed again. The interior lights snapped on.

"Cherijo?" Xonea saw me on the floor. "Cherijo!"

When he reached for me, I cowered. Gentle hands carefully lifted me to my feet. That was when I realized I was shaking all over.

"Xonea."

He pressed me against his chest, tucked me under his chin. Slowly he rocked me in his embrace. "You are safe, Cherijo. You are safe now."

The only thing I could say I repeated, over and over. "I thought it was you. I thought it was you."

*   *   *

No one challenged Xonea's right to assume command of the *Sunlace*. Pnor's ruling, I learned, became void at the moment of his death. Someone else would have to accuse Xonea of trying to kill me before he could be removed from command. No one did that, either. Apparently my Choosing Xonea had convinced the crew the whole banishment thing had been a mistake.

Since Xonea suspected the Furinac First Scion had betrayed our position to the League, our convoluted course to Joren was immediately altered and recharted. His first official act as Captain. His second was to schedule all Senior crew members for a strategy session. I was to report to the meeting as well.

Xonea told me about it as I was getting dressed for work.

"What about the murderer, and Rogan? What are you going to do about them?"

"Defense planning must take priority."

I didn't agree. "Xonea, you can't ignore this problem and hope it'll go away."

"I will deal with it."

I wasn't going to pick a fight with him. "All right. But I don't know why you need me to attend this meeting. Ship defense isn't my area of expertise."

"Your input will be valuable."

"What input? All I can say is stuff like, 'Don't stand there bleeding when you get hit, report to Medical.'" I pulled my tunic straight and sat down at my vanity console to attack my snarled hair. "I'm not a combat veteran, like some people I know."

"Stop. You are making it worse." Xonea came up to stand behind me and took the brush from my fingers. "As Senior Healer, your presence is mandatory."

I sighed and sat there as he patiently detangled my knots. "What sort of strategy are we talking here?"

He chose his words carefully. "There is a main item to my agenda: our current response to the League threat. Pnor felt swift retreat alone was the appropriate response to these mercenary attacks."

"And you don't."

"No. The *Sunlace* was commissioned by our HouseClan primarily for extended deep-space survey. The ship is not, however, defenseless. I will invite opinion on our current procedures, and propose changes."

He might have sounded all Captainish saying that, but I knew what was behind the words. After all, the man had a warrior's knot in his hair. Pnor, I suddenly recalled, had never worn one.

"Changes that include fighting back."

"If the Senior crew members agree," he said, "yes."

"Hooray for democracy. I may have something to contribute to this meeting after all." Such as how many more casualties we could expect if the *Sunlace* did return fire. "Where and when are you having this meeting, so I can be sure to be late?"

"Tomorrow morning before your shift begins. You will not be late. I will escort you myself."

"Gee, Captain, what's next? Time drones?"

His lips quirked as he separated my now-smooth hair into three sections. "If necessary. You do seem to have an abhorrence to punctuality."

"I have an abhorrence to a lot of things." I shivered as the frightening assault replayed in my mind. "What are we going to do about last night?"

His eyes met mine in the mirror. "I will assure it does not happen again."

"You can't baby-sit me forever."

"I will find the traitor," he said. His hands skillfully wove the long black strands into a braided cable. A rather *tight* cable. "Until then, you will not be left alone."

It was time to be blunt. I waited until he took his hands off my head. I liked my hair attached to my scalp. "Xonea, we need to access my memories."

"You were drugged," he said.

I bit my lip, then jumped in the rest of the way. "Reever was able to get to them once before. He can do it again—"

Xonea grabbed my braid and used it to pull my head back. Upside-down, he still looked furious. "No. I forbid you to do this."

"You're being unreasonable, Xonea. Reever—"

"No!" Xonea shouted. I found myself yanked out of the seat and spun around. "Duncan Reever did not Choose you. I did!"

So he was angry. He wasn't alone. "Choice has nothing to do with this!"

A muscle in his jaw twitched as he glared down at me. "Stay away from him, Cherijo." Dark rage transformed his features. Maybe becoming Captain made him think he could order me around. He needed a wake-up call.

"You don't own me, Xonea."

"You will do as you are told!"

"How many more people have to die before *you* do something?"

He flung me away from him. Not a shove. Not a push. I literally flew through the air, and landed on the sleeping platform ten feet away. What the hell was wrong with him? Getting the wind knocked out of me didn't improve my mood. As soon as I could, I sat up to blast him.

Too late. Xonea was already out the door.

I shoved myself off my bed and locked the door. A few moments later, the door panel chimed. Sorry for tossing me across the room, was he? I went to the console, slammed my fist into it, and planted myself in front of the opening door.

Darea stood there with Fasala.

"We thought to invite you and Xonea for a meal . . ." Darea looked over her shoulder. Apparently my raging roommate had passed her in the corridor. "Perhaps another time—"

"No. I mean, come in, please." I stepped aside, and forced a smile for Fasala's sake. "You know how it is once the honeymoon is over."

Darea looked puzzled. "What is a honeymoon?"

"What I'm not having today. Come in, sit down for a minute."

Jenner, who had been hiding during all the fireworks, came out to inspect my visitors. Fasala went into raptures at once, and soon the pair were playing a vigorous game of catch the toy mouse. I smiled at their antics.

"We would not have intruded on your privacy, had we known, Senior Healer," the Jorenian woman said.

"It's okay. I just don't think Xonea and I will be accepting invitations to visit anyone in the near future," I said. "I suppose you and Salo never argue."

"On the contrary. My bondmate can be extremely obstinate, nonverbal, and often forgets to equally participate in parenting activities." She made a short, rather direct gesture. "I merely remind him I am his mate, not his drone."

I tried to imagine Salo and Darea quarreling. "Are your furnishings made out of plasteel?"

"No," she said, and smiled. "There have been rare incidents of . . . damaging them. It is better than harming each other."

Maybe Xonea should talk to Salo. He could have seriously injured me with that thoughtless little toss. "Your Senior Healer sincerely agrees."

"It is part of the bond. Salo is a fine warrior and communications officer, but there are moments he is simply a man," Darea said. "As I am sometimes sorely lacking in patience."

"I could use some lessons on how to live with a Jorenian man."

Darea stood and beckoned to Fasala. "Come to our quarters after your shift concludes," she said. "Xonea need not accompany you. You may observe how I live with Salo and still maintain my sanity."

"I accept," I said on impulse. Some of my furnishings *were* going to end up damaged, I thought, if I didn't try something.

I walked my visitors out to the corridor. No sign of Xonea. After confirming a time with Darea, I went to work.

Medical Bay was operating at full capacity. I walked in to find Rogan in deep discussion with one of the nurses. Apparently he was very interested in knowing the hierarchy structure of the *Sunlace*. He was muttering words like "incompetent" and "mutant specimen." He didn't realize a Jorenian was usually too polite to comment on inappropriate or rude behavior from someone considered a guest. When he saw me, he went into auto-sneer.

"Dr. Torin," Rogan said. And here I thought he was going to address me as *incompetent mutant specimen*.

"Squilyp?" I yelled as I stood there and watched him. The Omorr appeared from the ward and looked from Rogan to me.

"Senior Healer?"

"Status report, please."

Squilyp recited the bed count, various stages of recovery of the critical patients, and projected discharges.

"You have a problem working a half-shift more on rotation?" I asked the Omorr. He shook his head. "Good." I addressed the nurse. "Nurse, go change someone's dressing." Then I turned to my smelly problem. "Dr. Rogan, your services are no longer required. Thank you for your assistance during the crisis. Get out."

"I will apply to the Captain for a medical position," he said as he strode past me. His polyps were whirring madly, making a sly, whispering hiss drift behind him. "He should be informed I have twice your experience. We shall see who gets out then, Doctor."

Rogan as Senior Healer? I'd blow up the damn ship first. Something of what I felt must have shown in my expression. Nurses scattered. Patients pretended unconsciousness. Even the Omorr took a nervous step backward.

"Oh, relax!" I said to Squilyp. "Let's take a look at Yetlo. Might as well let everyone who wants to take a shot at me do it now."

Yetlo Torin was making excellent progress, considering I'd patched up a hole in his ventricle big enough to fly a starshuttle through. The jagged chest wound showed no signs of infection. His surgery had been completely successful. All indications of a full recovery.

Well, there was one hitch. He still wanted his Speaker.

"My . . . right . . ." he croaked the words out as I passed the scanner over him. "Bring . . . Speaker . . ."

Beyond my shoulder, the Omorr suddenly got very busy checking the already perfectly functioning monitor.

"Yetlo. Your scans look very promising. Odds are you're going to be just fine."

"Speaker . . ." he said.

Stubborn man. "Yetlo, as your physician, I'll go out on a limb and guarantee you will recover. You'll recover if I have to sit and hold your hand until the day you're ready to walk out of here. Satisfied?"

He frowned at me. "Why . . . deny . . . me?"

"Why?" I pursed my lips and consulted the deck overhead. "I don't know, maybe it's because I dislike my patients committing suicide. Especially after I've spent six hours with my hands in their chests. Call it my little quirk."

I could see he didn't understand. I didn't understand, either. What was so alluring about death? It came soon enough for most beings. I'd seen two men kill themselves already. I had no intention of letting Yetlo become number three. Enough was enough.

I put a hand on his healing chest. Beneath my palm, his repaired heart beat slow and strong. "Feel that? It's life. Should something so precious be so easily disposed of? Don't throw it away, Yetlo. Embrace your *life*."

When he would have spoken, I pressed a finger to his lips.

"Senior Healer," Squilyp said. He sounded nervous. I glanced back, and saw a whole row of Jorenian nurses standing beyond him. They were whispering back and forth.

Not this again.

Adaola stepped forward. "Senior Healer, this patient has repeatedly expressed his wish to embrace the stars. We cannot disregard his request."

"Watch me," I said, and turned back to Yetlo. If reason didn't work, maybe blackmail would. I grabbed his hand and pressed it against my throat. "Feel that, Yetlo? That's *my* life. I love my life." I bent closer. "I've never wanted to give up my life."

"You are . . . not . . . me. . . ."

"I know that. But, if you Jorenians are right, what's the point in prolonging *my* life? Death is just another journey. You're not making this one alone. If you divert your path, I'm going with you."

Squilyp made a strangled sound. One of the nurses stifled a small cry. Patients who could hear me began sitting up in the berths. Yetlo's hand tensed under mine.

"That's right. If you die, pal, so will I. In fact, why should I wait for you? I'll go first." I stared into his widened eyes as I called out, "Nurse! Bring me a syrinpress." I smiled at Yetlo. "Have you ever seen a perfectly healthy human die of a myocardial infarction, Yetlo? Watch this." I turned my head when the nurse arrived at my side, and took the instrument. I deliberately dialed an overdose of heart stimulant. "This little shot will make my heart speed up until it bursts. I'm told it's a very painful way to die."

"No . . ." The Jorenian moaned.

"Think of it as a preview. When I'm dead, you can have some."

"That's enough, Doctor!" The Omorr tried to take the syrinpress out of my hand. I smacked Squilyp's membranes away and put the instrument in Yetlo's hand. With my own behind it, I guided the nozzle to my throat.

"That's it, Yetlo. All you have to do is press the button under your thumb. Go ahead, do it."

"Please . . ." He tried frantically to pull his hand away from my neck.

I held it firmly in place. "What's the matter? It's a simple procedure. I'm telling you *I want to die*. Just press the button and watch."

"Healer . . ."

"Press the goddamn button!"

"I . . . can't." All the color was gone from his face.

"No?" I pretended to be surprised. "It's not that simple, is it? To help someone to die, when you know how easy it is to let them live?" I let go of his hand. The syrinpress fell to the deck. With my palms, I framed his face. "Now you know how I feel when you ask me for your Speaker."

His hand curved around my neck, and he pulled me down against him. He was shaking. So was I, for that matter. When I lifted my head, I saw tears streaming down his temples into his dark hair.

It appeared the score would be Cherijo—one, the stars—zero.

"Still want your Speaker?" I asked. He shook his head and openly sobbed. I stood and turned toward the ogling nurses. "Everybody see that?"

Everybody nodded.

"Good. Squilyp." The Omorr was so intent on Yetlo's tears that he looked at me, dazed. "Let's move on to the next case."

I marched to the adjoining berth, and picked up the chart. Sniffed. Blotted my face with the edge of my sleeve. Squilyp hopped up alongside me.

"Senior Healer, that was the stupidest thing I've ever seen a physician do." His gildrells undulated madly. "Also one of the smartest. No one suspected you were bluffing."

I switched the chart to display and sniffed again. "Who said I was bluffing?"

By the end of my shift, Yetlo was showing remarkable improvement. Maybe it was the return of his will to live. Maybe he was terrified he might *accidentally* die and be responsible for my suicide anyway. Whatever the reason, his vitals never looked better. I'd have to write an article on *Death Threats as an Alternative Method of Postoperative Therapy for Jorenian Surgical Patients*.

My surgical resident spent a lot of time muttering to himself and staring at me when he thought I wasn't watching. I suspected he wanted to request a transfer to another ship with a more rational Senior Healer.

Poor Squilyp. Working for me was going to give him a permanent gildrell-twitch.

CHAPTER FOURTEEN

Part of the Connection

After final rounds I went directly to my quarters to get cleaned up. I was looking forward to the meal with Salo, Darea, and Fasala. My anticipation had nothing to do with the argument I'd had with Xonea. Nothing at all.

Xonea walked through the door panel as soon as I'd finished dressing. He appeared quite formidable in his new Captain's tunic. Jenner streaked across the desk and did his best to wrap himself around Xonea's ankle. I resisted the urge to salute. He picked up Jenner and studied me.

"Why are you wearing that garment?"

I glanced down at the red dress Ana Hansen had given me long ago during my tenure on K-2. "Why not? I like it." I did a small twirl, making the bottom half flare out around my thighs. "What do you think?"

He leaned back against a wall panel and cradled my cat against his chest. Narrow white eyes noted the fact I had put sparkling red accessories in my ears and around my wrists. My silver-sheened dark hair was piled on the top of my head.

"You look beautiful," he said as he stroked Jenner. A familiar expression of discomfort passed over his strong face, and I glared at him.

"You still haven't gone for that internal scan yet, have you?" He shook his head. "It's going to look very odd when the Senior Healer's roommate keels over from an untreated, perforated ulcer."

His mouth curled. "I am sure you will endeavor to save me."

Maybe not. "Of course I would."

Xonea gestured toward my outfit. "Is this your method of apologizing for provoking this morning's altercation?"

The man had thrown *me* across a room and thought I should apologize. One simply had to admire that kind of gall.

"No." I stuck the last pin in the sleek coil. Stepped back to check my appearance in the mirror panel one last time. "Feed Jenner for me, will you?"

I walked past him toward the door. Six fingers stopped me with little effort. There was a dangerous set to his features, one I'd seen earlier. Jenner shot out of Xonea's arms with a yowl.

"Where are you going?"

I smiled brightly. Picked his hand off my arm. Dropped it the way I would a soiled glove into a disposal unit.

"Out."

Xonea didn't follow me. I was almost disappointed. We could have had a rip-roaring fight right there in the corridor. Let the crew in on our little secret. I wondered who they'd side with. The defiant little woman, or her abusive ball-and-chain.

Darea and Salo's quarters were on level twelve. I arrived just in time to greet Salo as he came off duty. He gestured for me to proceed him, then held out his arms for the little girl who came barreling past me. Fasala flung herself on Salo.

"ClanFather!" She squealed as he picked her up and tossed her in the air. The little girl was caught, kissed, and returned to the deck. Darea came to her bondmate at a more sedate speed, but her greeting was as warm and loving as their daughter's.

All three turned to give me belated and apologetic greetings.

"Okay, okay," I said, and laughed. "Consider me welcomed!"

"Your pardon, Senior Healer," Salo said.

"Please, call me Cherijo," I replied. "If you keep calling me Senior Healer, I'll have to make chart notations!"

They all laughed as we walked inside. Salo excused himself to get cleansed and changed for the evening meal.

Fasala proceeded to haul me at once to her room. I was shown each of her HouseClan flags, the vast selection of toys she kept in a tidy storage compartment, and her favorite sleep cuddler, a stuffed fabric *t'lerue.*

"So that's what they look like." I examined the benign-looking model of the ponderous creature. Fasala explained that on Joren, the slightly dull-witted *t'lerue* often planted itself in front of a reservoir and would not move sometimes for months. I recalled Tonetka calling Roelm a *t'lerue* several times, and smiled sadly.

Darea chided Fasala for monopolizing me and escorted me through the remainder of their quarters.

"You've got a beautiful dwelling," I said as Darea gave me the tour. Family quarters were arranged to render both efficiency and privacy: A large living and dining area were combined, while separate bedrooms were partitioned on either side with their own individual cleansing units.

Salo, I learned, was an amateur geologist. He had a display case full of interesting specimens from a dozen worlds. Darea, in keeping with her profession, collected actual paper documents and showed me a shelf of real *books.*

"I've never held a book in my hands before," I said as Darea urged me to examine one ancient volume. I was afraid to touch it. Fasala bounced on my lap and flipped open the old animal-skin binding.

"Look, Healer, see?" She pointed to a bewildering block of Jorenian pictographs. "This says, *Be aware always, for the path changes beneath your feet.*" She grinned. "Our HouseClan once made such odd things. It was all they had to preserve their knowledge."

"Primitive idea, isn't it?" I said, carefully tracing a fingertip over the dried, pressed leaf of plant pulp. "My people used books in ancient times, too."

Fasala frowned. "But . . . *we* are your people, are we not, Healer Cherijo?"

Darea and I exchanged a glance.

"Yes, Fasala, you are my people. But I was born on a planet called Terra. Before I was adopted by HouseClan Torin, I was Terran."

"You won't go back there, will you?" the little girl asked.

"Perhaps we can make your skin blue, and remove the spots from your eyes. Then you will belong to us."

She was precious, I thought. And thoroughly confused. "My skin will never be blue, honey. Nor my eyes white. But I'll tell you what: It doesn't matter. Because I am Jorenian in here." I tapped my chest.

"Oh." Fasala thought this over, and smiled. "Smooth path, Healer Cherijo." It was "okay" with her.

I was invited to the dining area for tea while Fasala was sent for her nightly cleansing. Darea refused to let me assist with the preparations for the meal. Instead, I was made to sit while she chatted over her shoulder about popular Jorenian recipe programs. Something that smelled delicious quickly emerged from her food unit.

"You are hungry?" she asked as she placed the heavy server of steaming vegetables on the table.

"I can't remember the last time I had a meal interval," I said. I was permitted to assist Fasala with her evening chore of setting places for the meal. Salo emerged just as Darea placed ice-cold servers of znobell juice at each plate.

"At this time we entreat the Mother," Fasala whispered, slipping her hand in mine after we sat down. "You have to close your eyes. My ClanFather says the words to offer our thanks for bounty and togetherness."

"Got it," I whispered back.

"Mother of All Houses, this day we are indebted to you as all days before and to come," Salo said. "For this meal, our friends and family, we give thanks. Smile upon our House forever."

Fasala nudged me. "You can open your eyes now, Healer Cherijo."

The meal, the main course of which Darea called g'loho dibnarra, was incredible. I had to take some programming lessons from this woman. I particularly enjoyed the dessert, which was a frozen, edible flower that was eaten one petal at a time. The sweet, delicate confection melted on my tongue like a candied snowflake.

"Don't give me the recipe program for the dessert," I said. "I'd outweigh Salo in a week!"

Another enjoyable aspect of the evening meal was simply watching the family interact. I remembered the meal intervals I had taken with my creator for years. Drones served our every need back on Terra, so all I had to do was sit, eat, and listen to Joseph Grey Veil lecture me on some aspect of Terran medicine.

In contrast, Salo and Darea discussed ordinary events of the day. Planned future schedules. Even disagreed over the amount of some spice Darea favored in her prep programming. Fasala wasn't left out, either. She was asked about her day at school. What work she had accomplished. The activities she enjoyed with her friends. Darea actually apologized for it as I later helped her clear the table.

"Your pardon, we did not converse with you very much. We always use meal intervals to remain knowledgeable of one other's activities." She made an embarrassed gesture. "As you can guess, we do not often have guests."

"I loved it," I said as I sterilized the servers and handed them to her to be replaced in storage. "You have nothing to apologize for. I envy you your family."

Darea glanced fondly at her bondmate and child. They were reading a display primer, Fasala laboriously forming the words, Salo regularly praising her efforts.

"They are my world." She looked back at me. "What say you of having children with Xonea? You would be an exceptional ClanMother."

I was exceptional, that much was true. I shook my head. "It isn't possible now." Or ever, I added silently.

"Xonea honors you, Cherijo."

"Xonea needs a good kick in the—" I bit my lip, then tried again. "Xonea wants what Xonea wants."

"He is a warrior," Darea said, as if that excused everything.

"So is your bondmate. How would your relationship with Salo be, if he . . . got physical when you argued?"

"I am warrior-trained as well." Darea's eyes danced. "Salo and I would alternate occupying berths in the Medical Bay, I think."

We giggled together like girls.

"ClanMother? Healer?" Fasala piped up from the living area. "What do you find amusing?"

"Your ClanFather," we answered her at the same time, and giggled again.

"Darea," Salo said her name with a warning rumble in his chest.

"My bondmate displays his warrior's pride for your bene-

fit," Darea said as we finished up in the preparation area.
"He is not half so dignified, or so fierce, when we are
private."

Fasala was sent off to bed soon after that. The little girl
would have protested more, but enormous yawns weren't
backing up her claim to be wide awake. I wished her pleasant dreams.

"Sometimes I do not," the child confessed. "I dream of
the time I was hurt with my educators. I am still afraid of
that place on level fourteen. Even walking past it fright-
ens me."

Fasala needed to face her fear, I realized, not tiptoe
past it.

"Tell you what," I said. "Why don't you and I go back
there together? You'll feel better when you see there's
nothing there to hurt you, and I bet it will make the nightmares go away."

"Will they, Healer Cherijo?"

"Sure."

I found myself being ferociously hugged by small arms
flung around my neck. For a traitorous instant, I imagined
she was my child.

Salo carried Fasala back to her sleeping platform. I
would have left myself, but Darea asked me to remain.

"I—we would like to show you something, Senior
Healer," she said. Her bondmate had returned to the living
area and frowned when he heard that. "Salo, you said I
might tell someone of it."

He ran six fingers through his dark hair. "I said you
might *tell*, Darea."

"Please. Healer Cherijo will appreciate the curious nature of this." She pretended to think for a moment. "Of
course, I could *tell* your ClanCousin Tareo. He often finds
amusement in—"

"Tell anyone—*show* anyone—but Tareo." Salo groaned.
"I beg you."

Darea jumped up and hurried out of the room. A moment later she returned, carrying a rather bulky, fabric-
draped object in her arms.

"Do you remember the sentient crystal given to us while
we sojourned at Garnot?"

I nodded. "It was truly the loveliest thing I'd ever seen."

Salo appeared supremely embarrassed as Darea placed the object on the deck in front of us. She placed her hand on it and looked ready to burst from excitement.

"The crystal we chose was shaped like our Clan-Daughter. Do you remember it?" I nodded. "When we returned to the ship, I placed it on a display stand near our sleeping platform."

"Thank the Mother." Salo scowled. "To think it could have been in this room, for all who entered to view!"

Darea glared at him, then turned back to me. "Healer, the crystal did not retain its shape. We believe it wishes to continue to be impressed by our thoughts."

"Really? What did it do? Make itself into a big question mark?" I asked.

"No. It did this." Darea removed the cover with a flourish.

What had once been a beautiful crystal statue of Fasala had changed into a precise replica of Darea and Salo. They were standing together, holding each other. They were also both completely naked.

"What say you?" Darea asked me. "Is it not beautiful?"

"Um, yes. Beautiful."

"This was an embrace Salo gave me last night," Darea said. "The crystal changes each day."

"How . . . nice." I leaned toward Salo and murmured, "Now I see why you were glad it was in the bedroom."

"*She* would put it in the center of the galley for all to gawk at, if I had not stopped her," he muttered back. "This is not the worst of it. You should have seen what it shaped three nights ago."

"Don't tell me," I said. "I have a great imagination."

"With this meddlesome rock, you need not have one at all."

Kneeling down beside the crystal, I put out a hand and held it an inch above the surface. I could feel warmth radiating from it.

"What makes it retain heat?" I asked Salo.

"I do not know, but the radiant heat is not harmful. I have examined it with every instrument I possess."

"Take my hands," Darea said, and joined her fingers to mine to encircle the crystal. "We will impress it together, you and I, Healer."

"Yes, please," Salo said. "Shape it into anything but what it has flaunted a predilection for."

"What do I do?" I asked.

"Close your eyes," Darea said. "Think of one you honor above all others. The crystal will interpret your thoughts into form."

I closed my eyes, and concentrated. Jorenian honor—the closest thing to love. So who did I love? Maggie was dead. So was Kao. I wasn't too fond of Xonea at the moment. Would it cast itself in Jenner's image?

Darea gasped. I opened my eyes.

"A most interesting interpretation," Salo said. If big strong male Jorenian warriors giggled, he'd be rolling on the floor. As it was, he was grinning widely.

The crystal had reformed into two figures: one male, one female. Both were in each other's arms.

Darea was puzzled. "What are they doing?"

I looked at the precise duplicate of myself in a long gown, and Reever in formal dress. The miniatures were atop a towering cliff. Tiny waves curled in below us.

"We're waltzing," I said.

The strategy session was already in progress when I made an extremely late entrance. I even had an excuse—it was twelve levels from my quarters to Engineering. If the Captain wanted me on time, he'd better get the gyrlifts fixed.

Xonea looked up from his central position at the conference table and glowered at me. "Senior Healer Cherijo."

He'd never come back to our rooms last night. Off sulking, I guessed. Probably slept in his old quarters. I waggled my fingers at him and slid into an empty seat.

"As I have indicated, the recent escalation of League hostilities against Jorenian vessels mandates a review and possible revision of our response procedures," my Chosen said. "I would hear your comments on this."

I made a show of stifling a yawn.

"We have not been sent from the homeworld to start a war with half the galaxies in the universe, Captain," the Executive Administrator said. "Pnor's nonaggression policy has preserved what peace remains between Joren and the League."

Now there was a comment I could stand up and cheer for.

"For how long?" the Senior Engineer demanded. "The League has no interest in preserving the peace."

"Violence is not the answer," the Head of Programming said. "Half my staff was wounded during the latest assault." He nodded toward me. "The Senior Healer can well describe the aftereffects of violence."

That I could. In exact, bloody detail.

Xonea ignored the Programmer's comment. "Our current policy is not protecting this ship or the crew. If the thought of violence disturbs you, what would you propose as an alternative?"

"We could try to renegotiate a treaty with the League," the Programmer said.

"We could enlist the aid of sympathetic species," the Head of Survey said.

I held up my hand and waved it at Xonea. "We could send me back to the League, Captain."

All heads turned toward me. No one seemed eager to agree. And for a moment, the Captain looked ready to throttle me right there on the conference table.

"The ruling Houses have decided against further dialogue with the League," Xonea said. He had composed himself and looked remarkably like Pnor. I had no idea he could do impressions. Maybe he could do a *t'lerue* for me later. "Thus, no treaty. We have enlisted the aid of species friendly to us, but can we truly depend on those who do not belong to the HouseClan?"

"What about my suggestion?" I asked.

Xonea looked pretty impressive when he flexed all his muscles like that. "No, Senior Healer. Turning you over to the League is not an acceptable alternative."

The discussions continued. I listened as proposals were presented, discussed, and ultimately rejected. It appeared there was no viable alternative. Once this was established, Xonea made his recommendation.

"I propose we respond to League attacks in kind. No longer shall the *Sunlace* transition away from a skirmish with these bounty hunters. We have a considerable arsenal at our disposal. The ship's structure can be reinforced to withstand most displacer fire. HouseClan Torin will fight back."

Half the room erupted into frantic speech.

Salo and some of the other warriors backed Xonea. "The Captain's plan is sound—"

Others were not so happy. "No HouseClan since—"

Xonea stood up, all seven-and-a-half feet of him. "Hear me! HouseClan Torin has been attacked. We know we will encounter more mercenaries on the path. Which of you will stand back and watch our kin die? Which of you will turn and run away?"

That definitely rallied the troops. Rumbling fury echoed around the room. Nice, peaceful administrators suddenly looked as though they wanted to gut someone. I even saw some claws emerge. Xonea appeared highly pleased with himself. His wording and delivery had been flawless.

Time for me to spoil the Captain's fun.

"Excuse me," I said. I had to repeat that a few times before I had the room's attention. "There is something you've forgotten."

"Please, tell us, Senior Healer." That was Xonea. "We would hate to forget something."

He was such a grump today, I thought. Sleeping in his old quarters definitely did *not* agree with him. I got up now.

"You're saying that we should stand and fight back. That's your whole strategy, Captain?"

"Of course not, Senior Healer," he said. "We will—"

I whipped up my hand. "Spare me the gruesome details. I suppose you expect the entire crew to go along with this."

"Success requires a cooperative effort," the Senior Engineer said. He frowned at me with censure. Maybe he thought I was unwilling to enlist myself in the cause.

"I'm not trying to get out of it," I told him. "In fact, you can't do this without support from me and my staff."

"Agreed," Xonea said. "Medical will be a vital resource."

"Glad to know we're appreciated." I walked to the center of the room. "I know you want to make all these big, bad battle plans, but there's one small detail you've forgotten. What about the kids?" Everyone went still. "Yeah, remember the kids?"

"Explain your meaning!" Xonea demanded.

"Captain, the *Sunlace* is not a troop freighter. We have

more than two hundred children on board. Last time I checked, most of them aren't old enough to qualify for warrior training."

"Do you question our ability to protect our children?" Salo asked. Not in a friendly tone, either.

"Absolutely not," I replied. "Your devotion toward the youngest members of this HouseClan is nothing short of slavish. That isn't the point."

I slipped a disc in the display module at the center of the room. I'd spent half the damn night working on it, they'd better pay attention.

"I'm telling you that you *can't* protect the kids."

Dimensional imagers projected an imaginary battle between four ships. The graphics were very realistic, thanks to some tips from Squilyp on adjusting the holopicells. Little blue figures inside the ships actually got blown to bits when a direct hit was achieved. You could even make out green blood and tiny dismembered blue limbs.

"Observe, if you would, a simulated counter-offensive, where you stand and fight rather than withdraw and escape," I said. "This conjectural scenario is based on hard data gathered from all mercenary attacks since we left K-2 orbit."

I identified the components. "Here you see the *Sunlace* under attack by three mercenary vessels." I pointed to the League vessels as they were destroyed, one by one. "Note the number of direct displacer hits the mercenaries are capable of making prior to the destruction of their vessels."

"Your data is inaccurate," Xonea said. "We will reinforce the hull."

"No, it isn't," I replied. "This model of the *Sunlace* already has the proposed structural bolsters in place."

"How could you know what we plan to do with the ship?" Xonea demanded.

I gave him a dazzling smile. "I'm touched that you used my name, but you need to think of a new password for your sensitive data files."

A few unwilling chuckles had Xonea dropping back down into his chair.

"Go on," he said.

"Thanks." I pointed to three different levels on the display model where the *Sunlace* was badly damaged. "Projections show total loss of life here, here, and here. That's, oh, say a hundred Torins, give or take a few." With a few key taps on the module console, I rotated the image of the cripple vessel. "Fifty percent more casualties on these five levels. Half of them will die."

I ended the simulation and inserted a second disc. This one was the clincher.

"This is a mock-up of what Medical Bay would look like after such an attack. At current staffing levels and equipment availability, we could not meet demand."

Everyone stared at the realistic drama the computer played out. Bodies littered the deck. Nurses ran from berth to berth. The residents and I performed surgery without sterile fields. Lots more blood and body parts. Life sized this time.

"We would treat the salvageable cases as top priority. In my experience, that category seldom includes children. Young bodies rarely tolerate as much punishment as mature ones." I projected a list of the names. "These individuals were not chosen at random by the computer. Death ratios are based on the routine locations of crew members, and which portions of the ship the mercenaries are likely to attack. More than seventy-six percent of the dead would be under the age of sixteen."

I enlarged the list until it filled the center space. "How many of you see the names of your own children?"

The room was silent.

"If you survived the firefight, and any subsequent injuries which could not be adequately treated by Medical," I said, "you would have the joyous task of shooting ninety-four dead children into some stars." I switched off the module, gathered up my discs, and addressed the pale blue faces staring at me. "Which of you will stand back and watch our kids die?"

No one said a word, so I walked out. The meeting adjourned soon after. I heard later the vote had been unanimous.

No change of policy.

When my shift ended, I thought about going down to the galley, or challenging Dhreen to a rematch at the whump-tables. I sighed as my feet took me to my quarters anyway.

I barely got through the door panel before Xonea started cursing at me in Jorenian.

"Hello, honey, I'm home," I said as I set down a stack of charts I'd brought with me. He was pacing back and forth in front of the viewport. "Things sure were busy at work. How was your day?" Another burst of violent swearing. "Sorry to hear that. Well, relax and put your feet up. I'll make us a nice dinner."

"Your tongue shall divert your path someday," Xonea said. Must have been hard to get out, too. Clenched teeth did not allow much in the way of articulate speech.

"That, or one of your policy changes," I replied. I went to the prep unit and eyed the main menu thoughtfully. "Are you in the mood for kcdarak, or some utolla? I see you've been drinking jaspkerry tea. Does that go with—"

He turned me around. Not gently, either. "I am not hungry."

"I am." I stood unresisting beneath his brutal grasp. "And don't even *think* about tossing me across the room again. You got lucky last time. My body isn't built to take that kind of abuse."

"Who are you to interfere with my policies? You are not the Captain of this vessel!"

"You're right, I'm not." I wasn't yelling. Yet. "Nor am I your drone, sparring partner, or punching bag. Now take those big blue hands off me, pal."

He let go and I went back to preparing our meal. The baked syntrout I was programming for myself would probably choke me, but I wasn't going to let Xonea know how angry I was. With a glance over my shoulder, I saw him standing by the viewport again. This time he was staring out into space.

"Cherijo, the other morning, when I threw you—" He faltered, then his voice dropped to a low mutter. "I have never hurt a female in my life."

"Am I supposed to thank you for starting with me?"

"We cannot continue in this fashion."

I placed our servers on the table. "No, we can't."

He came to the table. Took my hands. His expression was anger and torment and need, all wrapped together. "Cherijo. Why is this happening between us?"

I shook my head. "Don't ask me. I'm no psych therapist."

"I honor you."

Well, at least he didn't say it like *I spit on you* this time. I was about to suggest a separation when the door panel chimed.

"Ignore it," Xonea said when I tried to move past him.

"You're the Captain, remember? We can't." I broke free of his grip and went to the door. The panel slid open to reveal Phorap Rogan waiting outside. "On the other hand, maybe you were right, Xonea. What do you want, Rogan?"

He walked in right past me. "Captain, I was hoping to have a word with you."

"Dr. Rogan," Xonea greeted him.

"The ultimate oxymoron," I muttered.

My roommate gave me a calculated glance. "Would you care to join us for a meal interval?"

"No, he wouldn't," I said. "Let him have his word and then he goes."

Rogan faked an anguished expression. "You can see Dr. Torin has a great deal of prejudice against me." His helpless little shrug made me snort. "I hope her Terran bigotry will not influence you in regard to your decision."

"What decision?" I recalled Rogan's last threat. "Oh, no. You're not putting him to work in my Medical Bay."

"It is not *your* Medical Bay," Xonea said. His voice was soft but rich with triumph. "You yourself stated we are grievously understaffed in Medical." He turned to the half-human. "I will permit you to work as a physician for the duration of your journey with us."

"Thank you, Captain." Rogan's four lips parted in a repulsive grin. "You're a wise man."

"I resign," I said.

"Resignation refused," Xonea replied. "Excuse us, Dr. Rogan. You may report to Medical tomorrow and review your shift schedule with the Senior Healer."

"Thank you again, Captain." Rogan nodded, and smiled even wider as he passed by me. "Doctor."

I almost spit on him then. My bad Terran blood. I waited until the door panel slid shut, then I secured it.

"I know you're getting back at me for sabotaging your meeting this morning." I stayed by the door panel, unable to look at Xonea. "What you don't know is how dangerous that man is. You're putting people's lives at risk."

"Dr. Rogan has already explained your personal aversion to him. You need more staffing, he is a doctor—"

"He is a *quack*," I said, turning around, my fists clenched. He wanted a battle, by God, he was going to get one. "That bastard nearly *killed* the first patient I saw on K-2 because he couldn't be bothered to follow procedure. His work is slipshod and neglectful. Hell, calling what he does malpractice would be a *compliment*. As for his personal aversion to me, did he tell you how many charges he invented and filed against me with the ruling Council on K-2?"

"No, he did not," Xonea said.

"Did he mention he was partially responsible for spreading the contagion that resulted in the deaths of over seven thousand colonists?" I advanced toward him. Xonea shook his head. "How about the time he led a mob into the hospital to kill me and a ward full of infected patients?"

"Cherijo—"

"No? Here's one more item about your new staff physician: Rogan appeared before the ruling Council one last time before I left K-2. You should remember him. You were there." I thought for a minute as I stopped in front of him. "No, now that I think about it, you and the others came in after Rogan had testified."

"I did not know he was there on your behalf."

"He wasn't. Rogan testified *against* me."

We stared at each other. Xonea looked faintly sick now. I didn't enjoy it as much as I'd thought I would, especially when I saw the very real pain in his eyes.

The physician behind my eyes spoke to him first. "You're showing all the symptoms of an aggravated ulcer, Xonea. Get Squilyp to run the series on you, soon."

"Cherijo—"

"Another suggestion. Step up your investigation into the murders, before this maniac finds another way to signal the League. And get Rogan off the ship. I guarantee that will prevent more mercenary attacks."

He frowned. Obviously he hadn't thought of that.

"I'm leaving," I said. "But when I come back to these quarters in a few hours—with all due respect, Captain—I want you and your junk gone."

*   *   *

After my fight with Xonea, I walked all the way down to the observation ring on level twenty-eight. The plasteel panels retracted to reveal transparent alcoves. It was probably the most breathtaking view of space available on the ship.

I didn't see a damn thing. I sat and stared at the pale reflection of my own face on the shielding.

A sudden surge of power rumbled through the hull of the ship. Here, three levels below Main Engineering, the engines were plainly audible.

I ignored them.

The situation with Xonea was becoming intolerable. Maybe it was starting to affect him. The deep core of anger seemed to be growing within him every day. A core that could erupt into violence at any moment.

I missed Tonetka. Would any of this have happened if she was still alive? Probably not. The Jorenian woman would have never allowed Rogan in her Medical Bay. She had always taken charge and remained in control. I was wasting my time trying to fill her shoes.

The engines quieted down. I spent another half hour staring at the stars, wondering what the hell I was going to do. Then someone joined me.

"Cherijo."

I wasn't surprised to hear Reever's voice. He usually showed up at some of the worst moments in my life.

"Go away, Reever." I wanted peace and quiet. Hopefully the engines wouldn't start screaming again.

"Why are you here?" His reflection appeared behind mine on the shielding. "You shouldn't be alone."

"Which did you hear about?" I asked. "Rogan, or Xonea?"

"Both."

I smiled. My reflection smiled back. Reever's didn't twitch a nerve cell. "Then you already know why I'm here." My smile faded as the engines made a transition. At least they weren't as loud as before. That sound . . .

He stepped closer and sat down next to me. The heat from his body reached mine. "That is not why I am here."

"It doesn't matter." I hunched away from him. "I'm leaving the ship. Getting off on the next non-League world we come to."

"That would be Dr. Rogan's homeworld."

"The second non-League world we come to." If the engines lasted that long.

He moved an inch closer. Now I could smell his skin. "Cherijo, it is never as hopeless as you may think."

He was right. It was worse. "The voice of experience." I frowned. The engines . . . what was it about that sound that bugged me so much?

"I am here, am I not?"

I turned my head to glare at him. "Very funny." His arm came up around me, and I let my head rest on his shoulder. "I'm terrible company right now. You really should go."

His scarred hand tightened on my upper arm briefly. "There is something I have to tell you."

Something in his voice warned me I wasn't going to like it. I sat back up and faced him. "*You're* not getting off on Rogan's homeworld, I hope."

"No. I was sent to find you. There has been—"

That sound! The same thing had happened after Fasala and the educators had been injured. After Roelm's death. After the mercenary had been killed. I had been unconscious at the time, but I felt sure the same surge occurred after Ndo died. That meant—

"God, Reever, someone's been murdered," I said. "The same way the others were."

"How did you—"

"Come on." I got up and started running. He caught me before I could reach the next level. "Let me go, Reever. I've got part of the connection now! I have to tell—"

"Cherijo. Listen to me. You need to hear this first." He took me in his arms.

"What?"

"It is Yetlo Torin."

"No." I pushed my hands against his chest, struggling free. "Nothing's wrong with Yetlo. I just left him a few hours ago. He's fine."

"He was murdered, Cherijo."

"No!" I shouted as I grabbed the front of his tunic. "I just left him! He was doing fine, he *wanted* to live! I swore I'd—" I broke off with a strangled sound, and buried my face against him.

Reever stood there with me for a long time, holding me,

saying nothing. When I finally regained my composure, I lifted my head from his damp tunic.

"Let's go."

Medical Bay echoed with silence. No one looked at me as I swept down the ward to where Yetlo's body lay. His outer derma had the same strange striae as Roelm's had, with a grisly addition. The stress of whatever killed him had torn his chest wound wide open.

"Senior Healer." Squilyp appeared with Yetlo's chart.

"Report."

"Yetlo was complaining of discomfort and trouble sleeping," the Omorr said. "I gave orders to administer the painkiller you prescribed an hour after you left the Bay."

"Who administered the dose?" I demanded.

"Adaola, under my supervision. We finished making rounds, and were treating outpatient cases when Yetlo's monitor went on full alert."

Outpatient cases? "How many walk-ins did you have in here?"

Squilyp looked uncomfortable. "Perhaps twenty. I had scheduled them in a group, to afford the most efficient processing and treatment."

"I want a list of everyone who was on this ward," I said. "What happened after his monitor went off?"

"I began resuscitation at once, of course, but it was too late. Tissues were flooded, possibly due to a reaction to the narcotic. Convulsions and heart failure were nearly synchronous. He died without ever regaining consciousness."

"Did you or the nurses see anyone do anything?"

He shook his head.

Reever accompanied me to the office. Squilyp followed after he retrieved the list of outpatients. Once the door panel closed, I sat down on the edge of the desk and rubbed my reddened eyes before I consulted the list.

"Tareo, Ralrea, Hado . . ." I continued to read the names until I reached the last one. "Is this everyone who was in Medical today, Squilyp?"

"No, Senior Healer. There were several others who reported for treatment," the Omorr said. "Dr. Rogan unfortunately did not make the proper chart notations on the patients he treated, so I am unable to provide a complete list."

Another reason for me to kill Xonea. "Gentlemen, we have a problem."

"What of Pnor's investigation? Was nothing discovered?" Squilyp asked.

"Pnor found no evidence to identify the killer." My fingers began thrumming on the desk top. "I have. There is a link between the power surges in the engines and every one of these killings. That, and a two-meter ring of light that mysteriously appears and disappears." I looked from Squilyp to Reever. "Yetlo is the last person who dies this way. I will take this damn ship apart piece by piece to find this maniac if I have to."

"How can you find someone when you don't know who it is?" the Omorr asked.

"We're going to try accessing my memories again. You, me, and Reever."

"The Captain has forbidden it," Squilyp said. "He was most specific."

"The Captain has no authority over my mind. We're going to do this, right here, right now."

"Doctor, at least give me time to set up one of the surgical suites as an isolation area. The last time we attempted this, there was an unpleasant aftermath."

And the unpleasant aftermath was now running the ship. "Locks on the doors are good," I said. "Reever?"

"Perhaps Resident Squilyp can requisition some weapons," Reever said. "I should not wish to encounter the Captain when he is in an emotional state again."

"If no one makes an announcement," I said, "we don't have to worry about ugly scenes. Agreed?" Both men nodded. I focused on my resident. "How long to set up, Squilyp?"

"I will need an hour."

"Great. Let's do it."

Chapter Fifteen

Breaking the Choice

We made arrangements to convene at the surgical suite in an hour. I left Squilyp to settle the ward down for the night. Reever had already disappeared.

Rather than returning to my quarters and facing the sight of Xonea moving out, I trudged down eighteen levels to level twenty-five. It was the lowest of the four levels providing access to the enormous engines and stardrive array. I found a number of engineers examining one of the huge housings. They looked like ants swarming over a giant barrel. One noticed me and hurried over.

"Senior Healer?"

It was Barrea, one of the men who was injured during the last attack. He had to shout to be heard over the sound of the exposed engine.

Broken arm, torn shoulder ligaments, my brain recalled. "How's the arm, Barrea?"

He appeared delighted that I remembered his case, and rotated the limb carefully. "Still stiff, but much improved!"

I beckoned to him and we walked far enough away to be heard without the yelling. "Barrea, did you report to Medical for outpatient treatment today?"

He removed his protective headgear. "No, I am not scheduled to report for three more days."

"Good." That meant he wasn't present when Yetlo was murdered, and it would be reasonable to assume he wasn't involved. "I need your help."

He was surprised. "Of course, Senior Healer. Anything."

"A short time ago I heard a sound coming from this level. The engines sounded like they were screeching."

"We experienced a power overload."

"What was that caused by?"

Barrea looked sheepish. "I do not know, Senior Healer. We cannot explain the power fluctuations as of yet."

"But it's happened before, hasn't it?"

He nodded.

I counted names: Fasala, Roelm, Leo, Ndo, and now Yetlo. "Five times before?"

"How could you know that?"

"A lucky guess," I lied. "Can you describe—in nontechnical terms—what has happened during each of these incidents?"

Barrea tilted his head as he considered my question. "I can theorize, if that is acceptable."

"Great. Go ahead."

"The engines draw power from the absorption grid and primary energy exchangers." He went to a console and waved for me to join him. On the display, he brought up a schematic of the *Sunlace*. "Here." He pointed to the ship's interior. "Each level of the ship forms an outer part of the central fuel core."

I peered at the display. "Are those circular symbols the transductors?"

He seemed surprised I knew the term. "No, they are transductor junctions." He pointed now to cylindrical tubes leading to and from the junctions. "These are the transductors."

"What do they do?"

"Transductors supply energy forms demanded by ship operations. The junctions are where raw fuel is converted before it floods the transductors."

"How big are these junctions?"

"They range in size, according to load and demand. They can be as large as twenty meters in diameter, or as small as—"

"Two meters?"

He nodded. I managed to maintain my composure. "Go on, Barrea. Tell me the rest of your theory."

"We believe that energy is being drained from the transductors. It goes in a definite cycle. Very little power is lost, and slowly at first. The power drain grows greater and more rapid over a period of time."

"What would happen if the power was drained all at once?" I asked, already sure I knew the answer.

"The engines would cease operation at once."

"Okay." I rubbed the back of my neck. "What happens next?"

"Once the engines are nearly drained of energy, the unidentified tap seems to heal itself. Power floods back into the cold engines, making them strain to compensate. The result is the sound you heard."

"You don't know what's doing this?" I thought I did, but I couldn't tell him that. Not yet.

"No, Senior Healer. We believe it may have something to do with the unexplained buffer breech in level fourteen some weeks ago."

"Why is that?"

"We discovered some sonic-based matter in the engines themselves after that incident. The matter was identical to the shards removed from the three females who were injured."

I related all I had learned from Barrea to Squilyp and Reever a short time later in Medical.

"Sit still," the Omorr said as he attached the monitor terminals to my head.

"But don't you see the connection? The smallest of these transductor junctions match the diameter of the light ring that flashed just prior to the murders."

"What has this coincidence of size have to do with the loss of power to the engines?" Reever asked. "Transductor junctions cannot generate power surges or breaches in the sonic alloy."

"Whatever is being used to kill our people apparently requires a tremendous amount of energy. Let's say the murderer can tap into the ship's own power and drain it off from the engines. Barrea told me the engines would shut down if the power was drained all at once. So the killer has to do it gradually—siphon it off a little at a time."

"Where would the power be stored during the draining process?" the Omorr asked.

My fingers flicked. "Tech details. Who cares. Let's say

the killer stockpiles the energy until he has enough to do this thing that kills the victim. After he attacks, the drain stops. The engines go into an immediate surge. Hence the engine rattle Roelm heard after the attack on Fasala and the two educators."

"An interesting theory," Reever said. "For which you have no evidence."

"Your support is appreciated, Reever." I glared at him. "What I can't figure out is how the transductors are involved. This two-meter circle of light, does it come from them? Or is it supposed to be some sort of artificial junction? Does it convert the power? Focus it?"

"Doctor." Squilyp sounded pained. "We must begin. Oblige me by tabling this discussion for the moment."

I obliged. "Did you secure the doors?"

"Yes, for the third time." He checked the monitor connectors and stroked his gildrells. "You are certain you want to do this?"

"No one else is going to die."

"Cherijo," Reever said from the exam table next to me. "Calm yourself."

I remembered something else. "I forgot to tell you about the stuff Barrea found in the engines."

"Not now, if you please," the Omorr said. "We can't leave the ward unsupervised for too long. The nurses are already suspicious."

"Oh, all right. I'm ready."

"NE levels are reading normal," Squilyp said as he checked the monitor display. "Limbic system neurotracer portals functional. Initiating continuous vital scans."

"Be prepared to apply cortical electristim." I lay down face-up. Reever turned on his side toward me. "Let's go."

The Omorr took his position by the monitor. "You may initiate the coupling."

Cherijo.

Reever, I thought back. *I didn't even blink this time.*

We improve with practice. Yield to me now, Cherijo.

As we had before, Reever and I entered the recesses of my memory. It wasn't as frightening this time.

Think of the third visitation. When you were injured. Remember, you are in control.

Someone had said that to me before.

Xonea's voice.

Take control of the dream, Cherijo.

Take control.

Take take take—

I was back in the golden, glowing chamber. I couldn't breathe right. It was there. I could feel it wrestling with me for control of my mind.

Look at the presence, Cherijo. See the face of your attacker.

Laughter mocked Reever's quiet command. "You think you see me, little human?"

It was different this time.

Reever? I called out, unsure of what to do.

Face your attacker.

I squashed the fear and turned back to the presence. My words were the same as they had been before. *Get it over with.* Again I watched as Ndo's busy image appeared.

"Pnor never knew Ndo's envy. Ever loyal, steadfast Ndo. Now only a speck on the face of a star. The one, true path."

The ring of light. The shattering attack. Ndo's collapse. The convulsions. Death.

I've been here, seen this. Come on out and face me.

"You are braver than before, little one. Remember our last encounter? I enjoyed watching your body writhe beneath my fists." The voice gloated. "Almost as much as I enjoyed caressing you."

You're a sick, twisted monster.

"Oh, yes."

I watched as an image of Yetlo appeared. He never opened his eyes, but deep inside me I sensed he knew he was dying, and fought for his life.

Yetlo. You did understand.

"You corrupted him. Diverted him from the true path. I gave him his greatest wish."

You murdered him!

Cherijo, you must open your eyes.

"Yes, little one. Open your eyes."

Anger gave me the last push I needed. I opened my eyes. Xonea stood before me. His open hands dripped with green blood. "Here I am, my Chosen."

Xonea?

"What say you, Cherijo? Is this not what you wanted?

The truth?" He came toward me. "I am here for you, my Chosen. Here to divert your path." For a moment, he seemed to hesitate.

Reever was trying to break through some barrier between him and the two of us. *Cherijo, it is not Xonea.*

Sure looks like Xonea to me. I wasn't going to let him get away with this. He'd played me for a fool more than once. I went toward him, and was surprised to see him take an uncertain step backward.

What's the matter? Afraid of the little Terran now?

"I will crush your bones to dust," my ClanBrother said.

I reached with a mental hand and grabbed the front of his tunic. With a tremendous effort I tried to swing my other arm, but he jerked out of reach. A handful of fabric remained in my fingers. The tear revealed a jagged purple mark over his heart.

Xonea doesn't have a birthmark on his chest. I came at him again. *Who the hell are you?*

"Death."

Reever broke through the barrier and thrust himself between us.

Remove this false image, he ordered the presence. *Reveal your true face.*

"Not yet," the voice whispered. Xonea's image melted into a yawning, empty hole. "But soon. For now, here is something with which you can remember me."

This time Reever shouted as we were jolted from the link back into reality.

Cherijo!

"Doctor!"

My eyes opened. The Omorr was pinning Reever to the exam table as he went into violent convulsions. I rolled off and tried to help him. Forgot about the hookups. I ended up sprawled painfully on the deck. By the time I untangled myself and stumbled to Squilyp, he had sedated Reever.

Someone began pounding on the outer side of the surgical suite's doors.

"Visitors," the Omorr said.

"Cherijo! Open this panel!"

"My ex-roommate." I sighed. "You got those weapons Reever asked about, right?"

*   *   *

I'd never realized what a propensity for claustrophobia I had. Or that I knew that many bad words. Of course, I'd violated my superior's orders before. I'd just never been thrown in jail for doing so.

Captain Xonea took his sweet time in coming down to the detainment cell. By then I knew it was approximately forty-feet wide. Thirty-feet long. Twenty-feet high. Driving me nuts.

I heard my two guards speaking quietly to someone, then Xonea appeared outside the barrier.

I stopped pacing. "This your idea of poetic justice?"

He turned his head. "Deactivate the locking mechanism."

I thrust my hands in my tunic pockets. "Don't I get to speak to my judicial advisor before you start beating me up?"

Cool white eyes inspected me. "No."

"Ha, ha, ha." I sat down on the edge of the rock-hard sleeping platform. "Go ahead, Captain. Yell your head off, slap me around, whatever you want. It won't change the facts. I've done nothing wrong."

"You knew my orders regarding unauthorized psychic experimentation, Senior Healer," he said. He stayed by the barrier. Xonea was becoming a careful man. Maybe there *was* hope for him. "You disobeyed me."

"Yep. I did. How is Reever? Is he okay?"

"He has recovered. Why did you disobey me?"

"To find out who the killer is, Captain. And we did." I rubbed my eyes. "Though Reever says I'm wrong."

"Who was it?"

I dropped my hand. "You."

The astonished horror on his countenance almost—*almost*—made up for what he'd done. The indignity of being arrested and escorted from Medical. Being pushed in a cell and locked up. Almost, however, was not good enough.

"Did you beat me? Try to rape me?" I rose. "Did you kill Roelm and Ndo? Did you kill Yetlo?"

"No!" Xonea said. He backed up against the barrier. Knocked into it with his shoulders. Guess he was appalled.

"No? You had plenty of motive," I said. "Everyone knows how jealous you are where I'm concerned. Maybe you saw them all as a threat. Whoever has been attacking me obviously has an obsession with me. You nearly got yourself exiled for the same reason. This monster enjoyed hurting me. You tossed me across a room just the other day."

Xonea dug his hands into the barrier mesh, fighting for control. "Cherijo, I would embrace the stars before I would harm you."

"Sure you would. That's why I'm currently enjoying these luxury accommodations, right?"

The Captain-of-the-*Sunlace* mask slid back over his face. "You are being detained for violating my orders."

"Oh, yeah. Almost forgot. The first time Reever and I tried to access my memories and reveal the killer's identity, you stormed into Medical. You never did tell Pnor how you knew we were linking. Same thing happened today."

"That is not how I knew what you were doing!" he shouted. "The information came to me through another source. I did not tell Pnor because it was a matter of honor!"

That was more like the Xonea I knew and wanted to push out a pressure lock.

"One of the nurses, I suppose." I dropped back on the platform and reclined. The deck above me had seventy-six individual panels and a small stain to the right of the third cross section of rows fourteen and fifteen. "You've had one of them keeping an eye on me."

"I cannot discuss the matter with you." His voice drifted closer. Soundless as always, Xonea crossed the thirty feet of deck until he stood next to the bunk. He looked bigger and meaner and more handsome than ever. "Cherijo. Do you remember when you came to me here?"

"This conversation is over." I closed my eyes. "Go away, Xonea."

He knelt beside the platform. "I was prepared to die. You shielded me."

"I have lousy judgment."

One big hand reached out, encircling my throat. "When you came back from Pnor, and I touched you—"

My eyes flew open. "Forget it, Xonea."

Fingers began releasing the front fasteners on my tunic. "I did not wish to stop touching you." He pushed his hand beneath the open edge. "You pledged yourself to me."

"Get your hands off, now."

He didn't. He was so close I could feel the heat coming

in waves from his huge body. He wanted me. Maybe locking up a woman tickled his libido.

"I honor you, Cherijo. I desire you more than my life."

"Well, I hate to disappoint you pal, but—" I yanked his hand off my breast and sat up. "Desire someone else."

The warrior replaced the lover. He seized me, hauled me off the platform, dragging me up every hard inch of his body.

"You want me," he said. "I can see the change in your eyes. Feel the heat of your body." He buried his face in my throat. Anger made his claws emerge. "You will be mine."

He wanted to get rough? Fine.

I put my lips next to his ear. "Maybe I'm still warm from being with Reever."

This time a sleeping platform didn't break my fall. My face did. I flew through the air, bounced off the detainment cell wall, and slid to the deck. Shock and pain made it hard to breathe.

Maybe my mouth *would* get me killed one day.

I touched my face with trembling fingers. Blood was running from my nose, mouth, and four shallow gashes on one cheek. Those claws were really sharp.

"Cherijo." Now Xonea was picking me up, his face all distorted. As if *he* was the one who had gotten up close and personal with the plaspanel.

"Guards," I called out, wincing as that made the cut on my lip split wider.

The guards appeared outside the barrier. When they saw what Xonea had done, they jerked open the access door and hurried inside.

"Captain, the Senior Healer needs to be taken to Medical," one of them said. He looked ready to shoot Xonea in the head.

"I will take her." The other one actually raised his rifle toward Xonea. "Release her, Captain."

It was an excellent opportunity to instigate a mutiny. Or observe my guards as they gutted the commander of the ship.

"No," I said to both of them. I *had* deliberately provoked him, knowing how angry he was. "I'll be all right. Get me a first-aid case, and get him out of here."

*   *   *

Squilyp and Reever came for me not fifteen minutes after the guards escorted Xonea from my cell. Both reacted to the sight of my bleeding face. The Omorr exclaimed loudly and pushed the guards out of his way.

Reever simply stood, quiet and watchful. His eyes had never been that color before, I thought. Raw ice crystals had more warmth.

"I'm okay," I said when the Resident crouched down and began scanning me. "Just some bumps and bruises." I let him clean and dress the lacerations, then reached for Reever. "Give me a hand, will you?"

Scarred hands carefully lifted me from the deck. I hadn't moved since I landed there. I didn't want to know what was broken and what wasn't. I moved my arms, legs, head, and bent over. No fractures. Lucky me.

"We'll take you to Medical," the Omorr said.

"Can't." Talking hurt my face. "I have to stay here. I violated the Captain's orders."

"The Captain ordered that you be released."

"He did? How considerate." I'd been giving the entire situation a great deal of thought. I looked at Squilyp and gingerly touched the dressing on my face. "How good are you with cardiac electristimulators?"

The Omorr looked confused. "I've used them dozens of times during training sessions."

I turned to Reever. "I want to access the cultural and judicial databases in Medical. I need you to find something for me in the Jorenian HouseClan laws and traditions."

He inclined his head in agreement. "How does this relate to cardiac equipment?"

"I'll tell you after we find the data I need."

We took a newly repaired gyrlift back up to Medical. Squilyp gave me a status report on the ward. Reever wouldn't let go of my arm. We passed a number of crew members, who reacted with varying degrees of concern and anger when they saw my face.

The mutiny might just happen without me saying a word.

"Clear an exam table," I told Squilyp. "Prepare for a cardiac case. I want you to make a full vid/audio record of this procedure. Set up the monitor over there."

Before he could ask me the dozen questions that order provoked, I took Reever into my office and shut the panel.

"Access the databases."

"What, specifically, are you searching for?"

"Laws governing the Jorenian right to Choose. I need to know exactly what is required to break a Choice."

Reever accessed the judicial database, cross-referenced with cultural, and found the applicable laws within minutes. I stood beside him and read it for myself. I was right.

"Download this"—I pointed to a case reference—"onto a disc." I told him the rest of what I wanted done and suggested he get Salo to help. He didn't say a word until I finished and tried to go back out to the ward. Reever pushed past me and blocked the way.

"I cannot permit you to do this," he said.

Now *he* was telling me what to do. "Get out of my way."

"Cherijo, you cannot—"

I pointed to the gashes on my cheek. "Look at me, Reever. I could have lost an eye. Or half my face. It ends, now."

He put his hands on my shoulders. "I want to stay with you."

"Okay." I let out a breath. "I'd like that, too."

We walked back out to the cardiac berth Squilyp had just completed preparing. I climbed up on it.

"Senior Healer!" The Omorr sounded horrified. "Are you experiencing angina? What—"

"Power up the stimulator, Squilyp," I said as I strapped my legs into the restraints. "Adaola?" I called out. "Are you on duty?"

The nurse appeared at the berth side. "Here, Senior Healer. What has happened to your face? Why are you—"

"I need two Jorenians." I waved at another nurse, who hurried over, then addressed her and Adaola. "You are my witnesses. You may be required to testify before the ruling Houses as to what you see here today. Do you understand?"

Both nurses nodded. I turned my attention to the Resident.

"Squilyp, I want you to charge up and hit me with a full stim."

The Omorr nearly toppled over from shock. "That will *stop* your heart!"

"I know. Once my heart has stopped, pronounce my death, wait three minutes, then revive me."

"Absolutely not." Squilyp dropped the hookups and hopped backward. "I won't do it."

"Okay." I turned to Reever. "Reever, you have to make sure the monitor reaches—"

"Stop it!" the Omorr shouted, and grabbed my arms with his membranes. "You're insane if you think I'm going to let this man kill you!"

The two Jorenian nurses came to my aid then. "The Senior Healer has the right to embrace the stars, Resident."

I grinned at them. "I never thought I'd like that damn custom, but it does have its uses. Now either you do it, Resident, or Linguist Reever does. You know my survival chances are a lot better if you handle the procedure."

"I know I should save myself some grief and *not* revive you," he muttered as he took position by my berth. His dark eyes were tormented. "You're sure about this, Doctor?"

"It's the only way I can free myself of Xonea."

When Adaola heard what I said, her eyes widened.

"Adaola. You were the one feeding Xonea the information about me and Reever, weren't you?" I asked.

"He is my ClanBrother, Senior Healer," she said. "I could not refuse him."

Well, learn something new every day, I thought. She and Xonea had kept that from me.

"That makes you Kao's ClanSister, right?" She nodded. "Then you're my ClanSister, too. Do you think you extend some of that loyalty to me today?" Evidently ashamed, she nodded once more. "Good. All right, people, see you in a few minutes." I nodded to the Omorr. "Anytime you're ready—"

"Wait." Reever bent over me. His lips felt cold against my ear. "Come back to me, Cherijo."

Ironically, Xonea had said the same thing the last time I risked life and limb. "I will."

I stared at the deck above me when Squilyp charged the stimulator. *I was doing the right thing.* Heard the hum of the electric as the terminals descended. *This wouldn't kill me. At least, not permanently.* Convulsed as the power slammed into my chest. *On second thought . . .*

My heart stopped.

At the very last moment, I felt the cold presence infiltrating my mind. I couldn't fight. Couldn't move.

"Now you will die, little one."

Everything around me grew very small and insignificant. Just on the edge of my field of vision, a woman appeared. I tried to move my head to see her clearly. She was smiling, and held out her arms.

"Joey. Come to me, baby."

"Maggie." Had I really told Squilyp to stop my heart? "Maggie, am I dead?"

"Shhhh, no, baby."

The berth, Medical Bay, and everything I knew was gone in a moment. I went deep within myself, to a place no one could ever touch. Not even the killer. How I knew that was a mystery. But Maggie was there.

There was no color or shape to the well of darkness I had fallen into. Only a warm security that I wrapped around me like an affectionate embrace. And Maggie's voice, soothing as she eased away the pain.

"It's okay. I won't let you fall, kiddo. It's okay."

When I was an infant, she had done the same. I knew this place. What I didn't know was how it was possible that I shared it with a dead woman.

The subliminal implants—had she put more in my mind? What were they for? What reason would she have had to do this to me?

"Always with the questions!" Maggie's rich contralto spilled over with laughter. "I think a damn drone makes less enquiries!"

"Maggie. What's happened to me? Why am I here?"

"That mop-faced pink guy was able to start your heart again. Problem is, someone interfered, messed with your brain waves, and you never regained consciousness. In reality, you're in a deep coma."

"That stinks."

"Yeah, it does." I could hear her blowing out smoke from one of the illegal cigarettes she thought I never knew about. "So what are you going to do about it?"

"Can't we talk somewhere else?" I shuddered. "This place is giving me the creeps."

"Voilá," Maggie said.

I was back on Terra. In the house of Joseph Grey Veil. In my old room.

Maggie stood there, as if still alive. She dusted off the mantel and scowled at a regal photoscan of my creator. Same old Maggie. She wore a gaudy tunic that was a little too tight. Lots of accessories. Her silver-streaked red hair glowed like a traffic drone signal.

I sat on the edge of my sleeping platform. A glance down found a childish body dressed in pajamas. My hair hung down my flat chest in two long braids. Bemused, I held up one chunky dark cable.

"Trying to turn me back into a kid, Maggie?"

"I liked you when you were ten. You weren't trying to be your father back in those days." She reached over, picked up a doll, and tossed it across the room at me. I managed to catch it. "Remember Crissy Credits?"

I examined the toy. "Yeah, I do. She came with her own credit chip and miniature shopping center." I fingered the doll's bright blond curls. "You bought this for me."

"Do you remember what Joseph gave you for your tenth birthday?"

I snorted and put the doll aside. "My first scanner. He made me practice using it on you. I identified that ingrown toenail with it." I smiled, then winced at the flare of pain that produced. "You were my first surgical patient."

"Goddamn it." She planted her hands on her hips. "What did that oversized blueberry ape do to your face?"

My fingers touched my cheek. "Long story. Why don't you tell me why you brought me here?"

"*You* brought you here. Once your heart stopped, the subliminal memories I implanted began to surface. It's important, Joey. Stop looking at me like that."

"I can't believe you stuck all this junk in my mind." I sighed. "So what gem of wisdom are you going to hand me this time?"

"Wisdom?" Maggie chuckled. "Is that what you think this is? Oh, no, honey. I'm no teacher."

"You were a great mom."

Her smile trembled a little. "Yeah, well, I tried. It wasn't hard; you were a sweet kid. Now, listen to me carefully. A lot of those blueberry people are depending on you. You've got to stop this nutso who's killing them."

"How?"

"Use your head, not your heart. It's like a dimensional puzzle game. You have the pieces. Put them together."

It seemed like we had only been speaking for moments, but suddenly I became aware of the passage of time.

"I've got to go back, now." Another sensation penetrated, a mind battering against the walls of the darkness. "Duncan."

"Now, him I like," Maggie said. "He has great eyes. How does he do that color-changing thing with them?"

"Maggie. Please." I stopped and concentrated for a moment. "How could you like his eye color? You died before I ever met Reever."

"You always think in such categorical patterns, Joey. When you get on this side of creation, you can lecture me all you want about existential paradoxes. Now go back. They think you're dying."

"Am I?"

"No, baby. You won't die."

I opened my eyes. "Ma . . . geee . . ." I croaked.

Adaola shrieked and dropped a chart down on the bed beside me. A moment later, Squilyp appeared. His gildrells stiffened like a bunch of exclamation marks.

"If you ever try that again, Healer, I will stop your heart for good!"

" 'Sokay . . . Squid . . . Lips . . ." My voice slurred, as though my speech center had been damaged. "Ho . . . long?"

"Thirty-seven hours since you entered deep coma."

"N-not . . . c-coma . . ."

I slid into the shallow darkness of natural sleep, and I spent a long interval there before I sensed another voice calling to me.

Cherijo. Cherijo.

Duncan.

I felt disoriented. Disconnected from my body. Barely able to contain the frantic thoughts pouring into my mind.

Out of my . . . Are you in pain . . . ? What went wrong?

Maggie. I managed a ghost of a chuckle. *Subliminal . . . implants . . . long story.* I smelled something warm and male close to my face. Heard the steady rhythm of a human heart. Felt the stroke of a gentle hand on my hair. *So tired.*

Then sleep, Cherijo. You are safe. I will stay here with you until you wake up.

I slept with my cheek against his chest, cradled in arms that kept me safe.

Two days later, Reever accompanied me to the Captain's office, along with Adaola. I carried the discs with the signals Salo had received, statements from Squilyp and the other Jorenian nurse, along with a copy of my chart.

Xonea got to his feet when we entered, every inch the polished, professional Jorenian ship commander as he made a formal gesture of greeting.

"Senior Healer. Are you recovered?"

We were going to be polite, were we? "My nose wasn't broken, and my face won't be scarred," I said. "My ribs, however, still twinge now and then."

That put a dent in his composure. "I regret what occurred in the detainment cell."

I didn't blink an eyelash. "I'll bet you do."

"I attempted to see you several times," he said. The slight change of tone revealed a flicker of anger. "I was not allowed to approach your berth in Medical."

Just as I'd ordered. "Then you met my personal guards. Nice guys, don't you think?"

He didn't appreciate my humor. "It was unnecessary to post guards, Cherijo. I will not touch you in anger again."

"Don't make promises you don't intend to keep, Captain." I placed the discs on his desk and activated a recording drone. "I am Senior Healer Cherijo Torin, presently meeting with Captain Xonea Torin, on board the Jorenian survey vessel *Sunlace*. Witnesses to this meeting are ship's Linguist Duncan Reever, and Senior Nurse Adaola Torin."

"You seek some sort of litigation against me?" Xonea sat back down.

"Captain, this"—I leaned over and nudged one disc toward Xonea—"is the audio/vid record of my death. I present this data as proof conclusive that at the time and date specified, my heart stopped functioning and I was declared dead."

"Declared *dead*?" Xonea asked.

Adaola stepped forward. "Senior Healer Cherijo chose

her right to embrace the stars. Her path was diverted as a result of cardiac failure induced by electristim."

"Indeed?" Xonea made a show of looking me over. "For one who has embraced the stars, you appear very animated, my Chosen."

"Correction." I nudged another disc toward him. "I died, and according to Jorenian law twelve, applications thirty-three through forty-seven, remained dead long enough to meet the criteria to break Choice. I am no longer *your Chosen.*"

Xonea's breath hissed out. "No."

"Let me quote: 'Only the death of either Chosen can break the bond.' I died. The bond's broken, pal."

"You are *still* alive!"

"There is a historical precedent," Reever said. "A Jorenian female of HouseClan Vaseran Chose a male shortly before he became grievously ill. At one point, his heart arrested. Although he survived, the resulting damage was considerable. His Chosen was permitted to Choose another, based on the fact that her bondmate's path had been diverted, and she could not accompany him."

"I know that case!" Xonea swept the discs from his desk with one flick of his hand. "The Vaseran male was paralyzed and catatonic. It was a merciful ruling so the female could have children and a normal life." His hair shimmered as he swung toward me. "You are not crippled, my Chosen."

"No, I'm not. Which is why Salo sent a transdimensional signal to Joren three days ago." I stooped and picked up one of the discs he had shoved off the desk. "The case was brought before the Ruling Council. Here's their judgment. Want to guess what they said?"

"No." He sat down, his eyes wide as he stared at the disc. "It cannot be possible. I Chose you. You are mine."

I put my hands on his desk and ducked until I was in his line of sight. *"Not—any—more."*

Xonea stared at me. "I will simply Choose you again. What say you now, Senior Healer?"

"You can't," I replied. "I've already been Chosen by someone else."

At his cue, Reever moved to my side and took one of

my hands. "Cherijo and I have discussed plans to be married. In Terran tradition, that is equal to Choosing."

"It cannot be thus!" Xonea bellowed.

I pointed to the data from Joren. "We asked the council for their opinion on that subject, too. They agreed. You can't Choose me again, Xonea. Reever got me first."

Adaola watched as her ClanBrother covered his face with his hands. Her reserve broke at last and she went around the desk to put her arms around him.

"Leave us, if you would," she said, her dark head close to Xonea's. "I will talk with him now."

Reever and I marched out. Only when the door panel closed did I let out the breath I'd been holding. "Do you think he believed that last part?"

Reever waited until we walked past a couple of crew members before he answered. "I dislike lying to the Captain."

"You didn't lie. You said we discussed getting married. You just didn't tell him I turned you down."

"Such an omission is still wrong, Cherijo."

We could debate this all day, but I had work to do. "I have to get back to Medical. Rogan is probably trying to kill off half the patients," I said. "Do me a favor. Don't go to Xonea and start confessing, okay? I'd hate to think I went through all that for nothing. And one more thing."

"What is it?"

I reached up and touched his cheek. "Thanks, Duncan. You're a true friend." I hurried off.

Medical was in smooth operation by the time I reported for my shift. Squilyp had managed to supervise Rogan and keep him busy while at the same time ensuring none of our patients suffered. He also arranged the schedule so that I rarely if ever worked the same shift with Rogan.

The Omorr had been apprised of our plans and was waiting anxiously to hear the result of my meeting with Xonea.

"It worked. It's over," I said. "Adaola is up there consoling him now."

"He must be devastated," Squilyp said.

"He'll live." I picked up the chart of our burn patient. "Well, someone looks ready to get out of here today."

The programmer, whose name was Lalona, slipped to her feet and stretched. It was wonderful to see her face and derma restored to their former flawless condition. "I am more than ready, Senior Healer. Give me leave, and I will vacate this berth before you can blink!"

"Seems no one appreciates the luxury of being cared for by the finest trained professionals in the universe," I said in disgust. "All right, Lalona, get out of my Medical Bay."

She thanked us both before she left. Squilyp, I saw, watched her go, and didn't hear a word I said until I nudged him with my elbow.

"What?" The Omorr's pink skin flushed puce around the gildrells. "I beg your pardon, Senior Healer. What did you say?"

"I said she's a very pretty woman." I studied the way his membranes contracted nervously. "You like her, don't you?"

"I have come to care very much for her."

"Well, what are you waiting for?" I grinned and waved a hand toward the door. "Go get her and ask her to share a meal with you."

"I would." He puffed out some air through his gildrells. "Unfortunately, Omorr and Jorenians are not compatible species."

"What a shame." It really was. "There's no way you and Lalona could . . . ?" I trailed off delicately.

"No. Even if I could Bond with a Jorenian, I could not . . ." He averted his eyes. "I must consider an Omorr female for purposes of intimacy. Perhaps someday, when my work does not require so much of my time."

"You can still be friends with her, right?"

He shook his head. "It is better that I maintain some distance from her; my attachment will fade."

"I'm sorry, Squilyp," I said. And I was.

We reviewed the day's schedule and caseload. Most of the patients were reporting for routine treatments, now that the injured cases had been cleared and discharged. Lalona had been the last of those recovering from the mercenary attack.

"Where's Rogan?" I asked just before the Omorr went off shift.

"Didn't you know? We'll be transitioning in a few hours, when we reach his homeworld system. He's getting ready to leave the ship."

"Oh. Right." I really needed to start accessing my relays more often. "What's it called?"

"Ichthora."

"Sounds like the right name. What are the natives called? The Ickies?"

"Ichthori."

"Hmmmm." I flipped a chart to display when it occurred to me there was more involved with dropping Rogan off on his homeworld than merely assuming an orbit. My head snapped up. "Why the hell are we sending a team down with him?"

"Captain's orders."

We'd just see about that. "Tell me you're on the sojourn roster."

Squilyp shook his head.

"Wonderful." I tossed the chart aside and went to stare through the ward viewer. "With my luck, the entire planet will be populated by Rogans. The Captain has a real sense of humor." I swung around. "Well, there's no way I—Squilyp? Squilyp!"

He had hopped out so quietly that I hadn't heard him, and made a clean getaway.

PART FOUR:

Betrayer

CHAPTER SIXTEEN

Rogan's Move

Xonea ignored the ten signals I sent to him about the sojourn. Guess he was still mad at me for dumping him. Salo and Reever were on the team, along with Dhreen and a couple of anthropologists. I agreed to go only if I could take one of my personal guards with me.

"There is no need for additional security," Salo said, trying to reassure me. "The Ichthori are a peaceful people. We will meet them, perhaps share a meal, and learn more of their culture."

"Yeah, well, if Rogan turns out to be the Crown Prince of the Icky People, I want someone with weapons at my back. Just to be on the safe side."

Ichthora, according to the database, listed tech trade as their main source of income. Salo had orders to keep bartering to a minimum, as the *Sunlace* had an overabundance of technology. From the way Rogan talked about the place, I expected some superbly modern, highly developed world populated by geniuses and paved with soaring alloy edifices.

We landed in a swamp.

I looked out of the viewport as the team prepared to disembark. "There are pools of water out there on the Transport docking pad," I said. "We're *sitting* in one of them."

"Biodecon results are negative," Dhreen called. "I'm opening the hull doors."

"Close them," I said a moment later, covering my nose and mouth with my hand. Ichthora was a world of rotten vegetation, estuaries of yellow, muddied water, and dense islands of stunted trees. It also *smelled* like it. "Please."

Thick, steamy heat accompanied the stench, while insects began buzzing in through the open doors. I couldn't resist the urge to swat at them. Rogan shouldered his one case and gestured toward the docking ramp.

"After you, Dr. Torin."

"I'll stay in the launch, thanks." I had no desire to go wading through the muck out there. I waved my hand at the swarm of tiny insects circling around my head. "Where are the envirosuits?"

Salo and Reever took positions on either side of me. Each grabbed an arm and made me get up. They walked me down the ramp the way they'd escort a prisoner.

"Where's my guard?" I asked.

"Directly behind you, Senior Healer," my guard said.

"Shoot these men."

Salo chuckled. "It is not so bad, Senior Healer."

"Oh, yeah? I happen to know a human's sense of smell is more developed than a Jorenian's is. So don't try to tell *me* it's not that bad." I looked toward the perimeter of the Transport area, and saw at least a dozen bodies lying facedown in the shallow pools. "Oh, my God!"

I would have run toward them, but Reever grabbed me first.

"There is nothing wrong with them," he said. "Observe."

I watched as the facedown bodies twitched, then moved a few inches. One raised on elbow-shaped fins and awkwardly dragged itself from one pool to another.

"*These* people trade tech?" I glanced around. "They can't even walk!"

"Native Ichthori do not manufacture or deal in tech." Rogan gave me a lofty sneer. "Half our population is made up of offworlders who have mated with natives. *They* are the ones who produce and trade."

That made more sense.

Rogan gestured at some of the partially submerged figures. "My family has gathered to greet us."

I had to ask the obvious. "What are they doing?"

"Why, they're feeding, Doctor." Rogan looked at one of the empty pools with what could only be called greed. His case dropped to the ground. "Excuse me."

A moment later he, too, had joined the Ichthori and was facedown in the mud.

I turned to Salo. "I am *not* sharing a meal with these people."

That wasn't the only strange revelation. Rogan's physical appearance did little to prepare me for Ichthora and its bizarre inhabitants. Compared to his nonhuman relations, he was erudite. Gorgeous. Perfumed.

I endured the long, very uncomfortable hours of the sojourn. Barely. I played Senior Healer, perspired freely, swatted insects, and stepped over the most of the natives. I did not partake of their diet, which they dredged from the swamp mud at the bottom of the tidal pools that littered the surface of the planet.

There was no sign of the League, but that didn't make me feel any better.

"Just where *is* all this highly developed tech?" I said to Reever. We had to pick our way through the pools of sludge and step over yet another filter-feeding Ichthori.

He pointed up, and I raised my eyes. The thickets of what I thought to be trees were actually organically formed structures, topped by a series of funnellike platforms that connected each group. Apparently the offworlder inhabitants lived in them. Their Ichthori mates used adapted hover lift technology to ascend, then slid from one "tree house" to another on their bellies.

The lethargic mud-dwellers made very little attempt to communicate with us. Reever attempted to translate some of the bubbling and snorting sounds we heard now and then. Apparently all they cared to talk about were the best spots to feed on the insect larvae and microorganisms that constituted the bulk of their diet. They must spend most of their *lives* on their bellies. Which explained Rogan's intense dislike of remaining vertical and active.

After feeding with his family for an extended period, Rogan returned and agreed to gather some of the "leaders" of the Ichthori to meet with us.

While we waited, I idly gathered some round, speckled stones that were piled around the base of each tree. The prettiest specimens I slipped into a pocket for the ship's geologist to examine later.

It took Rogan a long time. Very few of the non-Icthori

inhabitants were willing to leave their climate-controlled tree houses to socialize with us. I couldn't blame them.

One squat, block-shaped Ramotharran trader passing by us stopped to chat. I had to find out why any sane humanoid would *want* to stay on this godforsaken planet.

"What keeps you here?" I wiped the back of my hand over my brow. "It can't be the heat, smell, or the bugs."

He gave me a shrewd look. "Do you know how an offworlder usually ends up staying here? They impregnate one of the Icthori."

"But how—never mind, I don't want to know," I said at first, then my curiosity got the better of me. "Of course . . . in the interests of science . . . okay, tell me."

"Happened to me my first trip here," the Ramotharran said. He pointed to one of the natives who had inexplicably turned over. From the diamond-shaped orifice on the thorax, I could tell this one was a female. Her face was, well, not as much *face* as it was *mouth*. Elongated versions of the polyps Rogan possessed heavily fringed a central aperture. A big, four-lipped, gaping aperture.

Too bad the Captain didn't make the trip this time, I thought. I'd love to see Xonea give *her* the traditional kiss of peace. She'd probably suck his whole head in.

"Watch now." The trader nudged me, his protruding black eyes grim. "Here comes a male."

Another native crawled over to the female, slid over her, and remained still for a moment. Then the male slid off and crawled away.

"He just inseminated her," the trader said.

"Did he?" That was it? Crawl on, wham, crawl off, we're having a baby?

"Yes. She'll flip back over now." And she did.

"Do the Ichthori generally mate in public?"

"They're not what you'd call a *modest* people. Nor do the females pass up any opportunity to get—"

"I see," I said. "You say something like that happened to you? You—er—crawled on to one of the females?"

"Not likely." He snorted. "I slipped in the mud, was all. Landed right on top of the wrong side of my mate. It was all over before I could say a word."

"Your mate?"

The Ramotharran nodded and heaved a sigh. "Ichthori

law requires an offworlder to mate with an Ichthori female if he impregnates her. I thought about denying the paternity charge, but as you can see . . ." he waved a hand behind him.

A young Ichthori crawled up to us. He raised his flattened skull, and between the polyps I saw two bulging black eyes staring at me. A rudimentary nose sniffed.

"The boy is undoubtably mine."

"Hello." I smiled at the child, who tried to imitate my facial expression. The Ramotharran sighed again. "He seems, um, very bright."

"Oh, sure, he's developing far ahead of the other full-blooded Ichthori young. It's only . . . " He spread his hands. "Can't exactly toss a romlo ball back and forth with him."

"I guess you get used to living here after a while?"

The trader's one nostril flared. "I used to be a geologist, until that happened." He nodded toward his son. "I went into trade just to have excuse to get off this miserable sludge ball occasionally."

A bubbling sound interrupted our conversation. I looked down to see one of the adult Ichthori clinging to the trader's leg, the notched fins clutching his boot. Her mouthace remained buried in the mud below our footgear.

"My mate," he introduced me. My vocollar wouldn't translate the sounds he made into anything but bubbles.

"Hello," I greeted her. I noticed a swollen sac protruding from one of her legs and frowned. "That's a bad tumor she's got there."

"It's not a tumor," the Ramotharran said, and gave his mate a glum look. "It's our second child. At least, I think it's mine."

We took a lift to one of the larger tree-house structures, where six of the Ichthori leaders (all clearly half-strains) had assembled. In our honor, the half dozen males had propped themselves in a half-slouch on some benches and invited our party to be seated. All six wore standard wrist coms.

There was no table between us, nor did the Ichthori wear any manner of garments. I got an up-close view of the anatomical varieties that offworld gene strains had afforded. The mud stains on my tunic sleeve, I quickly decided, were much more riveting.

One large, green-yellow Ichthori with less facial fringing than his colleagues stood for a moment. He had three pairs of visual organ stalks protruding above his feeding polyps. Unlike the others, he wore a sort of girdle that didn't cover anything but sported a number of bladed weapons.

"Krugal," he said, and pointed a flipper/hand toward the triple clusters of broad nipples on his chest. I darted a look down. Yep, three of everything else, too. "We hear you want to talk."

Salo, as the appointed Jorenian representative, stood and made a brief bow. "We are honored you have taken time to speak with us."

Krugal plopped back down and waved at Salo. "We have fed well today. There was nothing better to do. Tell us, have you come to trade, or simply marvel at life on our world?"

Marvel? My jaw sagged. Did this bottom feeder actually use the word *marvel*?

"Our interest lies largely in surveying and recording data about Ichthora," Salo said, his expression diplomatic. "We will have to return to our ship very soon."

Yesterday couldn't be soon enough for me, I thought.

"Sit, sit. Our kinsman Phorap" —Krugal nodded toward Rogan—"tells us you travel to Varallan. That is quite a distance from our divine Ichthora. Why not stay, enjoy the pleasures of our world? Life is good here." His eye stalks bobbed, their ends glowing bright red.

Salo sat down. Diplomacy was beginning to wear on him. The *good* life on Ichthora, I suspected, had very little in common with a Jorenian's view of the same.

"We thank you for your gracious offer of hospitality. However, as our people have responsibilities, we must depart." Salo made an eloquent gesture. "I am certain you understand."

"No, I don't," Krugal said, and yawned. I wished he hadn't. Who would have guessed teeth could sprout all the way back there? "That blue skin of yours is unusual. Can we buy you from your Captain?"

It took a lot to shock a Jorenian warrior, but that did the job. "Our crew is not for sale."

Krugal didn't stop there. His six red eyes inspected Reever, then me. The Ichthori leader grinned. If you could call what he did with that gaping hole a grin.

"Terrans don't often visit Ichthora. We would welcome the opportunity to learn more about your species."

Reever shook his head. "No, thank you."

I was no diplomat. "Not even if you drugged me."

"Dr. Torin bears the burden of being a true Terran," Rogan said. "She is a hostile xenophobe."

"You always say such nice things about me, Phorap." I gave him a sweet smile.

Salo rose. "Our time, as I have indicated, is limited. If you will excuse us, we will complete our surveys and return to our vessel."

"Sell her to me," Krugal said.

Salo looked from me to the Ichthori. "What say you?"

"The Terran female—she is not one of your species. I'll buy her from you. Name your price."

"Salo, let's go," I said, rising to my feet. My guard and Reever flanked me.

"I must refuse your request," Salo said through his teeth. "Excuse us." He looked at Dhreen, who had just entered the structure. "Pilot, prepare the launch for departure."

"No," Rogan said, and got up at once. He held a small weapon in his hand, and pointed it toward me. "None of you are leaving Ichthora just yet." His four lips stretched. "Except the good Doctor."

"I'm going to kill Xonea when we get back to the ship," I said as Reever's fingers plucked at the knotted vines around my wrists. "I knew Rogan had it in with the League. I *knew* it."

Reever sighed. "I cannot do this if you keep twitching."

"I'm not twitching, I'm agitated."

"Stop being agitated. Krugal said he would return shortly."

We stood tied together, back to back, locked in one of the small chambers away from the center of the colony. Salo, Dhreen, and the others had been hauled off to similar structures. They left me and Reever tied together on Rogan's orders.

"Keep the humans together," he told some alert-looking

half-strain Ichthori. About a dozen of them had come in with weapons and taken all of us hostage. "Krugal wishes to interrogate them both."

That had been two hours ago. Now Reever was patiently loosening the last of the intricate knots binding my wrists to his.

"Hurry." My own patience was in short supply. "He'll be back any minute."

"It is almost done. There. Try to pull free."

I strained, and my wrists slowly separated. Quickly I worked them from the vines until I was free. The return of unrestricted circulation made numbing pain shoot up both arms. I whirled around and began working at untying Reever's hands. Too many knots, not enough time. I looked around the interior for anything I could use as a weapon.

"Krugal is coming," Reever said.

I turned, put my arms behind my back, and pressed up against him. My fingers continued plucking at the knots.

"Whatever you do," I murmured, "don't let him know I'm loose."

Krugal slid through the door and propped himself in front of us. His body left a trail of slick brown mud. The swamp smell rolled off him. He appeared highly pleased with himself.

"I've fed well tonight in celebration," he said as he awkwardly rose to his vertical stance.

"How nice," I said. "Celebrating what?"

He shuffled over until he was only a foot from me. His body wasn't the only thing that was erect. "Our triumph over you, my kinsman's enemies."

"We saved your kinsman's life, and brought him here to Ichthora," Reever said. "Do you consider those the actions of an enemy?"

"It doesn't matter," he said, and rubbed his handlippers together. "Phorap says the League will pay handsomely for this female." He stepped closer to me, which made it necessary for me to breathe through my mouth.

"Leader Krugal, the beings you believe to be your friends are dangerous," Reever said. "They will take Dr. Torin without paying the Ichthori."

"Then we will tie some of *them* up until they do." Krugal

didn't seem concerned. He studied the way my tunic fastened. "You know, I've never had a Terran before."

"Don't hold your breath, lover boy," I said, and let go of Duncan's hands.

He laughed. "She is eager to fight. Good. That adds zest to the play. Our females are too passive." His flipper reached for my tunic.

Just before he touched me, I swung my fist out. I drove it low, hard, and directly into the three things Krugal seemed to treasure most.

"Aarrggghh!"

I followed through with my other fist. Air bellowed from his lungs. A strange, high-pitched whine emerged from his fringe.

"How's that for zest?" I asked as he sank down to the flooring. I waited until I saw his eyes stalks wilt, then bent to retrieve one of the blades on his belt. "I'll just borrow this for a moment."

With a rapid series of slashes I cut Reever's hands free.

"You're very capable with a blade," he said, and rubbed his arms briskly.

"Trained to be." I handed the knife to him. After I took the belt from Krugal's unconscious body, I slung it over my shoulder. "You never know when you're going to be somewhere without a lascalpel."

After we tied up and gagged the Ichthori leader, we slipped from the small chamber. Confident, indolent, and negligent to the bone—if they had any—the Ichthori hadn't even bothered to post guards. We went from tree to tree until we found and released every member of the sojourn team. I turned Krugal's belt over to Salo.

"You left him unconscious?" he asked. He had pulled out one of the blades from the belt and was fingering it with a lover's caress.

"Not now," I said, and grabbed his arm. "We've got to get to the launch and get the hell off this planet. Rogan signaled the League mercenaries and offered to sell me to them. They're coming."

It took nearly an hour before we located the launch in the darkness. No one attempted to stop us or even question why we were loose. What few Ichthori we stepped over simply kept on feeding or snoring or whatever it was they were doing. Perhaps Krugal hadn't been missed. Maybe no one cared if their hostages escaped.

Or not.

"This is too easy," I said to Reever.

My suspicions were confirmed when I saw the launch was waiting with the hull doors still open. I grabbed Salo's arm and waved Dhreen over to us.

"Dhreen?" I whispered. "Did you secure the launch after we disembarked?"

"Of course I did, Doc," he whispered back.

"It is a trap." Salo said something else to the other Jorenians, too low for my vocollar to translate. He pulled all the blades from Krugal's belt and distributed them, then turned to me, Dhreen and Reever. "We will board the launch. Stay here and keep watch. The natives move quickly, when they have reason to."

Salo and the others melted into the shadows. Reever indicated a sheltered spot by a tree and we huddled there. Dhreen took position on the other side of the launch. A choked cry, cut off in the middle, floated from the launch cabin, and I winced.

"The Ichthori are coming," Reever said, and pointed. A long line of prone bodies were crawling through the muck toward us. In the middle of them was one figure, walking upright.

"Rogan." I started toward him. Reever jerked me back into the shadows.

"No, Cherijo. We must warn Salo."

I nodded with regret. I had a knife, Rogan still breathed. Life wasn't fair. "I'll go, Reever. I don't think you want to see Salo's handiwork."

With as fast a sprint as I could manage, I avoided the tidal pools and crossed the distance to the launch. Cautiously I looked inside. And immediately regretted it. "Oh, my God." Salo paused for a moment. Large pools of blood covered the deck around his feet. I swallowed hard. Remembered not to look at what the other Jorenians had done.

"Excuse me, Salo." I averted my eyes from the grisly thing hanging limply from his big hands. "We've got company."

Salo dropped the dead body of the mercenary he was

. . . decorating, and wiped the excess blood from his strong hands on the front of his victim's tunic. "We have to but dispose of the bodies, and we can depart."

"Hurry," I said, then climbed back down the docking ramp. I waved toward Reever, then hurried around the launch to find Dhreen.

I saw him struggling with an Ichthori female who had attached herself to his leg and was trying to pull him down into the mud. I kicked her, yanked his arm, and pulled him free of her grasp.

"No time for romance, Dhreen," I said, pushing him in front of me toward the launch. "We're leaving."

He shuddered with relief. "About time."

"We want the Terran," I heard Rogan shout. "The rest of you can go. Leave her."

Oh, good. I didn't have to leave this waste heap without getting a shot at Rogan after all.

Silently I motioned to Dhreen. "Here." I handed him one of the smooth round stones I had picked up near the tree houses. "Watch."

I dropped down and dug my hands in the brown muck. Dhreen imitated my actions. When we were armed, we darted across the open ground for the shuttle.

Pulses of energy smashed into the mud all around us. Rogan was only a few meters from us now, firing at our legs. Didn't want to damage the merchandise, I thought. We danced around the beams, but it was obvious we weren't going to reach the launch.

"Surrender!" Rogan yelled.

"Okay! We surrender!" I called, approaching Rogan slowly. I kept one hand behind my back. Just a little closer. "I give up! Let the others go!"

"Krugal is very unhappy, Doctor Torin. You may be on your back for days." Rogan leered. We were close enough now to catch a whiff of his stench.

"I don't think *I'm* going to assume that position, Phorap," I replied. I nodded to Dhreen. "Now!"

We volleyed our mud balls directly at Rogan. Mine hit him in the head with a solid thunk. Dhreen's curving pitch delivered his to the side of Rogan's thick neck. The heavy rocks we had packed in the center of each sphere did the job, and Rogan landed facedown in the muck. He wasn't going to be feeding for a couple of hours.

The prone Ichthori swarmed around Rogan, making bubbling snorts and trying to prop him up. Dhreen and I raced for the hull doors. The engines were already firing. Two of the team members literally dragged us through the closing panel.

"We have them, Salo!"

Dhreen and I were thrown to the bloodstained deck as the launch ascended sharply upward. When we cleared the upper atmosphere, the Oenrallian caught my hand and squeezed it with his spatulate fingers before he helped me up.

"Thanks, Doc."

I squeezed back. "You'll have to teach me that curve pitch someday."

We arrived back at the *Sunlace* in time to see the crew making final preparations for transition. Salo and I exchanged a few words before I took a gyrlift to Medical Bay.

Squilyp barred my path before I had taken six steps through the door panel. "Doctor! What has happened?"

"Did you prep the patients for transition? I—" I glared at him. "Get out of the way, Squid Lips."

"You are filthy," he said, his dark eyes eloquent.

I looked down. Ichthora muck covered my tunic. "Squilyp—"

"I can *smell* you, Doctor." He shuddered. "The bacteria alone . . ."

"Okay, okay. I'll go get cleaned up. Get the patients ready."

I ran down to my quarters. Jenner hissed as I darted inside.

"Just me, pal," I said as I stripped off my clothes and jumped into the cleanser. Two minutes later, I stepped out, free of dried mud and dripping all over the deck.

"Here."

Reever stood there, holding out a towel. I snatched it from him. Dried off fast. Wound it around me. Thought of where I'd like to hurt him.

"My door chime not working?" I asked.

"I didn't use it," he said as he sat down. I pulled my clothes on, awkwardly keeping the towel in place until I was covered. I had gotten used to living alone again, that was all.

"Why?"

The door panel opened before he could reply. Xonea stood just outside, along with Salo.

"That is why," Reever said.

"May we come in, Senior Healer?"

"Sure," I said. "Invite some of the crew. We'll have a party." Neither man reacted to my sarcasm. "Aren't we supposed to be transitioning right about now?"

"We cannot leave yet," Xonea said. "Fasala Torin is missing."

"There was no place for her to stow away on the launch," Dhreen said as we checked the interior for the third time. "I went over the storage holds myself. They were empty, except for the gear."

"What about Dr. Rogan?" Reever asked. "He was carrying a heavy pack."

"Not large enough," I said. "Fasala is nearly five feet tall, and weighs almost as much as I do. Even if she was tied up, Rogan's pack didn't have enough room in it to carry her."

Salo appeared, carrying rifles. "Here." He tossed a weapon to Dhreen, then Reever. "Arm yourselves. The mercenary fleet is approaching."

"Fleet?" I reflexively caught the rifle he tossed to me.

"Twenty-two ships. Half are comparable to the *Sunlace*."

I carefully put down the weapon. I healed people, I didn't shoot them. "We have to get out of here."

Salo nodded. "If Fasala is on Ichthora, we will come back for her." He said it with all the hopelessness of a parent unable to protect his child. "I must go to Darea."

"I'll go with you," I said.

He nodded. "She may need some . . . professional aid."

As we hurried through the corridor, we checked with the other search teams we encountered. No one had found a trace of the child, who had disappeared just before the launch left the *Sunlace* for Ichthora.

Darea was waiting in their quarters, in the event Fasala came home. When Salo told her we had not found their ClanDaughter, tears streamed down her beautiful face.

"Is there nothing we can do?"

Their door panel chimed. Darea shot to her feet and had it open before I could blink. She sagged as she saw who it was.

"Oh, come in, Navigator."

Hado Torin entered, and his good arm went around Darea. They hugged briefly, then the older man helped her to a chair.

"She will be found, my ClanCousin. Have no fear of that." Hado glanced at me. "Senior Healer, perhaps you can leave us? I will sit with her until Fasala is found."

"Yes, please." Darea nodded. Salo went to her and would have taken her in his arms, but she stepped back. "Go look for our child, Salo. I will wait for your signal."

He lifted her hand to his lips. "I will find her."

"Speaking of signals, has anyone checked your console lately?" I asked.

Salo hurried over, and scrolled through the intership file. "No, there is—" He paused, then pulled up a data-only screen. "There is a message here for Fasala. From you, Senior Healer."

I looked over his broad shoulder. "Salo, I never sent this." I read through the brief message. Someone pretending to be me had requested that Fasala meet them on level fourteen. The exact place where Fasala had been injured. "Has anyone checked the storage area on that level?"

"She would not go there," Salo said. "Fasala knows the area has been restricted."

"She might do it for me." I was thinking of the talk I'd had with her about facing her fears.

Salo immediately signaled Operational. "Send a team down to fourteen at once."

We ran. Two levels down from Salo's quarters, an impressive display of warning signs and portable barriers barred access to the storage facility. I noticed there was enough space for someone my size or smaller to duck under and crawl through. One of the barriers stood slightly askew.

"She's been here." I pointed to the jostled unit. Salo began ripping the equipment out of his path, tossing the heavy units aside like toys. I stayed out of range until he cleared the entrance panel.

"Fasala? Fasala!" he shouted as the door panel slid open. "Answer me, child!"

I picked my way around the discarded barriers and followed him into the storage facility. There was an eerie hollow feeling here, where weeks ago the buffer had shattered backward and hurt the little girl. Something was wrong. The fine hair on my arms and nape felt the ghostly brush of energy gathering around us.

"Salo! We have to get out of here! Now!"

"I must find her!"

I saw a faint ripple in the buffer covering the repaired hole in the hull.

"No!" I shouted, and tackled the Jorenian. Surprise was the only reason I knocked him down behind one of the large cargo bins. I landed right on top of him. He rolled me off and thrust me behind him.

A flash of blinding light appeared above us. The smell of melting alloys stung my nose, while a two-meter circular section of the cargo bin began to dissolve right next to us. I pushed myself up, and yelled as I yanked on his arm. "We have to go! Come on!"

We staggered away from the damaged bin. I looked back and saw a solid beam of energy pouring from the buffer itself into the metal where moments before we had been standing. The beam was nearly transparent, but hummed with menacing power. I glanced back at the buffer.

Just as the beam cut off, I saw a flickering, rainbow-fringed circle of light.

Salo hauled me out of the facility and sealed the door. He panted and his face dripped sweat. "What was that?" he demanded.

"That's what killed Roelm and Ndo," I replied, gasping for breath. "The same thing that hurt Fasala and her educators."

"It has done something to me as well." He lifted the edge of his tunic, and I saw his abdomen rapidly turning a mottled purple.

"Medical." I pointed to the gyrlift. "Right now."

"My Fasala—"

"We'll find her. Right now I have to see what kind of damage that thing did to you."

He nodded, already pale and shaking with reaction. I

pulled one of his long arms around my shoulders and got him into the gyrlift.

Salo collapsed just as we reached Medical. Immediately two nurses and Squilyp were there to help me maneuver his big frame onto an exam pad. Adaola gasped when I opened his tunic. His entire abdomen was badly bruised.

"Scan him for internal damage," I told the Omorr. "I've got to signal the Captain."

At the display, I waited impatiently until my emergency relay was put through. Xonea listened as I reported what had happened.

"Have you located the girl yet?" I asked.

"No," he said. "Search teams have been recalled. We must transition now."

"Someone has to tell Darea," I told him, then looked over my shoulder. "Report on Salo!"

"His spleen and pancreas are ruptured!" Squilyp yelled back. "He needs surgery, now!"

"Prep him. Surgical team, prepare for emergency procedure!" I turned back to the display. "How long until transition?"

"Fifteen minutes."

"I can't do this kind of surgery that fast!" I told him. "Can you transition sooner?"

Xonea's mouth thinned. "Five minutes."

"Do it, if you want Salo to live." I reached for the keypad.

"Cherijo." I looked up at the screen. "Will he remain on the path?"

"Salo has Fasala and Darea. Two very good reasons to stick to the path." I gave Xonea a half-smile. "Not to mention one of the best cutters in the quadrant working on him."

"Keep me advised. Prepare for emergency transition."

I yelled at the Omorr and the surgical team, who were frantically readying for the operation. "Hold it. The ship is going to transition first. We need to put Salo in sleep suspension, *now*." I gestured to most of the nurses and my resident. "Prep the patients. Adaola, you're with me. Move it, people!"

Adaola and I just managed to get Salo under as the ship

transitioned. We helped each other off the deck once real- ity righted itself and checked Salo.

"He's going into shock anyway!" Adaola cried out as we pulled him back out of suspension. "Blood pressure is dropping!"

"One hundred ccs of synepinephrine," I said as I in- creased oxygen flow. Salo's damaged tissues had begun to flood with fluid. I injected him with the bronchodilator drug. "Get his legs up, Adaola. That's it. Vitals look bet- ter." I stared at the monitor for a moment. "That's how they died. That's why Fasala went into shock. Proximity to the beam creates stress on the system. Direct exposure causes the cellular disruption."

"Senior Healer?" Adaola asked. She looked worried. I shook my head to clear it.

"Never mind. Prep him for surgery. I want him ready in two minutes." I put down my scanner and ran into the scrub room. My team was already geared and waiting. The Omorr hopped in after me. "Report."

"Minor injuries keep coming in, but we can handle it on the ward," Squilyp said. "Salo?"

"Anaphylactic shock brought on by proximity to intense sonic-based energy. Someone tried to shoot us with it."

"There is no such thing as a sonic-based weapon—"

"Oh yeah?" I finished scrubbing and snapped on my gloves. "I saw it, Squilyp. Salo used his body to shield mine. It melted a damn cargo bin right in front of us."

The Omorr's expression was comical. "But the only thing capable of doing that is—"

"—a resonant harmonicutter, I'll guess."

He nodded.

"Squilyp, I know you said these things are huge, that they couldn't fit one inside the ship. What if someone found a way to make one out of available materials here on the ship?" I put my mask and the rest of my gear on. "Is it possible someone is using this thing to kill our people?"

His gildrells flared. "If they could build it, we'd see it. It would have to be nearly as large as the entire ship."

"So what is almost as large as the ship that we see every- day that could be a harmonicutter?"

"Nothing. I've never seen a single piece of equipment that size—"

Neither had I. That was it. "Maybe we *can't* see it."

The Omorr looked at me. We were thinking the same thought. Said the same words together.

"The buffer."

Salo's surgery lasted six hours. I successfully avoided a complete pancreatectomy, by repairing the small ruptures in both the head and body of the organ. The Jorenian exocrine tissue was remarkably resilient; the same damage would have killed a Terran. Once I'd salvaged the main duct, I removed the pancreatic tail and linked the remainder of the repaired organ with part of Salo's small intestine.

The larger problem during the operation was presented by Salo's spleen. In a Terran, the tiny organ usually weighed no more than seven ounces. In a Jorenian, it was five times that weight and triple the volume. Standard procedure on Terra required a splenectomy; in adult humans there were virtually no ill effects after complete removal.

My friend Salo, however, had not one but three arteries leading into his spleen. He hemorrhaged from two of them. Jorenian spleens not only removed worn-out blood cells and fought infection, but also regulated their digestive and immune systems, too. If I removed it, he would die in a matter of days.

Operating to repair a spleen compared to the most delicate of neuro repairs. Once I clamped off the bleeders, I had to work through the tiny forest of arterial branches, suturing the torn lymph tissue itself. I imagined sewing a sponge back together without leaving any stitch marks. This ranked slightly below that. I was working against time as well. We had lowered Salo's body temperature, but the spleen would not survive being cut off from the blood supply very long.

"Tissue looks healthy," I muttered as the nurse blotted my brow. "Salo may be a nice guy and regenerate some of this on his own." I finished repairing the torn arteries and released the clamps. A near-black color returned at once to the pale organ. In this species, black meant healthy. "Looks good." I inspected the remainder of his open abdomen. "Anyone have an objection to me closing this patient? Anyone really brave enough to tell me, that is?"

Everyone chuckled.

"Good. Let's wrap it up."

After I finished suturing the long surgical incision down the center of his torso, I stripped off my gloves and rubbed the back of my neck.

"Move him into post-op," I said. "I want two nurses monitoring him until he regains consciousness."

I went out to the scrub room and cleaned up before I returned to the ward. I was surprised to see Xonea there. Adaola was running a scanner over him. I went over and gave him a brief summary of the operation on Salo.

"Has someone informed Darea?" I asked once I'd finished.

Xonea shook his head. "We could not locate her."

"She's in her quarters. I left her there with Hado just before Salo was injured."

"You don't understand. While you were operating on Salo, Darea disappeared. Just like Fasala." He grimaced and leaned forward, favoring his abdomen.

"For God's sake!" I snatched the scanner from Adaola and checked the display. "Just what I thought. All the stress is eating holes in your stomach."

"I do not require an examination!" Xonea grated, and pushed off the table. I checked the last of the readings and caught my breath.

"Get back on there. Now."

"Cherijo—"

"Now!" I ran the scanner over him one more time to be sure. While he sat there, digging his fingers into the exam pad, I went to the database display and entered the scanner readings. What the diagnostic array returned made me want to spit. I went back over to the exam table and planted my hands on my hips.

"What the hell are you doing, eating jaspforran? Are you trying to kill yourself?"

Xonea's wrathful expression faded. "Jaspforran? I have not taken any of that wretched herb. Why would I?"

"Don't lie to me! You've got so much in your blood-stream it's starting to penetrate your gastric lining!" I said. "No wonder you've been so out of control! That stuff will . . . that will . . ." I halted at the obvious confusion he displayed. "You really didn't eat any?"

He shook his head.

I ran the scanner a third time. Found nothing in his stomach, except for traces of jaspkerry tea and the high levels of the warrior's herb.

"What does this stuff taste like? Jaspkerry spice?" He nodded. I ran the scanner over myself, then put it down. "Well, that explains a lot."

"What say you?"

"I'll tell you later." After I administered a mild tranquilizer to Xonea to counter the effects of the jaspforran, I signaled Hado. The navigator responded from his duty station.

"Hado? Weren't you going to stay with Darea?"

"I was, Senior Healer, until I was signaled to return at once to Command Level." He made a slightly frustrated gesture. "In error, as it happens. I will return to her quarters now."

"Don't bother, she's not there." The next person I tried was Ktarka. The educator appeared to have just stepped out of her cleansing unit.

She smiled at the screen. "Yes, Senior Healer?"

"Is Darea there with you?"

"No, she is not. After I heard the news about Fasala, I signaled her. She wished to be alone, she said." The Jorenian woman frowned as she tugged her towel higher. "Has the child been found?"

"No, and now Darea is missing." I tried to smile reassuringly. "Sorry, Educator. It's a long story. I'll get back to you when I find her."

"Signal me if you need my assistance."

Squilyp had been listening and now waited for me as I walked from the display. "You're going to look for Darea?"

"Yes. Something isn't right about all this. Why would two members of a ClanFamily disappear, and the third receive serious injuries, all on the same day?"

"Unfortunate coincidence?" the Omorr said.

"Or they all have a connection to the killer."

I went directly to Salo and Darea's quarters, to see if Fasala or her ClanMother had returned there. The rooms were silent.

I went into Fasala's room, and even checked under the sleeping platform. Nothing but a rather dusty plasball under there. I opened the storage containers, and even the compartment where the child had carefully put her clean garments. Aside from the usual contents, they were empty.

When I returned to the living area, I smelled a trace of something odd. Cleanser? I stepped past the sofa, and heard a faint squishing sound. Beneath my footgear, the loose, fluffy weave of the area rug was damp. I bent down and sniffed at it. The odor was much stronger. Had Darea spilled some tea? The wet area disappeared beneath the bottom edge of the sofa, so I pushed it back to see what was under it.

There were several green splotches on the rug beneath the sofa. My fingers gingerly touched one of them.

Jorenian blood. Wet. Fresh.

I got to my feet and ran into the larger bedroom, calling Darea's name. I pulled the room apart, opening everything large enough to contain her body. The cleansing unit was empty. Nothing under the bed. I sagged against it for a moment, resting my cheek on the soft coverlet. When I opened my eyes, I saw what had happened to Darea.

I contacted Barrea in Engineering first, then sent a coded signal to the ship's linguist. It took a moment to receive his reply.

"It will work, but why do you wish to do this, Senior Healer?" Barrea asked over our secured channel.

"I know who the killer is."

An hour later I sent out five more signals. Within minutes, Hado, Adaola, Xonea, Ktarka, and Reever showed up at Darea's door panel. They looked at each other, then at me. Adaola appeared nervous. Hado and Ktarka seemed bewildered. Reever's expression never changed. Xonea glared at me.

"Come in, please." I gestured to the empty room behind me. "I need to speak to all of you."

Xonea folded his arms. "Senior Healer, I have no time—"

"Shut up and sit down, Captain." I set out servers of tea and sat down in the chair I'd set a foot back from the rest of the furnishings. "Try the tea. It's real jaspkerry," I told Xonea. "I programmed it myself."

"Senior Healer, have you word of Darea or Fasala?" Ktarka asked.

"Not exactly. I came here looking for Darea, and found some blood on the floor." I pointed. "Right there where Adaola is sitting."

The Jorenian nurse lifted her footgear at once.

"Don't worry. It's under the sofa. When I found the blood, I scanned it. The DNA matches Darea's perfectly. Is she dead?" I looked at each intent face. Not a flicker of reaction. "Well, I suppose if I was a cold-blooded killer, I'd hardly volunteer the information."

That icy formality the Jorenians were capable of settled over my little group. They became big blue statues. Reever stood to one side, silently watching me.

Hado's gentle eyes narrowed. "You believe one of us diverted Darea's path?"

"Cherijo, this is not amusing," Xonea said. "If you have information about the murders, tell me now."

"I'm getting to that part. Hado, let me ask you a question: What's the first thing you do after you invent a weapon?" The navigator appeared confused. "You test it. In a remote place, like the storage compartment on level fourteen. On a live subject, like Fasala Torin."

"No one could want to deliberately hurt an innocent child," Ktarka said in protest.

"The killer had a reason for using Fasala as a test subject." I smiled at her. "But I'll get to that later, too."

"What weapon do you speak of, Healer?" Hado asked me.

"The killer created a resonant harmonicutter here on board the *Sunlace*."

"No level on this ship is large enough to contain a harmonicutter!"

I smiled. "You're right, Hado, you can't fit a harmonicutter on the ship. But you can use the ship's *buffer* to store energy, and act *like* a harmonicutter."

"That kind of technology doesn't exist!"

"It does now. I'm no engineer, so I checked with someone who is. A smaller device would have to be placed on the buffer to release the power in a focused sonic beam. Once the victim was located and targeted, a remote unit could be used to trigger the beam."

"Then why wasn't Fasala killed?" Adaola asked.

"What the killer couldn't predict was that Fasala's educators would come looking for her. My theory is that the killer tried to protect the two adult women and reversed the power flow. The sudden stress from the backlash made the buffer shatter."

I sipped my tea as I let that sink in, then continued.

"Before the killer could try again, Roelm Torin noticed the engine surge. Did you know Roelm was one of the *Sunlace*'s original designers? He knew those engines better than anyone. He must have figured out what the killer was doing. He was on his way to Engineering when he was murdered."

"How did you discover these facts, Senior Healer?" Hado asked.

"I have proof, but for now I'll save that, too. Let's talk about motive." I turned to the Captain. "Xonea, you aren't going to win any awards for self-control. And when Reever accessed my subconscious, I saw you as the killer."

"I have wronged you in the past," he said, the words forced and stiff. "Yet the only injuries I have inflicted have been upon you."

"I know," I acknowledged. "But that wasn't your fault. Someone removed the jaspkerry stores from the prep units in both our quarters and the galley, and replaced it with pure jaspforran."

"What?" He clenched his fists and struggled for control. "By the Mother, that explains the ungovernable rage I have been enduring."

"From the way that stuff affects the Jorenian central nervous system, I'm surprised you haven't punched a hole through the hull," I said. "I also found micro-encapsulated artificial enzymes had been added to my Terran tea and all the Terran stores in the galley. They stimulated my sympathoadrenal response and made me, shall we say, slightly more aggressive than usual? The few times I had Xonea's tea only made it worse."

"Who has done this?" Xonea wanted to know.

"I'm getting to that." I turned to the senior nurse. "Adaola, you were on duty when Roelm and Yetlo died in Medical. Off duty when Ndo was murdered. Plus you were in the launch bay when the mercenary was killed. You had access to all the victims."

Adaola paled, but said nothing.

"I could see you killing Ndo because he might threaten Xonea's succession in some way. Or Yetlo, because you disagreed with my decision to stop him from committing suicide. But why Roelm? Why the mercenary? They presented no threat or connection to Xonea. And why would you poison your own ClanBrother if you were trying to protect him?"

Adaola shuddered. "I could never do such things."

I gave her a smile. "I know it wasn't you, Adaola. A killer doesn't spend double shifts watching a sick kid if she wanted her dead, or smash a desk because she believes she may have accidentally killed a patient. Nor does she try to destroy the mind of a much-loved sibling."

"I can imagine why I am here," Hado said. "I was a patient in Medical when Roelm's path was diverted, and like Adaola, present when the mercenary was killed."

"Whoever did this had an unusual mark over their heart—something you certainly have, Hado." I watched him press one hand to the location of the surgical scars on his chest. "Plus you discovered Ndo's body. You could have taken his data pad and planted it in my quarters." I shook my head. "The problem is you were still recovering from cardiac surgery when Fasala and the educators were attacked."

Xonea turned toward Reever. "And the ship's linguist?"

"I don't know where he was during the other murders, but he was there when the mercenary died," I said. "It's also true Reever's never been happy about you Choosing me, Xonea, or me going along with it. I might have suspected him, had I not been linked with him when the killer tried to alter my brain wave patterns." I decided not to bring up the time when I'd offered myself to Reever, and he'd turned me down. "It wasn't him."

Reever's and Xonea's eyes met mine, then Adaola's, then Hado's. We all turned to the only person in the room who had not touched her tea.

"That leaves me," Ktarka said. She was very calm.

"Yes." So was I. "It does."

CHAPTER SEVENTEEN

Game Over

"I have heard no evidence that would indicate my involvement."

It was interesting, the way Ktarka said that. If someone accused me of murder, I'd be screaming my head off. Protesting my innocence. Telling everyone to stop wasting time and go after the real killer. I might even throw things. I didn't see myself being really concerned with the *evidence*.

"After Fasala was injured, you came up to me in the galley and introduced yourself. Why?"

"I merely wished to acknowledge your work with our children," Ktarka said.

"Or was it that you'd just tested your weapon and nearly killed two of your colleagues? Did you decide then you needed someone to take the blame? Who would be ideal? A Terran outsider who had already killed one Torin, maybe?"

She took a sip of tea. "Your theory proves nothing."

"Later, while you were in Medical gloating over Fasala's injuries—or trying to make another attempt on her life, I don't know which—you must have overheard Roelm making a fuss about the engines. After he questioned the little girl, you followed him. Did you kill him to protect your secret?"

"Another groundless speculation."

She sure was hung up on validation. I guess that was the usual mind-set of a murderer. How can I kill and get away with it? Make sure there's no damn proof.

"After Roelm died, I had a dream. A dream that began

as part of a very calculated campaign to set me up for the murders. But you got a little sidetracked, didn't you?"

Hado made an ugly sound. Xonea's fists bulged. I motioned for both of them to stay calm.

"The next victim was Leo, the League mercenary. You killed him for obvious reasons—he nearly beat you to death." I looked at my Jorenian nurse. "Adaola, did you see Leo abduct Ktarka from Medical that day?"

"No," the nurse said. "I noticed his berth was empty and went out into the corridor. From there I followed the marks of blood on the deck."

"Didn't you find any blood in the isolation room?"

"No," Adaola said.

I turned to the educator. "You offered to help him, didn't you? That's why you released him and smuggled him out of Medical. But Leo waited until you got out in the corridor before he turned on you. Why did you let him go? Did you want to watch him rape me, or help him do it?"

The Educator made a curt gesture.

"Reever? Would you mind getting the two items I left on Darea's sleeping platform for me?" Reever disappeared, then re-emerged carrying two wrapped objects: one large and bulky, one small and flat. "Put them on the table for me, will you?" I picked up the small one first and unfolded it. "Do you remember this, Educator?"

She gazed at the pendant, then at the place on my vocollar where it used to be attached. "Yes."

"What a gift it was, too. I found out ten minutes before you five got here that this isn't a mere bauble. A scanner picked up some very tiny, very interesting tech imbedded in the stone." I held it up for everyone to see. "The stone itself is a genuine Jorenian antique. Centuries ago, it was used to signify a Choice had been made."

My nurse frowned, bewildered. "Jorenians do not Choose members of the same gender. They cannot produce offspring together."

"Someone who could never bond because she'd botched her first Choice wouldn't be worried about having kids." I leaned forward and wrapped the pendant again. "In my second dream, the killer told me we shared our aloneness. When I resisted the sexual overtures, I was beaten." I placed the pendant back on the table. "Then Xonea Chose me. How did it feel, Ktarka, finding out you'd screwed up again?"

"I did not Choose you," she said. Her voice was low and furious. "I am Chosen; you are female. I *cannot* Choose you."

"No, you couldn't. Xonea already had. You decided to play more games. You'd already poisoned everything I ate or drank with enough artificial enzymes to keep me hostile. So you switched the jaspkerry tea stores and assured Xonea would be in a near-constant state of rage, too. You killed Yetlo after I'd given him a reason to live. I didn't understand why Ndo had to die, at first. Until I found out where on Joren the resonant harmonicutters are used to fit buffers to space-going vessels."

"The Talot province shipyards," Xonea murmured.

"I checked the com logs. Just before he died, Ndo signaled you. He'd discovered you once worked in your HouseClan's main business. Outfitting ships for deep-space exploration. You and your immediate family are expert engineers. Highly skilled in the use of harmonicutters."

Ktarka's hand knotted in her lap. "That has nothing to do with these path diversions!"

"When you were burned, you clutched your tunic over your breasts. When I signaled you today, you covered your upper torso. Why?"

"I have no—"

"I checked your medical records, Ktarka. Stabbing yourself in the chest leaves a big, ugly scar. But you don't think of your botched suicide attempt as a failure, do you? It was the day you were reborn. That's why it looked like a birthmark to me when you pretended to be Xonea in my dream."

"Stop this!" Ktarka's beautiful face contorted with rage.

"You planted Ndo's data pad to frame me, and used a beacon to signal the mercenaries. If Pnor was still alive, he would tell me it was *you* who suggested I was the killer to him—several times. You also reported to him when Xonea had stormed the Medical Bay while Reever and I were linking." I glanced at Reever. "Roelm tried to tell us the killer was 'one who is not one of us.' The only thing that sets Ktarka apart from everyone else is the fact she was born to *HouseClan Zamlon.*"

Xonea rose to his feet. "Why harm Fasala? Why attack Salo?"

"It's simple." I stared at the seething Educator. "Salo is Konal's ClanBrother. His only ClanSibling."

Ktarka's entire body tensed. Time for the big finale.

"That's why you joined the crew," I said to her. "You needed the *Sunlace*. Time to design and build the weapon. Long before your little infatuation with me, you knew exactly who you were going to kill. Salo and his family. Your revenge against Konal."

"No!" she shouted, tearing at her tunic, baring her breast and the twisted scar bisecting it. "Not revenge! Justice! Konal shamed me! Took my family from me!" Ktarka flung her hand out toward Xonea, Hado, and Adaola. "Cursed be HouseClan Torin!"

Someone had to say something. Might as well be me.

"Game over," I said. "You lost. Where's Darea and Fasala?"

She drew back. "You dare question me?"

"I'm going to dare to do a lot more," I said, and got to my feet, "unless you tell me what you did with Salo's family. Right now."

"You will never find them." Ktarka reached up and took her pendant in her hand. "Nor will you escape my revenge!"

Behind my back, I gave Reever a thumb's up. He turned and nodded slightly toward Fasala's bedroom.

"End this, Ktarka," Adaola said.

"No." The educator's fist tightened around her pendant. I felt the air beginning to change within the living area. At the same time, Dhreen silently appeared behind the Educator. "I will show you the true inner path."

"Everybody down!" I yelled, jumped across the table, and slammed into Ktarka. The combination of the Jorenian woman's weight and my momentum knocked us to the deck. I rolled, snatching the pendant from her loosened grasp and snapping it from her vocollar. It glowed red-hot against my skin.

"Dhreen!" I tossed it to him, and he raced out of the quarters into the corridor.

"No!" Ktarka tried to get up and follow the Oenrallian. I jumped on top of her, but she thrust me aside with one hand. I landed against Salo's display case, shattering the protective plass panels. My arms covered my head as I huddled, protecting myself from the sharp shards raining over me.

When I eased my arms down, I saw Xonea had Ktarka by the throat. She hung suspended a good foot above the deck.

He was shouting and shaking her. "Where are they?"

"Xonea!" I got up, and the plass shards rained from my tunic to the deck. "Don't kill her!"

He released her, and Ktarka dropped to the deck on her knees. I went to her, took her by the shoulders.

"Ktarka, it *is* over. Where are Darea and Fasala?"

"I wanted you," she said, sobbing. She lifted her hand to touch my face. "So small, so perfect. So like me within." Her hand fell to the floor, then came up again. Before I realized what she was doing, a jagged piece of plass slashed across my face.

Hado yanked me back, shielding me with his body. Blood spurted from the gash under my right eye through the fingers I pressed against it. Ktarka crawled backward until she hit a wall panel.

"You will never find them. This I vow."

She rose unsteadily, and before anyone could stop her, plunged the knife-shaped shard into her heart.

An hour later, Adaola finished temporarily repairing the damage to my face. Ktarka's body had been removed from Salo's quarters, and I sent a grey-faced Hado to Medical, to have a complete exam. Xonea and Reever remained, quietly discussing options.

"Cherijo," Xonea said at last. "How did you discover Ktarka was the one responsible?"

"I got lucky." I winced as Adaola sprayed skinseal over the deep gash. "Ouch."

"It requires sutures, Senior Healer. You must return to Medical," the nurse said, then gazed at the bloodstained deck where Ktarka had fallen. "I can hardly believe it myself. She seemed so gentle a person."

"Hardly," I said. "Never got to make my big finish, did I?" I waved at Reever. "Let Duncan show you."

He reached over and pulled the covering from the bulky item still sitting on the table between us. The sentient crystal from Garnot had shaped itself again. This time, it portrayed two figures during a terrifying assault. Darea on her knees, arms flung out as a decidedly *un*gentle Ktarka struck her from behind.

"That's one very smart crystal," I said. "Maybe we can make it a member of the crew." Dhreen walked in, looking satisfied. "Well?" I demanded.

"I deactivated it, Doc. It's over."

Xonea turned to me. "We must find Darea and Fasala."

"I shook my head. As crazy as Ktarka had been, I held little hope of finding them alive. "Could she have ejected them through one of the pressure locks?"

Xonea made a swift gesture. "We would have picked up the ejections on our perimeter scanners."

"Are there any gyrlifts that have been sealed off?" Dhreen asked.

Reever rose to his feet. "Perhaps we should search her quarters."

Xonea went with us. While he and I searched through Ktarka's sparse belongings, Reever went to work on her personal console. Evidently he gained access to her personal files, and I noticed him scrolling through screen after screen of what looked like engineering schematics.

I went to stand behind him. "Find anything?"

"Ktarka was a brilliant woman. Her designs will revolutionize Jorenian ship-building techniques."

"Excuse me if I don't applaud her genius." I peered at the complex diagrams. "There must be a thousand places on this ship to hide someone." Something I saw made me grab his shoulder. "Wait. Go back two screens." He did, and I pointed to a pair of long, capsule-shaped objects. "What are those?"

"According to her notes, they are receptacles made of sonic alloy."

"Receptacles for what?" I checked the dimensions listed. They were too small to hold any of the stardrive equipment. "Probes?"

"They are approximately the same size as the ceremonial receptacles the Jorenians use for their dead," Reever said.

"But why make them out of sonic alloy?"

Xonea joined us, and I filled him in. He studied the pods.

"Ktarka could have used these to conceal the bodies of Darea and Fasala."

"That doesn't answer my question. Why put them in sonic alloy capsules? If they're dead, why bother?"

Reever glanced up at me. "Perhaps they are not dead yet."

"Okay. We know she knocked Darea out. Then she puts Darea in the capsule, and takes her somewhere on the ship where she won't be found. Maybe the same place Fasala is." I thought about what Ktarka had said. *You will not find them.* Suddenly it all came together. "There's only one place on the ship we wouldn't search."

Xonea went still. "The power core."

A few minutes later, I finished making the same proposal to the Senior Engineer. He stared at me as if I'd lost my mind.

"It is inconceivable, Senior Healer. No life-form could survive more than a few minutes inside the core."

"Let's take a look anyway."

"You cannot simply 'take a look' at the core!" one of the engineers protested. My pal Barrea, however, was busily exercising some brain cells.

"Inspection portals," he said. The Senior Engineer now stared at him. "We access them to examine the structural constitution before we flood the core."

"Don't be foolish!" Barrea's boss made a blustering gesture. "No one could enter a fully flooded core!"

I ignored him and turned to Barrea. "What if I was wearing a full envirosuit?"

Barrea nodded. "That should provide protection, for a few minutes."

The Senior Engineer threw up his graceful hands. "After which you would receive a fatal dose of radiation!"

"I'll hurry up," I told him. To Barrea, I said, "Will you back me up on audio?"

"Even if Darea and Fasala are still alive in the core," Xonea said, "how can you get them out?"

"Ktarka got them in, right? She must have accessed one of the larger transductor junctions and shoved them through it."

"No, not through the transductors. There are access domes in the inspection portal. They are very much like gyrlifts," Barrea said. "If she put them in one of them, and dropped them into the core . . ."

"The domes are not designed for use in a fully flooded core. They would dissolve in minutes." The Senior Engineer was emphatic. "This is a useless exercise. If they were placed in the core, they are both dead." He stomped off in rigid indignation.

I turned to Barrea. "Well?"

"I'll rig the suit myself." He looked thoughtful. "I might be able to fit some addition shielding, gain more time for you."

"Let's go."

Xonea caught my arm and kept me back as Barrea hurried off. "I will go."

I made a show of looking up and down his large body. "You're too big. You need someone small, and fast."

His fingers tightened. "You will be killed."

I looked at his hand. "You're making more bruises."

His fingers fell away from me. "I hurt you even when I am trying to keep you from harm."

"You're a warrior," I said. "Maybe you should start looking at some of the big, strong warrior women on this ship." The despair in his eyes made me stop teasing him. "Look. What happened wasn't your fault. Ktarka had us both pumped full of drugs."

"That is over," Xonea said. "Perhaps in time you will forgive me."

"I already have, Captain." I gave him a smile. "Now let me do this."

"Senior Healer?" Barrea yelled.

Xonea nodded. I shouted back. "On my way!"

It took time to modify the Jorenian envirosuit, but at last I was enclosed in the bulky, heavily armored gear. Barrea dropped the helmet over my head as we approached the panel leading to the largest inspection portal.

"Testing audio relay," I heard him say.

"Clear signal." I turned and waved him off. "Go back to the monitoring station now. I'm going to open the panel."

He nodded, then put a hand on my shoulder. "Gods of Luck be with you, Senior Healer."

I put my thick glove over his fingers. "You'll do just as well."

Once Barrea was back behind the heavily shielded monitoring equipment, I keyed the panel to open. The dark plas faceplate cut most of the glare from the raw energy streaming just beyond.

"Entering access dome," I said, and stepped through the panel. I activated the autonomous unit and was immediately enclosed in an oval ball of alloy. A maneuvering console appeared in front of me. Barrea had instructed me at length on how to use it. "Activating access sequence now."

"Your suit's levels are reading in the high tolerance range even now, Senior Healer," Barrea said over the audio as the dome's systems powered up. "You will have but three or four minutes before radiation absorption begins."

"Okay. I'll hurry." I grabbed the control stick and eased it forward. "Entering power core."

It was a sheer drop at first into the seething amber fuel, until I remembered Barrea's instructions and maneuvered the dome to ride the power currents to the center. The dome dipped and shuddered as it was bombarded, then found the central stream and floated slowly upward.

"Senior Healer? Status?"

"Inside the core," I replied, my voice soft with wonder. Raw fuel swirled and undulated around me, like a fountain of liquid gold. "Barrea, it's beautiful in here."

"Do you see them?"

That jolted me back to reality. I scanned the enormous, twenty-eight-level tall storage unit. "No readings at lower position. Going to ride up the stream now."

I used the dome's hull plates as resistance flaps and felt myself rising higher. I thought I saw something flicker toward the left of the dome. I scanned. Nothing appeared on my console.

"Radiation levels are now at maximum," Barrea said.

The problem with radiation poisoning is you can't feel it. "I'm okay, Barrea. Still rising. Halfway to top level."

I spotted something there: two indistinct, shadowy figures. As the dome drew level with them, I saw the perfectly preserved figures of Darea and Fasala.

"Found them. The buffer pods are connected to the same transductor portal." I peered through the golden power stream. "They're breathing!"

"Use the grappler units," Barrea said.

I jabbed a gloved finger at the keypad on the console and two large maintenance arms extended from the sides of the dome. The mechanical grapplers, or "hands," opened and eased around the buffer pods.

"Here we go." I was getting sick to my stomach. Not a good sign. "Retrieving Darea and Fasala."

Carefully I eased the grapplers back. Fasala was unconscious, but I saw Darea staring at me, her eyes wide and frightened. Dried blood painted her throat with green streaks.

"Senior Healer," Barrea said. He sounded really worried now.

"Got them. Returning to inspection portal. "

It was harder to get the dome's controls to respond. The alloy that made up the small unit was beginning to degrade. I had maybe a minute, I decided as I shot up through the golden power stream. A docking clamp extended as I approached the open portal. With a final hard thrust of the control stick, I skimmed the dome over the falling fuel streams and bounced over to the clamp. We just made it.

The bubble of alloy around me began to undulate. I extended the grapplers until both Darea and Fasala's pods were inside the portal. The bottom of the dome unexpectedly dissolved, and I yelled as I grabbed on to the console. My gloves were slipping as I punched at the melting unit.

"Barrea!" I shouted. "The dome is breaking up!"

"Try to climb out onto the docking clamp! I'll pull you in from here!"

I didn't climb as much as fall onto the docking clamp. Barrea closed it around me, and the boiling power around me pulled at my envirosuit.

"Hurry, Barrea!"

I swung up and into the inspection portal. With relief I saw the aperture close behind me. I fell to the deck, panting. Next to my helmet, Darea looked at me through the transparent capsule. She was crying. I put out a gloved hand, touching the surface of the pod. On the other side, Darea flattened her hand next to mine.

Thank you, she mouthed.

I managed to nod my head before I fell over.

*   *   *

Acute radiation poisoning was no picnic. I woke up in Medical to find myself bent over, vomiting into a basin held by Squilyp. His membranes were gentle but firm as he supported my head. Once the spasms passed, I peered at him.

"Will I live, do you think?" I asked.

"With my luck? Yes," he said as he set the basin aside.

"Salo? Darea and Fasala?"

"All doing well." The Omorr wiped my face and eased me back on the berth. "You, however, are a madwoman who needs to be forcibly detained and treated with extensive psych-therapy."

"Love you too, Squid Lips." I closed my eyes and fell asleep smiling.

Days passed while I slept and healed. Apart from exhaustion, extreme nausea, and one other annoying side effect, I recovered.

"At the energy absorption of one joule per kilogram," Reever said, calculating the figures during his first visit, "you absorbed over two hundred fifty grey units."

That was more than three times the amount of ionizing radiation that would normally kill a human being.

"I should glow in the dark, right?" I awkwardly rose to a sitting position. I still felt weak and disoriented. "Have you seen Darea and Fasala?" I was being kept in isolation until Squilyp decided I wasn't a threat to my own recovery. Which might take several revolutions. Reever nodded. "How are they?"

"The child suffered a high dose of radiation, but Resident Squilyp's bone-marrow transplant appears to be a success. Darea endured less exposure, but Ktarka's attack caused her to suffer a severe concussion as well. The Omorr tells me he expects both to fully recover."

"Salo?"

"He frequently wishes he had been present when Ktarka admitted to attacking his ClanDaughter and murdering the others," Reever said. "He was most expansive. I was not aware a Jorenian warrior could use an enemy's internal organs to—"

"They get pretty creative," I agreed in a rush. "How was Barrea able to get Fasala and Darea out?"

"The betrothal stone pendant Ktarka gave to you was a

receiver, tuned to the voice-activated transmitter imbedded in the one she possessed. She used it to artificially disrupt your brain waves as well as trigger the sonic beam."

I wondered if she'd used it to signal the League, too. "How do you know all this?"

"We found her design schematics on the personal terminal in your quarters. Barrea was able to use the device to release Darea and Fasala."

"Why were the schematics on *my* terminal?"

"She transferred them, just before attacking Darea. Perhaps she planned to switch the pendants, and have you blamed for the murders."

"That bitch."

Reever simply nodded.

"Well, it's over." I nestled back against my pillows. "I hope Xonea has done something to recognize Barrea's efforts. The man saved all three of us."

"After the rescue, the Captain made Barrea Senior Engineer."

"Do you approve?" a deep voice asked, and we both turned to see Xonea standing at the door panel to my isolation room.

"Absolutely," I said. "He's more than earned it."

Reever rose and looked from me to Xonea. "I will go now."

"No, stay, Linguist Reever," Xonea said. "I wanted to inform you we will be reaching the homeworld tomorrow."

"Joren? Already?" My voice squeaked. "I couldn't have slept that long!"

Xonea's lips twitched. "You have. We have also risked taking a more direct route. The buffer was not designed to act as an energy storage unit; the ship requires a complete retrofitting." He inspected me with casual interest. "Do you think you will feel well enough to join the sojourn team?"

"I'll start getting dressed now," I said.

Reever pushed me back on the berth. "We will see how her condition is tomorrow, Captain."

"Keep me advised. Cherijo"—his eyes crinkled—"thank you. Salo will remain in your debt forever. As will our House." He squinted at the one remaining side effect of my exposure. "I like the change. It gives you a . . . distinguished air." He bowed and departed before I could throw anything at him.

My hand automatically went to the inch-wide, silver streak newly appeared in my black hair.

Reever studied me thoughtfully. "I did not think you were particularly vain about your appearance."

"Shut up, Duncan." I made a disgusted sound as I flopped back against my pillows. "I can't believe this. I'm not even thirty yet!"

"The effects of the radiation could have been far worse," Reever said. "Your hair might have fallen out completely."

"Don't try to make me feel better." My fingers plucked at the edge of my berth linen. "That reminds me. Has Dhreen found a transport?"

He nodded. "I have also signaled the ruling Houses, as you requested. We can have the succession ceremony when we land tomorrow."

I glared. "No one has screwed up and let it slip, have they?"

Reever smiled. "No one would dare."

The Omorr reluctantly discharged me from Medical the next day.

"You are still very weak," he said as he finished the last of the million scans he felt compelled to perform. "You must rest, or you'll be right back here stuck in a berth again."

I made a face. "Yes, Mommy."

He sighed. "Go. Damage yourself again. I see my career being based on treatment of deranged Terrans with a multitude of self-inflicted injuries."

I knew better. "Thanks, Squilyp." I patted his cheek and hopped off my berth. "Did you hear the Captain's announcement about the sojourn?"

"Yes. What I do not understand is why we must wear formal garments. Or why my presence is required, as you are determined to go yourself."

"Darea, Fasala, and Salo are being transported down to their homeworld facilities. Most of the crew is getting off so they can land the ship and have it repaired. Do you see yourself having much fun at the vessels docks?"

"No, but formal garments . . . " He winced. "They are not very flattering on me."

"Stand next to me at the reception," I advised him. "I look worse."

Joren was the seventh planet in a single-star system. I expected it to be as big as Kevarzangia Two. It was bigger. I expected it to be as cultured and sophisticated as Terra. It was better. When the *Sunlace* transitioned and began to orbit above the planet, I stood at the viewport for a long time.

From space, it was a lovely, multicolored ball of rainbow pigments and thin cloud "rings." Irregular dark patches marked the oceans that divided the land masses into distinct continents. One sea stretched from polar cap to polar cap. Kao's family lived next to it, on the north shore of Marine Province.

Joren loomed like a giant next to the tiny *Sunlace*. Here was the place I'd heard so much about, and I began to get nervous about going down there.

"Sojourn team Alpha, report to launch bay immediately," my display announced.

I was ready. I put on the stupid tentlike sojourn robes (for good reason, I reminded myself) and hoisted Jenner's carrier from the deck. I took a peek through the grid.

Blue eyes stared back at me sullenly. *I don't want to go on a sojourn.*

"I can't leave you here," I said. "We're not coming back to the ship. The rest of our stuff will be transported down tomorrow." I looked around my quarters. I had spent close to a year living here. In spite of all the terrible things that had happened, I was going to miss it.

Reever, Squilyp, and Xonea met me in the corridor. The Captain politely offered to carry Jenner for me. I turned my pet over to him with a sigh of relief.

"He needs to go on a diet," I said as I huffed and puffed. I wasn't feeling weak. Jenner was getting fat. That was all.

"Why are you taking the animal?" the Omorr asked me.

"The Jorenians have never seen a Terran cat before," I replied. That much was true.

Dhreen piloted the launch down to the planet with his usual deftness. I found myself wedged between Adaola and Xonea, trying to ignore the plaintive yowls coming from my beleaguered pet.

"Marine Province is very beautiful during this cycle," Adaola said.

"Prepare for final docking sequence," Dhreen called back.

Squilyp looked uncomfortable and was more quiet than usual. Reever, sitting next to him, seemed content to stare at me. I avoided the now blue eyes. I hadn't forgotten the time we almost didn't make it back from a sojourn.

He'd held my hand as the mercenaries fired on our launch. What was it he said? *Don't worry, it will be quick.* I had kissed him, before yanking a breather over his face.

The blue eyes darkened, and I knew he'd picked up my thoughts, remembering the same moments.

"Biodecon complete. Sojourn team may disembark."

Dhreen's announcement startled me out of my mesmerized stare. Reever got to his feet, looking very sophisticated in his formal black robe.

I got up and looked down. Nope. No difference. I still resembled a small tent with feet.

Xonea opened the hull doors, and we filed down the docking ramp into what surely had to be Heaven in terrestrial form.

The huge sky was a rose color, too dark to be pink, too pale to be red. The only red was the solar sphere passing from one horizon to the other. Straight lines of cloud marched in symmetrical columns around the scarlet sun. Clouds that were every color of the rainbow, and more.

"Welcome!" a chorus of voices called.

I glanced down from the amazing show overhead to see a large group of Jorenians waiting at the other end of the ramp. They were dressed in HouseClan Torin blue.

"Relatives?" I asked Xonea.

"Relatives," he said. "The pair waving so energetically at you are my ClanParents." Which made them Kao's ClanParents. Mine, too, for that matter.

They were a handsome couple, and abandoned formality to race up the docking ramp with eager, open arms. Kao's family squashed me in a sort of group hug between his ClanParents and Xonea and Adaola. What choice did I have? I hugged them back. By the time they were done demonstrating their affection, my tent-robe was a little wrinkled.

"You are so tiny!" Adala, the ClanMother said. A handsome, sturdy woman, she looked too young to be the mother of three adults. She was right, too. I barely cleared her waistline.

"Such exquisite coloring," Xonal, the ClanFather, said. He was even taller than Xonea and had nearly solid-purple hair. When he smiled, I saw Kao as he would never be—a mature man.

The couple addressed the rest of the sojourn team. "We welcome you all," Adala said. Xonal beamed as he took Jenner's case from my hand and carried it down the ramp for me.

"They know we're not engaged anymore, right?" I muttered to Xonea.

An odd expression flickered over his features. "They know."

Before I could get specifics on just what our ClanParents knew, we stepped down onto Jorenian soil.

The few simulations of this world I'd accessed on the ship paled next to the reality. Everything was sharper, clearer, more overwhelming. The stretch of purple sea flavored every breath with salt and moisture. Colors, from scarlet flowers to sapphire skins, shone deeply and vitally alive. Even the air seemed more like a deliberate caress than the usual mix of oxygen/nitrogen/carbon dioxide/helium/water vapor gases against my skin.

Here was my adopted world. Where the plants sang. Where huge families dwelled together in tight-knit, serene communities. Where the ruling Houses were as benevolent as they were wise.

So why was I itching to run back up that docking ramp and hide in the launch until it was time to go?

"Senior Healer?" Squilyp looked like I felt—ill and ready to leave. "Do you feel it?"

"The effects of the additional gravity," Reever said. "Terra has 14.7 pounds per square inch, Omorr has 13.8 pounds psi. The *Sunlace* maintains pressures at exactly 14.3 pounds. The atmospheric pressure here is at least 16.7, two pounds over what you're used to, Cherijo. More for you, Squilyp."

"No wonder they're so strong out in space. Walking around the ship must feel like floating to them." I groaned as my ears popped. "I think I'm going to be sick."

"Me first," my Resident murmured. His gildrells were hardly moving when he spoke.

"You will grow accustomed to it. Come," Xonea said. "We will take you to our pavillion, and there you can rest."

Reever didn't seem affected by the change at all.

"You're human," I said to him when we arrived at a large, beautiful, shell-shaped structure that served as headquarters for HouseClan Torin. "Why aren't you turning green?"

"I spent two years on a world with twice this atmosphere," he replied. "This is vaguely irritating compared to that experience."

"I bet." One of the many relatives I now had gestured toward a suite of rooms, and I groaned in relief. "At last. See you later, Reever."

The rooms were spacious and simply furnished, with the style of Jorenian minimalism I was beginning to appreciate. There were square-shaped vases of many different flowers, all in the exquisite shades of HouseClan Torin blue. Furnishings were fashioned from dried, woven plant fibers that looked airy but were surprisingly strong. Even the fabrics covering the cushions of the chairs were soft and sank deliciously beneath my fingers. I opened Jenner's carrier, and he darted out.

I'm going to get even with you for this, he glared at me before he darted under a chair. I was too tired to go after him.

I didn't realize Reever had walked in behind me until he closed the door to the bedroom I had entered. I stopped my direct path to the sleeping platform and whirled.

"I appreciate the offer of company, Reever, but—"

"These quarters have been assigned to both of us," he said. "I'm told they are reserved for those who have recently Chosen."

"Why would they—" My jaw dropped. "You told them we were getting married?"

"No. I believe Xonea did." He crossed the distance between us and invited me to sit down on the bed. I flopped on it, falling on my back and burying my face in my hands.

"This is *not* happening to me." I peeked through my fingers. "Let me guess. They want us to follow Jorenian tradition?" He nodded. "Have they already prepared the

usual week-long celebrations?" Another nod. "And you intend to go through with it?"

"You made your Choice public, Cherijo."

"Why is it always my fault?" I dropped my hands.
"Okay. You can stay here and sleep on the sofa. But I am
not, repeat, *not* bonding with you."

"You may have no other option." He got up and went
to the triangular set of windows overlooking the sea view.
The rosy light from outside softened the harsh set of his
features. His lips curled in an imitation of a human smile
as he pointed at something. "Look."

I squinted against the strong light and saw a group of
Jorenians putting the finishing touches on what appeared
to be an enormous heap of flowers and vines.

"*What* is *that*?" I asked, already dreading the answer.

"Our bonding chamber."

Adala interrupted our discussion to inquire if we desired
to dine in our rooms or join the communal feast. I had put
down Jenner's food and water, but had no success in coax-
ing him out from under the sleeping platform. Adala
thought he simply needed time to adjust to the alien
atmosphere.

I was sure he was plotting his revenge campaign.

"After the succession ceremony, we will be celebrating
your Choice, Cherijo," my adopted ClanMother said. "I
have been told the arrival of our HouseClan's vessel has
spurred ten more Choices. Xonal and I will be on the chamber grounds for the next month in preparation!"

Her protests didn't fool me. Like most moms, I bet she
loved the fuss and ceremony.

"I'd like to have permission to visit your medical facility
before the ceremony begins." I glanced at Reever. "With
my . . . Chosen."

"Ever the dutiful professional." Her white eyes shone
with pride. "Of course, a ship's Senior Healer would do no
less. You are free to do exactly as you wish." She held up
a finger. "Until tomorrow."

"Thank you, Adala," Reever said, seeing me fumbling
for a reply.

"Call me ClanMother," she said, and stared at his eyes.
"Why, they change color!"

"A human mutation." I quickly pulled Reever out of our

rooms, then called back over my shoulder, "We'll see you at the ceremony, ClanMother."

We walked down through the lower level and out of the main house. "You've got to stop doing that," I said.

"Doing what?" Reever asked me.

"That color-changing thing with your eyes." I peered into his face. "They're green again."

Reever didn't comment on his annoying habit. "Where is the medical facility?"

"Over there." I pointed to a smaller building set back from the HouseClan colony. "Xonea showed it to me earlier."

"There is something I must do before the ceremony. I will meet you later." He abruptly turned and headed off in the opposite direction.

Was I relieved to have some time to myself? *Yes.*

From what I saw, the Medical Facility was even finer than the ship's accommodations. Out of courtesy, I went first to the facility director's offices. A smiling administrative assistant escorted me to see the Director, an older man named Sberea, who embraced me like a long-lost daughter.

"I have received many, many signals detailing your work, Healer Cherijo." Sberea released me with a smile. "Tonetka thought you the most gifted surgeon she had ever known."

"She probably grumbled about how stubborn and opinionated I am, too," I said. Feeling the usual intense depression that thoughts of Tonetka always brought on, I asked after my three patients.

Sberea insisted he take me to them himself. As we walked to the inpatient wards, he discussed the individual cases with me.

"Salo continues to improve. I was astonished by your work, especially to the spleen. Few Jorenian surgeons would have attempted that operation." We halted by Salo's berth, and Sberea offered the chart for my inspection. Since the big man was sleeping, I made only a quick scan to confirm he was rapidly healing without complications.

From there, Sberea and I made our way to the isolation chamber. Until Fasala's weakened immune system was stronger, she remained quarantined to prevent potentially lethal infections.

"Greetings, Senior Healer, Cherijo." Darea put down the book she was reading to Fasala and both walked over to the transparent chamber barrier.

"Hello, Darea." I bent down to hold a hand to the plas wall. On the other side, Fasala did the same against mine. "Hi, Fasala. How are you feeling?"

"Much better." The little girl rubbed her head. "Only this feels strange, Healer Cherijo. ClanMother says my scalp is prettier than my hair was. What do you think?"

"I think you look great, honey." Alive was better than anything, I thought. And her beautiful black hair would grow back in. We chatted for a few minutes, then Fasala went back to her berth. Sberea asked her mother a few questions as he made chart notes.

"She eats very well now. The nightmares . . . are less." Darea made a frustrated gesture, then rubbed her left arm absently and continued in a lower tone, "If only I had known Ktarka meant to . . . strike back at Konal through us. All of this could have been . . . avoided."

Sberea made a commiserating sound. "She is gone forever from us, Darea. Her own madness punished her more than you or Salo could have."

I doubted that. I'd seen Salo taking a mercenary apart before. I looked over their charts as Sberea excused himself to take a direct signal in his office. I frowned when I came across a notation where Darea had complained of occasional migraines.

"Excuse me, Darea, these headaches Sberea has noted—are they unusual for you?"

She nodded. "I have never had many, or with such . . . frequency."

Darea had never been a woman to mince words, so her new habit of searching for a phrase concerned me. So did the way she had been rubbing her bicep before. "Did you hurt your arm?"

"No. It feels . . . numb at times," she replied, and looked around her. "This chamber is quite cramped."

"Any numbness in your legs?"

She patted her left thigh. "This one, but like my arm . . . infrequently. Why do you ask, Healer?"

"Just checking. Would you excuse me for a moment?" I

left them and returned to Sberea's office with Darea's chart. "Can I discuss something with you, Senior Healer?"

"Of course. Come in."

I went over his chart notations with him, and he frowned. "It did not occur to me that the headaches were unusual. She has been uneasy over Fasala's progress, and the enforced confinement. I believed they were wrought by tension." His brows drew together as he read my notation about the numbness complaint. "Both on the left side. She never mentioned it to me."

"She thinks it's from lack of exercise. Have you noticed the occasional aphasia she's experiencing?" He nodded. "When was the last brain scan . . ?" I flipped through the chart display, and frowned. "She hasn't had one since the initial eval."

Sberea's wise gaze met mine. "We should perform one at once."

CHAPTER EIGHTEEN

To the Last Warrior

We returned to the isolation chamber together, and donned envirosuits before entering. Once sealed inside, Sberea and I scanned Darea several times. Through the protective headgear, I saw Sberea's reaction to the display. Mine was the same.

We told Darea we would return after a brief discussion, and left her with Fasala. In Sberea's office, he shook his head as he transferred the scanner data onto his main display.

"I never saw it on any of the previous scans."

The image of Darea's brain showed a crescent-shaped bilateral extra-axial fluid collection, a mass of blood leaking from one or more ruptured bridging veins in the subdural space of the cranial meninges.

"According to the database, Jorenian physiology can render the hematoma isodense for quite some time after the initial injury." I checked Darea's chart. "That made it look so much like the rest of her brain that anyone could have missed it."

"You are kind to an old man, Healer Cherijo. Will you perform the surgery?"

I nodded. "We'd better go tell her."

Darea listened carefully as I explained the source of her headaches and muscle weakness.

"When Ktarka struck you, it caused a rotational movement of your brain. That stretched and ultimately tore a blood vessel between the brain parenchyma and the dural sinuses, inside of the dura mater." I indicated the affected area on her chart display. "Over time, the vessel has been bleeding into the space between the dura mater and the arachnoid, or middle meningeal layer. The trapped blood formed a clot. We refer to it as a subdural hemorrhage, Darea."

"What must be done, Senior Healer?" she asked.

"I'm going to perform a surgical procedure called a craniotomy," I replied. "We'll drain the blood clot, then I can repair the torn vessel. We need to do this surgery as soon as possible." Darea looked frightened. I hurried to reassure her. "I've performed this procedure a hundred times, Darea. Don't worry."

"And if I do not have this surgery?" Darea asked.

Sberea and I exchanged a glance before I answered. "Then in all likelihood Fasala will grow up without her ClanMother."

She visibly collected herself. "Very well. Please do not tell Salo, he will worry." I wasn't crazy about that—he was her mate, after all—but nodded. "And I would see my Speaker before the operation."

I saw red at once. "You are not going to start that let-me-die nonsense, are you?"

Darea shook her head. "No. But I would like to make my wishes known, in the event I do not survive the surgery."

"She has so much confidence in me," I said to Sberea, then eyed my patient. "Okay, Darea. Talk to your Speaker. We'll have a good laugh about it when you're in post-op recovery."

She looked back at her sleeping child. "I will wish for nothing else, Healer Cherijo."

I sent a signal back to the pavillion informing Xonal and Adala of the impending procedure on their ClanNiece. We scrubbed while Sberea's nurses completed the preparations. He assembled a scrub team with experience in open cranial procedures, and discharge-sterilized the surgical suite. An hour later, we were in place and ready to begin.

Darea's shaved head was in the secluding halo that would hold it completely immobile during the delicate operation. I powered up the laser rig and made the primary incisions.

That exposed the portion of Darea's skull that I had to temporarily remove.

"Stats, please."

The nurse rattled off Darea's vitals, all normal.

"Here we go," I said, and began cutting carefully inside the markers. "Clamp." I pinned back the outer layers, cauterized two bleeders, and instructed the nurse to suction the small amount of blood from the site. The dark grey gleam of Darea's cranium shone in the bright light. "She's looking good." I checked her stats again, then said, "Parietal drill."

I made a series of burr holes in the parietal plate. Those allowed me to safely cut through the skull. Once all the holes were drilled, I placed a plasguide around them, adjusted the lascalpel, and cut out the section. I lifted the bone away and set it aside on a tray for later replacement. Darea's brain was now completely exposed, along with a large, dark green clot.

"There's the culprit," I said, and carefully drained away the coagulated blood. Beneath it, I saw not one but three tiny vessels still seeping from ruptures. "Make that a trio."

Sberea leaned close. "You'll have to go carefully with the center vessel. That one appears to have the greatest damage."

A gigantic crash behind us made both of us jump and swing around. Salo came hurtling through the observation panel and landed heavily on the floor. Before I could react, he was on his feet and coming at me, his white eyes slits of rage.

"Salo?" I handed Sberea the lascalpel and pushed him behind me. "Calm down."

"My mate." He was clutching his abdomen and breathing heavily. He looked at Darea, and growled like an animal.

"No, Salo. Darea is all right. I'm not hurting her. I'm operating on her." I winced when he hit the sterile field, and the resulting bioelectrical charge sent him staggering backward. "Don't do that. You can't get through it."

"I declare you . . . my ClanKill." Salo thrust himself against the barrier again, and this time bounced off and collapsed.

"Salo!" I yelled when he pushed himself up. New blood stained his dressings. "Stop it!"

Behind me, I could hear suction being used. "Healer, he will not stop until he kills you, or dies," Sberea said.

"I don't *think* so." I reached over, grabbed what I needed from the set-up tray, then deactivated the sterile field. Sberea made a startled sound. Once I'd stepped outside generator range, I immediately reinstated the field. That protected Sberea and Darea, but left me locked out with Salo.

Once he got to his feet, he immediately lunged toward me.

"Salo, listen to me." I quickly stepped out of the way. "I wasn't hurting her. Darea needs this operation. She—"

"You lie." He came at me again, and this time caught the front of my gown. His claws slashed through the outer layers of my gear as he threw me to the floor and straddled me.

There was no reasoning with a rampaging male bent on protection. I got one arm up, feigning a block, and used the other to push the syrinpress in my hand against his throat.

We stared at each other for a long moment.

"Sorry," I said.

A moment later, the big warrior toppled over, unconscious.

Sberea deactivated the field just as another doctor and two nurses appeared outside the ruined panel. "Get this man back to his berth, restrain him, and run complete scans. Report back to me at once if he has sustained further internal damage." As they removed Salo, Sberea bent down and lifted me to my feet. "Healer, are you injured?"

I wasn't, but my gear was ruined. Since we'd both been contaminated through touch, Sberea and I had to scrub and gear up all over again. A worried assistant monitored Darea until we returned to the table.

I took a steadying breath and recalibrated the laser. "All right. Here we go."

Two hours later, I finished sewing Darea's scalp back in place and watched her monitor. She was strong; her levels never wavered throughout the delicate procedure. Sberea looked exhausted. I flexed my cramped hands as I stripped off my gloves and deactivated the sterile field.

"That's all, people. Take her into post-op. I want her revived in thirty minutes." I walked out to where Xonal and Adala were waiting.

The ClanMother touched my arm. "How fares Darea?"

"She made it through the procedure without a problem. She's going to be fine." I looked down the rows of inpatient berths. "Salo, however, jumped through a plas panel and tried to kill me."

Xonal and Adala stared at me, shocked.

"It's not Salo's fault. We didn't tell him about the surgery. Between the drugs still in his system from his earlier surgery and the instinct to protect, he could hardly have done otherwise." I gave them a tired smile. "You can see Darea in a few hours, once we're sure she's going to remain stable. In the meantime, why don't we go tell Fasala the good news?"

Once Sberea and I returned to recovery and finished the post-op examination, we roused Darea from her drugged sleep. She automatically tried to put her hand up to her head. I caught her fingers and gently placed them at her side.

"No touching, pulling, or poking," I said. The sleepy white eyes tried to focus on my face. "Darea, the procedure went beautifully. I removed the blood clot and repaired the vessel damage." I deliberately left out the details of Salo's attack. "The rest is up to you."

She nodded. "Thank . . . you . . ."

When Sberea and I came out of recovery, we found a recovered Salo hovering just outside.

"How fares my mate? Is she well? Does she feel pain?"

It was useless to order him back to his berth. "She's stable, pain-free and recovering like a pro." I exchanged a look with Sberea. "Would you like to go in and see her?"

"Yes." Salo demonstrated his thanks by ignoring his injuries, picking me up and hugging me. "I will never be able to adequately express my gratitude, Healer," he said. "Never."

"You could start by not breaking my spine," I said, voice muffled against his broad chest. I was returned to my feet at once.

"Your pardon." Salo straightened the edge of my tunic the same way he would for Fasala. Then he pressed his brow to mine, a gesture usually reserved for immediate family members. I was touched. "I will find the words someday. Until then, my life is yours." He went in to see Darea.

Sberea stared after him. "I don't believe I've ever heard a warrior pledge his life to anyone but another warrior before."

I pressed a hand to my lower spine, and groaned. "It's better than having them come after you in surgery."

After I wrote up my procedural notes, I returned to Sberea's office and we spent another hour talking shop. After I related the story of Roelm's secretive basket weaving and Tonetka's reaction, Sberea wiped tears of laughter from his eyes.

"I can see her image even now," he said, and sighed. "I will miss that old woman more than I can tell you."

"Me, too." To keep from blubbering myself, I checked out his office. The combination of efficiency and grace made me sigh. Plenty of space to hold a conference, work on charts, or interview a patient. Woven tapestries on the walls and airily woven furnishings gave it a comfortable, warm feel. "Did you design this space yourself?"

He shook his head. "My bondmate did, some years ago. I lost her to the stars just before the *Sunlace* left on its survey jaunt." His white eyes gleamed. "You know, of course, we celebrate death instead of mourning it."

"Yes. And I'd love to know why," I said. "I can't find a single rational explanation in the database."

Sberea smiled. "You know how fiercely protective we are of our kin."

I sputtered out a laugh. "Boy, do I."

"Before the HouseClans formed, it was a matter of survival. A threat to one's kin was a threat to the tribe. Our species developed this unreasonable ferocity as part of the process of proliferation." He made an elegant gesture. "What is the greatest threat toward the proliferation of a species? Death. Can one take revenge for what is a natural process?"

"No," I said. "But you don't have to like it."

"Our people were unable to change that integral part of their character, Cherijo. That is why we had to develop a separate concept of death, or risk madness and even extinction. Thus, death is celebrated with joy."

"And everyone stays sane."

"Most medical practitioners, by their constant exposure to injury and illness, have developed a different view. We try to encourage our patients to embrace life."

I smiled sadly, thinking of Yetlo. "I've resorted to accidental sedation and death threats, myself."

A knock at the door panel startled me, and I turned around to see Reever through the viewer.

"Another human?" The Senior House Healer was curious.

"My . . . Chosen, Duncan Reever." I made the introductions. "Duncan, this is the Director of the medical facility, Senior HouseClan Healer Sberea."

Reever nodded politely to the Jorenian. "A pleasure to meet you, Senior HouseClan Healer. I regret I must ask Cherijo to leave with me now."

"Ah, yes, the celebration commences," Sberea said, and rose to his feet. "Please visit us again, Cherijo."

"Thank you, Sberea. I'd like that very much."

As Reever and I left, I squinted at the rapidly darkening sky. Sunset on Joren bathed the world in gold and crimson light. "We'd better hurry or we'll be late." I surveyed him. "Where did you go?"

"Dhreen is discreetly arranging our transport. He wanted me to look over the vessel being offered by the Jorenians."

"What's it look like?"

"Small, but fast. We will need both if we are to evade the League's mercenaries."

"Don't make an announcement to any of the Torins," I said. "They won't be too happy to hear I'm leaving almost as soon as I got here."

"I agree," Reever said as we walked by the ceremonial bonding grounds. The chamber being erected in our honor was reaching the dimensions of a small mansion. "Have you changed your mind about the bonding ceremony?"

I should have said no. "Yeah, I guess I have."

"A Jorenian ceremony would not be considered binding under current Terran legislation."

"Oh, as if I'm worried about what Terra deems legal and illegal," I said. "Reever, I'm doing this for one reason and one reason only." We had reached our rooms, and he closed the door silently. "I get the cleansing unit first."

I almost made it before he blocked my way. "What reason?"

"I want to."

He started backing me up against a wall. "Why?"

"Reever . . ." His hands were cradling my face, tilting it up. I closed my eyes. I didn't want to see what was in his. "I'm going to be a terrible wife, you know. My hours—"

"You don't have a job anymore. Why?"

"My temper is worse—"

"Tell me, Cherijo."

The door panel chimed. Saved by the bell.

It was Adaola, looking beautiful in her ceremonial robe. "Senior Healer, are you not ready?"

I looked down at my formal robe. Wrinkled. Wilting. Nope, it wasn't even in the same neighborhood as ready. "Give us a half hour, will you, ClanSister?"

"Make haste!" she said as she went back out.

"I will sterilize our robes."

"I was hoping you'd say that," I said, and turned to find myself an inch away from him. When I drew back, he offered me a small, black box he pulled from a pocket in his robe. I frowned at it.

"What's this?" I fingered the smooth, glasslike container.

"Open it and see."

I found the tiny hinge and released it. Inside, a band of gold gleamed, intricately carved with a flowing alien symbol.

"A ring?" My fingers shook as I touched it.

"On Terra, human males once gave such hand ornaments to their betrothed." He took it from the box and slid it over the fourth finger of my left hand.

I stared at the ring, which fit perfectly. "It's lovely. Thank you." I was doomed, even before his arms came around me. "Duncan—"

His hands pressed me closer. "Tell me why you want to bond with me."

"We belong together." There, I'd said it. Only the words kept spilling out of me. "I can feel it, when I touch you, when I look at you. When I hear your voice. It started on K-2, but I didn't understand then. You always got under my skin, yet I never stopped to wonder why. When I got hurt after the attack on the *Sunlace*, all I could think about was finding out if you were alive or dead. When I saw you—" I pressed my brow against his shoulder, shuddering as I remembered the terrified relief I'd felt that day. "I just knew."

Reever's hand settled against the back of my head. He could have linked with me, read my thoughts for himself, but instead he simply held me.

Finally I lifted my face. "Well? Are we going to do this, or not?"

"Yes." He kissed me. "We will do this."

The first item on the evening's agenda was a surprise we'd been planning for weeks. Once Reever and I presented ourselves at the communal great room (late, as usual), the festivities began.

"HouseClan Torin, live forever!" Xonal said from the ceremonial dais. Hundreds of voices echoed the blessing.

I looked around me. There were more ClanAunts and ClanUncles and ClanCousins than I could count. Just one big, happy family.

"We initiate our celebration this night with a ceremony of succession," Xonea said. "Senior Healer Cherijo Torin, rise and join me!"

I shook out my tent as I stood, and walked with what dignity I could manage under all that fabric to the dais. Visions of me tripping and falling flat on my face kept my pace slow, and my head high. When I reached the dais, I accepted a rib-splintering hug from the ClanFather.

"You are lovely, my ClanDaughter," he said against the top of my head.

"I am suffocating," I said into his tunic, then chuckled as he set me back down on my feet. When I was sure I didn't have a collapsed lung, I stepped forward and held out my hands.

"I have served as the Senior Healer on board the *Sunlace* for some time now," I said. "Tomorrow my path continues, but in another direction. In accordance with the traditions of our people, I've chosen my successor."

I looked around the room, and saw the confidence and pride shining on the faces of my adopted family. It was nice to work a receptive crowd.

"My successor is more than worthy to bear the title of

Senior Healer." I went on to detail some highlights of my replacement's career, then added, "The only problem is, I have to make him a doctor first." I smiled down at the Omorr. His gildrells were splayed in absolute shock. "Squilyp, come on up here."

My former Resident ascended the platform with short, nervous hops. He came to stand next to me and looked out at the approving crowd.

"I will get even with you for this," he said under his breath.

"Dream on, Squid Lips," I replied, just as quietly. In a louder voice, I announced his doctorate. "Squilyp, native of the Omorr world in the Niabac system, having successfully completed your final year of residency on board the Jorenian vessel *Sunlace*, I now bestow upon you the title of Medical Doctor, in accordance with the standards set forth for all humanoid practitioners." I pinned the small gold tunic pin that identified his title. "Congratulations, Doctor." I clasped his membranes with my hands.

HouseClan Torin rose to their feet, and in their version of applause, gave a rousing, musical shout.

"Now, Doctor, I am leaving the *Sunlace* and select you as my successor. Will you accept the position as Senior Healer?"

He nodded. "I would be honored."

Well, that was the right word to use. HouseClan Torin made so much cheering and noise only Squilyp heard me as I said, "I appoint the Omorr, Dr. Squilyp, to the Jorenian survey vessel *Sunlace* as Ship's Senior Healer." I shook his appendage again. "Good luck, Doctor."

I left Squilyp on the dais and sat back down. He gave a brief but thoroughly appropriate acceptance speech, then joined me and Reever in the front row.

"That wasn't so bad, was it?" I nudged him with an elbow.

"You are most devious, Healer." The Omorr gave me a sly look. "Your turn."

I saw Sberea, Xonal, and Adala walk up to the dias. Uh-oh.

"HouseClan Torin, you may have heard by now of the adventures experienced by our kin on board the *Sunlace*," Xonal said. "During their struggles, one of our HouseClan strove tirelessly to aid our kin in moments of crisis and disaster. Though not born to us, this woman has always sought to preserve the honor and traditions of our HouseClan."

Well, no one had spilled the beans about me ignoring that suicidal bent of theirs, I thought.

He gestured to me. "Please, Healer, join us now."

I walked up and saw Adala holding a beautiful circlet of some sort of twisted golden alloy. When I drew close enough, she placed it on my head.

"The Mother of All Houses blesses you, ClanJoren," Adala intoned solemnly.

ClanJoren? What was that?

"To be known as ClanJoren is to be honored by all of the Houses on Joren," Xonal said. "Wherever you journey on this world, the HouseClans will welcome you." He handed me a lovely fiber scroll bound with yiborra cord. "With honor and gratitude for your service to our world, ClanJoren."

While everyone was calling their blessings from the crowd, I considered this new twist. I had an official title now. Okay. I could deal with that.

"As with all those blessed by the Mother, the Healer is now considered a genitor," Xonal said. "This night she bonds, and thus the newest HouseClan will begin. We salute HouseClan Reever."

I saw Duncan Reever rise and approach the dais. They had planned this, I decided. All of it. Without telling me a damn thing. Now we weren't just getting married, we were starting a whole new HouseClan. That only happened once or twice every century on Joren.

"Nice going, Reever," I said close to his ear as he bent to kiss my cheek. "We are *never* going to get off this world."

"We will discuss it later."

"You're damn right we will, ClanFather." What did that make me? ClanMother? Cherijo Torin-Reever? ClanJoren? I'd never be able to get it all out in the same breath.

The celebration would last for days, I'd discover later that evening. Reever and I were toasted, Squilyp was toasted, the Mother of All Houses was toasted. Then Adaola and Barrea, who unknown to all of us had been having a torrid romance, announced their Choice.

"I never even suspected," I said to my ClanSister, who sat with the new Senior Engineer at our table. I passed a jug of some very potent floral wine over to Squilyp, who was doing his best to polish off the dregs of another. I was surprised to learn he ate and drank as elegantly as he hopped. The gildrells performed each function with very dainty, graceful precision. When he wasn't drinking floral wine, that is.

"How are you doing, Doctor?"

He peered at me, his dark eyes slits of amusement. "Better than I was on that dais up there, Doctor."

"I thought Omorr are like Oenrallians, and can't get intoxicated," I said.

Squilyp shook his head and nearly fell off his chair. "Naturally we can get intox . . . intoxi . . . int . . . *drunk*," he said, *then* fell off his chair. Two of my sympathetic relatives helped him up and escorted him to his rooms. As he departed, he waved all three appendages back at me.

"Better take Squilyp some analgesics in the morning," I told Adaola as I waved back.

"Did he hit his head when he fell?" she asked, concerned.

"No. But he'll feel like he did when he wakes up."

At that point, my adopted ClanParents appeared at the head of our table. "Dear ones," Adala said, and gazed down the rows of family members with affection. "It is time to escort those who will bond."

That was me and Reever. I rose to my feet, only to find Adaola, Adala, and a half dozen other female relatives lifting me up in their arms. When I jerked my head around, I saw the men doing the same to Reever.

"Don't drop me," I said as we were carried off from the great communal room. "Terran bones don't bounce the way Jorenians' do!"

In a very formal, ceremonial procession, Reever and I were carried across the chamber grounds to the towering, floral-covered structure where we would be bonded.

At the small entrance, we were lowered down to the ground and placed to stand next to each other. Xonea appeared before us, and placed yiborra grass garlands around our necks.

"May the Mother give you children," he said. "May she bless your path together from this day until eternity comes." Gently, Xonea touched my cheek with his hand, and leaned forward. "Be happy, Cherijo," he added, for my ears alone.

Reever drew me in through the small entrance, and those assembled outside sealed the opening with armfuls of loose flowers. We were alone, in total darkness, when a small light overhead glowed into life.

"Oh, look."

The interior of the dome-shaped structure was carpeted with flower petals of every shape, all the identical shade of rose. It represented the sky, the marching cloud columns symbolized by streaks of petals in other hues—green, blue, yellow, and violet. More pools of violet petals surrounded us—the Marine sea. I spotted several baskets heaping with enough provisions to feed an army.

"It's like our own little world in here," I said.

There were no furnishings, only a small, sectioned-off unit that on later inspection revealed a cleansing unit, lavatory, and a week's supply of clean garments for both of us.

Reever didn't seem impressed. "Appropriate description."

"So now you're my . . . *husband*." I tried out the word. It felt strange on my lips. "Sounds like something strapped on a strained joint for support, doesn't it?"

"*Wife* is no better. In Svgana, that word means small, poisonous snake."

"I'll have to remember that, if we ever jaunt to Svgan." The light above began to dim. I was feeling a little desperate, and looked around. "Hungry? There's enough food here to feed the entire HouseClan."

"No. I'm not hungry." He took my hand, and I jumped. "Calm yourself, Cherijo. Here." He guided me to mound of flowers. "Sit down."

I knew what that petal heap was meant for, and it wasn't sitting. "No, thanks. I think I'll just . . . stand here for now." Three minutes down, six days, twenty-three hours, and fifty-seven minutes to go.

"Are you afraid of being alone with me?"

Despite the fading light, I could still see his face. Not that it helped. "No." His arm came up around my shoulders. "Uh—Duncan?"

Before I could ask him just how he felt about me, the

mound of flowers blocking the entrance shifted, then started falling away.

"Your pardon, Healer Cherijo, Linguist Reever." Xonal stepped inside. "You must return to the pavillion at once. Marine Province security grid has detected several battle cruisers entering orbit."

"What kind of battle cruisers?" I asked as we hurried back to the main complex.

"According to the defense monitors, they are League troop freighters."

Celebration had been replaced by organized chaos, I saw as we entered the pavillion. Children were being herded into sub-surface shelters. Warriors were distributing arms. Every console was being used to monitor reports from planetary defense command.

"How much time do we have before they attack?" I asked Xonal. A sudden explosion from outside gave me my answer. "Do you have an emergency medical facility?"

Xonal nodded, and pointed to a passage across from us. "The wounded will be brought there, through underground shafts." One of the warriors came up to him and murmured something. "Excuse me, Healer. I must respond to a signal from the Ruling Council." He hurried off to a nearby console.

I turned to Reever, who was discussing something with two of the older Torins, and touched his arm. "Duncan, I have to go."

He nodded, then pressed his palm to my cheek. "Be careful."

I descended into the sub-surface medical shelter, which was a maze of emergency supplies, equipment, and temporary berths. Nurses were already setting up instrument trays and laser rigs. I checked in with the harassed Senior Resident supervising the setup, who was only too happy to let me take over surgical preparations.

More muffled explosions went off as we got ready. We were nearly done when a huge blast thundered just above us.

"Displacer fire," one of the nurses beside me said. Her blue skin paled. "They must have targeted the pavillion itself."

We hurried to the surface access passage, only to find it completely blocked off.

I looked down the opposite tunnel. "Is there another way out of here?" The nurse nodded. "I'm going up to see what's happened."

One of the residents and a couple of nurses went with me. When we emerged a few hundred yards from the main pavillion, I gasped. The night sky was brilliant with flares of red, illuminating the huge building, which had partially collapsed.

"Did everyone get out of there?" I yelled to someone taking cover behind what was left of my bonding chamber.

"No!" a voice shouted back to me.

I could see HouseClan members rushing to pull the injured from the structure. Some badly wounded were being carried from the site toward us. We ran to assist them. Somewhere along the way Adaola and Barrea joined us.

It took time to evacuate the injured from the collapsed wing of the pavillion. We uncovered four dead and two so critical I knew there was no saving them. Once there were enough people to help search the rubble, I helped carry one of the litters back down to the medical shelter.

Where was Reever? Had he gotten out in time?

"Healer!" Sberea had his hands full. The nurses had lined up the cases according to severity. All the cots were occupied, and they were resorting to stacking litters on the floor now. "Patient prepped in room three for you. Team is waiting."

"Got it," I said, and ran to scrub.

Just as I finished snapping on my gloves, Xonal's voice rang out through the underground facility's multiple audio consoles.

"HouseClan Torin. There has been an attack on our province by the Allied League of Worlds. More than twenty ships are now in orbit, ready to recommence the assault." His voice went flat and hard. "Reinforcements from other Provinces will arrive shortly. All warriors have reported to defense stations, and we are prepared to return fire."

"Bastards," I muttered under my mask as I backed into the makeshift surgical suite. The patient was prepped, the team waiting. "Okay, people, what have we got?"

"It is our ClanMother," one of the nurses said.

Adala lay unconscious. Scanner reading indicated compression injuries in three major organs. The nurse beside me positioned the instrument tray. I made the initial incision, then held out my gloved hand.

"Clamp."

Ten hours later, I finished the last surgical case and stripped out of my green-stained gear. I was bone tired but still tense, waiting for the explosions of displacer fire that never came. Xonal had only sent a signal for me to report to defense station one when I could be spared.

"Go," Sberea said. "We have matters here under control. Healers from other provinces have begun to arrive."

Defense stations were cleverly hidden tactical units which controlled orbital fortifications and ground-to-orbit systems. I was escorted by armed guard through the maze of corridors to the nerve center of the operation, where Xonal was plotting the next move in repelling what appeared to be a planetary invasion.

Xonea stood at his side, pointing out details on the grid. Everyone looked up when I entered. Most of the warriors silently filed out of the room. Only Xonea remained. The door closed, and the three of us were alone.

"They've come for me, haven't they?" I asked.

"Yes," Xonal said.

Xonea was grim. "We do not intend to let them have you."

I joined them at the strategy table, where he had displayed a satellite view of the League ships hovering above Joren.

"I believe the attack on the pavillion was merely a way of getting our attention," Xonal said.

"Nice guys. Why couldn't they just signal us?"

"The League has a reputation for ruthlessness when it is crossed," Xonea replied. "You, I fear, have crossed them more than once." His stony expression softened for a moment. "Our ClanMother?"

"Adala is in post-op, and she's in stable condition. I had to repair a punctured lung, among other problems. Most of her ribs are broken." I smiled wanly at Xonal. "No hugs for a few weeks, okay?"

My attention was diverted when the display on the table flickered, and was replaced by a live vid signal.

"Xonal," the audio crackled as the signal was adjusted in frequency. "ClanFather of HouseClan Torin." The face of an emotionless mercenary filled the screen.

Xonal took the precaution of coding his own signal so his location would not be pinpointed. "I am here, cowards."

"Give us the Terran test specimen."

"That's fairly direct," I said to Xonea.

"There is no Terran test specimen on this planet," Xonal replied. "Leave orbit at once or face counter-assault."

"We will exchange a member of your species for the Terran test specimen designated Cherijo Grey Veil."

"What are they talking about?" Xonea demanded.

"You have a Jorenian in custody?" My ClanFather's voice acquired a deadly tone.

The vid switched to the interior of a detainment cell.

"Oh, my God." My legs wouldn't hold me anymore, and I sagged back into a chair.

The display showed an image of Senior Healer Tonetka Torin, very much alive and well. She stood at the detainment barrier, yelling her head off. There was no audio, but I didn't need one. I'd seen her do that too many times to doubt it was her.

Xonea looked ready to kill anyone wearing a League uniform. "They must have removed her from the ship during the attack."

Xonal didn't waste time. "Release our ClanSister."

"Give us Cherijo Grey Veil."

"You have no authority to detain Tonetka Torin. Release her at once!" Xonal shouted.

"On the contrary. Senior Healer Torin was rescued during an encounter with the Jorenian vessel *Sunlace*. We consider our actions humanitarian. In order to release her, we require our property be returned. If you cooperate, we will consider the matter to be settled."

Xonal glanced at me. "No. Unlike your League, Joren does not trade in living beings. We refuse."

"Cherijo Grey Veil. The remainder of this signal is addressed to you." The face on the vid disappeared. It was replaced by the stern, austere features that were an older, masculine version of my own.

"Dr. Joseph Grey Veil," I said for Xonal's benefit. "My creator." I addressed the vid now. "I guess you can't take 'no' for an answer."

"I am here to take you back to Terra."

"What I can't figure out is how you got Tonetka off the *Sunlace*. Mind telling me how you managed that, Doctor?"

"One of our operatives gained passage on your vessel. He tagged you with a targeting device which allowed us to locate and retrieve you. Unfortunately, it was discovered after we retrieved Tonetka Torin that you gave her the device."

"The trader." I remembered the bracelet he'd sent me, just before the attack.

"Precisely. Our operative and your Senior Healer were removed from the ship. By the time we realized we had the wrong physician, it was too late."

"Jewelry gives me a rash," I said. "Try something else the next time."

"This is finished. Surrender to the League at once."

"Threatening Joren isn't very wise, you know," I told him. "Our warriors will hunt you down and take you apart, organ by organ."

"We will remain in orbit and continue the assault until the Jorenians turn you over to us."

I eyed Xonea and Xonal. Both looked ready to do some intestinal decorating. "They *aren't* going to do that."

"Thus far minimal harm has been done. That will change, Cherijo—"

"*Minimal* harm?" Xonea's fist slammed into a console, creating a large dent in the alloy. "Six of our people are dead!"

"What is six compared to six million?"

"More than six people were harmed," I said. "Twenty more Jorenians are in critical condition. Twice that many were injured during your unprovoked attack. Seven of them are children." I clenched my hands on the edge of the table. "I just spent ten hours in surgery patching together what you blew apart. Don't talk minimal to me, Doctor."

"No one else has to die."

"The other Provinces have mobilized. Jorenian defense systems, I understand, are also very efficient. You're right.

You'll be blown out of orbit before you have the chance to kill anyone else. Goodbye, Doctor."

"A warning, Cherijo. Forty more League vessels are due to arrive within the hour. All are fully manned, heavily armed planetary cruisers, more than enough to overload the defense grid. Joren is, I'm told, a lovely planet. How will it look after the surface has been bombarded with displacer fire?" He sneered at me. "You have one hour to consider your answer."

The vid went blank.

Xonal suddenly looked very old and tired. "Forty more of them. Mother of All Houses."

"We will fight them, ClanFather." I noticed Xonea didn't say anything about defeating them. He looked unwell.

I didn't feel so great myself. "No. There's only one solution."

"No!" Xonea grabbed my arms and shook me. "I will not allow you to sacrifice yourself!"

"That isn't your decision," I said as kindly as I could. I looked at my ClanFather. "Xonal, you know what I'm saying is right."

Xonea released me. His hands bunched in frustration and he dropped them to his sides. "Tell her she is wrong, ClanFather!"

"Xonea. Listen to yourself," I said. "It goes against everything Jorenians believe in."

"'The House is greater than any one of its Clan,'" Xonal quoted with great bitterness.

I nodded. "You can't forfeit your entire world for one former Terran physician."

"I would forfeit my honor if I let you do this," Xonea whispered.

"There are times for honor, Captain. This is not one of them." I looked down at my tunic, which was splotched green from our rescue efforts. "I have enough Jorenian blood on me already. Let me go."

I saw the stubborn denial on Xonea's face. He was going to be a problem.

Salo was standing outside when I left the room.

"What are you doing out of bed?"

"I was told they demanded your surrender," he said. I nodded. "What will they do when you refuse?"

"Forty more cruisers are due to arrive shortly. They'll have enough firepower to knock out surface defense systems. They'll destroy the planet."

"We will not let them take you, Cherijo. We will fight them, to the last warrior."

"I know, Salo. I simply can't let my people do that. One life in exchange for an entire world? Sounds like a pretty good deal to me." I reached out and touched his sagging shoulder. "Hey, I got away from them once, remember?"

He said something as I walked toward the Medical Facility. It sounded a lot like, "My life is yours."

Xonea *and* Salo were going to be a problem.

The League was feeling rather benevolent, once they had more than sixty ships in orbit. As a result, I was given a standard day to put my affairs on Joren in order. I spent the first half of it working at the Medical Facility.

Dhreen arrived later that day with a fast, sleek transport that was of no use to me anymore. I was doing post-op rounds, and he came up as I finished my exam of a patient.

"Got a great little shuttle," he said. He was miserable. Flushed dark yellow. Scuffing his footgear around on the floor. "We could jaunt out of here before they knew it."

"Sixty ships up there, on full scanner sweeps? I think they'd catch us in about ten seconds," I said. My patient was sleeping, so I lowered my voice. "Thanks, anyway."

"This has a foul odor," he muttered.

"Yeah, I know it stinks. I can't let them decimate this planet, Dhreen. You know that."

"Cherijo." The Oenrallian grabbed me and gave me a hard hug. Without another word, he left.

Reever caught up to me toward the end of my rounds. "I must speak with you."

"Heard the news, have you?" He nodded, and took my arm. "Reever—"

"There are other Healers who can see to the patients." He hauled me down the ward toward the facility's entrance. "I must speak with you now. Come with me."

He led me out of the building and over to Dhreen's shuttle at Transport. She was pretty and looked like she could zip between the stars. I was almost sorry I wouldn't get the chance to jaunt on her.

We walked up into the main cabin and Reever closed the hull doors and secured them.

"You're not thinking of kidnapping me, I hope," I said. "Not when the fate of an entire planet rests in my two little hands."

Reever leaned back against the hull to watch me. "Your humor is—"

"Inappropriate, I know." I grabbed his hand and pulled. "Come on, show me where we would have been cooped up together for weeks at a time."

He led me back to the small, tidy section allocated for our quarters. What would have happened, if I'd left Joren with Reever and Dhreen before the League had shown up? Would I have had a good life with Duncan? What would it have been like? Would we have had children together?

Now I'd never know.

Maybe it was all for the best, but I wasn't going back to Terra without finding out one thing first. I glanced around. The sleeping platform was on the small side, but it would have to do. I went to the door panel, closed, and secured it.

Reever watched me. "Cherijo?"

I sat down on the mattress and patted the space beside me. "Come and sit down, Duncan."

He lowered himself next to me. "There is something I have to tell you."

"Later." I put my arms around him, and moved closer. "I know this is hardly the time or place—"

"You are correct." He pushed my hands away and got to his feet. "It is not."

"Your compassion is breathtaking," I said, his rejection making me sarcastic. "Would it really be so terrible to grant your wife's last request?"

"I have negotiated space on a merchant vessel. The Captain plans to transition before it can be detected by the League."

Why did that make me feel abandoned? After all, I was leaving, too. "Good idea."

His eyes were flat ice again. "Come with me."

"And let the League blast Joren into dust? No. I can't." The offer made me feel a little better. But not much. I wondered why I'd expected him to want to stay with me. "Thanks for the thought."

"You are very loyal to these people."

"Who wouldn't be?" I caught the slight change in his expression, and frowned. "You wouldn't do the same thing?"

"I have no loyalties."

No loyalties. God, that hurt. "Then why ask me to come with you?"

"You are my mate."

"That's right, I am." And I had just enough time to find out what that felt like. I stood up and began unfastening my tunic. "Start treating me like one."

"Cherijo." He strode over to me and grabbed my wrists. "Come with me. Now."

"I can't." I jerked my hands away. "For God's sake, Duncan, how can you ask me to turn my back on these people?"

"Very well." He stepped away from me. "I must go."

My breath solidified in my lungs. "You're leaving? *Now*?"

"If I do not, I will miss the launch slot."

Dumbfounded, I sat down on the platform. Without another word, the man who had no loyalties, not even to me, walked away.

I spent my last hours with my patients after all. When my time was nearly up, I returned to defense station one. I found Xonal alone in the planning room, and a vid of the mercenary leader staring up at me.

"We have waited long enough, Doctor Grey Veil."

"My shuttle is leaving within minutes. You can track us by scanner."

"Do not think to escape, I warn you. We will begin surface bombardment the moment you take evasive maneuvers."

"I figured you would. Don't worry. I'll be there." I terminated the signal and turned to Xonal. "Keep your defenses ready until the last ship is out of this system. I don't trust them to keep their agreement. Dhreen will bring Tonetka back to Joren. Tell her I'm glad—she's—" My voice broke as my ClanFather drew me into his arms. "Thank you for everything, Dad."

"Is that what Terrans call their male parent?" he asked,

and I nodded against his chest. He kissed my brow. "Then remember me as your 'Dad,' my honored ClanDaughter."

Adaola waited by the shuttle with my animal carrier.

"I forgot about Jenner," I said, hitting myself in the forehead with my palm. Some devoted pet owner I was. "Again."

"Perhaps they will let you keep him," my former nurse said.

I shook my head. "No, they'd only use him to control me." Like Reever, I thought, had he decided to stick around. "Tell you what, pal"—I dropped down and looked through the front of the carrier—"you stay here. I know a certain little girl who will love you and take good care of you." I held my fingers to the mesh. Jenner sniffed, then rasped his rough tongue against them. I rose to my feet. "Take him to Fasala. When she gets better, she'll look after him."

Adaola enveloped me in a crushing hug. "The Mother Bless You, Cherijo Torin."

"Kiss the baby for me," I whispered back, patting her flat stomach. "Go on now."

I climbed up the docking ramp and took one more look at the beautiful colors of Joren. On the other side of Transport, silhouetted against the scarlet sun, was a tall, muscular form standing alone. I lifted my hand.

Xonea didn't wave back.

CHAPTER NINETEEN

One Way or Another

Inside at the shuttle control console, Dhreen was preparing to launch. I strapped into the empty seat beside him at the helm. He looked surprised.

"Want to fly her yourself?" he asked.

"No, just some company," I said. "Yours will be the last friendly face I see for a long time."

He initiated launch sequence and nosed the shuttle up into the sky. The sheer density of ships hanging over Joren made me shudder.

"They don't clutter around, do they?" Dhreen said, and whistled.

"No, they don't."

"I want you to have something before you go to them." Dhreen withdrew a small package from his tunic pocket and handed it to me. I unwrapped it, and made a shocked sound when I saw it was Ktarka's pendant, attached to an ornamental chain.

"Wear it. They might think it's only jewelry." He spent the rest of the flight explaining the tiny mechanism inside to me. I hung the chain around my neck and slipped the pendant under my tunic.

"Thanks, Dhreen."

"Find a power source, and it could help you escape."

We reached the designated exchange site, and Dhreen signaled for permission to dock. A cold voice granted it. Before our shuttle touched down in the enormous launch bay, I looked for Tonetka. I saw her standing just beyond, three guards surrounding her, more mercenaries behind them.

"There she is." Why had I been worried the League had starved or tortured her? She never looked better. "I bet she hasn't given them a millisecond of peace since they kidnapped her."

The launch touched down. Every rifle in the bay was now pointing at me and Dhreen.

"Whatever you do," the Oenrallian muttered, "don't insult them."

Dhreen escorted me off the shuttle, to be at once surrounded by League troopers. I saw their leader standing a little apart from the rest of his men. He was a spare, smooth-skinned humanoid with ancient eyes and heavy, canine features. From all the decorations on his Commander's tunic, I gathered he was both experienced and important. Or needed to feel that way.

"You want to call off your thugs?" I asked, which made Dhreen cringe. "We're not armed."

One of the men handed me a wristcom—I'd forgotten my vocollar wouldn't work here—so I strapped it on and repeated my request.

"At ease, men," the leader called out in a rumbling baritone. His fleshy lips parted over an impressive amount of sharp teeth as he approached me. Men got out of his way so quickly they nearly stumbled in the process. When we were a few feet apart, he halted and gave me a thorough visual inspection. "You're what all the furor is about?"

"Hard to believe, isn't it?" I gave him the same appraisal. "And you are—who? The Head League LapDog?"

He laughed. "They warned me about your mouth. Colonel Patril Shropana, League Troop Commander." He made a shallow bow.

"Healer Cherijo Torin," I replied. I didn't bow. "My pilot, Dhreen."

"I'm delighted to meet you, Doctor. After hearing all that is said about you, I must admit, I expected you to be . . . larger."

"Really?" I sniffed the air. "I expected League Troops to smell better."

"Perhaps we should continue this discussion—"

"First things first, Colonel. You have a prisoner to exchange."

"Of course." He made a languid motion with his hand. The guards holding Tonetka dragged her forward. Literally *dragged*, for she fought them with every ounce of the considerable strength she had, despite the bonds on her wrists and ankles.

"Hey, boss," I said. "I'm glad I didn't go to your death ceremony now."

"How—are you—Cherijo?" Tonetka tried to smash her bound hands into one of the guards' faces. They finally had to pick her up and carry her the last few yards. "Let me go, you—" The rest of what she said scrambled my wristcom.

The guards placed her on her feet. One of them handed me the remote key, then both of them scuttled away from her. I unlocked the tight bonds and tossed them aside.

Tonetka flexed her arms and legs before she gave me a stern look. "Did you save all the children?"

I nodded. "Every one of them, thanks to you. Next time I offer you jewelry, refuse, okay?"

She chuckled, then glowered at Shropana. "Would the League Commander be generous and allow me a private moment with my colleague?"

The Colonel nodded. "A moment."

She rubbed at dark bruises on her wrists as she pulled me out of hearing range. I found myself in her arms, her mouth against my ear. "Chamber twelve, level sixteen. What I was to show the children before the bracelet."

"Uh-huh." I hugged her tightly. "I'm glad to see you, too." I reluctantly drew back. "I gave your job to Squilyp. Sorry."

"I am more than ready for retirement now."

Shropana's voice rang out. "Your time is up, Healer."

Tonetka eyed the silver streak in my hair. "I would have enjoyed hearing how you received that."

"Salo will tell you the story. Go now. Tell Xonea—" I hesitated as Dhreen joined us. "Tell him I'll be okay."

My old boss took Dhreen's proffered arm. "You are HouseClan Torin, Cherijo." She pressed her fingers to my cheek as I nodded. "Be strong and survive. I will think of you every day of my life, ClanDaughter. Walk within beauty."

I watched until the shuttle cleared the launch bay. Shropana came to stand next to me. "I would like to confirm when Tonetka safely reaches the surface, Colonel."

"Of course." Everything civilized now, he personally escorted me to a display. I keyed in the signal myself after the proper amount of flight time had passed. Xonal's weary face appeared.

"Did they make it back all right?"

He nodded. "Both are well, Healer."

"Thanks, Dad." Colonel Shropana seemed a little too interested in observing my ClanFather's pain, so I abruptly terminated the signal and looked at him. "All right. I'm here. What next?"

"I believe you should be asking me that question."

The voice was unmistakable. I swung around and sure enough, Joseph Grey Veil stood behind me.

He had aged. His once-dark hair was heavily silvered now. The lines around his eyes and noses were deeper. Erect as his posture was, he seemed smaller, too. Probably because I'd spent the last two revolutions around truly *impressive* people.

I'd dreaded this meeting for a long time. Played it out in my mind, over and over. Thought of what I would say. Agonized over the betrayal that had changed my life.

I discovered I was walking toward him. Now that the moment had arrived, it didn't seem frightening. I kept seeing the dead bodies this man had left behind in his quest to capture me. Heard the cries of all the injured children. Smelled the decaying flesh of the dead. All in the name of his endless pursuit of perfection.

"Dr. Joseph Grey Veil." I halted a foot from his position. He was staring at the streak in my hair, the change in my weight. I could almost hear him making clinical notes in his head.

He never saw my fist coming. He fell straight back, and was unconscious before he landed heavily on the deck.

I rubbed my bruised knuckles and walked back over to Colonel Shropana. "What next?"

The Colonel threw his head back, and roared with laughter.

I taken to my assigned quarters and left there. The furnishings were comfortable. My favorite foods stocked the prep unit. Even a collection of jazz recordings was placed for my enjoyment. I noted every single album in my collection had been duplicated. Joseph kept excellent records.

I had to get out of here. I accessed the door panel, but it wouldn't open. They had locked me in the cozy, attractive little cage.

Mistake number one. I spent my first hour in captivity methodically smashing the music discs. Each and every one of them.

"Dr. Grey Veil?" someone called over the display.

I ignored it. I had finished with the music discs and was unloading all the stores from the prep unit. It was interesting to see how much bulk food a disposal unit could handle. I wondered if it could chew up metal and wiring.

"Healer?"

They finally figured out how to address me correctly. "What?"

"Are the music discs and food stores not to your liking?"

I should have known they'd stick recording drones in here somewhere. Mistake number two. I was mad now. I began looking for them. The nasty little things are almost impossible to spot.

"Healer? Answer the inquiry, please?"

"Where are they?" I started ripping the fabric and underlying foam from one of the free-formed sofas. I didn't like the warm brown and orange tones of the decor much, I decided. I'd grown partial to blue. "Tell me now and you'll save yourself a bunch of unnecessary recycling."

The disembodied voice sounded dismayed. "What are you looking for?"

I sighed. "Your surveillance devices, stupid."

"I cannot give you that information."

"Then I can't answer *your* questions." My fingers hurt, so I stopped to rest. I turned full-circle and smiled at the whole room. "I have plenty of time. I'll find every single one of them."

"You would do better to cooperate, Cherijo." That was Colonel Shropana's gravelly voice.

"Really, Colonel?" I started ripping again. "I didn't agree to cooperate with you. I just traded myself for Tonetka."

"We can assure you will cooperate."

"Not without messing up Dr. Grey Veil's tests. He dislikes me performing under the influence of drugs. Ask him about the time I accidentally took too many decongestants when I was fourteen. I thought he'd suspend my entertainment privileges ad infinitum."

No other comment was made. Guess Shropana had to think things over, I thought, and continued ripping.

I found the first miniature recording drone embedded in a chair cushion. It smashed to irreparable pieces under my footgear. It took an hour to determine there were no more devices in the living area. I left the demolished room and moved on to the next.

Once I got the sleeping platform apart, I found an even tinier device implanted at the foot of the bed. Probably wanted to watch me snore. I immersed the unit in water, and chuckled as it short-circuited. Somewhere in the big League ship, I knew someone had just yanked off their headgear. The feedback would not have been music to their ears.

A voice came over the display again. It sounded pained. "Healer?"

"I'm busy," I yelled. I began dismantling the cleanser. I wondered how much I'd get to destroy before they got exasperated and came for me. Wanton destruction was kind of fun.

"You will not be reassigned new quarters," the voice said.

"Good. Save me the trouble of having to do this all over again." I wrenched the cleanser port from the wall and sure enough, found a third drone busily monitoring. "Well, well."

"Healer, please cease this activity at once."

"No. Why put one in here? I'm not much to look at." I wrenched the drone out of the recess. "Naked, I mean."

I took this one to the overworked disposal unit. It sputtered and made some ominous grumbling noises, but eventually reduced the drone to small bits of metal and wiring.

"Vandalism is punishable under League statutes."

"I'm so scared. See, I'm shaking," I said, holding up my steady hands. "Or can't you see anymore?"

"Are you hungry, Healer?"

I sat down on some mounds of cushioning I had ripped from the furnishings, curled over, and closed my eyes.

"Are you hungry?" the voice repeated.

"There's no more food in here."

"We can bring you more supplies."

"No. Thanks."

Shropana's voice took over again. "Dr. Grey Veil wishes an interview with you."

"If Dr. Grey Veil so much as comes within spitting distance of me, I'll make what I did on the launch bay look like a love-tap."

"That would not be wise."

"Maybe I'm not as smart as he tells you I am."

"Your hostility will not make your stay with us a pleasant one, Cherijo."

I loved the way he said that. Like this was some kind of resort and I was on vacation. "If I wanted pleasant, I would have stayed on Terra."

He produced a frustrated growl. "You are your father's daughter. Of that I am convinced."

"Thanks. I know Xonal would appreciate you saying that."

I slept. How long, I had no idea. Sleeping and destroying things composed the majority of my immediate plans. That was how I spent the first three days of my captivity, until I became so dehydrated I couldn't do much more than sleep fitfully or toss bits of shredded fabric around while I was awake.

They came for me, of course. Weak as I was, they still drugged me with a mild tranquilizer. When I woke up, I was in a medical berth, my limbs pinned down by tight restraints. Intravenous tubes were pumping colorless liquid into my arms.

Mistake number three. Now I was *really* getting mad.

Colonel Shropana appeared as soon as I opened my eyes. So did a humanoid nurse, who began wordlessly spooning glucose into my mouth.

"Feeling better?" he asked.

I spat the glucose in his face. "Yeah. I am."

Strong, claw-tipped fingers encircled my throat. "I've killed men for less," he told me.

It was good to see the League's Chief Jerk lose control. I grinned as his grip tightened. "By all means." My laughter croaked. "Do me a favor."

The claws eased from my neck as he released me. "I see." He grew quiet as he wiped the glucose from his face with a cloth the appalled nurse handed him. "You're intent on suicide."

"If that's what you want to believe, sure."

"Will you talk to me, Cherijo?" He tried to appear earnest and caring. It might have worked if he'd had some prior experience, I thought. Or a lot more practice in front of a mirror. "How can I help you adjust to this change in your life?"

"Gee, I don't know." I pretended to think it over. "Put me off on the first non-League world the ship passes?"

"You know I can't release you." The old eyes glittered in contrast to the entreating words. "I am quite serious. Let me help you."

He needed my cooperation and would now do a lot to get it. Which is exactly where I wanted him. "Here's a helpful hint, Colonel. If you don't want someone to act like a hostile prisoner"—I lowered my voice so he bent close to catch my words—"you stop *treating* them like one."

"You feel you have been mistreated?"

I made my eyes wide. "Wouldn't you? Locked up in a cage with drone monitors all over the place? Never being consulted as to what you want to eat, drink, or listen to? No freedom offered whatsoever? Can you blame me for being angry?" I even managed to work a pathetic little throb in my voice. "How could you do that to me?"

Shrewd, experienced Colonel Shropana fell for it. "I had no idea you felt like this."

"Try detainment sometime. Come back and tell me how *you* like it." I heaved out a sad sound. "You know, you people have spent an enormous amount of credits tracking me down and getting me to surrender. What do you do the minute you have me in custody? You treat me like a large, dumb, lab specimen. The League doesn't send sixty ships out after just anybody, do they?"

"No." Now he showed some of his inner perplexity. "To my knowledge, no mission short of full-fledged war has required so many resources."

"There you go. They think I'm important. So what will you do for me, Colonel? What do you have to offer to entice me to even think about cooperating?"

Talk was easy for him. Concessions weren't. "I can allow you to have access to most areas of the ship," he said, without much enthusiasm.

"Good start."

"You may select your quarters, furnish them as you like from ship's stores."

"Even better."

"We will endeavor to give you a measure of privacy."

He was lying, but I nodded. Two out of three wasn't bad. "That's more like it."

"If I do this, what will I get in return, Cherijo?"

He might be fooled, but he wasn't stupid. I mimed his thoughtful expression. "In return, I'll eat and drink."

"That's all?"

"That's better than keeping me restrained, on tubes, and getting glucose spit in your face."

The fleshy lips parted in a canine grimace. "You are a very shrewd young woman. Very well. I will put these new measures into effect immediately."

"Fine. When I see that you've done it, I'll have lunch with you."

"What about your father?"

"He's back on Joren."

He corrected himself quickly. "What about Dr. Joseph Grey Veil?"

"If you want him to make it to the end of this jaunt in one piece, keep him away from me."

"He wishes to conduct tests on you."

"Tell him his tests should be used as an enema."

"He will not accept that."

"Big deal. Why are you all so terrified of him? He screwed up nine times before he got his little experiment right."

"He has all the experimental data."

I smiled. "I *am* the experiment."

Whatever they pumped into my veins worked. The effects of three days without food or water soon disappeared. The cranky nurse refused to give me my chart, so I had to guess it was the standard saline/glucose shock cocktail. Within hours I regained enough strength to walk out of Medical to join Colonel Shropana for lunch. I snagged my

chart from the nurse without asking and tucked it under
my arm on the way out.

"Hey, Colonel."

Shropana waited in the outer corridor for me, and
glanced at the chart I carried. "Is there a problem with
your treatment?"

"I'll make a list after I read the physician's notes."

The galley was regulation freighter design, which meant
it was a big open room with a bunch of tables and benches.
Everything was in stanissue League colors (unpainted grey
alloys), and even more depressing than the stark confines
of their Medical section. I could smell the mingled odors
of a hundred meals, none of which appealed to me.

"Ever think of hanging a few botanicals around here?"
I asked the Colonel. "Maybe a picture or two?"

"The League discourages reminding space-bound troops
of the pleasures of planetary service," Shropana replied.

"Pity. This place is killing what's left of my appetite."

The crew scattered like frightened mice as we approached a smaller series of tables reserved for the officers.
One brave soul lingered, evidently meaning to offer his
assistance. Shropana's steady gaze sent him scurrying along
after the others.

"Do they always do that?" I asked.

The Colonel nodded. "I never have to wait for a table
to become available," he said.

I made my mouth go round and pressed a hand to my
heart. "Why, Colonel. A League Commander who can actually make a decent joke. I'm stunned."

"Call me Patril," he said, at ease with my sarcasm now.
"What can I program for your meal?"

I wouldn't let him serve me. Being polite was one thing,
but the man commanded sixty League cruisers and God knew
how many troopers. Him waiting on me was a bit ridiculous. Plus I didn't want him slipping some unknown substance into my food or drink. To my surprise, the main
menu included a complete selection of native Jorenian
recipes.

"You have food stores from Joren?"

"Synthetics. Even with those, your Senior Healer refused
to eat anything that was not prepared in classic Jorenian

style." The Colonel sighed. "It took days to adjust the prep units to that woman's specifications."

"Oh, so that was where you got the recipe programs." I programmed the d'narral, waited a moment, and removed the result. I tasted it carefully. "Yep. This is Tonetka's, all right. She never uses enough safira."

We returned to the table with our trays and sat down. With my peripheral vision, I saw Joseph Grey Veil approaching us. I casually picked up the fork on my tray (the Colonel wasn't ready to trust me with knives, I noted) and poked the steaming vegetable mound. Shropana watched my creator approach without a word to me.

I made a humming sound as I tasted it again. "I think she overcooks it a little, too."

"Really?" The Colonel pretended interest.

"Here, try some." I offered a forkful to him. He sampled it with a great show of concentration. That's right, indulge the little lab specimen, I thought. "Too limp, right?"

"Well, perhaps—"

"I would speak with you, Cherijo," Joseph Grey Veil said, all preemptory arrogance. Like he had a right. I saw him place a hand on the table beside my tray. Felt him hanging over me. My, wasn't he confident?

Joseph forgot who I'd been living with for the last year.

I immediately turned the fork and rammed the sharp tines through the back of his hand. I never felt this surge of feral satisfaction before. Maybe there was something to that Jorenian tradition of violent revenge. His scream was a top note of joy to my ears.

My creator fell back, clutching his wrist, using language I'd never heard issue from his prim lips before. Guess Joseph had picked up a few bad habits, too. Colonel Shropana half rose from his seat, then slowly sat back down. I used my napkin to blot up the small drops of blood from my side of the table.

"Sorry, Patril," I said, the epitome of courtesy. "You were saying?"

Shropana gestured to the two guards that shadowed him everywhere and pointed to the fallen Joseph Grey Veil. They helped the wounded Doctor to his feet and escorted him from the galley. I saw all of this from the corner of my eye, and had to bite the inside of my cheek to keep from laughing. The Colonel rose and got another fork for me.

"Healer, I gain respect for you by the day." He handed me the new utensil. "You make Jorenian warriors seem subdued in comparison."

"Not really," I replied. "The only interest I have in someone's viscera is repairing damage to it. In Dr. Grey Veil's case, however"—I let my voice go flat—"I can make an exception."

The heavy features darkened. "You are determined to keep him at bay?"

"Among other things."

"I applaud your perseverance, although I can't condone your methods or intent." The Colonel sipped some of the noxious-smelling beverage he'd chosen. "I thought the Terran Hippocratic Oath required you not to deliberately inflict harm on other human beings."

"I don't consider that thing I just stuck my fork in to *be* human," I said.

There were no further interruptions. Colonel Shropana ate sparingly. When he thought I wasn't looking, he gave me odd looks. It didn't bother me. I happily demolished the d'narral. I liked the way Tonetka programmed it, soggy layers and all.

We finished our meal, and two crew members rushed in to clean up after us. Being a Commander did have its perks. From the galley, Shropana took me on a tour of the enormous troop freighter. I wasn't surprised to find out it was nearly ten times the size of the *Sunlace*.

"Command levels and engineering sections are off-limits, I'm afraid," the Colonel said. "I am willing to give you freedom to access the rest of the ship, including our medical facility. Your consultation will be more than welcomed by our staff physician."

I suppressed the urge to snort. I'd play consultant. In his dreams. "Where are we headed? Terra?"

The Colonel was convincingly regretful. "I'm afraid that's out of the question, although Dr. Grey Veil insists his research can only be carried out on your homeworld."

"You're not giving Dr. Grey Veil what he wants? My, my. He'll have a terrible tantrum. You may have to put him in sleep suspension to keep him from developing an embolism."

Shropana cleared his throat. "We are coordinating our jaunt and will leave orbit tomorrow to return to the Pmoc Quadrant." We passed a trio of engineers in the corridor. They flattened themselves against the plaspanel walls to get out of the way. "Fendagal XI will be the site of the League Conference in regard to your future."

That was news. "The entire League is holding a conference just for me?"

"You're the only genetically enhanced Terran in existence." He gave me a thorough survey. "Your unique DNA makes you of vital importance to every member of the League."

"I hope they've heard the story about the goose who laid the golden eggs," I said.

By that time we had reached level fifteen, where League tech programmers were busy maintaining and monitoring the huge ship's internal systems.

Chamber twelve, level sixteen, Tonetka had said. I had to get that far today. I didn't know if I'd have a fork handy the next time Joseph Grey Veil tried to put his slimy hands on me.

"What's on the next level?" I asked. Acting nonchalant was easy. I did it with patients all the time.

"Communications, resource management, and our gymnasium and recreational imagers." He counted off each with a claw. "I understand you are an excellent simulation programmer."

"I prefer reality these days," I said. My lips curled. "Still, can't be too picky, can I?"

"I'd hardly call you indiscriminate. Come. I'll show you some of the best the League has to offer its members on extended space jaunts."

Level sixteen, like the rest of the ship, was extensive. I counted eleven chamber entrances down the starboard side of the corridor and made note of the twelfth. The gymnasium. Perhaps they had given Tonetka routine access to it? What kind of weapon could she have hidden there? Had to be something small she could conceal on her person. I couldn't anticipate finding a large calibre displacer rifle. I could always *dream*, though.

The Colonel steered me toward the simulator room, which was equipped with a sophisticated array of dimensional imagers.

"Show me something you've enjoyed in the past," he said.

Probably all part of Joseph's test. "Sure."

The tech fell short of the Jorenian environomes, but it was adequate enough. I programmed a simple loop I'd once spent a great deal of time in while I lived in my creator's house.

Once inside the simulation, Shropana stopped and admired the detail. The damp, heated air was filled with the sounds of a dozen different birds and twice that many animals creeping about the dense undergrowth. The tropical rainforest, canopy soared three hundred feet above our heads.

"Well done, Healer." Shropana's smooth skin was already beading with sweat.

"Not really. The parameters could be more defined." I pulled aside a low frond, revealing a solid block of green where there should have been shoots and root clusters. "I can get most of the leaves and trunks right, but I always screw up the details." I inclined my head. "Half the birds are indigenous to North America, not the Amazon basin." A large, amiable white bear ambled past us. "Did I mention how much I liked polar bears?"

Shropana grinned. All those little daggerlike teeth made me shudder inside. "It is good to know the most-developed being in existence makes mistakes, too."

"Is *that* what he told you I am?" I made a *tsking* sound with my tongue. "I don't think the theory culminates in fact. Like my program here." I reached out my hand, and my polar bear reappeared. The triangular black nose snuffled my palm. "On Terra, a real version of this would be *dining* on my hand, not licking it. We'd also have to be in the Arctic, not Brazil."

"Healer, I suspect you can twist theory into any fact you desire," Shropana said, patting the rump of the placid creature.

"Or maybe I'm not so brilliant." I went to the control alcove and terminated the loop. The rainforest disappeared. "The League has spent a great deal of valuable time and resources based on—what? The wild promises of one mad scientist."

He spread his hands. "What he promises could change the nature of existence on many worlds."

"For who? Tell me, Colonel, do you believe the League will make the technology that created me available to say, a crop cultivator? How about a data input clerk? Someone on subsistence? Or do you think they'll reserve genetic enhancements for the inner circle of power?"

He shook his head. "I cannot answer. The League directors make policy. I am simply a soldier."

"Good point. Maybe the soldiers will benefit the most. Imagine what could be done with an army that was genetically programmed to never stop fighting. They'd never have to eat or sleep. Never have to be pensioned off. Just fight until they drop."

Shropana didn't like that. I suspected he was far more intelligent than he wanted anyone to know. That might be valuable to remember when I put my escape plan into action. Smart men had a tendency to think too much.

"Let's see your gymnasium," I said. "I'd like to get some exercise. My sweat glands are shriveling."

Once inside the gymnasium, I pretended to be fascinated with the weight-resistant equipment and began planning a vigorous exercise regime.

Shropana excused himself. "I have duties to attend to. Please remember to avoid all prohibited areas."

I grunted as I pressed a heavy tension coil between my hands. "Will do."

"Enjoy yourself." He left.

I kept working my protesting muscles as I examined the room. The League probably hadn't wasted recording drones on Tonetka while she exercised. I suspected I didn't merit the same luxury, but they'd already screwed up once. I touched the pendant that still hung around my neck. The idiots had never even checked it.

Where could she have hidden it?

Visual inspection revealed nothing but a profusion of equipment, a cleanser unit, diagnostic console—I nearly dropped the weights.

The image of Squilyp and me arguing in Tonetka's office popped into my head. *"Tonetka has a habit of doing that*

when she's in a rush to access the database," I'd told him.
*"She drops what she's holding and it ends up jammed
somewhere."*

I casually finished examining the last machine and
strolled over to the diagnostic console. I slipped under the
scanner and ran a cardiac series on myself, the whole time
searching the upper console board with my eyes, looking
for the gleam of Jorenian alloy.

No, I thought, she wouldn't have jammed it into an open
seam. She wanted to keep it safe, for later retrieval. Where
could it be? I sat down and scooted the chair forward until
my legs were beneath the edge of the console. I let one
hand fall in my lap as I leaned forward to study the displayed results of my scans. My hidden fingers danced lightly
underneath the console recess.

Cold, sharp metal bit into my thumb. I controlled a yelp
and the urge to snatch my hand back. Carefully I felt along
the opposite, blunt edge until I knew how it was placed,
then tugged it free.

It might be small. Hundreds of years old. Good only
during close proximity to an enemy. But the archaic Jorenian scalpel was a weapon. Where to hide it was my next
dilemma. I ran my open palm over my hair, hesitated for
a moment, then smiled.

I dropped the knife in my lap. After I sucked the drop
of blood from my thumb, I used both hands to release the
thick cable of my braid. As I shook my loosened hair, I
slipped the knife in my palm, holding it in place with my
thumb. I raised my hands to my hair again, gathering the
heavy mass into a bundle at my neck.

No one would question the wide, thick Jorenian warrior's
knot I now wore. They'd attribute it to my love of my
adopted people.

The League believed it had me in its pocket. The biggest
mistake of all.

I killed a couple of hours the next day by selecting furnishings for the quarters I had no intention of occupying
for very long. Once we were out of the Varallan Quadrant,
I planned to appropriate a launch and dive into an asteroid
belt the same way the Potnarch's pilot had done. They'd

damage their ships in pursuit, while I made my getaway. I was planning on staying lost for good.

My abused stomach finally pleaded feebly for nourishment. I had just decided to access the new prep unit when the ship went on alert status. Curious, I opened my door panel and looked out. Warning beacons blared. Orange lights flashed. Crew members ran back and forth.

Damn. Had Xonea tried something stupid?

I couldn't try to escape now. It would only put Joren back in the line of fire. I went to my display and signaled Shropana.

He responded after a few seconds. "Yes, Healer?"

"What's all the excitement about?"

"We are under attack." He turned his head and gave a sharp series of orders to someone. "Excuse me, Healer."

"Wait! Who's attacking?" I demanded. "Someone from Joren? Tell them I said—"

"It isn't anyone from Joren. It's the Hsktskt." He terminated the signal.

The Hsktskt? Attacking a fleet of sixty League ships?

I punched the display keypad until my display showed the external view of the ship. Beyond the thick field of cruisers, a solid wall of heavily armored Hsktskt transport and attack vessels were bearing down on us.

"God." I didn't have to count. There were a lot more than sixty vessels out there. Try two hundred. Three hundred. So many that I couldn't see clear space behind them. "Looks like we're not going to Fendagal XI after all."

I was sure Shropana would try to negotiate with the raiders. Typical League first response. He may have even sent the initial "truce-request" signal out before the displacer fire began. Did the Hsktskt want Joren, and the other neighboring worlds in the system? Was the League simply in the way?

I saw the other fleet vessels dodging the Hsktskt attack, felt the deck rock beneath me as the displacer blasts smashed into the hull. I wasn't afraid. I rather liked the irony of the situation.

"Blow us to Kingdom come," I whispered as I watched the approaching tide of vessels. "Be sure you get all the Terrans."

"Cherijo!"

My door panel was forced open. Salo stood in the opening, panting, and bleeding in several places.

"Cherijo? Are you well?"

"Salo!" I jumped up and ran to him. "What are you doing here? Are you crazy?"

He gulped in air and shook his head. "We must go."

"You're hurt," I said and began assessing his injuries. "How did you get so far into the ship? Did anyone come with you?"

He tucked an arm around me and hoisted me up the way he would a child. "Your pardon," he said, held me against him, and ran.

I didn't have time to argue. My job was to hang on while Salo dodged the frantic crew members running past.

Salo carried me down two levels to the ruins of a launch bay. I saw Dhreen and Xonea using one of the League launches as cover while they held off a small security team with pulse rifles. Salo didn't hesitate, but shot his way through to the launch pad. I tried not to look at the writhing, screaming bodies on the deck as he waded through them.

"I have her!" he shouted.

Xonea and Dhreen climbed back into the small, fast shuttle Dhreen had used to transport me here. Salo literally tossed me in and dove through the hull doors just before they closed.

We were out in space, dodging the crossfire between the Faction and the League before I could get up off the deck. Salo apologized profusely for his rough handling, until I smacked an uninjured area on his arm.

"You did a wonderful job rescuing me. Shut up. Xonea, get me the medical pack."

Salo had suffered only moderate lacerations and a few pulse burns. I cleaned him up and temporarily dressed one bad gash. I looked up and saw Joren looming in the viewer. "We're going back to the homeworld?"

"Yes," Salo said. "Let the Faction and the League destroy each other."

"Oh, I've no doubt the League will end up littering space, but the Hsktskt won't stop with them," I said. "They're here for more than target practice."

"Someone signaled them directly." Xonea sat down beside me.

"What?" I was aghast. "Are you kidding? Why would anyone want to signal the Hsktskt?"

"With the League in orbit, Joren is vulnerable. The Ruling Houses have ordered all offworld traders be detained until we discover who betrayed us."

"It doesn't matter who did it. They'll destroy the planet anyway," I said. I closed my eyes. Wished I had let them take me back to Terra a year ago.

"We can try to evacuate as many of our people as we can. If the ships scatter in different directions, transit to other dimensions, most will escape." Xonea was bleak. "There are not enough ships, however. Only enough for ten or twelve percent of the population."

No Jorenian was going to celebrate the death of their world.

We landed just before the League began bombarding the surface again. Xonea instructed Dhreen to escort me to the underground medical facility that had been prepared. He and Salo then hurried away to their defense stations.

Tonetka, Xonal, and Sberea were waiting for me. I rushed into my old friend's arms.

"I thought I'd never see you again," I told her when she finally let me go. "Has she been driving you crazy, Sberea?"

"As much as she ever has, Cherijo."

Xonal smiled sadly at us. "Cherijo. It appears you will be free of the League, but not for very long."

That was better than being a League prisoner. "Have you started the evacuation?"

"Yes. Members of all HouseClans have been selected at random to take the escape vessels. They are reporting now to their Transport assignments," Xonal said. He looked at Tonetka. "Your name was on the list for our HouseClan, my ClanSister."

Tonetka sniffed. "Another, younger Torin may have my position. My place is here."

He nodded. Displacer fire boomed above our heads. "The League is being decimated. They have been signaling for you, Cherijo. Their leader demands a response."

Shropana was a known threat, the Hsktskt only theoretical at this point. I might be able to buy time for the evacuees if I answered the signal. "I'd better talk to them while I still can."

Xonal took me through the underground network of tunnels to his defense headquarters, where a vid of Colonel Shropana appeared an instant after he signaled the League.

"Healer. You have reneged on your bargain."

"I was rescued from a Hsktskt attack."

"You may still save yourself. I have managed to negotiate a temporary ceasefire with the Faction. They are willing to allow us to leave Varallan space, with you, in return for not interfering in their raid on Joren and the other occupied worlds in this system. That, and a considerable amount of our available supplies."

"You're a real humanitarian, Colonel. Forget it."

"Joren will be destroyed, by one force or another," he said. "Surely you can see that."

"I'll die with my people. Good-bye, Colonel." I went to terminate the signal.

For a moment, Shropana seemed wistful. "I enjoyed meeting you, Cherijo."

"Wish I could say the same." I cut off the transmission. It looked like there was no way out of this. Then something Shropana had said made me smile.

"Xonal," I said, turning to my ClanFather, "I have an idea."

CHAPTER TWENTY

The Last Betrayal

Several hours after I arrived on Joren, I left again with Dhreen. Our shuttle flew directly to Shropana's ship, which looked battered, but remained in full operation. A few vessels had been disabled, but the bulk of the fleet remained intact. We were received in the same launch bay, minus the pomp and ceremony of my last visit.

Colonel Shropana and a small detachment stood waiting as Dhreen landed. We climbed out of the shuttle. I made the introductions.

Shropana nodded to Dhreen, then turned to me. "When you signaled, you indicated you had a specific request before we departed."

"Yes. We are evacuating approximately eleven percent of the surface population from Joren. If you allow the refugees to accompany us to Fendagal XI, I will cooperate fully with the League for the remainder of my existence."

Shropana's cynical eyes glowed with triumph. "I will grant your request. We will have to disperse the Jorenians among all the fleet ships, however."

"Thank you. Signal your ships to expect to receive them in one hour." I gestured to Dhreen. "My friend, of course, will be staying with me."

"Of course. I'll show you to your quarters."

"There's no need. I remember the way." I led Dhreen off, keeping my head high and back straight until we were out of sight. "Do you think he believed me?" I murmured.

"I don't know, Doc." Dhreen looked ill. "I hope this works."

All we had to do now was wait. We remained in my quarters, Dhreen near the door panel, me by the viewport. I'd offered to prepare tea for us, but Dhreen declined.

"Last thing I want to do is regurgitate in the middle of this," he said. He gestured to the interior of my new quarters. I had redecorated—everything was in shades of HouseClan blue. "They must like you."

"A comfortable cage is still a cage," I said.

The door panel slid open and Joseph Grey Veil strode in. Only Dhreen's quick movement diverted the trajectory of the server I threw, and it smashed into a wall panel. Two strong arms clamped around me.

"Cherijo!" Joseph visibly seethed with wrath. "You will cease attacking me every time I approach you."

I fought to twist free of the Oenrallian's hold. "Let me go, Dhreen. I won't kill him. Not right away."

"Quell down, Doc." Dhreen gave my creator a hard look. "You should leave."

I kept struggling. "Five minutes. That's all I want. Just five minutes."

My creator addressed the Oenrallian directly. "Perhaps you can persuade my daughter to change her unacceptable behavior."

"I'm not your *daughter*!" I yelled.

Joseph Grey Veil contemplated me with mild surprise. "Is this your idea of complete cooperation?"

"When the refugees are safe," I told him. "Not until then."

His arms folded. "I am weary of your childish tantrums."

"Oh? What are you going to do about it? Kill someone else?"

"There will be a great number of Jorenian children traveling with us to Fendagal XI," he said. "I can arrange to have them brought to the lab."

"Two minutes, Dhreen!" I struggled wildly. "Give me two minutes!"

My creator decided he'd said enough, or realized he was courting serious injury. He walked back out.

"Why did you stop me?" I yelled when Dhreen let me go. I pushed him out of my way and ran to the door panel.

Outside, the corridor was deserted. I whirled around. "Do you have any idea what he's capable of doing?"

The Oenrallian's pallid skin was nearly white. "We have to maintain, Doc. At least until the launches arrive safely."

I flung myself down in a chair. Well, there was that, too.

"Don't perspire over it." Dhreen reached over and patted my arm. "You'll get another chance."

An acid taste rose in my mouth. "No, I won't. In a few minutes it won't matter, I guess." I huddled in the chair, drawing up my knees, resting my brow against them.

The sense of imminent catastrophe was no surprise. I'd arranged everything. This time, I couldn't put the responsibility on anyone else. Not even the League.

A signal came to my display.

"Healer." It was Colonel Shropana. "Please report to launch bay. The Jorenian vessels are on final approach."

I stood at the side of the League Commander while the large Jorenian launch eased into the bay. Shropana's men were setting up to help the refugees report in and get their quarters assignments. The Colonel's stance was that of the omnipotent, benevolent despot—hands folded behind his back, spine straight, chin elevated.

"I might earn a seat on the Supreme Council for the success of this mission," he said. "Delivering you, now saving the Jorenian refugees from the Hsktskt. All I need is to discover some uncharted world rich in mineral deposits on the jaunt to Fendagal XI. I can store my uniform for good."

"I hope you get everything you deserve," I said with complete honesty.

"You have done well, my dear. Not only for yourself, but for these people." He nodded toward the launch as it touched down on the docking platform.

"I'm sure they think the same thing." I wondered how long it would take. Maybe another minute. "Tell me, Colonel, do you know anything about prehistoric Terra?"

The thick lips stretched over his teeth. "Only that your people spent centuries trying to annihilate one another."

"That we did," I said. "Terrans have always been very good at wreaking havoc. Some of our idioms are based on events that occurred during such conflicts."

"We should discuss it in the future," Shropana said. "My people have similar linguistic oddities."

"There's one expression that comes to mind at the moment. Do you know what a *Trojan horse* is?"

"No, I don't believe I do." Shropana's gaze sharpened as he noticed my expression. "Perhaps you would explain it to me. At once."

"Oh, I don't have to." I nodded toward the Jorenian vessel as its hull doors opened. "You've just let one land inside your ship."

The Colonel's powdery hair flew as he whipped his head around and saw what had stepped out onto the docking ramp. "No," he whispered. Then, with a terrible shout, "No!"

The occupants of the launch streamed out into the bay. I dropped to the deck and covered my head with my arms as soon as weapons began firing. The Colonel seized me and yanked me back up. His claws cut into my flesh as I struggled to free myself.

"What have you done?" he shrieked as he shook me.

I gazed into his rounded, terrified eyes. "It's called payback, Commander."

He shoved me aside. I hit a wall panel and let myself slide to the floor. Weapons discharged heavy, ceaseless streams of deadly energy, and bodies thumped as they fell beside the launch and all around me. I peeked through my arms and saw Shropana charge directly into the fray. His Commander's tunic probably saved his life. He was captured and disarmed in seconds.

Once the weapons stopped firing, something picked me up from the deck. I regained my balance and looked around me.

Monsters surrounded me. Ten-foot-tall, six-limbed, nasty-looking monsters. One of the giant reptilian beings stepped toward me. The grey uniform it wore over its monstrous frame bore the insignia of what appeared to be a high-ranking command officer.

A Hsktskt officer.

One sinuous limb aimed a rifle at my head. Huge, lidless yellow eyes inspected me. Just like old times, I thought, and held out my empty hands.

"I'm not armed," I said.

The Hsktskt removed something from an inner fold of his uniform and tossed it to me. It was translation gear, to be worn on the head. I slipped it on, and positioned the tiny receiver in front of my mouth. The fate of Joren depended on what happened in the next few minutes.

"I'm not armed," I repeated. "Stop pointing that thing at me."

The Hsktskt warrior's enormous jaw dropped open, and a thin, sinuous black tongue lashed out. "You haven't changed, Doctor." He barked out a series of orders and the bulk of his troops disappeared into the bowels of the ship. He made a curt gesture with his rifle, and Colonel Shropana was dragged in front of me. "The fleet leader?"

"Yes. Colonel Shropana. League Troop Commander." I looked at the Colonel's colorless, twisted features. No one had bothered to strap a translator on his head. "I'd introduce you, Colonel, but I don't know how to pronounce this Hsktskt officer's name."

"These vessels are now property of the Hsktskt Faction," the monster announced. He jabbed the end of his rifle into Shropana's belly. "I am OverLord TssVar. Tell him to remember the name or die."

I told him.

"What have you done?" Shropana said, this time choking the words out in a raw croak. He was forced on his knees before me by the soldier holding him.

Diplomacy time. I checked with the monster in charge. "May I speak with this one, OverLord TssVar? Just to explain things."

The Hsktskt nodded.

I turned to Shropana. "You came here, attacked my people, held them hostage by threatening to destroy their world unless I surrendered. I've just returned the favor, times sixty."

"Sixty?" The Colonel closed his eyes. "The other refugee launches."

"Bingo." I pointed toward the external viewer. "As we speak, your entire fleet is being boarded and taken over by OverLord TssVar's soldiers."

"But they are Jorenian launches!"

"OverLord TssVar and his soldiers needed a way to infiltrate the Fleet with minimum resistance. Jorenians are a very hospitable people. They invited the Hsktskt to land on the opposite side of the planet a few hours ago."

"The Hsktskt will invade Joren anyway," Shropana muttered.

TssVar's gear picked that up, and he didn't like it. I could tell from the way he stuck his rifle barrel into the Colonel's face. "Does this fool think he speaks for the Hsktskt?"

"The OverLord wants to know if you've appointed yourself spokesman for the Faction," I said to the Colonel. I never thought diplomacy could be this much fun.

Shropana gulped and shook his head.

"Tell the coward a Hsktskt does not violate his oath."

"OverLord TssVar has given his oath he and his troops will *not* invade Joren," I said. "He wants you to know the Hsktskt keep their promises."

TssVar walked away to consult with one of his officers reporting back from the initial occupation assault.

"You see, Colonel, League cruisers are a valuable commodity," I told Shropana. "The Hsktskt were happy to negotiate with me for them. They'll get more for sixty of your cruisers than they would for whatever was left after the attack on Joren, slaves included. The bonus is they won't have to kill the entire crew. They'll keep them alive to pilot the vessels back to the Faction."

"Why would the butchers negotiate with you?" the Colonel growled. "You're nothing but a Healer! You know nothing about war!"

"Patril, Patril. Rule number one: Never mess with a Hsktskt. Rule number two: Never mess with a Hsktskt's *obstetrician*."

That really confused him. "What has that got to do with this?"

TssVar trudged back over to us. The deck shook with each heavy footfall. When he reached Shropana, the viewport-sized eyes revolved toward me.

"I do not need this one," TssVar said. "I will kill him."

"He could be useful. Keep the others in line," I said. Not that I cared, one way or another. I simply didn't want to get League blood all over my tunic. "As you can see, he's easily motivated."

TssVar appeared to be thinking it over.

"Why is he listening to you?" Shropana asked.

"I told you." I smiled. An insulting grin cuts deeper than displacer fire. "Never mess with a Hsktskt's obstetrician."

"You delivered one of these monsters' whelps?"

OverLord TssVar took exception to the insult. One of his limbs lashed out and caught the Colonel across the face. Shropana yelped and cowered away.

"I wouldn't talk about his children like that, if I were you," I said.

"You mean—"

"Yep." I turned to the Hsktskt Commander. "I meant to ask you, OverLord. How *are* the kids?"

The League Fleet surrender was rapid, nearly bloodless, and complete. All communications were immediately jammed, so no one got a message off for reinforcements. None of the other planets in the Varallan system was going to signal the League. They were quite happy with the arrangements we'd made. The Trojan horse had worked perfectly.

The Hsktskt stationed several officers on board each ship to supervise the jaunt back to Faction-occupied space. Crews were surprisingly cooperative. I discovered why when I overheard one Hsktskt giving orders to some captive League troops.

"You! Move this cargo bin or I will rip out your liver!" the Hsktskt bellowed. All captives were now wearing the headgear that allowed them to understand the Hsktskt language. "You there! Your flesh looks tender! Hasten your pace or I will dine on your fat limbs!"

After my startling revelation, Colonel Shropana had dissolved into hysterics. TssVar had him dragged off to detainment.

Soon after, I was summoned from the launch deck to the new command center.

TssVar sat behind a display, studying the schematics for each of his newly acquired vessels. The soldiers with him trudged out of the room, leaving us alone together.

He nodded toward the seat before his desk. "Sit, Doctor."

By now I felt a little nervous myself. To TssVar, I might be just another commodity. The question was, did he know *how* valuable a commodity I was?

"My troops prefer battle, yet I favor an acquisition effected with little conflict." TssVar blanked out the display he was studying and turned his huge head. Monster and Terran stared at each other. I tried not to fidget. "It has been some time since we last met."

"Not so long. It seems like only yesterday you were jabbing a rifle at me and making a bunch of nasty threats."

"The sharp tongue," TssVar said. "That I remember of you, SsureeVa."

"What does 'SsureeVa' mean?"

"Thin-skinned." His jaw couldn't bend into a smile, but I heard the ghost of humor in his hiss.

"What does 'TssVar' mean?"

"Fearless."

Yep, that pretty much summed it up for me. "So—Over-Lord TssVar—where do we go from here?"

"League vessels will be taken to our space. Some crew will be sold with the ships. The others will go to the slavers." He saw my tiny reaction and rubbed his claws against the side of his thick neck. "You knew their fate."

"I knew. If you're waiting for me to cheer with joy, don't hold your breath, OverLord."

My sarcasm seemed to amuse him more than anything. "You are a mystery to me, Doctor. Small, fragile, and bolder than any warm-blood I have known. You are . . . unique among your kind."

"Thanks. I think."

Two of his limbs lashed lazily around his massive head. "A Terran male has been demanding dialogue with me. He resembles you, uses some of your name."

"My parent. Doctor Joseph Grey Veil."

TssVar pressed a keypad on the console before him. "Bring in the Terran."

I enjoyed watching the guard toss Joseph Grey Veil into TssVar's office. His limbs flailed wildly until he landed on the deck and collapsed.

The OverLord sighed. "Your kind are too flimsy, SsureeVa. You there. Terran. Get up!"

Joseph awkwardly scrambled to his feet. His wrists and ankles were bound with short lengths of alloy chains. On his head he wore the same headgear I had. He didn't so much as glance at me.

"OverLord TssVar." He bowed as elegantly as his bonds allowed him to. "Dr. Joseph Grey Veil, Terran research scientist. Thank you for seeing me."

"This one uses mannerly speech," TssVar said to me.

"He's good at talking," I replied.

"What do you want, Terran?"

"I beg a private audience with you, OverLord."

"He begs, too."

"Not for long," I said.

Joseph stiffened and peered down his nose at me. "This Terran female is a habitual liar. She attempts to create a conflict between us before I can state my case to you."

"SsureeVa, you are a liar?" TssVar asked me. "I thought you but short-tempered, arrogant."

"Dr. Grey Veil would have you believe otherwise." I wasn't going to confirm or deny. Let my creator dig his own hole.

The Hsktskt Commander seemed bored. "Terran, beg or get out."

"Very well." He assumed a posture I was very familiar with. It was the same way he stood behind a podium when he was about to deliver a lecture or commencement speech. I yawned. "Two years ago . . ."

He gave TssVar a severely edited version of the facts. The OverLord listened with genuine interest. When he finished his summary of the events leading to my rescue by HouseClan Torin, Joseph gestured toward me.

"I have no knowledge of her activities during the past year, but with your permission, I will continue my analysis and turn all findings over to the Faction for their scientific advancement."

Sure he would. When there were alien matchmaking agencies on Terra.

TssVar rose from his chair. "Terran, you may go."

That surprised my creator. "Will you not grant my request, OverLord?"

The Hsktskt looked from Joseph Grey Veil to me. "No."

"Why not?" Joseph demanded.

"You question me?" TssVar came around the desk so fast my creator fell backward on his posterior trying to scuttle away. With one limb the Hsktskt raised him from the floor, then *off* the floor. "You claim this female your test specimen. Your property. You wish freedom to experiment on her again. Have I understood your begging?"

Joseph nodded frantically.

"The female is the Designate of my brood. Do you understand *me*, spineless one?"

"Cherijo, what does he mean?" Joseph was frantic. I studied my fingernails. "What is a Designate?"

"Godmother to his children," I said. "Good-bye, Dr. Grey Veil."

TssVar tossed my creator out of his office and closed the door panel. He returned to his console and inspected me closely.

"How long did he experiment on you?"

I lifted my eyes to the yellow stare. "Twenty-seven years."

"My condolences, SsureeVa."

I had expected the Hsktskt to be heartless butchers, and here one was sympathizing with me. I would have laughed, but the image of a NessNevat child appeared in my mind. My good humor evaporated abruptly. "OverLord, may I ask what will happen to Dr. Grey Veil now?"

The Hsktskt towered over me. "I could have him gutted for you. I will allow you to decide."

I thought it over. It was a tempting offer. Some small spark of humanity made me shake my head. "No. If anything kills him, it will be his own ambition. Will he go to the slavers along with the others?"

"No. That tongue of his makes him of small value. Less if I remove it. He will be my messenger to the League." He moved to the desk and selected a data pad from the assortment.

I frowned. "I didn't know you wanted the League to be aware of this assault."

"We have captured sixty of their vessels. It is an indignity the League will not ignore. This time they will retaliate."

I saw his motives clearly at once. "You're trying to draw them out."

The OverLord's tongue lashed out quickly. "You claimed you knew nothing about war. You *are* a liar."

"And bad-tempered. And arrogant," I said. Time to find out what my future held in store for me. "What will happen to me, OverLord?"

He seemed startled by that. "I had assumed . . ." His yellow eyes narrowed. "Of course. I see the wisdom of it."

"Maybe you could let me in on some of that wisdom?"

"You will be informed. Go to the ship's Medical Facility. There are wounded you may tend to."

I rose and bowed as I had seen the other soldiers do. He made a sweeping motion; I turned and keyed the door panel open.

"Doctor."

I hesitated.

"My debt to you is satisfied."

He was telling me I would get no preferential treatment from him anymore. "I understand, OverLord."

There were no wounded Hsktskt soldiers, only battered League troopers with broken bones, pulse burns, and plenty of lacerations and bruises. I sterilized and went to work.

The nurses and staff physicians weren't openly hostile— they were furious, not stupid. We were all watched closely by a heavily armed Hsktskt guard.

It took most of the day to treat the injured troopers. I neither saw nor heard from Dhreen. I finished updating the last of the charts. While I worked out a temporary shift schedule for the jaunt ahead, Dr. Grey Veil made his entrance.

The bonds on his wrists and ankles were gone. His escort stood by the Medical Bay guard and exchanged a low series of grunts and clicks. Probably speculating on how to best prepare a Terran flank roast, considering what an ass my creator was.

The great man wasted no time but came directly at me. I put down the chart I was annotating and picked up a syrinpress. In plain view, I dialed an overdose application of sedatives and held it out like a weapon.

"Back off."

He halted several feet from me. "You persist in this hostility, even now."

"You wouldn't be alive if it wasn't for me," I said. "Don't push your luck."

"I am being sent back to the League to inform them of this incident. Your OverLord TssVar intends to provoke a war."

"Have a nice trip." I held the syrinpress steady. "Don't bother to write."

Behind him, I saw the door panel slide open and Dhreen walked in.

"Dhreen!" I smiled and waved to him. "Don't let me keep you from your journey, Dr. Grey Veil." I allowed myself a small, triumphant sneer. "Send my love to the League."

The Oenrallian stopped when he saw Joseph turn around. Dhreen would have made it back out the door panel, but one of the guards stepped in his path.

"No, Oenrallian. Come here," my creator said.

I glowered at Joseph. "Don't do anything stupid."

Dhreen trudged over to us. He had a miserable dark-yellow flush on his face. His eyes wouldn't meet mine.

"Hey, Doc." He gave my creator a disgusted look. "Grey Veil."

"Dhreen. It's good to see you again."

My breath caught in my chest. A terrible thought came to me, and I dismissed it at once. Not Dhreen. No.

Joseph watched the dawning horror on my features with immense pleasure. "Yes, Cherijo. I know your friend here very well. As a matter of fact, I hired him to work for me, two years ago."

A cold, numbing dread settled over me.

"Dhreen?" It came out of my mouth like a whimper. I tried again. "Dhreen, tell me he's lying. That it's just another one of his games."

Dhreen opened his mouth. Closed it. Hung his head.

I went from numb to pain. This was how it felt to have your heart broken. It felt like dying inside. I wanted to scream. Throw up. Weep.

"We came to a very amicable agreement, Dhreen and I," Joseph said. "It cost a great deal of credits to set up the meeting. I had to buy off all the independent pilots in New Angeles. When you went looking for transport from Terra, Dhreen was waiting. I paid him to take you to K-2, become your friend, and track you."

"Doc, I never meant to hurt you," Dhreen said.

"How could you?" I whispered. Anything louder would have ended with a shriek. "You were my friend."

"Why do you think he took you to Caszaria's Moon?

Why would a trader give up a lucrative route to join the crew of a survey vessel?"

"I stopped reporting to him after the *Bestshot* crashed!" Dhreen said. "I—I—"

"How do you think we were able to track the *Sunlace*?" my creator asked.

"Don't lie to her!" Dhreen shouted, and jumped at Joseph. One of the Hsktskt guards moved quickly, and pulled the Oenrallian back just before his spoon-shaped fingers reached my creator's throat. "Let me go!"

I walked up to Dhreen, and stared at his contorted face. So young. So innocent. So deceitful. "Take him with you, Dr. Grey Veil."

Joseph nodded. "He has been assigned to me as my pilot. When we return to the League, he will get his payment for a job well done."

"He's lying, Doc! I didn't do it for that—I never—"

"Get him out of here," I told the Hsktskt guard. "Please."

I turned my back and waited until I heard the door panel close. I looked at Joseph. Saw the pleasure he took in savoring my pain. "You can go now, too."

"I wanted you to know," he said. "Only *I* cared what became of you. Now I will return to Terra, and begin work on the eleventh trial. You will remain a Hsktskt's slave." He laughed in my face. "A fitting end to this farce."

I wandered from Medical an hour later, walking the corridors until I reached my quarters. I was still in shock over Joseph's revelation. When the door panel opened, I faced the emptiness with blank eyes.

Dhreen had betrayed me. Had been betraying me all along. Why hadn't I seen it? Why hadn't I known? The signs were there.

After the attack on Caszaria's Moon, Reever had told me what happened. *"The Terran pretending to be a Dervling drugged you and attempted an abduction. Dhreen heard you scream, and fought off your assailant, but the Terran escaped."* Or had Dhreen been helping my assailant when Reever came in? Did he let the Terran deliberately escape?

Joseph Grey Veil contacting me almost immediately after the attempted abduction on Caszaria's Moon. *"Cherijo. The*

incident on Caszaria's Moon was made known to me."
Dhreen must have signalled him.

Norash, the Commander of Colonial Security, interviewing me.

"—now this alleged attempted abduction during your off-planet furlough . . . confirmed only by Chief Linguist Reever's account." Dhreen had not made a statement. Afraid he'd say *too* much.

Dhreen leaving K-2, infected with the contagion. His ship crashing. Me and the medevac team at the crash site, pulling him from the wreckage. Yelling at him for running away. Dhreen coughing, in agony. *"Couldn't . . . take the . . . chance."* Of getting caught.

The worst was the clumsy cohab proposal he'd made after the epidemic. *"I just wanted to tell you I've gotten a position on one of the system long-ranger haulers . . . now that the* Bestshot *is gone, I need steady work . . . you saved my life . . . you've been a good friend . . . see, when I heard the Council was trying to get rid of you . . . I have cohab rights on the hauler . . ."* I had been charmed, I remembered. *"We don't have to bond for life . . . we've always coexisted well . . . I don't like leaving you here. . . ."*

Yeah. I bet he hadn't.

I was beyond tired. When I closed the door panel, I saw the signal indicator on my display and punched the keypad.

OverLord TssVar's grim visage filled the vid screen.

"Doctor."

"OverLord. What can I do for you?"

"Report to Command."

"Okay."

I wandered back out. How I arrived at the correct level without getting lost, I don't know. I had a vague sense of direction, but I really didn't care what was happening to me.

TssVar saw it the moment I was admitted by his private guards.

"What has happened?"

"May I sit down?" I asked, and he nodded. "I just found out one of my best friends has been betraying me for the last two years."

"Who do you speak of?"

"Dhreen, the Oenrallian pilot. Orange hair. Red horns. Lying mouth."

"I am sending him back to the League with the scientist."

"That's nice."

The Hsktskt's claws tapped on the desk as he lowered his limbs. "It is not good. To be betrayed."

"No, it's not."

"Warm-bloods make a habit of it," he said. "Yet you are always surprised when it happens to you."

My cynical smile burned on my lips. "Perhaps we should be more like your people."

"That would be an improvement." He watched me stare at my footgear. "You display no curiosity about my summons."

"Sorry." No, I wasn't. "Why did you want to see me?"

"We have kept our bargain. I have the Fleet ships. The planets of this system will not be raided." He said it carefully, as if making sure I understood every word of the agreement clearly.

"You've been extremely generous." He had. After all, he had over four hundred ships at his disposal. He didn't have to keep any promises he didn't want to.

"You made no bargain for yourself," TssVar said.

I looked up from my footgear. "No, I didn't. You have satisfied your debt to me by sparing the inhabitants of this system."

"It is good you acknowledge that." His hissing changed in pitch. Became more menacing. "SsureeVa, you have not been forthcoming with me. About your personal value."

"I rarely volunteer information about myself," I replied. "Being on the run from the League has made me somewhat paranoid."

"I would have done the same," he said. "Yet my task remains the same. I now know you are of infinite value to the Faction. You will not be returning to the planet."

I wasn't surprised. Joseph must have added some interesting details to what he'd already told the Hsktskt about me. I'd expected he would.

"Our rules are specific," TssVar said. "As Hsktskt property, you have no special privileges. Yet you were instrumental in our success. I will not require you remain in detainment with the other captives."

That was nice of him. I didn't relish getting my throat cut while I slept.

"Are you truly . . . a genetic construct?" he asked. His tongue lashed as he said it, relishing the words.

The truth might save or kill me. I didn't seem to care. "So I've been told."

TssVar stood. "It will be determined. Our scientists are extremely knowledgeable."

I bet they were. I rose to my feet, too. "Will that be all, OverLord?"

"For now. You are to report to level six, chamber one."

"Thank you." I turned to go, hesitated, then swung back around. "Tell me something, OverLord. Would you have let me go, if I had asked that as satisfaction of your debt?"

"I am grateful, SsureeVa. Not foolish."

A new guard was waiting to escort me to my holding cell. He snapped something around my wrist. It was the same metallic device the other prisoners were wearing.

"What's this?" I held up my arm.

"Detainment cuff. It tracks you. Disciplines you."

I didn't ask any more questions. He might want to demonstrate the discipline function. We walked briskly to level six. The business end of his rifle never moved from the small of my back.

Crew's quarters took up most of level six. The officers, if I remembered correctly. Chamber one had once been assigned to Colonel Shropana, according to the panel designation.

"You will remain here until summoned."

I nodded to the guard and stepped through the door panel. Shropana must not have spent much time here. No personal decor. Little beyond stanissue furnishings. I sat down on a rigid, uncomfortable chair and waited.

My thoughts bounced between relief and rage like a plassball.

Relief. *Joren was safe.*

Rage. *Joseph Grey Veil was free.*

Relief. *My people would not be destroyed.*

Rage. *Dhreen had betrayed me.*

I decided to take a long, hot cleansing. The throbbing in my head made it impossible to consider sleep. If I didn't relax, I'd work myself right up into a tension migraine. I doubt anyone from Medical would send me so much as an oral analgesic.

When I released the warrior's knot in my hair, Tonetka's blade dropped to the deck with a clatter. I'd forgotten all about it. I stared at it for a moment, then picked it up. It wouldn't hurt to hold on to it.

I might not like being Hsktskt property.

It felt good to be clean. I hunted through Shropana's stores and found a tunic that fit me like a long dress. That was all I needed. Something to cover my flesh. I lay down on the sleeping platform. Stared at the deck above me. Wondered how it would be. Life as a lab specimen in some Hsktskt research facility.

"Doctor," a voice called from Shropana's console. "Prepare to be escorted to your OverMaster."

"Acknowledged," I said. OverMaster? That was news. Apparently I was going to be put to work by one of TssVar's soldiers. I worked the knife into the warrior's knot in my hair, then presented myself by the door panel. The guard appeared almost instantaneously.

"This way." He jerked his weapon toward the descending corridor.

We walked quickly down three more levels. My fingers felt cold, my throat dry. I wasn't afraid. I always acted like this when I had a rifle shoved in my back.

"Halt." A door panel was keyed open. "In there."

The rifle jabbed me. I stumbled over my own feet, and tried to grab the corridor panel to stop from falling. The guard misinterpreted my clumsiness for resistance. A painful blow landed across my shoulders and drove me to my knees. Before I could say a word, he picked me up and tossed me into the dark chamber.

I landed facedown, my cheek and mouth throbbing, my upper back on fire. Why the hell had he done that? My headgear lay askew, so the disembodied voice that came to me sounded distant and garbled.

"Wait a minute." Furiously I straightened the device. "Want to repeat that?"

"Get up."

I did. The darkness prevented me from seeing much at first. Gradually my eyes adjusted, and focused on a seated figure at the other end of the chamber. I caught the metallic of a Hsktskt uniform.

"You're the OverMaster?"

"Yes."

It didn't sound right, the voice. There was none of the hissing or sonorous breathing the Hsktskt did when they spoke.

"Okay. I'm here. What now?" I squinted at the figure, but it rose and moved back into a deep pocket of shadows.

"Silence."

Being a captive wasn't going to be easy. All right, calm down, I thought. Hsktskt didn't like getting socked in the jaw. Very important I remember that.

I heard something being tapped. A bright, blinding light focused on my face.

"State identity," a drone audio announced.

"Cherijo Grey Veil, medical physician." They knew all this. Why the drone?

"Identity confirmed. Prisoner designation 1471428. Repeat the designation for future voice recognition."

"Designation 1471428," I said. My tongue felt thick, my lips stung.

"Correct. You are now property of the Hsktskt Faction. All former rights and freedoms are terminated. You have been assigned to OverMaster HalaVar. Repeat the assignment designation."

"I'm assigned to OverMaster HalaVar," I said. My face felt hot. I raised my fingers, discovered the warm wetness trickling from my mouth and nose. I wiped a sleeve across my face, smearing the blood on the fabric.

"You will obey the orders of your OverMaster and all free citizens of the Hsktskt Faction. There are no exceptions. Penalty for failure to comply is termination. Acknowledge these instructions."

Do what they said, or die. Pretty simple. Wonder if they had programmed the drone with standard responses. "Acknowledged."

"Prisoner 1471428, remove outer garments for physical scan."

Undress? I lifted my fingers to my fasteners, releasing them as slowly as I dared. It took a few minutes, but at last everything dropped on the deck and I stood naked in the light.

"Hope you enjoy the view," I said.

"Do not speak unless you are ordered to!" the drone's audio screeched. "Commencing physical scan."

A thermal beam swept over me, front and back, from crown to feet. I could feel something else scanning me, too. The OverMaster. I wondered if he found naked Terran females appealing. If he meant to hurt me. If I looked like a small pale-pink appetizer in his eyes. How hard would it be to dislocate his jaw.

"Minor injuries detected. Epidermal contusions. Facial lacerations."

If you don't like the damage, I thought, stop knocking me around.

"Scan complete. Replace outer garments."

I replaced them.

The light snapped off. The sudden return of darkness blinded me again. I stood waiting for what would come next. The time seemed endless as nothing happened.

Don't speak unless you are ordered to? Stand here forever? What was this guy's problem?

"OverMaster?"

"Silence."

I felt him then. Not from the voice, but the heat growing closer. Behind me. I didn't dare turn around.

"SsureeVa." Something cool touched my neck. I flinched, but rammed my hands at my sides and kept still. As still as was possible, considering I was shaking inside like a leaf in a strong Terran wind. "My prisoner."

What was it about the voice? The headgear I wore only translated the words into automated Terran. The sounds I heard beyond the earpieces weren't Hsktskt.

Worse. They seemed almost *familiar.*

The coolness encircled my throat. A collar of some type snapped against my flesh. My inner shaking began to emerge. My knees weakened, my throat went tight. I fought for air and courage.

"TssVar gave you to me," he whispered against my ear. I shuddered at the touch of his warm breath. "Remember that, SsureeVa."

"Yeah, right."

Something nudged me between my shoulder blades. The cold edge of a weapon's barrel? "Walk forward."

I walked. I found myself in front of a viewport looking down at a rapidly dwindling Joren. Tears stung my eyes.

I pressed my fingers to the icy surface. "Bye, Jenner," I whispered.

"You saved them. A life for a world."

What was he talking about?

"Close your eyes."

Oh, God, what was this monster going to do to me? I closed my eyes. Pressed my forehead against the viewport. The sudden press of light against my eyelids told me the darkness was gone.

"Open your eyes."

I did. Joren dwindled to a small speck now. Full lighting illuminated the room. The Hsktskt stood directly behind me.

I wasn't going out with a whimper. I turned as my hand tugged the blade hidden in my warrior's knot. If I was going to die, the OverMaster could be a gentleman and go first.

I launched myself toward the blurry figure in the grey uniform, arm up, blade high. Something knocked me away. Something that felt like a humanoid limb. I hit the deck, rolling over and over until my head struck an interior panel. New pain flooded in shimmering waves over the old.

I rested for a moment, wiped more blood from my mouth. Propped myself up with one hand. Tried to focus my eyes.

"Get up, SsureeVa."

My headgear lay on the deck next to me. What I heard wasn't Hsktskt. The OverMaster spoke to me in my own language. I got up slowly. Carefully.

I could be hallucinating. I'd hit my head pretty hard, twice now. So I stood and stared until my eyes burned from not blinking. The blood dripped from my mouth to my tunic like tears.

One word left my lips. Soundless. Incredulous. "You."

I realized why the Hsktskt negotiated with me. Why TssVar knew so much about me. The most effective treachery comes from the one you least suspect.

He wore a modified Hsktskt military uniform. His fist

curled around Tonetka's blade. No emotion animated his flat, steady gaze.

"You signaled the Hsktskts."

The drone went bananas. "Do not speak unless you are ordered to! Do not—"

"Terminate prisoner indoctrination program." The drone shut off. "Yes," he said to me. "I signaled them."

"You told TssVar about the League attacking Joren. About what my father did to me."

"Yes."

I nodded. After what Joseph Grey Veil had done to me, it seemed silly to find myself so shocked by another betrayal. This one, I thought, was the last. The worst.

"Cherijo. Get up."

I buried my face in my arms so I wouldn't have to look at OverMaster HalaVar anymore. "Go to hell, Reever."

I heard him move across the room. A panel opened. "Guard. Bring it in."

More footsteps. Something touched my hair, and I jerked my head up. "I said—"

I'd been wrong. That wasn't the last, or the worst. This was. Shock shut me up. Horror made me shake.

Reever had done the unthinkable. He'd abducted an innocent being. Stripped it of the only freedom it had ever known. Subjected it to its own worst nightmare. This was beyond betrayal.

This was obscene.

Sad, colorless eyes looked down at me. "I am sorry, Cherijo."

"Me, too, Alunthri. Me, too."